the
Making of Us

LISA JEWELL

the
Making of Us

arrow books

Published by Arrow Books 2012

2 4 6 8 10 9 7 5 3

First published in Great Britain in 2011 by Century

Arrow Books
Random House, 20 Vauxhall Bridge Road
London SW1V 2SA

www.randomhouse.co.uk

Addresses for companies within The Random House Group Limited can be found at:
www.randomhouse.co.uk/offices.htm

The Random House Group Limited Reg. No. 954009

A CIP catalogue record for this book
is available from the British Library

ISBN 9780099533696

The Random House Group Limited supports The Forest Stewardship
Council (FSC®), the leading international forest certification organisation.
Our books carrying the FSC label are printed on FSC® certified paper.
FSC is the only forest certification scheme endorsed by the leading
environmental organisations, including Greenpeace.
Our paper procurement policy can be found at:
www.randomhouse.co.uk/environment

Typeset in Baskerville MT by SX Composing DTP, Rayleigh, Essex, SS6 7XF
Printed and bound by CPI Group (UK) Ltd, Croydon, CR0 4YY

This book is dedicated to Sarah and Elliot Bailey.

Acknowledgements

Thank you to Sarah Bailey, Jonny Geller, Kate Elton, Louise Campbell, Georgina Hawtrey-Woore, Claire Round and absolutely everyone at Arrow and Cornerstone, to Google, Wikipedia, my family, my children, my husband and to all the superb people on the Board.

Thank you to Marae for typing skills and to Maggie Smith who let me use her name in return for a donation to the excellent charitable concern, Room to Read. It was a very lovely name to work with.

Thank you as well to all my lovely friends and supporters on Facebook and, on occasion, in real life too. In particular, thank you to Yasmin, Janet and Denis for loyalty, enthusiasm, bear hugs, playlists and champagne. To my followers on Twitter all I can say is I am sorry. Not a natural born tweeter.

1979

GLENYS

Glenys Pike was thirty-five years old. She had long dark hair and a neck like a swan. Her husband was called Trevor and was five years younger than her. The idea was that he would keep her feeling young. The truth was that the fact that he had not yet reached his thirtieth birthday made her feel about as old as her grandmother. Trevor meanwhile still had all the swagger and sway of a young man, his hair a fat plume of mahogany, his stomach as smooth and hard as set cement. He lived like a young man, too; still went to clubs with his mates until the early hours; last summer he'd even taken a Club 18-30 holiday, just because he could. Trevor was fit and strong and smoked a cigarette like a cowboy. Trevor was a god.

But Trevor was also, Glenys had just learned, shooting blanks.

Well, she didn't know that for a fact. God, no, Trevor Pike would never wank into a jar, not for anyone, least of all a female doctor. But she had to assume it because there was nothing wrong with her. Nothing whatsoever. Five years they'd been trying to make a baby, five years of phantom symptoms and two-week waits and false hopes and lying with her bloody legs in the bloody air after bloody sex, and nothing. Not even a miscarriage to show for it. And this morning she'd been to see a doctor up at the fertility unit for some results and there it was, plain as your face: Perfect Working Order.

'What about your husband, Mrs Pike, has he been to see us for tests?'

Glenys had snorted laughter out of her nose. 'God, no,' she'd said, 'I don't think my husband even knows that there's such a thing as male infertility.'

'Macho man?' asked the doctor.

'And some,' agreed Glenys. 'Party animal. Good Time Guy. *Carouser.*'

'Well,' the doctor had sighed, and leaned back into a chair as though she'd heard it all before a thousand times, 'in that case I suggest you try and change his lifestyle. If he's living that kind of life, it's probably not doing his sperm any good. Does he smoke?'

'Forty a day.'

'Drink?'

'Forty a day.' Glenys had grinned. 'Just kidding. Though some Saturday nights, probably not far off.'

'Healthy diet?'

'Chips? Are they healthy?' Glenys winked at the doctor who just blinked back at her unsmilingly. 'No,' she continued, somewhat unnecessarily, 'I'm just kidding with you. He does like his chips, but he likes pasta, too. His grandmother was Italian. Says it's in his blood. And he does like two veg. Peas. Potatoes. Carrots. He always eats his veg.'

'Exercise?'

'He is fit, I'd say. He plays football of a Sunday. He walks to work. He's got amazing stamina, you know, when we're at it.'

'Well, anyway . . .' The doctor ignored the unwanted insight into her patient's love life. 'It sounds like there is plenty of room for improvement. Try a bit for another six months or so, no smoking, no drinking, and if there's still no change, we'll have to get your husband in for tests.'

'Six months?' Glenys had squeaked. 'But in six months I'll be thirty-six. I thought I was going to be a grand-mother by the time I was thirty-six! I can't wait six months! My eggs—'

'Your eggs are fine,' the doctor had reassured her. 'You are fine. If you can just get your husband to change his lifestyle. Oh, yes, and no tight trousers, no tight under-wear, you'll need to get him some cotton boxers.'

Glenys had snorted again at the thought of her Trevor in cotton boxers. Trevor was proud of his packet. He wanted people to be able to admire it, not cover it up in baggy old vicar knickers. And rightly so. 'You know,' she said to the doctor, 'I know my husband. And I know for a fact that he won't go for any of this stuff. He won't go for baggy pants and no fags. In fact, it's the tight pants and the fags that make him feel like a man. Without them he'd feel like, well, he'd feel like a nancy. You know.'

The doctor leaned across the desk towards her. 'Well, then,' she said, 'you might need to start thinking about some other options.'

'Options. What sort of options?'

The doctor sighed. 'Well,' she said, ticking them off on long fingers, 'fertility tests for your husband, lifestyle changes, those would be the first things to think about. But after that, well, there's adoption, sperm donation, IVF . . .'

'Sperm donation?'

'Yes.'

'What, like, some fella just gives you their sperm, like?'

'Well, no, he doesn't give it to you. Not directly. He donates it to a fertility clinic and the clinic matches the right sperm to the right recipient.'

'And, golly, how does it . . . you know?'

The doctor sighed again. Glenys knew she was just a silly girl from the valleys, she hadn't given much of her life over to thinking about the big, wide world. She didn't really follow the news or anything like that, just lived in her lovely little bubble of Glenysness. She'd heard about a woman in the next village who'd stolen some sperm from her boyfriend, sucked it out of a used condom with a turkey baster and blasted it up herself. Got pregnant but the baby didn't catch. Almost like it knew it was the result of some badness. But this, men giving away their sperm to strangers, this was news to her.

'It's inserted vaginally, using a syringe. Obviously when a woman is at her most fertile.'

'Wow, a strange man's sperm. And my egg. Fancy that. So, how do they decide whose sperm to give me? I mean, how do they choose?'

'Well, I wouldn't say they *choose*. But you are given a few salient details about the donor. Height. Hair colour. Eye colour. Nationality. Education.'

Education. Glenys liked the sound of that.

'What, like, they could be a professor or something?'

The doctor shrugged. 'In theory. Though more likely to be an out-of-work actor or a student.'

Actors. Students. Professors. The very thought of it. She did love her Trevor. She worshipped her Trevor. He was the sexiest guy in the world. He was cool and handsome and rough and tough and everything a man was supposed to be. Every time he looked at her she got goose skin. But he wasn't clever, her Trevor, not in that way. He knew a lot about the things he liked, like rugby and cricket and football and fish. He could even speak a few words of Italian. '*Ti amo, mi amore.*' Made her want to stick her hand down the front of his trousers and just grab him when he said that to her. But in some ways, well, it pained her to say it, but in some ways he was really quite stupid.

She hadn't been able to shake the idea of another man's sperm from her consciousness after that. Walked around for the rest of the day, imagining herself on a white bed, legs in stirrups, introducing the fruit of a stranger's loins to the darkness of her waiting body, imagining the eager little things scurrying their way up there towards the golden light of her radiant egg. Then she thought of Trevor's sperm. Drunk sperm, too busy showing off to each other to find their way through the gloam. She imagined them squaring up to each other: D'you want some? Well, do you? Stupid sperm. Stupid, lazy, macho sperm.

By the time she got home from the clinic she was really quite angry with Trevor and his sperm and had all but made up her mind that she was going to do it, she was going to go to a sperm clinic and ask for some sperm from a nice, clever teetotal man. But there he was, as she walked in the door of their cosy little flat just outside Tonypandy. He was filleting a fish on the kitchen counter, wearing his silly apron, the one with the picture of the naked woman on it that his brother had bought him for Christmas the year before, and his face lit up at the sight of her and he was so gorgeous and so silly and so damn perfect, she couldn't help it, she just wanted to cuddle him and kiss him and not talk about sperm or babies or cotton boxer shorts.

It wasn't until she woke up four mornings later and felt the wetness between her legs, the arrival of another monthly curse, that she began to feel angry again. What use was a man who fired blanks? What use was a man who could fillet a flounder and kick a ball into the back of a net if he couldn't even stop drinking for long enough to let his sperm sober up?

That was the morning when Glenys Pike decided that she wanted a baby more than she wanted a man. That was the morning that Glenys Pike decided to do it herself.

RODNEY

Rodney Pike had been in love with Glenys since the very first day he'd laid eyes on her. It was in his mum's front room, the day before Rodney's birthday. Not that that was why Glenys was in their front room. She was just waiting for Trevor who was upstairs fiddling with his hair in front of the bathroom mirror. There was often a girl on the sofa waiting for Trevor to finish fiddling with his hair. Usually they were blonde, trendy-looking types with fringes and cheap plastic earrings. But this one was different. She had sleek black hair, and a long, elegant neck. She was wearing plain clothes; a white shirt with a belt round the waist, sky blue cotton trousers and silver shoes like a ballet dancer might wear. And she sat very straight, as if someone had taught her how to do it properly. He'd expected her to open her mouth and talk like Audrey Hepburn, but she hadn't. She had a broad valleys accent and when she smiled her face turned into a caricature of itself. But for that first formative moment, Rod had looked at Glenys Reeves and thought that she was an exotic creature sent from another world to steal his soul, and he never quite lost that feeling.

Trevor showed more intelligence in the thirty seconds it took him to propose to Glenys Reeves a year later than he'd shown in the rest of his life put together. Rod had nodded approvingly when Trevor and Glenys had sat on that same green sofa and he told the family: 'I've asked Glenys to marry me, and, well, you'll never guess what – she's said yes!' He would have been mad not to. The girl adored him, that much was clear, and not only was she the prettiest girl that Rod had ever seen, she was kind and loving too. And you didn't stumble upon a girl like that every day. Rod had never stumbled across a girl like that. He'd never stumbled across any girls at all really. He was too small for most of them. Welsh girls liked big men and Rod was not a big man: 5′ 6″ and built like a forest imp. He had the same even features as Trevor, just on a smaller scale. He'd always assumed he'd grow to be as big as his elder brother, but it wasn't to be. Stuck the size of a schoolboy forever more.

Over the years Glenys had always done Rodney the great service of flirting with him mildly. She'd say things like: 'Oh, maybe I married the wrong brother,' and always insist on sitting next to him in pubs and restaurants. Rodney, unlike his brother, was not stupid. He knew she was just being kind. He knew that she knew how he felt about her, and he knew that she knew how he felt about himself and was just trying to give him a little confidence boost, a little fillip. It worked. Rodney always felt about 5′ 8″ when he was with Glenys.

And so, when she came to him one morning in early

1979, elegant as ever in a tailored skirt and frilled chiffon shirt, and put her hand over his and said: 'Rod, I need you to help me. I'm desperate,' he'd known already that whatever she was about to ask of him, he was destined to say yes.

It hadn't made any sense at first, what she was saying to him.

'It's Trevor . . . It's his sperm. They're no good. That's why we haven't had a baby yet, Rodney.'

He pushed his glasses higher on his nose and peered at Glenys through them. 'What do you mean, they're no good?' He found it very disconcerting to be in a room alone with Glenys and for her to be using the word 'sperm'. He'd never heard her using dirty language before. It made him momentarily deaf to the essence of what she was trying to say.

'They're duds, Rod. He's firing blanks. You know, a *Jaffa.*'

'Oh, my goodness gracious.' Rod slapped his hand to his mouth, realisation dawning. 'Are you sure?' he said next, because really and truly, how could Trevor be a Jaffa? You only had to look at him to see how virile he was.

'Well, yes, I'm pretty sure because I've been up to the clinic at Llantrisant, like, and they turned me inside out and upside down and hung me from the ceiling and there's nothing wrong with me and it's been five years, Rod. Five years, and it's not, well, you know, it's not for lack of trying.'

Rod blinked slowly, wanting the image of Glenys and his brother 'trying' gone from his head.

'And the doctor up there said it's his drinking, you see. And his smoking. And I can't tell Trevor he's not to drink and smoke. And the tight trousers. I mean, imagine Trevor in baggy strides? Really.' She shook her head sadly. Rodney shook his head, too.

'Have you told him?' he asked.

'Oh, my goodness, no! Can you imagine! He'd be *apoplectic*. I don't think he'd ever forgive me, do you?'

Rodney nodded slowly. She was right. Trevor was not the sort of man who would take a suggestion that he was not fully the man he thought he was very lightly. Rodney caught his breath. There was something massive coming up, something seismic attached to the end of this conversation. He could feel it in the air and see it in the tight contours of Glenys' lovely face. He tried not to let the obvious thing take root, it was too mind-blowing. There was no way in a thousand, million, trillion years that Glenys would ask him to father her child. Absolutely no way. He shook his head subconsciously against the thought. No, that would mean either betraying his brother or getting involved in messy mechanical stuff with tubes and syringes and God knows what and, really, the thought made Rod feel quite queasy. He and Glenys were of a like mind, he knew that. Gentle people, they were, wholesome you might say, not given to swearing and talking about filth like some. Glenys wouldn't countenance it and neither would he. So he sat and he waited to find out what she would say next.

'I'm going to a sperm bank,' she said eventually, 'I'm going to a sperm bank, in London. And I want you to come with me.'

Rodney had heard about sperm banks, even thought about donating a few years back, when he was out of work and desperate for some quick cash. But then he'd thought about it again: little Rods running around the world, cursing him for their skinny bodies and their fine hair and their poor eyesight and, really, what woman would want his sperm when they were told that it had been donated by a myopic 5′ 6″ tree surgeon from Tonypandy?

'Right,' he said, rubbing his chin gently with his fingertips. 'I see. You're not going with Trevor, then?'

Glenys threw him a look which he immediately understood.

'No,' he said, 'of course you're not.' He stared at the floor for a moment, considering the request. Then he glanced up again at Glenys. She looked hard. No, not hard, *resolved*. She had no doubt at all that this was what she wanted to do. 'So, you've thought about this then, have you?'

She nodded, firmly.

'And if I don't go with you?'

'Then I'll go on my own. But I don't want to go on my own, Rod. What'll they think of me? They'll think I'm some kind of crazy woman, showing up without a husband, demanding a baby. I mean, what sort of person would do that? I need you, Rod. I need you to come to London with me and sit with me and pretend that we're married.'

'But, if I do that for you, Glenys . . . and, believe me, I really would like to do it for you . . . it means lying to Trevor, to my brother.'

She nodded, her eyes wide with desperation.

'Gosh, Glenys. I don't know . . .'

'Think about how happy your brother will be, Rod. Think about when he holds that baby in his arms. When he can call himself a *man*.'

He blinked and gulped. She had him cornered. When she put it like that, well, she had a point. Trevor would never say so but Rod knew that it galled him that he hadn't made a baby yet. Everything came so easy to Trevor and he'd assumed that a baby would be the same. He talked about having four or five. But then he also talked about the joys of his child-free life, the clubs and the holidays and the nights out at the pub. But maybe that was just talk, thought Rodney, just macho bluster to keep away the demons of self-doubt.

'So, will you?' Glenys stared at him beseechingly. 'Will you come?'

'Where is it?'

'London,' she said, 'Harley Street.'

'Well, I never . . .' he mused.

'Don't want to do it near here. People talking, and that. And you never know, could turn out it's someone I know. Imagine that! Imagine it, having a kid who turns out looking like the guy in the electrical shop!'

They laughed then, extra loud, to blow a hole through the nervous tension. Once the laughter petered out,

Rodney sighed. 'I'll have to think about it.'

'Yes. You will. It's a big deal, Rod. I know that. And I wouldn't ask you if I didn't trust you.' She laid her hand over his and brought her face close to him. 'I wouldn't ask you, Rod, if you weren't the man you are.'

Rod smiled and inside him something expanded and grew and he knew that he would do anything for this woman, even betray his big brother.

1998

LYDIA

Lydia Pike wrapped her arms around her knees and closed her eyes against the hot sun. The dog sat alongside her, tall and panting, overdressed in his thick coat of hair. The grass was long, longer than she'd ever seen it before, and the air in this little dip on the disused railway track was thick and sweet with the scent of cow parsley. Lydia brought the dog here every day, it was part of her regular walk from the flat to the shops and back again. Usually she kept walking, at other times of year this place was dank and unwelcoming, but now, after six weeks of summer, the hottest summer in recent history, the earth had dried to a gentle crust and butterflies ornamented the wild flowers that burst from the banks. A ladybird crawled up Lydia's wrist and she brushed it gently to the ground. The silence was absolute. She lay back with her head in the soft grass and felt it wriggling beneath her hair, alive with the creatures of summer. She closed her eyes and the big sun strobed through her eyelids, a golden-red symphony.

A few moments passed and then Lydia sat up again, felt inside her rucksack and pulled out the quarter bottle of vodka. It was already half empty, she'd had the rest on the way here, tipped into a bottle of Diet Coke. She brought the bottle to her lips and drank from it thirstily. The alcohol brought even more piquancy to her situation, here on the banks of a long-dead railway line, escaping from home, escaping from life. The sense of loneliness and desperation whispered away, and Lydia felt colour return to her soul. She put her arm around the big German Shepherd; girl and dog, side by side, as they had been for the past ten years. Her dad had bought her the dog, to keep her safe. Not because he was the sort of dad who thought only of his child's safety, but because he was the sort of dad who couldn't be arsed to do the job himself. Arnie had been Lydia's sole responsibility from the age of eight. She had fed him, walked him, groomed him and slept with him at night in her single bed. Arnie. Her best friend.

People thought she was weird. Lydia *pikey* they called her: *of course they did*. Lydia was also the Goth with the Dog. Not that she was a Goth. She just liked black. She wasn't pierced or tattooed, but still, she was the Goth with the Dog. And the Grunger. That seemed more fitting. She did like Nirvana, she did like Alice in Chains and Pearl Jam. It had been Greebo before, when she was fourteen, fifteen. She preferred Grunger. Greebo made it sound like she was into Motörhead and Whitesnake. Made it sound like she hung around with smelly fairground boys and never washed her hair. But nobody knew, nobody really knew, what Lydia really was. Lydia barely knew what Lydia really was. She was eighteen. She lived in a third-floor flat in a small village outside Tonypandy with her father who was forty-nine. Her mother had died when she was three. She'd just sat her A levels and was fully expecting three A grades (another reason to hate Lydia, she was clever, too). She had a big dog called Arnie. She wanted to be a scientist. She drank too much.

An hour later Lydia returned to the small block of flats where she lived with her father. Outside the flats was a playground. In these high days of summer, halfway through the school holidays, it was full of teenagers; girls in crop tops and baggy jeans huddled on to swings, boys in singlets and combat shorts. Some of them were smoking. One of them had a beatbox on his shoulder. 'The Boy Is Mine' by Brandy & Monica, the soundtrack to their summer but not Lydia's. She'd known most of these kids since they were toddlers, been to school with some of them, even pushed one or two of them around the estate in their buggies while their mothers sat and gossiped. But none of them was a friend.

Lydia braced herself, but the teenagers were distracted by themselves, not looking for that moment outside their own immediate circle for entertainment. Lydia pulled the dog's lead closer to herself and the two of them walked, fast and quiet, past the playground and towards the flats. Lydia's eyes dropped, as they always did, to a patch of tarmac just below her flat, a smudge of pink paint, containing within it the merest outline of a hand, the curl of a finger. And Lydia's nose filled, as ever, with the scent of paint, thick and noxious and terrifying.

She walked on, around the corner and into the concrete well of the external staircase. Two teens turned their faces briefly towards Lydia as she passed by, making room for her and her dog, too interested in the contents of small plastic bags clutched in their fists to care much about the girl in black making her way to the third floor.

She turned her key in the lock of her door, number thirty-one, pushed it open, held her breath. Her father was attached to his oxygen tank. He was suffering from chronic obstructive pulmonary disease, which was hardly surprising given that he'd smoked forty cigarettes a day since he was fifteen. The oxygen tank was a new development and he was attached to it for fifteen hours a day. It frightened Lydia to see him like that. He looked bizarre, oddly perverted, like a character from a David Lynch movie.

He glanced up at her as she walked in and smiled wanly. 'Hello, love.' He'd pulled the mask from his mouth.

'Hello.'

'Nice walk?'

'Yeah, bit hot.'

'Yeah,' he said, his gaze drifting towards the window, 'yeah.' He'd been indoors for thirteen days now, on that sofa for most of them. If he wanted, he could sit on the balcony, sit in the sun, but Lydia's dad had locked the door on to the balcony fifteen years ago, locked it and never opened it again. She made him a cup of tea and brought it to him. He held out two big hands, thin-fleshed and cold as a reptile's. Lydia asked him if he needed any-thing else, and when he said he didn't she took her mug of tea and her dog into her own small bedroom and sat on her single bed and tried not to feel guilty about leaving her dad like that, out there on his own, dying for all she knew. She battled the guilt for a moment or two but then she remembered the man he'd been before his lungs had caved in and his body had started to collapse. Not a bad man, but not a good father. But he was nice to her now, nice now that she was all he had.

Lydia stared around her room, at the grubby magnolia walls with the hint of cyclamen pink skulking beneath. Her father had painted Lydia's room only a few days after her mother died. She'd watched in despair as the dun-coloured paint had been slopped over the bright pink. It was as if he was painting away her happiness. Nowadays the magnolia suited her. She found it hard to imagine she'd ever been the kind of little girl who would have wanted her bedroom to be pink.

Lydia was almost four when her mother died. She could remember very little about her. Dark hair. The little silver swans she would make for her daughter out of the lining of her cigarette packets. A skirt with blue roses on it. Long fingernails up the back of Lydia's top, scratch-scratch-scratching away an itch for her: 'Harder? Softer? There? There? Ooh, let me scratch that away for you.' Her name was Glenys. Lydia remembered music, Terry Wogan on the radio, a sink full of washing up, a cigarette left burning in an ashtray, the smell of chips in a fryer, the bars of a playpen, a cardboard box big enough to hide in, the *TV Times* on the coffee table, shows circled in blue biro, and a little yellow bird in a cage that pirouetted with joy every time Lydia's mother looked at it. After her mother died these things disappeared, one by one, like stars going out in the night sky. The yellow bird, the *TV Times*, Terry Wogan, the chips, the back scratches, the delicate silver swans, the pink paint in the bedroom. All that remained was the ashtray.

Lydia heard her father coughing next door. She tensed. Every cough sounded like it could be his last. The thought left her feeling torn between joy and panic. If he died she'd be all on her own. *All on her own.* She wanted to be alone. But she didn't want to be all on her own. She glanced at her dog, at his big strong skull, his soft ears. She wasn't all on her own. She had her dog. She closed her eyes against the sound of her father's rasping, the thoughts of her future, and let herself fall into a deep, vodka-induced slumber.

2009

LYDIA

Bendiks hoisted Lydia's leg over her shoulder and ran his hands up and down her calf muscles, squeezing as he went. A fine thread of sweat trickled from Lydia's hairline, down her temple and into her ear. She stuck a fingertip into her ear and rubbed away the itch.

'How does that feel?' said Bendiks.

Lydia clenched her teeth together and smiled. 'That feels great,' she said, 'absolutely great.'

'Not too much?' asked Bendiks, his oddly beautiful face softening with concern.

'No,' she said, 'just right.'

He smiled and lifted her leg a little higher. Lydia felt the latticework of muscles behind her knee pulling against the movement and winced slightly. Bendiks had one knee at her crotch and his thick black hair was almost brushing her lips. Gently he lowered Lydia's leg and rested it on the floor.

'There,' he said, 'finished.'

Lydia smiled and sighed. Bendiks stood above her, his hands on his hips, smiling down fondly. 'You did good today,' he said, helping her to her feet. 'Really good. You want we do it in the park on Thursday. Yes?'

'The park?' said Lydia. 'Yes, why not?'

'Great.' He smiled at her again. Lydia smiled back. She tried to think of something witty or conversational to say but, finding nothing inside the cavernous cathedral of her head that seemed to fit the job, just said, 'See you on Thursday,' then turned and walked away.

She saw Bendiks' next client loitering in her field of vision. It was the Jewish woman, the one with the over-stretched Juicy Couture trousers and the fake tan. Lydia knew she was Jewish because her name was Debbie Levy. From behind she looked like a cheap sofa and Lydia despised her, not for her resemblance to a cheap sofa but because of her slinky way with Bendiks.

'Morning, gorgeous,' she heard the woman growling behind her, 'are you ready for me?'

She heard Bendiks laugh, slightly nervously, and then Lydia pushed through the swing doors towards the changing rooms, her personal training session over for another day.

Lydia Pike lived not far from the exclusive health and fitness club where she was trained every other day by a beautiful Latvian man called Bendiks Vitols. The club was so exclusive that it was almost impossible to guess it was there, tucked away up a small St John's Wood mews, looking for all the world like someone's rather pretty house. Lydia only knew it was there because it was where Bendiks worked. She'd read about him in a glossy magazine that had been slopped through her letterbox three months ago. 'Want to get fit for spring?' said the by-line. 'We talk to three local fitness experts.' And there was Bendiks, a head-and-shoulders shot, thick dark hair in a side parting, a black fitted t-shirt, smiling at a third party out of view as though disturbed by a cheeky comment. At the time Lydia had dearly wanted to get fit for spring. She'd wanted to get fit not just for spring, but for summer, autumn and winter too, and the moment she saw Bendiks' face she knew that she'd found the person to do it. It wasn't just that he was beautiful, which he was, but there was a softness to his features, a sort of humour about him. She knew he'd put her at her ease. And he had.

From her external appearance you might not imagine that Lydia was in much need of fitness training. She was lean and spare, there was no extra meat on her, except perhaps for a little softness around her belly button. But Lydia knew the truth about her body. She knew that it was a shell behind which ticked a time bomb of un-nurtured organs and neglected arteries.

Lydia dropped her gym bag in the hallway and said hello to Juliette, her housekeeper, who was halfway up the stairs with an armful of freshly laundered clothes. She stopped when she saw an Ocado delivery man approaching the front door. 'You want me to take care of this?' asked Juliette.

'No, no, it's fine. I've got it.'

Juliette smiled and continued up the stairs. The man from Ocado unpacked Lydia's shopping on to her kitchen table while Lydia fingered the contents of her purse for a couple of pound coins with which to show the Ocado man her appreciation for sparing her the inconvenience of doing her own shopping. After the man had left, Lydia began to sort the goods into her kitchen cupboards. Lydia rarely dealt with her kitchen cupboards. She had a vague idea what each cupboard contained, had herself allocated each unit a function during the unpacking process, but really, some of them were slightly mysterious. Where, for example, she wondered to herself, do I put rice vinegar?

Juliette came upon her, a moment later, wafting vaguely around the kitchen with a packet of rice noodles in her hand. 'Here.' She took them from Lydia and placed them deftly in a pull-out cupboard next to the fridge. 'Let me finish.'

Lydia acquiesced and pulled a bottle of sugar-free Sprite from the fridge. 'I'll be in my office,' she said in the strange new tone of voice she'd developed for talking to the woman she paid to deal with her domestic affairs; it said, 'I am not your friend, no, but neither am I the kind of heartless, overpaid St John's Wood resident who sees you as nothing more than a paid-for slave. I know that you are a human being and I am aware that you have a meaningful and real life outside my home, but I still do not really wish to discuss your children with you, or to find out what brought you from the palm-lined shores of a Philippine island to our dirty old city. I am a nice person, and I too have travelled a long way to get where I am today, but I would like to keep our relationship purely professional. If that's OK with you? Thank you.'

23

Lydia had only had a housekeeper for a few months. It hadn't been her idea. It was her friend Dixie's idea. She'd been happy with having a cleaner once a week, but Dixie had taken one look at Lydia's over-sized new St John's Wood palace and said: 'Housekeeper. You'll have to.'

Lydia's office was at the top of her house. It was painted white with an eaved ceiling and a small Velux window from which, if she stood on her tiptoes, Lydia could see the cemetery and the otherworldly white bulges of the Lord's Pavilion. It also looked out across a playground, and sometimes when the wind was blowing in her direction Lydia could hear the shouts and calls of small children playing down below, and for a moment would be transported back to another time and another place, far, far away from here.

She twisted open the bottle of Sprite and drank it fast from the neck, thirsty after her workout. The sky seen through her window was densely coloured and strangely mottled, almost like a framed piece of marbled Venetian paper. On her desk was her mail, left in a neat pile by Juliette while she was out. Also in her office was a green plant of some description, and two abstract paintings that rested on their frames against the walls, waiting for nails and pieces of string. She'd been to an 'affordable' art fair just after she moved into the house and spent £5,000 on art. In fact, the whole experience of moving into her first home had involved alarming amounts of expenditure. A lamp at a price of £280, which in the context of Lydia's life pre-house might have seemed offensively expensive, in the context of having spent nearly £4 million on a house seemed something of a bargain: that little? Wow! I'll have two! Spending £5,000 at an art fair had felt a little like grocery shopping, throwing things into a metaphorical trolley, barely glancing at the price tags.

Lydia had taken a giant leap up the property ladder, from a flatshare in Camden with Dixie, to a St John's Wood semi, almost overnight. The flatshare in Camden could have gone on indefinitely; neither woman could see any point to mortgages and space and rooms they didn't use. But then Dixie had met Clem and very quickly she had got pregnant and clearly neither of them had any interest in sharing the joys of parenthood with a flatmate. And Lydia did have a stupid amount of money sitting in her bank account. Most millionaire entrepreneurs did not share flats in slightly scuzzy Camden back streets. She was nearly thirty. It was a sign. It was time. She would have liked to have stayed in Camden, oddly comforted as she was by the proximity of kebab shops and drug dealers and places to get drunk in at three in the morning. But St John's Wood seemed a sounder investment, a surer place to lump her money, a place that had never been fashionable so could never be unfashionable, just a big, clean, comfy place for rich people to live.

It wasn't Lydia's fault that she was rich. She had not intended to be rich. It had happened to her purely by accident.

The kitchen smelled like a Shanghai back alley. Juliette was making rice noodles with seafood and a chicken and cashew nut stir-fry. Not for herself, for Lydia. And Clem. And Dixie. And Viola. Not that Viola would be eating noodles and chicken, she was only five days old. Lydia had offered to come and visit them and their new baby in their own home but Dixie had said: 'I've seen enough of my own home these past five days to last me a lifetime. And I'm sick of eating frozen lasagne. Please can we come to you?'

Lydia could not cook. She had tried. She could make a fairly decent breakfast, particularly scrambled eggs, but after 11 a.m. she floundered. She hadn't even had to ask Juliette if she would prepare occasional meals for her; Juliette had taken one look at Lydia and said, 'I cook for you, too, yes?'

'Smells great,' Lydia said now appreciatively.

'It is great.' Juliette smiled. 'Delicious. Taste.' She waved a fork in Lydia's direction.

Lydia speared some flaccid noodles on to the fork and popped them into her mouth. 'Mm,' she said, 'mmm, mmm, mmm. Amazing.'

'And, please don't mind me asking,' said Juliette, patting her hands against her apron, 'but have you bought a gift for the baby?'

Lydia puckered her lips and her brow. 'Er, no, actually.'

'No,' Juliette insisted, 'you must have gift for the baby.'

Lydia shook her head. 'I, er . . . God.' She ran her hand across the crown of her head. 'I didn't think.'

'It's fine,' Juliette smiled at her, reassuringly. 'BabyGap is just here,' she indicated the back of the house, 'one-minute walk. Pink.'

'Pink?' repeated Lydia.

'Yes. Pink. Or even white. But not blue.'

She turned her back on her employer then and faced the sink to wash her hands. Lydia shuffled from foot to foot for a moment, hoping for further instructions, but none came so she found her shoulder bag and then headed from the house towards the High Street.

Luckily, Lydia felt, she had some basic statistics to work with. The baby was female, so yes, as Juliette had suggested, blue was to be avoided; also the baby was five days old which fell, it transpired, into a size range referred to as nb, or 'newborn'. So at least Lydia knew which ones she should be looking at. It was also the middle of January, so warm clothing seemed the order of the day. Finally, after a long and rather discombobulating traverse of the shop, Lydia arrived at the cash desk holding a small pink cardigan and a pair of pink fleecy trousers decorated all over with tiny teddy bears.

'Is this a gift?' said the sales assistant.

'Er, yes,' said Lydia, resisting the temptation to say: No, they're for me, don't bother wrapping them, I'll wear them out. It then occurred to her that the asking of the question signified that the sales assistant thought that perhaps the garments were intended for Lydia's own child. The thought stunned her momentarily. Did she actually look like the sort of woman who might recently have brought forth her own child into the world? Did she actually look like a mother? It seemed unlikely. She was so far from the reality of motherhood – the concept sat on the horizon, strange and unattainable – that the idea that someone could look at her and imagine for a moment she was that type of person made her feel disturbed and oddly flattered all at the same time.

She took the boxed-up gift in the blue carrier and headed back home, stopping on the way at the smart wine shop on the corner where she spent £27.99 on a bottle of Gewürztraminer on the recommendation of the salesman. In Camden she would have expected a minimum of three bottles of wine for that amount of money. It was almost, Lydia contemplated as she typed her pin number into the salesman's machine, as though money had lost its context, had been stretched out of shape. This, she assumed, was what it was to be rich.

An hour later, Lydia paced the kitchen fitfully, peering down the hallway towards the opaque glass of the front door every few moments until finally she saw their outlines. She breathed in deeply. Not only was she unused to entertaining, she was unused to entertaining people with new babies. She pulled open the door and smiled at her friends. 'Hello!' she exclaimed. 'Come in!'

She knew that somewhere in the midst of her friends there was a baby, but as neither of them appeared to be holding one in any easily observable manner Lydia ushered them through, accepting the usual citrus-noted kisses from Dixie and an avuncular slap on the back from Clem, taking coats and steering them towards the kitchen. It was only as they began to seat themselves at the dining table that Lydia could see that they had brought in with them a moulded plastic car seat containing a small sleeping infant. She immediately felt a sense of social unease. It was as though Dixie had arrived with a new facial scar or a malodorous fiancé, something new and permanent about which Lydia was obliged to say something positive and encouraging. She set her face to soft and eyed the contents of the car seat. 'So this is little Viola?' She smiled.

'Vee-ola,' Dixie corrected.

'Sorry, Vee-ola, yes, I did wonder. Vee-ola. Well, hello, aren't you small?'

Dixie snorted. 'You wouldn't say that,' she began, 'if you'd had to push her out of your body single-handedly. Without any drugs, of any description.'

'Well, no, I'm sure . . .' Lydia wrinkled her nose and trailed off. This was exactly the sort of thing she'd been worried about. Talk of pushing and drugs and, soon, no doubt, of bowel movements and putrid milky burps.

The baby appeared to be involved in a very vivid and involving dream, her eyes pressed shut as though against her will, her face twitching occasionally, her hands held out claw-like in front of her body. Lydia remembered that she was supposed to say something complimentary. 'Well,' she said after a moment, 'she's sleeping, that's good.'

Clem smiled and eyed the infant fondly. 'That's all she does,' he said, 'sleeps. Dreams, feeds, shits, sleeps. She's an angel.'

For a short while all three adults sat and smiled fondly at the oblivious Viola until eventually they recovered themselves and Lydia turned her mind towards drinks and snacks.

Dixie, she was surprised to notice, as she handed her a glass of sparkling water, still appeared to be pregnant. She was dressed in a kind of smock top and narrow-legged jeans and, as far as Lydia could tell, didn't look all that different from how she'd looked the last time she'd seen her, two weeks ago, before they had their baby. Lydia wondered about this, and felt worried for a moment that maybe her friend had something wrong with her, a tumour perhaps, but thought better of asking about it.

She passed Clem a can of Grolsch and a glass and poured herself one and then sat down with her friends.

'So, is this the first time you've been out, since she was born?' Lydia began.

They both nodded and Dixie said, 'I mean, I've taken her out to the corner shop, but this is officially her first car ride and her first dinner party.'

'Well,' said Lydia, 'I must say, you both look great. I mean, a bit tired, but still, great.'

She wasn't sure what she'd been expecting; skulls for faces, sick-splattered clothing, empty expressions, drained of anything that had previously made them what they were. But, no, they seemed jolly and bright and reasonably normal.

'Knackered,' agreed Dixie, untying the laces of some rather battered Converse plimsolls and kicking them off beneath the table, a relaxed and somewhat untidy gesture that betrayed their previous incarnations as flatmates. 'Though she's in our bed so at least I'm not getting up and down in the middle of the night to feed her.'

'And it is rather *brilliant* for me,' agreed Clem, 'as I don't have to wake up at all!'

Dixie threw him a withering look. 'Your time will come,' she said. 'Once she's off the boob, you will be getting very familiar with the bottle steriliser and the Cow and Gate, I can assure you.'

Clem smiled wanly and stroked his beer glass. Lydia got to her feet and lit the gas beneath the two woks on the hob, as per Juliette's instructions. 'Well,' she said, smiling across the hob towards her friends, 'haven't we all come a long way? Seems like only yesterday we were all squashed into that little flat together, and now you two are parents and I'm over here in this huge place. Is this it?' She smiled. 'Are we grown-ups now?'

Clem and Dixie laughed. 'Never,' said Dixie, 'perish the thought. I keep thinking someone's going to realise how immature we are and come and take the baby away from us. I'm sure the midwife thinks we're a pair of losers.'

Clem and Dixie laughed and Lydia glanced across the hob at them again. Her friends. Clem was a sweet-faced man with too much thick dark hair, scuffed cheeks and a slight paunch. Dixie was small and trendy with peroxide-blonde hair, currently showing two inches of pale gold roots after some kind of pregnancy-related bleach ban. They looked like a pair of overgrown students. They *were* a pair of overgrown students. Lydia had met Dixie (her real name was Suzanne Dixon but she'd been Dixie since she was a very young girl) at university in Aberystwyth. Dixie was studying film-making. Lydia was studying Chemistry. Neither of them could really remember how they'd come together, chalk and cheese as they were in every respect. But they'd co-existed quite happily for ten years, first in a shared room above a shop in Aberystwyth and then, as Dixie and Lydia's careers had taken off and led them to London, in the two-bed place in Camden Town. An old married couple, that's how they'd seen themselves, and in that scenario Dixie, cute and domesti-cated, the sort of person who randomly decided to make cup cakes, for no particular reason, had been the girl and Lydia, lean and formidable and with no notion whatso-ever of the difference between caster sugar and icing sugar, had definitely been the man.

Clem had come into their lives a year ago and Lydia had liked him immediately. She liked that he was unfashionable and wholesome and had views on things other than trendy film directors and club nights at Camden dives. He took Dixie out for walks on the Heath and made her eat meat (she was a rather woolly, uncommitted vegetarian type). And then quickly, rather too quickly in Lydia's opinion, he got her pregnant. Dixie was twenty-nine. It seemed far too young to be having a baby. And a year seemed far too early on in a relationship to become a parent. But from the moment they'd found out, there'd been no doubt in either of their minds that a baby was the way forward. 'Why not?' Dixie had said. 'It'll be an adventure.'

Adventures, Lydia felt, weren't always necessarily good things.

The baby started to stir in its seat and she felt herself bristle. It wasn't that Lydia disliked babies, it was just that she didn't know babies. She had not held a baby in her arms since she was a teenager, and even then she wasn't sure if she really had or if it was some kind of false memory. She busied herself extra-zealously to avoid the possibility of Clem or Dixie attempting to foist the baby upon her, keeping her gaze from the baby's face as it was unclipped and raised from its seat. Suddenly, though, she was face to face with it, its tiny little face a few inches from hers, staring at her with some alarm. Lydia stared back at her with some alarm and then the baby began, quite understandably, to wail. Clem immediately clutched the small bundle to his chest and whisked her away.

'Traumatised for life,' said Lydia, flatly. Of course the baby had cried. She had fully expected the baby to cry. Lydia was not a baby person and did not have the kind of face or demeanour that a baby would like.

The baby spent the duration of the meal slurping from one of Dixie's vastly over-inflated breasts, and then some time draped over her shoulder staring pathetically at the wall behind her. Lydia felt sorry for the child. She was so new and ill-equipped. Every day her eyes would see more of this strange place, every day her brain would process more reality, her tiny limbs would stretch and swell, she'd learn and absorb and empathise and understand and grow and grow and grow . . . until one day she'd wake up and she'd be just another human being. The length and magnitude of the journey seemed to bear such pitifully small rewards.

After her friends had left, taking the infant Viola and her new pink clothes with them, Lydia felt curiously sad. She loaded her shiny Miele dishwasher with large Royal Doulton platters and scraped sticky noodles into the very clever German-designed concealed bins. She dropped the empty wine bottle (it had not been worth £27.99) and beer cans into the recycling compartment and she wiped all her silky, off-white surfaces with a stack of folded kitchen paper. She washed the woks and dried them and put them away, and with every movement she felt something thick and sour sloshing around in the pit of her stomach and it wasn't her supper. It was a kind of melancholic longing.

It was the baby, something to do with the baby. She too had once been a baby, she too had been a tiny miracle, kept safe and nurtured, talcumed and clothed in doll-sized clothes. She'd been, it was hard to imagine now, a fat baby, with dark ringlets and cheeks like cherries and whey. She had pictures of herself in cotton romper suits with elasticated legs that cut into the meat of her thighs, smiling into the camera as though she were truly the loveliest thing in the world. She had other pictures of herself, dandled on knees like a catch of the day, held in arms like a football trophy, always the centre of the universe, always the reason for the photo having been taken. She remembered nothing about it, of course, nothing about being a baby, but she'd been wanted, she knew that much, wanted and needed by her sweet soft mother, even if her father hadn't cared.

The longing she felt was not so much for the baby she'd once been as for the life she'd been promised back in those rosy, unknowable days. The promise of gentle voices and warm embraces and a safe place to be. Nearly all babies were made these promises, given these false notions about the world, but few had them ripped away from them as painfully and suddenly as Lydia had. It wasn't, she now realised, that she didn't like babies, or that she didn't find babies interesting, and it wasn't even that she resented the baby for taking her friends from her and into a strange and unreachable realm, although she did, it was more that instead of feeling joy when she looked at a new baby, all she felt was fear.

On Thursday Lydia met Bendiks in Regent's Park. He was dazzling in a white t-shirt and a thick red hooded jacket. Lydia was less luminous in off-black joggers and a grey hoodie. She felt the familiar leap of happiness at the sight of her personal trainer. She didn't know why Bendiks made her feel this way. Lydia wasn't usually attracted to incredibly pretty men who looked like they should be wearing sailor suits in arty aftershave commercials. Lydia wasn't, as far as she was aware, usually attracted to any-thing, these days. Lydia was a scientist. Lydia was a businesswoman. Lydia was wealthy. Lydia was lonely. But

Lydia had barely thought about men, women, sex or anything in between for years.

'Good morning!' Bendiks beamed.

'Morning,' said Lydia, rubbing her hands together against the January chill.

'How are you this morning?'

'Oh, I'm fine, not bad. You?'

'I'm *fantastic*,' he declared.

Lydia nodded her agreement.

'Right,' he said, 'it's cold this morning, so let's warm up nice and quickly. Let's jump.' He smiled at Lydia and Lydia swallowed a groan. Jumping at the gym was one thing; jumping out here, in public, was quite another. Bendiks had a special jumping technique: hands at knee-level, knees bent, hopping around the place like a great gangling frog.

'OK,' she said, 'but only if you jump with me too.'

Bendiks smiled. 'For sure,' he replied.

And so the two of them clasped their kneecaps and began to hop, Lydia resisting the urge to say, Ribbit. Ribbit. After a moment her blood began to run warm and fast and her cheeks found some colour and her heart hammered against her chest and she laughed, despite herself. Ribbit. Ribbit.

Lydia's last sexual encounter had been eight years ago, with a fellow student, a man called William. It was William who'd suggested to her that she should take her ground-breaking chemical compound and her business acumen and make a product that would appeal to millions. It was also William who had broken her heart for the very first and only time.

'So,' said Bendiks, as they jogged sedately towards the outdoor training circuit in Primrose Hill, 'you are a scientist?'

'Well, yes,' said Lydia. 'Sort of. I used to be. Nowadays I seem to have become more of a business consultant.'

'Wow,' said Bendiks, 'and how does a scientist become like a business consultant?'

Lydia smiled. 'That,' she said, 'is a long and very dull story.'

'I don't mind dull,' said Bendiks, pursing his pretty lips together and turning to face the path once more. 'I am a personal fitness trainer!'

His body was extraordinary. Lithe and toned, yet still soft-looking. Lydia didn't like the thought of those very hard bodies that some men had, she didn't like the feel of muscle too close to flesh. It was, thought Lydia, the perfect male body. This, she assumed, may be what lay at the root of her strange fascination with Bendiks, just the sheer unlikely perfection of him.

'So,' said Bendiks, 'tell me.'

Lydia caught her breath. 'Oh, God, honestly, it really is so boring. I invented a chemical compound at uni, result of some strange obsession of mine, a compound to take the smell out of paint.'

'Paint?'

'Yeah, you know, for walls. It was for my final year. But actually I'd been working on it non-stop since school, in my free time, not sure why, just . . . hate the smell of paint. Anyway, I found this compound by a total fluke. I was working on something else at the time, and it completely eliminated the odour. And then a couple of years later I was decorating my flat, and I noticed this gap in the market for organic paint. So I took out a business loan and launched a small range of odourless organic paints. Just five colours to start with, then those sold really well so another five. After five years I had a range of forty colours and was selling through Homebase, B&Q. Then, eighteen months ago, Dulux bought my brand. For a lot of money. And I still get royalties for the original compound because I patented it and sold it to other paint manufacturers. So I have the money from Dulux, plus a regular income from the royalties . . .'

'So you just sit back and money arrives in your hands, is that what it is like?'

Lydia laughed again. 'Well, no, not exactly,' she said, 'I do a lot of work with small businesses . . . with the petro-chemical industry . . . write for a couple of trade papers. It's all quite unglamorous but, I don't know, for some reason, since I sold the paint business, I just haven't wanted to go back to science. It's almost like . . . it's like I had a mission and I've accomplished it and now I'm just swimming along in the wake of that. I tried taking some time off when I sold the business but, well, I wasn't very good at time off. So ever since, I've thrown myself into anything and everything that comes my way.'

'Wow.' Bendiks turned his head towards Lydia and

regarded her with awe. 'So you are a workaholic? You are very impressive. I am very impressed.'

Lydia smiled. She was quietly delighted to have impressed Bendiks.

In the circuit park, Lydia rained a few blows against the outstretched leather-gloved hands of Bendiks. Her fists made a sound like someone falling to the floor every time they connected with his. She didn't feel right hitting Bendiks. She didn't feel right hitting anyone. She'd heard other women talk of this practice as liberating and empowering. To her it just felt slightly undignified.

A mother sat with a baby sleeping in a buggy while her toddler larked around on the circuit-training equipment. The mother stared at a newspaper spread out next to her on a bench. She turned the pages slowly and rhythmically, as though she was exercising her wrist rather than her mind. With her other wrist she moved the buggy back and forth, an inch forward, an inch back, an inch forward, an inch back. Every few moments she would glance up from her paper, eye the slumbering baby, eye the rampaging toddler, eye the newspaper, turn another page; back and forth, back and forth went the buggy. It was rare for Lydia to see anything about parenthood that appealed to her. It all looked so mechanical and wearisome.

Suddenly the toddler was in front of them. He stopped in his tracks and watched as the thin dark woman hit the handsome man again and again and again. Lydia glanced down at him, willing him to walk away. Go, she thought to herself, go away. But he didn't. Clearly there was something spellbinding about the sight of the two of them. But suddenly the boy's interest turned from fascination to concern, and then from concern to distress, and his face crumpled and he ran sobbing back to his mother who finally snapped out of her paper/pram/peruse cycle to encircle him in her arms and protect him from the sheer horror of watching the scary lady hit the pretty man.

Lydia sighed. She no longer stalked around in threadbare jumpers with an oversized dog at her side, she no longer drank vodka on sidings and washed her hair with Fairy liquid. She was a grown-up, elegant, some might say, verging on stylish, when she could be bothered. She flossed her teeth, she wore perfume, she waxed her toes, she shopped on the high street and she did nice things to her skin. But still it seemed, to those with an eye for what lurked under the surface, to children and babies and animals and the more perceptive, she was the Scary Lady in Black. Just like she'd always been.

Bendiks looked across at the crying toddler and threw her an amused glance. 'He thinks we are fighting,' he laughed. 'Poor boy. He is traumatised. He will have to find counselling!'

Lydia smiled grimly and let her arms drop to her sides. Their training was over for another day. She suddenly wanted to reclaim some kind of healthy input from their session instead of the appalling sense of herself she'd been subsumed by.

'So, you,' she began, 'why did you become a personal fitness trainer?'

Bendiks laughed, showing off his square white teeth. 'Because,' he said, packing away the gloves and a towel into a holdall and smiling up at Lydia, 'unlike you, I was too stupid to do anything else! OK, I go this way, you go that way, have a great weekend and I will see you on Monday at the club. OK?'

Lydia stood, damp and dishevelled, with quickly cooling sweat rolling down her face, and watched him leave; solid buttocks, strong shoulders, off to be Bendiks somewhere else, with somebody else. She felt it for a moment then, the desperate ache she sometimes felt looking at other people, the ache of never being able to be them, not for even a moment, of always having to be herself.

Lydia arrived home fifteen minutes later and as she stepped over the threshold to her house, she saw a large manila envelope on the stairs, left there, she assumed, by Juliette to be taken up later. It caught her eye because unlike most of the mail that came to her this one had a hand-written address and looked kind of ungainly. She sat down upon the bottom step and pulled the envelope towards her. The postcode read Tonypandy.

She gasped.

All her adult life she'd been half-consciously waiting for someone from home to contact her. Now finally that moment had arrived. She stared at the handwriting for a moment longer. She knew whose handwriting it was. Not because she recognised it, but because she knew there was only one member of her family who would be interested enough to have managed to track her down. And that was her uncle Rod.

Uncle Rod had once been the closest relative they'd had because he was single and childless and because he was good with Lydia and helpful in ways that Lydia's aunts, with families and commitments of their own, could not be. But then, within a few days of Lydia's mother's death, Uncle Rod disappeared and was never seen again. Lydia was too young to wonder why or even really to notice. But she'd thought of him sometimes, and then she'd seen him at her father's funeral, fourteen years later, slipping away from the crowd through the trees, dressed in a cheap black suit, the sun glinting off a silver hoop in his ear, and she'd asked someone who he was and they'd said: 'That was your uncle Rod, that was your dad's brother.' She'd wondered briefly why he hadn't stayed but not thought much about him since.

She stared through the opaque panels of the front door as her head filled with memories of those last few days of her father's life. She could still smell the hospital, hear the wheels of trolleys heading to dark unknown places, feel her father's cold hand grasping hers, as tight as a clamp, whispering words into her ear that made no sense. 'You'll always be mine,' he'd said, 'always. No one can take that away from me. I raised you. You're as much mine as anyone's. Do you hear me? Do you understand me? As much mine as *anyone's.*'

They were no more than words to Lydia. She wasn't looking for meaning at that point. She wasn't looking for answers. She just wanted him to die so that she wouldn't be spending her first term of university sitting by his bed in this mouldering Victorian hospital or making him cups of tea in their damp loveless flat. She wanted him gone so that the rest of her life could begin. A clean break. From her village. From her past. She was ready to let go of him. And he, she could tell from the look in his eyes, was ready to let go, too, not just of her, but of the whole pointless, unhappy business of existence.

He finally passed away in the last week of August. Outside the hospital the air was sweet and hot. Inside it was stagnant and stale. There was no one else there. Just her and her dad. His last words to her were: 'Tell them it's stopped hurting. Tell them.' She'd watched the last breath leave his mouth. She'd expected it to leave his body like a small puff of grey-black smoke, a tiny toxic cloud, but instead it rushed from between his lips like a lizard escaping from his soul, panicky and desperate.

His hand went limp in hers and then his head fell slack against the pillows and he was gone and Lydia was still there, suddenly an orphan.

She hadn't looked back much in the years following her father's death. She never returned to the village outside Tonypandy, not even when well-intended invitations to her cousins' weddings arrived in the post, nor when her aunts pleaded with her to join them for cosy Christmas afternoons in small terraced houses with dry turkeys and fresh grandchildren. She lived her life in Aberystwyth, stayed in the flat above the shop during all three annual holidays, even when Dixie was away. She worked as a barmaid at her local pub for the full three years of her time at university, evenings and weekends. And when she wasn't at the pub she was in the lab, methodically and obsessively searching for something to take the smell out of paint, thinking that she was working towards a clear commercial goal, little realising that she was trying to scour away a whole film of putrid childhood memories from her subconscious.

And now she was here, twenty-nine years old, the merest undulation of a Welsh accent still present when she spoke, a millionaire, a self-made woman, tall, dark, clever, mysterious, a million miles away from her sad and rather humble beginnings . . . and suddenly a piece of her past was sitting in a brown envelope upon her lap. She took a deep breath and then she opened it.

Lydia stared at the newspaper cutting. It lay on her desk, spread out flat. Her right hand rested against the dewy coldness of a tumbler of iced gin and lime. The light in her office was inky and warm, still some smudges of daylight left in the sky. All the lights were off except for the Anglepoise lamp with which she was illuminating the cutting. She'd been sitting here for half a day. Six hours. Staring at the cutting, working her way methodically, coolly, through a bottle of Bombay Sapphire. Everything felt stretched and twisted and distorted. Her house didn't feel like her house. Her legs didn't feel like they belonged to her. Juliette felt like a stranger. Lydia had sent her home early, turned every light in the house off and made herself drunk.

The contents of the fat brown envelope had been both shocking and simultaneously unsurprising. Some paperwork from a fertility clinic in central London confirming that she had been conceived by means of artificial insemination, using the sperm of a French man whose occupation was classed as that of Medical Student. Also inside the envelope was a newspaper article torn from the pages of the *Western Mail and Echo*. It was a story about a woman in Llanelli who'd discovered at the age of twenty-five that not only had she been conceived in a fertility clinic under the glare of dazzling halogen lights, but that she had four half-sisters all living within a hundred miles of her. Lydia squinted and stared again at the happy gang. They had their arms around each other and their cheeks pressed up against one another's. They all had brown hair and they all had slightly fleshy-looking noses. They were clearly sisters.

The anonymous sender of this fun-pack of seismically life-changing information had also included a leaflet about a website called the UK Donor Sibling Registry. Adults who knew they'd been conceived by donor insemination and knew the name of the clinic where the procedure had taken place could sign up, have their DNA tested and be put in touch with children conceived from the same donor's sperm. In other words, they could be introduced to their brothers and sisters.

Lydia had never had to wonder why she had no brothers

and sisters. It was obvious. Her mother had died before she could have any more. Being an only child was absolutely, intrinsically, who she was. She could not have imagined her childhood, her persona, herself, in any other way.

She stared desperately at the sisters in the paper and then filled her glass again. She hadn't drunk gin since she was eighteen years old, not since her father had died. The minute he'd gone, so had the sore, tender spot in the pit of her belly that she'd been trying to anaesthetise. The smell of the clear spirit, the vapour at the rim of the glass, the tang of bitter old fruit, made her feel it again, all the pain and discomfort of being a tragic, unloved eighteen year old.

She thought of her father, the once strong man made of breeze blocks and Bacardi, batter and testosterone, shrivelling and shrinking in the room next door to hers, desiccated, drained and mummified as the life seeped out of him. She thought of the way he'd raised her to look after herself, because nobody else was going to do it. To watch her back. To trust no one. To believe no one. To stand alone. She thought of every last moment she'd spent in his company; the meaningless words they'd exchanged, the thoughtless gifts on Christmas Day, the brusque phone calls, the pills gracelessly administered, the silences that sang of secrets, the endless rolling moments that had felt like nothing at the time, just air, just space, just fug, now suddenly filled with meaning and poignancy. She wasn't his. *She wasn't his.*

Her real father was a medical student. A medical student from London with dark hair and dark eyes who stood at 5′ 11″ and hailed originally from Dieppe. Her real father was French. Her real father was a doctor. Her real father was not Trevor Pike. She felt something fluid like relief go through her bones. She felt something like *delight*.

And out there, somewhere, maybe on the street below her window, maybe in a flat in Llanelli, maybe in a briny bar in Dieppe, there were others like her. Brothers. Sisters. *People like her*. She had never met a person like her before. She was not like her mother, what little she could remember of her, and she was not like her father, although, ha, how he had talked about his 'Italian ancestry' over the years, how hard her father had tried to instil in her a sense of pride in her Latin roots. Roots which she now knew were non-existent. Roots as real as fairy dust. She'd never felt it anyway, her supposed Italian-ness. Always raised her eyebrows impatiently at any mention of it. *Just because that's the only thing that's interesting about you*, she'd think to herself, *don't try and make it the only thing that's interesting about me*.

She'd known she was more than the daughter of a semi-literate fishmonger. She'd known it. Deep down inside herself. She'd felt more related to her old dog Arnie than to her father. The guilt she'd carried for half her life, the guilt of wanting her father to be dead so that she could get on with her life, it lifted and it floated away from her, like an exorcised demon. All that was left was a jumbled sense of strangeness and newness and sadness and delight. She drank another tumbler of gin and lime and she typed the address of the Donor Sibling Registry into her address bar. As the page loaded she felt a quickening in her chest, a sense of rising panic. She wasn't ready. She closed the browser, shut down her computer and headed for a deep and unsettling sleep full of dreams of strangers.

She phoned Dixie the next morning. Her friend sounded startled to hear from her.

'Sorry,' said Lydia, 'were you in the middle of something?'

'No, no,' said Dixie, stifling a yawn, 'no, I was just, er, just having a sleep.'

Lydia considered the hour. 11 a.m. It was not like Dixie to be sleeping at 11 a.m., not with shelves to be rearranged and books to be read and people to be having potentially career-enhancing conversations with. Dixie took sleep very much as something forced upon her against her will, something she submitted to once a day and then emerged from groggily and crossly, as though sleep had stolen her soul.

'Yeah,' she continued, 'Viola had a bad night. She's out for the count now so I thought I'd catch up on some lost sleep.'

'Oh, shit, Dix, I'm really sorry. I didn't think.'

Dixie cleared her sinuses loudly, almost, Lydia couldn't help feeling, to ram home how utterly, deeply asleep she had just been and how much it had taken out of her to rouse herself for this phone call. Lydia bridled slightly and said, 'You should have kept your phone switched off.'

'Yeah, you're right.' She snorted again, and yawned. 'I wasn't thinking. Don't seem to be able to do much of that these days.' She laughed drily.

These days. That laugh. Lydia bridled again. She hated it when people had babies. No, not when people had babies. When *Dixie* had babies. Everyone else could sod off and have a hundred babies each for all she cared. She just didn't want Dixie to have one. She'd only just got used to Dixie having Clem. 'Boyfriend' was foreign terrain to Lydia but she could make a tenuous grasp on it, having had one of her own at one point in her life. But 'Baby' was another planet entirely. 'Baby' was consuming in a way that even the neediest boyfriend was not. 'Baby' changed *everything*. And 'Baby', unlike 'Boyfriend', was irreversible.

'That's all right,' she continued, trying her hardest to sound perky, 'I didn't want to disturb you but . . .' She stopped. Before 'Baby' she would have been able to launch straight into the topic she'd called to discuss. Now there was this spectre hanging over everything. Would Dixie even *care*, she wondered, now that she lived in the land of 'Baby'? Would it even register? *Sorry, a sperm donor, you say? Anyway, did I tell you about Viola's last nappy?*

'How are you all?' she managed.

'We're fine. I think. Are we fine, Clem?' Lydia heard him grumbling something in the background. 'Yes,' Dixie came back on the line, 'we're fine. How are you?'

'OK,' she said. 'Hungover.' The minute she'd said it she'd known it was the wrong thing to have said, insinuating as it did a night spent drinking sparkling wine and tequila-based cocktails somewhere fun and jazzy and nowhere near a new baby or a dirty nappy.

'Oh, lucky you,' sighed Dixie.

Lydia sighed too and thought about hitting Dixie with the reality of her night swallowing gin alone in the dark. 'Not really,' she said. 'It was . . .' She paused. It was horrible, she wanted to say, but before she could muster the first syllable a plaintive shriek cut into their conversation and Dixie was mumbling something about feeding time at the zoo and could she call her back in a minute, and Lydia said, yeah, sure, even though she knew it wouldn't be a minute, it would be a hundred minutes at least, and wondered silently why Clem couldn't take the squealing infant away for just a moment or two, but then knowing anyway that the physical absence of the squealing infant would not render her friend any more able to concentrate on anything beyond the realm of her current situation, and with a sense of dread and sadness Lydia realised that she was not going to be able to talk to her best friend about the most important thing that had happened to her in over a decade.

And so she hung up and Dixie disappeared in a metaphorical puff of smoke leaving Lydia feeling abandoned and alone.

Dixie didn't call back a hundred minutes later. She didn't call back three days later. She sent Lydia a text message on Saturday morning that read: *I just sprayed milk six foot across the room and hit the cat in the eye. What are you up to?* With every inch that Dixie stepped forward into the world of babies and normality, Lydia felt herself step an inch back, into the world of strangeness and solitude. She typed back: *Give the cat some goggles! I'm just hanging.* Dixie didn't reply and Lydia didn't expect her to. She spent the day alternating between working and drinking.

That night she pulled a photo album from her storage room and took it to bed with her. It was the one she'd kept when she'd moved out of the miserable flat she'd shared with her father. It was all she had of Glenys. Mum. There were no mothball-scented dresses or heirloom pearl earrings or locks of hair for Lydia to finger thoughtfully, her father had cleared out every last trace of her mother after her death, but he'd kept this. Lydia could not begin to fathom what sort of aberrational thought process had led to his putting it away for her, but he had and it was now her most treasured possession.

In the past she'd stared at these photos almost as though she was staring at photos of Marilyn Monroe or Queen Victoria, at a dead superstar; charismatic, unattainable, unknowable, powerful and gone. But she looked at them through different eyes that night. She'd always thought of her mother as just a girl. That's what everyone had always said about her: She was a great girl. A fun girl. A sweet girl. A lovely girl. Ah, yes, Glenys, she was a *lovely girl.* But *girls* didn't go to Harley Street to make babies out of thin air. Women did that. Women who wanted babies. 'Your mother worshipped me, d'you know that? Worshipped the ground I walked on.' Her father had said that. Not once, but repeatedly, his way of keeping her all for himself. But as Lydia stared at the photographs it suddenly struck her that her mother had loved her much more than she'd ever loved him. After all, she'd been prepared to risk absolutely everything for her.

On Sunday Lydia went for a walk. She was sober and tired and the pavement felt like sponge beneath her feet. The light was watery but she wore sunglasses, feeling as she did like a small half-blind creature emerging from hibernation. She walked three times round the old cemetery, averting her gaze from the playground where Asian nannies pushed French babies on swings and American power mummies tapped data into BlackBerries while their offspring slurped organic juices out of recyclable cartons. She walked up and down St John's Wood High Street, past boutiques and bagel shops and baby clothes shops and double-parked four-wheel-drives, and she stared at every person she walked past with a kind of animal curiosity. Here she was, two miles from the place of her conception. Here she was, potentially, walking through herds of relations. She scrutinised the noses, the gaits, the hands, the eyes, of everyone she looked at. She spotted a similarity in the curve of someone's jaw and found herself subconsciously following the hapless woman across the street and into a patisserie. She stopped herself at the entrance and turned back towards the street.

Lydia had always felt divided from the rest of the world,

elevated almost. She'd always felt cleverer and quieter and stronger and more self-sufficient. Her dad had made her that way. He'd built her up to believe that she was invincible. And alone. And she was. She always looked on the remainder of humanity as just that, an amorphous mass, a sprawling splodge, of flesh and bone. Nothing to do with her. And still, at the age of twenty-nine, she had not had a connection with anyone as strong as the one she'd once shared with her childhood dog.

After an hour of this aimless, eccentric wandering, she headed home. She appraised her house from the pavement. A shiver ran through her. It was so big. So soulless. So unwelcoming with its opaque windows like blind milky eyes. It was, she realised with a sudden discomfiting burst of perspective, a true reflection of herself. Even Dixie said it to her sometimes: 'You're *scary*!' And that was fine. Lydia was happy to be scary. Being scary kept the world away from your door. But now there was a tiny fleck of possibility that the world was on its way in, and that there was nothing she was going to be able to do to stop it. But more surprising than that was the realisation that she didn't actually want to.

That night, she took a plastic bottle of Sprite and a bag of Haribo Tangfastics up to her office. She twisted the lid of the bottle and waited a beat for the initial puff of sweetened gas to escape before removing it and taking a greedy gulp. She spent a few moments examining the contents of the bag of sweeties, testing her responses to the various options therein. Eventually she settled on a green and red bottle and chewed it contemplatively for a while. She thought about phoning Dixie. This seemed to be such an alarmingly big step to be taking in her life without a single soul knowing about it. The weekend had been long and intense. She felt absolutely removed from reality. She felt scared and excited and sick. On the other side of her next action was another existence. She imagined Dixie sitting with a baby on her gigantic breast, staring mindlessly into space, sighing at the sight of Lydia's number on her phone display. No. She would do this alone.

She typed in the web address and she filled in the on-line forms. Then she ate another sweetie, this one in the shape of a baby's dummy.

Days passed after Lydia posted her details on to the Donor Sibling Registry. They passed slowly and tire-somely, like plodders on the high street, blocking her progress. January became February. She couldn't seem to focus on anything. She couldn't see beyond her in box. All day she hovered over her computer, eating sweets, ignor-ing the phone, checking and checking and checking again her e-mail. The only sparks of life inside this blanket of hibernation were her thrice-weekly sessions with Bendiks and an invitation on her desk to a *Welcome to the World* party for Viola in three weeks' time.

She was at home now, waiting for Bendiks. He was training her here today because he'd parted ways with the health club in the mews. Lydia hadn't asked why. But she was feeling oddly nervous now as the minutes crawled their way towards eleven o'clock. In only moments Bendiks would be here, in her home. She would open the door and he would smile and she would invite him in . . . and in another parallel existence it would be evening and she would open a bottle of wine and they would talk across a flickering candle and then retire to bed to explore each other's bodies for half the night under Lydia's freshly changed bedding. But in this existence, this existence of stark, unupholstered reality, she would lead him into the wellness room in the basement (yes, she had a wellness room. It had already been here when she bought the house) and he would make her do boring and repetitive things for forty-five minutes and then he would go and she wouldn't see him again for forty-eight hours.

She glanced at herself in the mirror before descending the stairs. She looked ghostly and vaguely demented. Juliette had jumped when she'd walked in this morning and seen Lydia on the stairs and immediately made her a roast chicken sandwich. Bendiks was less fazed.

'Good morning, Lydia,' he said, swinging through her front door with a gym bag and a scent of cinnamon and musk. 'You have a very nice house.'

'Thank you,' she replied, allowing him past her and into the hallway.

He was, as usual, pristinely turned out. It was wrong on so many levels for Lydia to feel the way she felt about Bendiks. He was probably gay. In fact, yes, of course he was. Of course he was gay. His manicured eyebrows, his immaculate black hoodie, his whitened teeth and his pretty tattoos. Of course he was. She hoped he was. If Bendiks was gay then she could stop feeling this way every time she came into contact with him. If Bendiks was gay then she could just carry on living her life.

'Can I get you anything?' she asked. 'A glass of water?'

'No, it's fine,' he patted his gym bag, 'I have my bottle.' He smiled at her and she felt it. He was not gay. A gay man would not smile at a woman that way. She was sure of it.

'So,' she began, leading him down the stairs to the basement, flicking a switch as she went, 'did you have a good weekend?'

'Yeah, it was OK. Pretty dull. How about you?'

'Yeah,' she replied, 'the same.'

He laughed. 'If this was my house,' he said, 'I would fill it every weekend with beautiful people and make a big, big party.'

Lydia smiled wryly. 'I don't know any beautiful people,' she replied, drily.

'You know me.'

'That is true,' she said. She flicked another switch.

'Wow, look at it down here, this is amazing.'

'Yeah,' she scratched her neck, 'can't say I come down here very often.'

'But it is like your own spa! You have a whirlpool!'

'Yes, and a sauna. And a treatment room, here.' She pushed open a door and showed him a small white room painted with cherry-blossom sprigs. 'And a home cinema, through there.'

Bendiks' perfect eyebrows were sitting somewhere within reach of his hairline. 'Wow,' he said. 'Wow.'

Lydia didn't feel any gratification at his reaction. Try as she might, she could not make this house feel like it had anything to do with her. In her head it still belonged to the slightly forbidding American couple she'd bought it from, to Caitlin and Tom Schnobel and their three handsome teenage sons. In her head the three spare bedrooms belonged to those boys, and this vast dug-out pleasure dome of a basement belonged to Caitlin ('Call me Cait'). Lydia half-expected them all to walk back in one day with a set of matching luggage and Caribbean tans and thank her for minding their house for them.

'I thought we could work out here,' she said, indicating a space by the back door with a ballet barre and a mirrored wall and built-in gym mats.

'Well, yes, your own personal home gym, I think, yes, that does seem the logical place to work out.' He smiled widely, explaining his joke to her. 'You know, in this job I have been in some amazing houses belonging to, like, celebrities and things, but I think your house is the best. It's the most . . . *me*, you know?' He smiled again and began to unpack his gym bag. 'Right,' he said, 'are you ready to go?'

She nodded wanly.

'You look . . . I hope you don't mind me to say this, but you look bad today.'

'Oh,' she said, 'thanks a lot.'

'No, I don't mean you look unpleasant. I mean, you

look like there are bad things in your head. You look weighted down, squashed, you understand?'

Lydia grimaced. Squashed and weighted down. He made her sound like a slug under a brick. 'Just stuff,' she muttered. 'Some weird stuff going on in my life, that's all.'

He arched an eyebrow. 'Anything you'd like to talk about?'

She laughed, louder than she'd meant to.

'What,' he teased, 'you think I can't talk? That I am just some big meathead?'

'No! Of course not. It's just . . . I don't know. We never talk. It would be weird.'

He smiled and folded his arms across his chest. 'Listen,' he said, 'I am here as your personal trainer, right? You pay me to make you fit. That is the deal. But also, I have to know that you are in the right place, mentally, for me to make you fit and I have noticed lately that you are not. That I leave you and then you go like this,' he collapsed his upper torso, pathetically, 'until the next time I see you. And that is no good. So, if you think it would help, talk to me. I am cheaper than a shrink!'

'Oh, God,' she said, drily, 'I wouldn't know where to start. I really wouldn't.'

'Try me.' He smiled. 'I think I've heard pretty much everything there is to hear. I'm pretty hard to shock.'

Lydia glanced at him. He'd crouched down on his haunches to her level. His skin was like chamois, matt and unblemished. She was sure she could see a hint of concealer under his eyes. That confirmed it. Bendiks was gay. And the fact of his being gay made him suddenly emotionally accessible. 'Right, well,' she began, slightly defensively, 'up until four weeks ago I had no idea that my mother, who died in suspicious circumstances when I was three, had used a sperm donor to conceive me. Someone from my home town sent me an anonymous letter. And last week I signed up to a website that promised to reunite me with any siblings I may unwittingly have dotted around the world. I have had a DNA test and been told that my father's name was Donor 32 and that so far no other children have signed up or registered, so now every single day I sit by my computer checking and checking and checking to see if anyone's added their details, to see if I have a brother or a sister. And I'm finding it really hard to concentrate on anything else. When I'm not hovering over my computer, I'm walking the streets staring at people like a loon, wondering if they look like me, wondering if they might be my . . . *family*.'

She felt her body relax as the words left her mouth. The physical feel of them was soothing and pleasant, like syrup.

Bendiks exhaled slowly from bellowed cheeks and lowered himself on to his backside. 'Wow,' he said. 'Unbelievable.'

Lydia nodded.

'So your father . . . the man who brought you up . . . he could not . . .?'

She shrugged. 'I suppose not,' she said.

'And he knew? That you were not his?'

She shrugged again. 'I don't know. He said something strange once, just before he died, said that I was as much his as anyone's. Never knew what he meant by that, I thought he meant I was as much his as I was my mother's. But that makes sense if he knew, doesn't it? And it would explain why he hated me.'

Bendiks began to make a scoffing sound.

'No, really, he did. I always knew he hated me and I always thought it was because I hadn't died instead of my mother. I always felt guilty, you know, that I wasn't enough to make up for him losing my mum. And then, well, now *I* know that he wasn't my real dad, and if he knew it too, which I think he probably did, well then – he didn't have to love me at all, did he?'

A heavy silence fell upon them.

'I understand,' said Bendiks, softly.

Lydia glanced at him.

'I understand you. My brother died. He got knocked down by a truck, outside our home.'

Lydia blinked and examined her fingertips. 'I'm sorry,' she said.

He shrugged. 'You don't need to be sorry. It is not your fault.' He smiled.

'No, of course it's not, it's just . . . it's just what we say, when we feel bad for someone. How old were you?'

'Fourteen. My brother was eight.' He shrugged again. 'So, you know, I kind of get where you're coming from. I used to have a brother. Now I don't have a brother and

I walk around and I still see him. I try to imagine him at fourteen, at twenty, at twenty-four. He'd be twenty-four now.' His eyes filled with sadness for a second. 'And, wow, if I thought there was a chance for me to find I had another brother or a sister, someone who looked a bit like me or sounded a bit like me, it would be a miracle . . . I understand,' he said, cupping her hand with his. 'I understand how you are feeling.'

Lydia glanced down at the hand that covered hers. She stared at the perfect fingernails, the smooth cuticles, and then she imagined that hand sliding from her hand up her bare arm, moving her hair from her shoulder, cupping the side of her neck, pulling her face towards his. Of all the people, she thought to herself, of all the people to have shared this with . . . *Bendiks*. Her trainer. The man who made her do frog jumps and punch him. This man from a foreign land.

There was a whole night's worth of talking between their two stories, but Lydia could feel herself closing up again, slowly but determinedly, like the jaws of a Venus flytrap. She felt exposed and raw. It was time to go back to basics. 'Come on,' she said, jumping to her feet. 'Time to make me sweat.'

'You are sure?' asked Bendiks, his voice soft with concern. 'We can talk some more?'

Lydia opened her mouth. Yes, she wanted to say, yes, I want to talk and talk and talk and then I want to take all your clothes off and have you take all my clothes off and then sweat and pump and grind and breathe and groan and then lie with your beautiful body wrapped around mine in pools of our own shared salty sweat and then talk some more.

'No,' she said, 'no. I'm done talking for now. But thank you,' she said. 'I thought I was going mad. And now I know I'm not.'

LAST SUMMER

ROBYN

Robyn Inglis celebrated her eighteenth birthday with a Voltz energy shot and the morning-after pill.

The night before she'd still been seventeen, but she wasn't having her birthday party on a Sunday night, no way. Besides it had been half legal, the party hadn't started 'til nine o'clock, she'd turned eighteen at midnight, the last four hours she'd been partying as a proper bona fide paid up member of the adult population, thank you very much.

The man, the *boy* (he was still only seventeen, poor fool), was irrelevant. She'd just had to do it, quickly as possible, christen herself and her *adultness*. Christian was his name. Jewish was his religion. Circumcised was his penis. Quick was his coming. But Robyn didn't care. He was pretty and smelled nice and she'd only missed out on ten minutes of her totally brilliant party. She'd been planning that party for nearly a year, it was like it was her *wedding* or something. Her mum and dad had given her £500 towards it and she'd put in another couple of hundred of her own money, saved up from her Saturday job in Zara. A limo, yes indeed, a limo had come to collect her and three of her besties from her house on Saturday night. They all looked like actual celebrities, they really did. Robyn was channelling Anna Friel's backstage look, in a proper prom dress with petticoats and everything. And red lipstick and her hair up. She looked *amazing*. Everyone said so. They all did.

Robyn's mum had gone all funny when she came downstairs in her prom dress, cupped her hands over her mouth and sucked in her breath and said, 'You look stunning, stunning. A real, true princess.' Her dad had just smiled his big dumb smile and looked a bit proud. And then they'd said all the usual rubbish about *don't go anywhere without telling your friends,* and *call us if you're in trouble, it doesn't matter how late it is,* and *never leave your drink unattended and don't accept drinks from strangers unless you've seen the barman pour it with your own eyes.* Yeah yeah yeah. It wasn't as if she'd never been out drinking before. She'd been out drinking since she was about *thirteen years old,* for God's sake. Robyn could take her drink.

Even when she was at it with Christian (why would a Jewish person call their son *Christian,* it didn't make any sense?) up against a wall outside the men's toilets, she'd been in control. Totally. Except that he wouldn't put a condom on. It didn't matter really because she knew she had two morning-after pills in her drawer, and she figured he smelled too good to have an STD. No one with hair that smelled of actual *roses* could have an STD. Anyway, she'd been in total control, pulled him over by his tie, taken him out of his trousers, kissed him hard, *really hard.*

'You're my birthday present to myself,' she'd whispered in his ear.

After the restaurant had kicked them out at 1 a.m. they'd streamed down the high street, gorgeous girls and boys, everyone with their arms around each other; they were singing, it was like a scene out of a film. She'd tried to get a photo of it on her mobile but the light wasn't good enough, just a blur of streetlamps and streaks of people. But she'd keep it forever, anyway. Good times. The best night of her life.

She swallowed down the pill with the energy shot and prayed that they would both stay down. She only had one pill left and if this one came back up, that'd be it, back to the GP. She didn't have a hangover, Robyn didn't get hangovers. Liver of steel. But she felt as tired as a dead person just crawled out of their grave. She pulled her black hair away from her face and gazed at herself in the mirror on her dressing table. Was it right, she thought, to think that you were so pretty? Was it normal? Did other eighteen-year-old girls look at their own faces in the mirror and think, Mmm, *pretty*? She did. Every time she saw herself she felt a little shiver of pleasure, of satisfaction. She was already worried about losing it. Already knew that come her late-twenties she'd be Botoxing the crap out of herself. Or whatever people would be doing in the year 2018. Sitting in tanks of Martian pee or something. Actually she'd rather have Botox than sit in a tank of Martian pee. But anyway, she'd definitely be on the case.

There was little in the world that Robyn could imagine being worse than looking bad. But as it was, she looked good, even on five hours' sleep and a bloodstream full of metabolising vodka. Her hazel eyes were shaped like fish, and her eyebrows were finely arched and a really nice shade of brown. She had a – well, there was no other word for it really but a perfect nose. Not turned up, not long, not short, absolutely straight, with nice little nostrils. And then there was her mouth. It was cushiony. As a child she'd looked almost alien: over-wide eyes and a huge pair of lips that looked like they'd been unpicked from the face of a thirty-year-old woman. She'd had to grow into her extreme features, had to grow bones and an underlying structure to support them. People sometimes said she looked like Angelina Jolie. And she wondered, she did wonder, about these lips and where they had come from. They looked like African lips. It was possible, she supposed. They weren't her mother's, that was for certain, her mother had a hard mouth, lips like tramlines. And her father, well, *obviously* she hadn't got her mouth from him, because he wasn't her real father and her mother had never met her real father so she had no idea what sort of face he might have had. Full-lipped, she'd have to assume. Full-lipped and dark, with cheekbones like boomerangs.

She knew a few things about her real dad. He was French. Lived in London. A medical student. And not just any old medicine but *children's* medicine. How amazing did he sound? And he was a – what was it they'd called him, her mum and dad? – an *altruist*. That's right. He worked with sick children and he gave his sperm away to strangers. Which was quite funny because apparently altruism was also something that occurred in the animal world where a creature forwent its own comfort and safety to ensure the dissemination of its genes. Not necessarily by giving its sperm to lady animals, but just, you know, looking out for its own kind. Anyway, he sounded like the nicest man in the whole world and Robyn was never going to meet him but she loved him all the same, loved him for his altruism and for making her the way she was, so pretty and clever and everything.

Everyone knew that Robyn's dad was a sperm donor. It was no biggie. There were three completely separate people at Robyn's school who lived with gay parents, you know, two mums or two dads, and there was a kid in year ten who was having hormone therapy to turn him into a girl, so really, all in all, an anonymous dad was totally nothing. Half the kids at the youth project round the corner probably had anonymous dads but Robyn would bet that theirs weren't French paediatricians.

Her phone vibrated across the top of her dressing table. She grabbed it.

'Nuah! Fuck! Did you get home all right? Christ, I thought that bloke was stalking you. Yeah, that weird one. I mean, did he have an actual *forked tongue* or was I just imagining that? Ha-ha! Yeah, no, I feel fine, you know me. Liver of steel. Yeah. Yeah. It was brilliant, wasn't it? Seriously brilliant. Totally. I know. Today? Oh, nothing much, lunch out with Mum and Dad and my aunty and cousins and stuff. Roast at the Hog's Head. No, it'll be nice. I'm wearing that dress from Kookai, you know, the one with the sash thing round the waist. Hair up, it'll have to be . . . aw, and thanks for the beautiful necklace, it's so gorgeous. I love it. I love you. Yeah, I do! I love you, Nush! I love you so much that it makes bluebirds fly around my heart. Yeah. Right now. They're flying round and round it right now, can't you hear them tweeting – listen . . .'

At the Hog's Head later that day, Robyn felt like a celebrity. She'd been coming to the Hog's Head with her mum and dad since she was a few months old and everyone round here knew her. Everyone had known about Robyn since before she was even born. There was a newspaper clipping on the wall in her bedroom headlined: *Baby Joy for Tragic Buckhurst Couple*. It was illustrated with a photograph of her mum with really bad hair sitting on the sofa in their old house, cupping her baby bump, with her dad stood behind her with his hand on her shoulder. They didn't look much like they were in the throes of baby joy, they looked really old and really tragic, but then they'd had a tragic few years and Robyn didn't suppose they were ready to look really happy just yet. Robyn's mum always said she wouldn't believe it was going to be OK until she'd held her baby in her arms. Understandable really, given what they'd gone through. But it was Dad's face in that photo that was really interesting to Robyn. What must he have been feeling, knowing that that wasn't his baby inside his wife?

She sat on his lap now, her big lovely dad. He was solid,

like an armchair, and he smelled of pillows and fabric conditioner. They were having a happy time. They were a happy family. She kissed him on the cheek and shuffled off his lap to take her seat at the head of the table.

'So,' said Jan, her father's sister, 'how does it feel to be an adult?'

Robyn smiled. She'd felt like an adult for years. 'I like it,' she said. 'I'm going to start voting in elections, every day. And having anal sex.'

Jan laughed out loud. Robyn's family was the kind that didn't feel uncomfortable talking about anal sex. 'Ha-ha,' she guffawed, 'yes, do it now, love, before you've had kids. Because you won't want to do it after!'

Robyn wrinkled her nose and tried not to think what she might mean.

She looked around at her family; her mum, her dad, cousins and aunt, and thought, not for the first time, *I'm different from you*. And not just that but: *I'm better than you*. It wasn't a good thing to think. It was a hideous, sick thing to think. But she couldn't help it. All her life she'd been different. Prettier than everyone else. Cleverer than everyone else. 11 GCSEs. 4 AS levels. 4 A levels. About to start studying medicine at University College London. Following in her donor father's mysterious and glamorous footsteps.

She stood in line at the carvery and smiled at Steve, the chef, who was sweating lightly under the hot lights in a white paper hat, brandishing a large sharp knife.

'Happy Birthday, Robyn,' he said with a shy smile.

'Thank you!' She smiled back.

Steve was in love with Robyn. They'd been in the same class at primary school and he'd been in love with her then too. Everyone knew that Steve was in love with Robyn. He'd probably asked to be at work today especially because he knew that she would be in celebrating her eighteenth.

'I got you a card,' he said, wiping the shine from his forehead with the back of his hand and then slicing her off some turkey. 'I'll give it to you later, when I've cleaned up.'

She smiled and nodded. She could tell he wanted to kiss her. 'Thanks, Steve,' she said, 'that's really sweet.'

'Do you want some stuffing with that?'

'No, thanks,' she replied. 'Just a bit of bacon.'

'You look lovely,' he said.

'Thank you,' she said. 'Will you have a drink with us? After you get off? We're going to be here for the long haul, I reckon.'

His face went soft as beaten butter and he nodded. 'Yeah,' he said, 'that'd be good.'

Robyn piled roast potatoes on to her plate and soggy florets of broccoli and a ton of sprouts and then drowned the lot in the thick winey gravy that the Hog's Head was renowned for. Then she carried the over-piled plate back to the table and everyone oohed and aahed at her man-sized appetite and said, 'Ooh, where do you put it all? You must have hollow feet,' and Robyn looked at her well-upholstered parents and her slightly more than curvy aunty who was prone to saying things like 'All I have to do is look at a slice of cheesecake and I've gone up a size', and her small-mouthed cousins with their doughy faces and their wide feet, and thought: *I am not one of you. I come from my own tribe, once-removed on the ladder of evolution.* It didn't mean she didn't love them. She loved her family with a ferocious passion. But then people loved their dogs with a ferocious passion; didn't mean they were the same thing.

'Did you have fun with your friends last night?' asked Aunty Jan.

'Amazing,' replied Robyn. 'Best night *ever*.'

'I remember my eighteenth,' she said, 'I wore a boiler suit and had a perm. Thought I was It – looked like Brian May,' she laughed. 'It was tough being young in the eighties. You girls get to dress so pretty these days. So many lovely things in the shops for you.'

Robyn's phone buzzed with a text message. It was Christian: *Hey babe, what you up to?*

She groaned: *Hey babe.* Didn't matter how good someone smelled if they sent you text messages that began *Hey babe.* She shuddered slightly and sent a reply, thumb working furiously over the buttons: *Having lunch with family. See you out and about.* She deliberately left the last line without a question mark. A question mark would suggest that she was *hoping* to see him out and about. She was *not* hoping to see him out and about. She would quite happily spend the rest of her life without seeing him out and about or anywhere else for that matter. Robyn was not interested in the men round here. Not in that way. They were fine for drinking with, partying with, sleeping with. But for the long haul, for the rest of her life, only a doctor would do.

'A toast!' said her father, holding aloft his pint of cloudy bitter. 'To my little girl. *Our* little girl.' He smiled at his wife. 'We are so proud of you, my darling, so proud of you for everything you've achieved. You've brought us nothing but happiness these last eighteen years, nothing but joy. We could not ask for a better daughter. Thank you, Robyn, for being you.' As the words left his lips, a tear slid from the corner of his eye and down his nose. He wiped it away and smiled apologetically at his little girl. 'I love you,' he croaked.

'Aw, Dad,' Robyn snuggled into him, 'I love you, too. Thank you.' She pulled her mother towards them, too. 'Thank you both for being the best mum and dad in the world, and I want you to know that I am going to go on and on and keep on making you proud of me.'

This was it, she thought, feeling her parents' warm flesh against her body, the glow of her family around her, the warmth of this August afternoon of togetherness, this was it. This was all she wanted and needed. She was eighteen now. She could make contact with her real dad, if she wanted to. But she wasn't going to. This man here was her real dad, this man in his green Blue Harbour crewneck sweater and Clarks shoes and shoulders like a brickie's. *Her dad.* She didn't want another.

Her other father, the French paediatrician, he would stay inside her head forever. He would push her, unknowingly, towards a career in medicine and he would make her feel forevermore just a little bit better than everyone else. But her attachment to him would go no further than that. She liked him as he was – a character in her very own fairy tale.

Later than night Robyn sat on the sofa, pressed against her father, her feet tucked beneath her, watching *Big Brother*. Her mother walked into the room, something clutched between her hands and held against her heart. Her face was smiling but oddly strained. Her father sat straighter at the sight of her and Robyn instinctively uncurled her legs and placed her feet upon the carpet.

'You all right?' she said.

Her mother nodded. 'I'm fine, sweetie, just fine. Got something to show you though. Budge up.'

Robyn glanced at the paperwork in her mother's hands. 'Oh, no!' she said, mock-dramatically. 'Don't tell me – I'm *adopted*?!'

Her mother smiled. 'This,' she began, 'is what they gave me at the clinic, when I got pregnant with you.'

Robyn put her hand to her throat and recoiled. 'I don't want it,' she said, 'take it away.'

Her mother sighed and rested her hand on Robyn's leg. 'You don't have to read it,' she said, gently, 'but I want you to have it. You're eighteen now. You're an adult. It doesn't belong to me any more.'

'Then put it in the bin,' said Robyn, 'shred it. Whatever. I don't want it.'

Her mother sighed again. 'It's just a letter,' she said.

'I've read it. There's nothing alarming in it. And there's his donor number and info, in case you want to contact him.'

'I don't! And I don't want to read his letter! I know enough about him already and I'm very grateful and everything, but I don't need him in my life, OK? I really, really don't want to know.'

Her mum squeezed her leg and smiled. 'You know,' she said, 'we won't be around forever, me and your dad. We're not old, but we're not getting any younger either. And when we're gone, you'll be all on your own. Take these papers, sweetie, keep them. At least then if anything happens – *which it won't –*' she squeezed Robyn again, reassuringly – 'but if it does and you decide you want to meet him, you'll have the wherewithal to do something about it, OK? And another thing to think about, even if you don't want to meet your donor father – what about siblings? Brothers, sisters? I know –' she cut into Robyn's half-formed protests – 'I know you don't want that now. But in the future. One day. Maybe. OK?'

Robyn eyed the folder of papers and exhaled. It was so charged with explosive potential she could almost hear it ticking. She thought of these nameless, faceless siblings and she hated them. She saw them as grotesque carica-tures of herself, all fat lips and attitude, all thinking they were something special because their dad was a sperm donor, their dad was a French paediatrician. That was *her* role, nobody else's. And besides, she'd had sisters, two beautiful sisters. It was irrelevant to her that they were dead; they were still there, inside her heart, and she didn't have room in there for anyone new. Robyn pushed her heavy fringe behind her ears and regarded the folder.

'What will you do with it if I don't take it?'

'Put it away,' said her mother. 'Somewhere safe. Somewhere you can find it. Later. When we're gone.'

Robyn thought about this. It was possible, she conceded, that she might, one day, for whatever reason, want to contact her biological father. Maybe she'd need a, you know, a liver transplant or something, or a future child might have some rare genetic disorder. She might one day need this man to stop being a two-dimensional Disney prince and become a fully functioning, flesh, blood and DNA human being. And maybe it would be better then to have these papers in her possession. She flopped back against the brown suede sofa and pulled an expression of resignation.

'Fine,' she said, 'OK. Give it to me.' She held out her hands. The folder felt heavy, as if it contained wet sand. 'But I am not even going to *sniff* this stuff unless I really, really have to. You know that, don't you? I so don't need this guy or his other kids. I've got everything I need. OK?'

She awoke in the night, clammy and unsettled, an unremembered dream pulsing in the corners of her consciousness. She felt lost and disoriented. Her stomach was full of undigested cake and carvery and cheap white wine. She immediately got out of bed feeling there was something she needed to do. She paced her room distractedly, rubbing her angry, distended stomach. Obviously she knew what she was about to do. She'd known it since she'd first felt the folder in her hands, taken ownership of them. She pulled the folder from the bottom of her chest of drawers and she opened it.

NOW

Robyn had her microbiology file tucked under her arm and was wearing her black-framed reading glasses, even though she wasn't reading. She had on a really cute checked shirt dress from Urban Outfitters with green tights and granny boots. She looked cool and clever. Geek chic. She dressed differently for college from how she dressed at home. At home, in Buckhurst Hill, she was more polished. Out here in the hard-nosed streets of London town she let it go a bit. She didn't want to look like an Essex girl. Still had on proper underwear, though, and was wearing Mac lipstick and Agent Provocateur Boudoir perfume.

She was on Gower Street, headed from a study session at the main library to a guest talk at the Institute of Neurology. She was alone. The sun was low and London felt strangely quiet, like it was early dawn and the tubes hadn't started running yet. Where was everyone? she wondered. But she liked it, it gave her a feeling of exclusivity, of owning the place, like when they clear the streets to shoot a scene in a film and all the ordinary people have to take detours or just stand around gawping at the much more important people, who are probably just best boys or gaffers or shutter loaders. Empty streets made Robyn feel like she was the star of her very own movie. She smiled, knowing that nobody could see, and let her walk become a sway. No one was watching but she acted like everyone was. She liked these in-between moments, when she was a medical student but she wasn't actually in the process of studying medicine. Halfway between lectures she was able momentarily to empty her brain of all the facts and jargon and names and numbers that she seemed to carry around with her perpetually these days and just enjoy the fact of her existence in this rarefied world. The rest of the time she was overwhelmed and petrified by the amount of learning she was being required to do. Books like breeze blocks full of vital information, tests every few days, studying, learning, remembering. It was not what she'd been expecting. She'd thought it would be all sitting in airy auditoria with a notepad at her elbow, listening intently to learned men and women whilst gently chewing the end of a pencil. She'd thought exams would be easy, that tests would be a doddle. It was starting to occur to her month by month, in small, discomfiting bursts of awareness, that maybe she wasn't as clever as she'd thought she was.

She turned a corner and found herself opposite the Brunswick Centre. She smiled, as the irresistible lure of unknown shops therein called to her. Inside the centre she found a dress shop called, rather aptly, Joy. Her eye was immediately caught by a flame-coloured dress hanging in the window. It was shiny, a kind of orange-red, with a crumb-catcher bodice and a full skirt. It would be perfect for Nush's nineteenth the following month. With a beaded cardi over and her strappy gold platforms. £89.99, though. Where was she going to get £90 from? Her mum and dad had given her £1,000 for her birthday, but that was intended for something mega, for a year abroad or a car or a deposit on a flat or something, not for chucking away on dresses. And exactly how many prom dresses did one girl actually need anyway? She resisted the temptation to go in and try it on. (It would look great on her, she didn't need to try it on to know that, but once you'd tried something on you were about sixty per cent of the way to the till, really.)

She felt pleased with her resolve as she passed the shop empty-handed. She was growing up. She was changing. She felt in her pocket for a folded piece of paper and rubbed it between her fingertips, for reassurance. It was the letter from her dad, her real dad, that her mother had given her back in August, when they'd got back from the pub after her birthday lunch.

Robyn kept it about her person at all times. She didn't know why. She didn't really want to know why. The letter was short, less than a page of A4, and she'd memorised almost the whole thing, word for word, all the little blips in his grammar, the occasional exclamation mark. The letter was innocuous. It had done nothing to dent her fantasy. If anything, it had augmented it, adding layers of texture and detail. She could already picture a full-mouthed, handsome doctor in a white coat and one of those cute patterned hats that paediatricians wore to put children at ease; she saw him smiling beneficently at a wan kid in a hospital bed, his hands in his pockets, possibly, *probably*, rocking back on to his heels. Now she could add a touch of personality to the vignette: a charming misuse of the English past participle, a tendency to end sentences on a note of amusement, a certain shyness and self-effacement.

The letter, far from rendering him unpalatably human, had merely served to make him even more unattainably fictitious. And that in turn made Robyn feel even more unassailably certain that she would never, ever want to meet him.

But that was on a quiet Tuesday morning in February, halfway between a study session and a lecture and exactly two weeks before she met Jack Hart and fell in love.

It was a Thursday night, late-night shopping on Oxford Street. Robyn was on the till downstairs, in menswear. The shop was closing in half an hour and she was so tired she felt like she'd been down a coalmine. She'd left her house at eight o'clock that morning, done a full day of intensive lectures, a gruelling late-afternoon study group, been for a much-needed drink with a friend and arrived at Zara at 6 p.m. for her late-night shift.

Jack Hart walked in at 8.31. He walked past Robyn without a glance and headed straight for a display of mushroom-coloured knitwear. Something about his sil-houette made Robyn stand a little straighter and lick her lips. He wasn't tall and his build wasn't overtly masculine, but there was something springy about him, as if he could spontaneously perform a somersault. He wore jeans and trainers, an overcoat and a sweater. His hair was black and cut in a shaggy style. Robyn hadn't yet seen his face but she was spellbound by his back, the cut of his overcoat, the angle of his shoulders, the way he stood with his bouncy feet set wide apart. There was nothing fey or uncertain about him. He stood as though the floor belonged to him, a king inspecting his subjects. He flicked through the cardigans with an air of disappointment. He was not browsing, he was looking for something specific, something he'd envisaged in his head and that did not, it seemed, exist in real life.

'Do you need any help?' she asked, taking the edges off her Essex twang and trying not to smile too hard.

The man turned around and looked at her in surprise, as though he'd imagined himself alone down here.

A smile flickered across his face. *Insouciant.*

'Um, yeah, actually,' he replied, as if the idea that a shop assistant might be able to assist him had never before crossed his mind. 'Yeah. I'm looking for a sweater, kind of like this one,' he opened his overcoat to demonstrate the sweater, 'but in a sort of mid-brown.'

Robyn smiled. 'That's a very nice sweater,' she said. 'I think we might have just what you're looking for.'

She let him follow her across the shop floor. She was wearing fitted taupe trousers and a chiffon tank top. She knew what she looked like from behind because she'd already checked out her rear view in a changing room when she got changed for work. Her hair was tied up and the back of her neck was visible and she knew that he would be able to see the tiny tattoo at the top of her spine, an enjoined curlicue of her sisters' initials: G and R, Gemma and Rachel. She'd had it done last year. Her parents had given their permission. 'You can always wear your hair down over it,' they'd said, 'if you regret it when you're older.' They'd cried when they'd seen it. Said it was beautiful and tasteful, a lovely memorial to their two girls.

'Hmm,' said the man, as she unfolded a third creamy-coffee-coloured jumper on a table at the back of the shop, 'almost, almost . . .'

'But not quite?'

'Yeah, it's just a bit too *gold*?' He pinched his chin and smiled. 'I'm being a total nightmare, aren't I?' he said.

Robyn laughed. 'No,' she said, 'not at all. It's good to know what you want. Means you make fewer mistakes in life.'

'Ah,' he said, 'am I talking to a fellow perfectionist?'

She smiled. 'Probably. Yeah. I know what I want and I know what I like and I'm not really prepared to compromise.'

He backed away from her, playfully.

She laughed. 'Now *I* sound like a total nightmare.'

'No,' he said, 'not at all. You sound like just my kind of girl, in fact.'

The comment was overtly flirtatious but it didn't throw Robyn off course. She'd been expecting it. And not just because she was pretty and she was used to men flirting with her, but because everything about this man seemed so familiar. The comment didn't feel to her as though it had come out of the blue, but more as though it were part of a longer and more intimate conversation.

She glanced up at him. She hadn't really looked at him before, had been too distracted by knitwear. He was lovely. There was no other word for it. Just lovely. His face was soft, almost feminine, but the right side of androgynous. His skin was clear and smooth and his eyes were a glacial greeny blue. He had a neat straight nose and a full mouth, but more compelling than the perfect loveliness of him was the intelligence and humour that radiated from him.

She passed over his comment and said: 'What's it for? The jumper?'

'Oh, nothing really. Just to stop me wearing this one the whole time.'

Robyn checked his left hand for a wedding ring. He seemed the kind of guy who might be married or settled down. People described the air of a single person as desperation. Robyn didn't see it that way. To her it was more a feeling of vulnerability. There was something fragile about a person looking for another person. Something breakable and filmy, like the shell of a sparrow's egg. It didn't matter how hard the single person tried to cover it up with bluster and bravado, it was still there, beneath the surface, the heart-breaking baby bird. But this man had no inner baby bird. He was solid, all the way through. He was either gay, married or not even remotely interested in meeting anyone.

'Where did you get that one from?' she asked, pointing at his jumper, resisting the temptation to press the heel of her hand against it as she did so.

'Here,' he smiled. 'Zara. About three years ago. And now the moths have been at it.' He pulled the hem round and showed her a small hole at the back.

She winced. 'I hate moths,' she said. 'They're evil.'

He laughed. 'Absolutely,' he agreed. 'So I thought it might be time for a new Zara jumper. And a perfect opportunity to move on from grey.'

Robyn sold him three jumpers in the end. A brown one, another grey one and a black one. Just because she was attracted to him it did not mean that she couldn't also spin some extra commission out of him.

The air between them at the till as she de-tagged, folded and bagged the jumpers was clogged up and edgy. She had by-passed his one attempt at taking their jumper conversation any further and he clearly didn't feel the need to make another one.

'That's one hundred and eighteen pounds, please,' she said.

He raised an eyebrow in a manner that suggested that £118 was a lot of money and passed her a Switch card.

'Thank you,' she said.

She tried to read his name from the card in the shred of

time during which it was visible to her before she slid it into the reader. She caught a 'Mr', two initials and the surname 'Hart'. Mr something something Hart.

Robyn Hart.

The thought streaked through her mind like a bullet train. She blinked, to make sure it was gone. She had never paired her name with a man's before. Not even as a schoolgirl. She had no intention of ever changing her surname. It belonged to her, to her mother, her father, her sisters. It was theirs. She would never throw it away, not for anyone. But here it was. Robyn Hart. *Dr* Robyn Hart. It felt like a concept beyond high-school fantasy. It felt like prophecy.

'If you could just put in your pin number,' she intoned, weakly.

She watched him pad in the numbers with a strong forefinger and she licked her lips. His bag sat on the counter, ready for him to lift it away. The card machine chuntered out his receipt and she ripped it off. 'Would you like the receipt in the bag?'

'Yeah,' he nodded, 'sure.'

Their encounter was fading away. In one moment he would loop his fingers around the handles of his bag, he would smile, and then he would be gone. And that, she suddenly knew, would be a tragedy.

'Do you work here? Full-time?'

She felt her tension ease. Mr Hart had thrown a life ring at their encounter. She grabbed it and smiled.

'Oh, no,' she said. 'No, just Thursday nights. And I do

Saturdays and Sundays at my local branch, near where I live.'

'So, what do you do the rest of the time?'

She smiled again. 'I'm a student,' she replied, 'a medical student.'

His brow registered his surprise. 'Wow. That's pretty cool. What are you hoping to go into?'

'Paediatrics.'

'Right, now you'll have to remind me – is that feet or kids?'

'Kids,' she laughed. 'I want to look after sick children. And work towards world peace.'

He laughed. 'So one day you'll be a doctor?'

'Yeah, that's the idea. Got a long, long way to go first, of course. I've only just begun. But yeah, work hard, fingers crossed, one day I might be looking after one of your unborn children.'

He grimaced. She thought at first that maybe he was grimacing at the concept of having children, but then realised what she'd just implied. 'Oh, God, well, no, I didn't mean . . . obviously, if you do have a child, I really hope I'll never ever have to meet it . . .'

'Unless it's yours.' He smiled.

Her brain raced as she tried mentally to recalibrate his words into some kind of form that didn't mean what it sounded like it had meant. 'What? You mean . . .'

He looked embarrassed. 'Nothing,' he said, 'just being silly. Ignore me. Anyway,' he brought the exchange to an abrupt close, 'thank you for being so patient and informative on the subject of brown jumpers. And, er, good luck.'

'Thank you,' she said. 'I hope you and your new jumpers are very happy together.'

He smiled tightly. Robyn could see more words straining against his smile. She willed them to fight their way out. They didn't.

She watched him leave, his countenance neither as mobile nor as light-hearted as it had been twenty-two minutes ago. The store was empty. The time on the till said 8.54. Time to cash up, switch off, dim the lights and leave.

Half an hour later she pulled on her overcoat, swapped her heels for sneakers, slung her bag across her chest and left the store by the front door, the primed burglar alarm wailing deafeningly in the background.

She was about to turn left and head towards Tottenham Court Road tube station with the manager and another girl when a figure appeared at her side.

'Sorry,' said Mr something something Hart, 'I've been hanging around outside for half an hour like a freaky stalker. I was just wondering, I know it's late, but do you have to get home? Or have you got time for a drink?'

Robyn looked at him. Then she looked at her friend. Her friend sent her a warning look. Robyn looked back at the man. She thought: *I trust you. I know you.* And then she acquiesced, with a simple nod of her head.

She had only met him an hour ago, but already she had dreamed of being his wife and already he had talked of fathering her children. It could be no other way.

DEAN

'You're fucking pathetic, you know that?'

Dean flinched. His forehead was pressed hard against his fists and his nose was pointed towards the ground. He stared at a spot of dirt on the grey carpet. The spot of dirt was hard to identify. It might have been a burn mark. It might have been a trodden-in lump of shit. Hard to say from this angle whether it was convex or concave. A vein on Dean's temple started to throb in rhythm with Sky's voice. You'd think, wouldn't you, that a girl called Sky would have a voice like larks and doves and butterflies? You'd think a girl with a name like Sky would wear flowers in her hair and smell of jasmine and rosewater? But no. This Sky, *his* Sky, was hard and tough. She was small, tiny even, a premature baby who'd never caught up. But what she lacked in volume she made up for in attitude. She was scary. Scary enough when she'd just been a normal nineteen year old with nothing more pressing to worry about than what she was going to wear on Friday night, but now that she was pregnant . . . it was like she'd been taken over by a devil, literally. She looked at him like he was dirt. Worse than dirt. Like he was disappointing dirt. Not what she'd been hoping for from dirt. Maybe not quite dirty enough.

'I'm making a baby in here,' she harried. 'An actual baby. I've given up booze, I've given up fags, I've even given up fucking Diet Coke. Yeah? And all I'm asking you to do is stop with the fucking weed, yeah? You can't afford it and it's bad for your head. Yeah?'

He lifted his head slowly from his fists and stared at her through his lashes. The worst of it was that she was right. He couldn't afford it. It was bad for his head. But it was all he had. He sighed. Leave me something, he wanted to say. You've taken my youth and my freedom. Leave me this. Just this. Instead he smiled at her. 'I'll finish this lot,' he pointed at the box on the table, 'and that'll be it. OK?'

She raised her eyebrows. 'Yeah. Right. I'll believe that when I see it. It's not fair,' she continued. 'All the fucking sacrifices I'm making. My body . . . I mean, look at these,' she lifted her tunic top, 'fucking stretch-marks. Those'll never go. I'll have those for life, you know? Nineteen years old and my body's already fucked. It's all just a big game to you.' She let the top drop. 'Just a big game. You're a little. Fucking. Boy.'

She uncurled herself from the depths of the sofa and then raised herself and her bump with some effort (and, Dean suspected, some added dramatic effects) from its edge. She then shuffled, in worn-out lambskin slippers and with one hand rested wearily in the small of her back, towards the bedroom which she entered, slamming the door behind her for effect.

Dean ran his hands across his shorn head and sighed again. One minute he'd been working a van job, earning in excess of £250 a week, had enough money for drinking, for weed, for anything he wanted. He had the fittest girl-friend, Sky Donnelly, sex on tap, the good life. Next minute the job had gone and Sky was pregnant and frigid and covered in stretch-marks. There was no way he was going to leave her to it, didn't matter how much of a bitch she was to him. No way. He hadn't been brought up like that. And besides, he'd grown up without a dad and there was no way he'd let the same thing happen to any child of his.

It was a girl. A little girl. Sky wanted to call her Isadora. Dean wanted to call her Katy, after his grandmother who'd passed away the year before. Dean knew who'd win the fight. Small but deadly, his Sky.

Isadora Katy Higgins. It didn't exactly flow but then it was a damn sight better than half the names kids got called round here these days. There was one of his mates from the depot who'd called his twins Gucci and Prada.

Sky emerged from the bedroom five minutes later. She was dressed to go out.

'Where are you going?' he asked.

'The hospital.'

'What for?'

'Oh, for a fucking pedicure. What do you think I'm going for?'

'I *don't know*. That's why I *asked*.'

'I'm bleeding.'

'What!'

'Yeah. I'm bleeding. OK?'

'Shit. What do you think . . .'

'I think I'm losing the baby, that's what I think, and I'm not about to sit around here waiting for that to happen. You coming or what?'

Within half an hour of walking into A&E Sky and Dean were told that not only was Sky in early labour, but that her placenta was lying dangerously low and she was losing a worrying amount of blood. They were sent straight to the birth unit at Queen Charlotte's where they were told that the baby would have to be delivered immediately.

'But I'm only thirty weeks!' she wailed.

'We've got one of the best neonatal care units in the country here. Baby will be fine.'

'But it's going to be tiny!'

'Well, yes, but we've had tinier. We've had babies born at twenty-two weeks who've survived and flourished.'

'But I was a preemie. I was in hospital for weeks. And I was always behind in everything. What if she turns out backward?'

'Listen, Sky,' said the nurse, 'if you don't deliver this baby now, you could both die. So really, we're just going to have to take our chances. OK?'

Sky grabbed Dean's hand and looked at him desperately. 'Oh, shit, Dean! Oh, God, I'm scared! I'm really scared!'

Dean squeezed her hand and forced a smile through

the rigor of terror constricting his face. 'It's going to be fine, baby. You heard what they said. It's going to be fine.'

'But, like, thirty weeks? She's going to be so small. We'll have to buy new vests and sleepsuits and everything. Oh, God, Dean. I'm not ready for this. I'm not ready!'

Dean wasn't ready either. He had never been ready and hadn't imagined that he ever would be. He'd been putting this moment on hold, hoping that if he didn't think about it, it wouldn't come, that somehow his life would just peter off into the distance, to a small grey speck. In a way it was good this was happening now. He would have got more and more nervous as the due date approached, less and less able to deal with the reality of it. And now reality had fallen on his head, like a brick. Better this than weeks of sickening anticipation.

'It'll be fine,' he said again. 'Honestly. I'll ask my mum to get some new stuff for the baby.'

'Oh, I wouldn't worry about clothes for the baby,' the nurse interjected. 'She'll be here for quite a few weeks while we get her nice and strong. We have clothes here and by the time you take her home she'll fit into all the lovely things you've bought for her.'

Dean thought about that. The baby was about to be born, but it was going to stay here. Other people would be looking after it. He'd still be able to go home and have a smoke and an unbroken night's sleep. This was all starting to feel weirdly manageable. Sky wouldn't be pregnant any more; there'd be ten fewer weeks of her being a bitch. Ten weeks when she would probably be here at the hospital all the time. And all the while he'd be getting to know his new baby girl in stages, slowly, not all at once. She would seep into his life, bit by bit, not just gatecrash it.

He smiled. 'It's going to be fine,' he said, and he really meant it.

'They're going to cut me open, Dean! They're going to cut my belly open. Shit! I'll never have a flat stomach again. Oh, God. I haven't called my mum . . . How long have I got?' she asked the nurse.

'They're getting surgery ready for you now. And the anaesthetist's on his way. Your baby should be here within the hour.'

'Dean! Shit! Give me my phone. Give it to me!'

'Where is it?'

'It's in my pocket. Of my coat. There. No, there. The other one! The other one, you spaz. Fuck!' She snatched the phone from his hand and dialled her mother's number. 'Mum! I'm in hospital! I'm in labour! I'm bleeding. Yeah. And they're going to take the baby out. No. A C-section. Yeah. Dean's here, yeah. Are you coming, Mum? Are you coming now? Please come now, Mum. I'm so scared. Oh, God, the anaesthetist's here. They're going to inject me. Hurry up, Mum. Hurry up!'

Sky was crying. Dean felt oddly moved by the sight of the tears glistening on his girlfriend's cheeks. Sky never cried. Not even when her stepdad died. Not even when there were really sad stories on *The X Factor*. She was hard and unsentimental. She passed her phone back to him and then turned and stared desperately at the wall to her left.

The midwife clasped her forearm and smiled sympathetically. 'Everyone here is the best. The best people. You're safe here. Trust me.'

Sky turned and smiled wanly at the midwife. It was her 'yeah, right' smile, the one she used on Dean all the time.

'Are you going to call your mum?'

Dean blinked.

'She'll want to know, *Dean*. This is her first grandchild, *I might die*. You need to tell her.'

He raised his eyebrows and stuck out his bottom lip. 'I guess so,' he said, feeling the inside pocket of his jacket for his phone. His mum's number went through to voicemail and he left her a message. 'Mum, it's me, give us a call, OK?'

He slipped the phone back into his pocket and noticed that Sky was looking at him aghast. 'Give us a call? Give us a call?'

'Yeah? What?'

She pursed her lips and shook her head. 'You're a fucking moron, Dean. Could you not have said something, you know, *relevant*? Like maybe where you were. Or what was happening. Or that I was fucking *dying*? Jesus!'

'What?' he countered, lamely. 'She'll call me back. I can tell her then.'

Sky rolled her eyes and then grimaced.

Dean got to his feet and clutched her hand. 'You OK?' he said.

'Yeah, yeah, just a twinge. A thing. A contraction, you know.'

Dean squeezed her hand and wondered what he should say or do to help. Everything felt potentially hazardous. But then saying and doing nothing felt even more dangerous. 'Can I get you anything?' he asked, thinking it felt like a reasonably safe call.

'Yeah. A normal placenta and another ten weeks to grow this baby.' She threw him her 'you total wanker' smile, folded her arms across her belly and turned away from him.

The anaesthetist arrived, an Asian man with a goatee beard and trendy shoes. He curled Sky into a foetal ball and injected her back. Dean couldn't watch. He was squeamish about needles, in particular needles that went into your actual spine. Sky made a total fuss about it but then, for a few moments afterwards, she was calm.

Looking back on the day his first baby was born, Dean could hardly remember anything after Sky was taken into surgery. Everything started going really fast. Sky's mum Rose pitched up at some point and immediately acted like nobody had been doing anything right until she arrived. His mum had called and said she wouldn't be able to make it for at least a couple of hours because she was in Brighton. He was too shell-shocked even to ask her what the hell she was doing there. He had a photo of himself that Sky's mum had taken, wearing a green tunic and trousers and a matching green hat. What do they call that? Scrubs. Yes, scrubs. At some point someone had put him in scrubs. Or maybe he'd put himself in scrubs, he couldn't remember. And then a nurse told him he could go into theatre and he remembered very clearly thinking, *Shit, no time for a quick smoke*, thinking how much better seeing your kid being born would be after a smoke. And then the next thing he knew, she was out. Isadora. There. Like a skinned lamb. All loose skin and blue veins and feet and hands the size of thumbnails. He barely had a chance to look at her face. She was stolen away and put under a light like an alien abduction and then someone came and passed her under their noses, very, very quickly, long enough for Dean to see wide-spaced eyes and a big mouth and dark hair that grew low on her brow. And in that brief moment, his daughter glanced at him with a look of such intense intelligence and knowing that Dean's breath caught and he felt as small and inconsequential as a fruit-fly.

Sky looked at him desperately as the baby was taken away again. 'Is she all right?' she cried. 'Is she OK?'

'She looks fantastic,' said a nurse, 'just taking her away now, just to be sure. But she looks fantastic. Really strong.'

'I want my mum. Where's my mum?'

'She's outside, waiting.'

'Can I see her? I want to see her.'

'You can see her when we've finished putting you back together. OK?'

'Dean, go and tell her,' Sky pleaded. 'Go and tell her the baby's here. She'll be freaking out otherwise.'

Dean did as he was told. The world seemed to have been torn into fragments and was whirling around his head. He couldn't get a grip on anything. He remembered Sky's mum jumping to her feet when she saw him, grabbing his forearms, almost shouting at him: 'Is it OK? Are they OK?'

Then he remembered people streaming out of the delivery room and a lot of shouting. He stood and watched, transfixed almost, somehow not putting facts together in his mind. They were shouting about somebody else, he told himself, maybe there was a door to another room off Sky's room.

'What's going on?' said Sky's mum to the next person to walk urgently past them.

The person looked at Sky's mum for a split second, said nothing and carried on walking.

Dean's mouth felt dry. He licked his lips. He could feel fear pulsing from Sky's mum like radiation. The more she panicked, the more Dean withdrew inside himself. If he didn't say anything and he didn't do anything then everything would be cool.

'How can you just stand there doing nothing? That's your woman in there! Find out what the fuck's going on!'

Eventually someone emerged and told them that Sky was haemorrhaging, that she had lost a dangerous amount of blood and that they were having trouble locating her blood type, but that they would begin a transfusion the moment they'd managed to locate some.

Still Dean felt it, a sense of calm resignation, that there was nothing he could do, that people were doing what needed to be done, that very soon he could go home. The thought crossed his mind, once again, that he would like to slip out for a smoke, but with Sky's mother there, stressing and fretting, he knew he would not be allowed to. It felt to Dean as if he suddenly existed in three different dimensions. Part of him was here, cool and calm, yet two other parts of him, his child, her mother, had been unstitched and put away somewhere out of sight. Every time he tried to give over some thought to one of them, the other demanded his attention, and then he'd be back in his own head, wanting a spliff. Sky, baby, spliff, boing boing boing.

And then, some time later, maybe an hour, maybe less, a doctor appeared and stood in front of Dean and Sky's mother, and Sky's mother immediately began to wail, *'No, no, not my baby, not my baby girl, no, no, no,'* and nobody used the word dead, but Dean knew that she was.

Sky was gone.

His pretty, stroppy girl was gone.

Sky's mother wouldn't touch him. It was as if he'd killed Sky. And maybe he had. He'd got her pregnant. If she hadn't been pregnant, she'd still have been alive.

His own mother arrived an hour after Sky died and Dean sat and let her hold him for a while, while Sky's mum shouted at people and screamed. Dean had not done anything physical yet. He had not cried or shouted or fainted or hit anyone or thrown anything. He had not, as far as he could recollect, even spoken. He hadn't needed to. Sky's mum had been doing all the speaking that needed to be done.

A nurse they had not seen before came to them after a

few minutes and Dean's mum released him from her embrace.

'The baby's doing well,' she said, 'would you like to come and see her?' The question was directed at Dean. He nodded. He did want to see her. He wanted to get away from this. His mum came with him but Sky's mum did not want to leave her daughter.

'I'll come later,' she said, 'take a picture for me. Give her a kiss. Oh, God.'

His mum held his hand as they walked down the corridor behind the nurse. Dean could feel his head reordering itself as they walked away from the mess of grief towards a blander landscape. 'She's a bit tangled up,' the nurse explained with a smile, 'lots of tubes and things, nothing to be scared of, though. She's very strong, she won't have to stay in long.'

'Will we be able to hold her?' asked his mum.

'Possibly. You'll have to speak to the nurse on duty.'

They had to scrub their hands clean in a low metal sink and go through two sets of security doors and then they were in a small sunny room filled with incubators.

Dean looked around. The scenario was otherworldly. Eight babies the size of puppies wired up to flashing machinery.

'There she is,' said the nurse, 'your little girl.'

Dean inhaled. She was on his far right. She was wearing a knitted white hat that was too big for her, and a gigantic nappy. Her legs emerged from the cavernous nappy splayed out like a supermarket chicken with the string cut off. Her arms were spread out and she looked for all the world as though she were sunbathing.

'She's beautiful,' said his mum. 'Oh, Dean, she's just beautiful.'

Dean glanced down into the box. She was sleeping. Her fingers furled and unfurled in her sleep. With her wide mouth and far-apart eyes she looked a bit like a Muppet, like her face would divide in half when she opened her mouth. She looked just like him. Just exactly like him.

'She looks like you, doesn't she?' said his mum.

Dean nodded. 'Can I touch her?' he asked the nurse.

'Yes, you can.'

'I'll be gentle,' he said, wanting to say it before she said it, before she made him feel like a big brute.

He stroked the palm of the baby's hand with a fingertip. Her skin was warm and so fine and translucent it felt almost like nothing. 'She's so small,' he murmured.

'Just under four pounds,' said the nurse. 'A good weight. For her weeks. What are you going to call her?'

Dean stared at the baby and moved his fingertip to her cheeks. They were covered in a minky down. Part-Muppet, part-werewolf.

'Isadora,' he said. 'Isadora Katy.'

The nurse smiled. 'That's beautiful,' she said. 'Had you already decided,' she continued, 'before, well . . .?'

'Yeah,' he said. 'That's what Sky wanted.'

'Ah,' said the nurse, 'that's good. Good that you'd already decided. Can we put that on her notes, then? Can we write it down? I-S-A-D-O-R-A? And K-A-T-Y?

Higgins? Lovely. Great. I'll leave you to it then, OK?'

His mum pulled a chair over for him to sit on and they sat together for a few minutes, staring at the baby. Dean was glad that Sky's mum wasn't here. She'd have been talking. Dean's mum was like him, quiet, contemplative.

'Amazing, isn't it?' she said eventually. 'She's got all of you in her. All of your Dean-ness. It's all in there. Like ingredients in a cake.'

Dean nodded. He hadn't expected it. Hadn't expected his baby to look like him. The whole pregnancy had been about Sky. Everything was always about Sky. It was her body, her baby, her pregnancy, her life, her flat, her world. Dean had just assumed that his daughter would be Sky in miniature. And there she was, four pounds nothing of him. Sky would have been gutted. She'd even said it: 'I hope this girl doesn't look like you, Dean, she'll be spending her whole life plucking her fucking eyebrows. And wailing at the moon.'

But his features sat well on her, tiny and undercooked as she was. She was pretty.

Another nurse joined them and smiled. 'Beautiful little thing,' she said. And then she turned to Dean and she said, 'I'm so so sorry for your loss.'

Dean felt like he'd been slapped. His loss. He hadn't realised until just then that he'd lost something. He tried to bring Sky to mind; not the Sky who'd just died on a delivery table, or the Sky who'd spent the last six months hating him, but the other Sky, the one he'd spent three years lusting after, fantasising about, the prettiest girl he'd ever been with. He wasn't sure he'd ever loved her, but he'd liked her, more than he'd liked anyone else he'd been with.

No, he hadn't lost the love of his life. He hadn't lost his soul-mate. But he had lost the person who was going to bring up his baby. That person had gone, taking her milk and her lullabies and her enthusiasm for buying small pink dresses with her. This baby had no mother. One day soon, this baby would be big enough to leave this sunny little room and someone would have to take this baby home and raise it. And everybody was going to turn and look at him.

Images flashed through his head: an empty flat, a screaming baby over his shoulder, the black night outside the window, a bottle of milk illuminated and rotating in the microwave, his life desiccated to an existence of shit and noise and solitude. Dean said he wanted to go to the toilet. Instead he slipped out of the building and into a canopied walkway where he rolled together a spliff with shaking hands and sucked the life out of it.

He contemplated walking home. It was just getting dark, the day had gone by without him even noticing. He glanced up at the building. He thought of what lay in there. A tiny, too-early baby with tubes and wires extruded from every orifice; the body of that baby's mother, floppy and drained of blood like a kosher calf; the baby's grandmothers, sick and bleached and aged ten years in half an hour. He thought of the expectations, the needs and demands that lay inside that building. He felt sick. He felt weak. The sky loomed above him, purple and low. The walls of the building squashed up against him. He was being compressed from every angle. He knew he had to run, in one direction or another.

He chose away.

MAGGIE

Maggie Smith pulled the clear wrapping from a two-pack of Rich Tea biscuits and snapped one in half. It broke with a sound like a twig being stepped on in a forest. She dipped the corner of the semi-circle into her mug of tea and let it soften for three seconds before transferring it to her mouth and sucking the soft bit off the end. She gazed at her mug. And it was *her* mug. She'd brought it with her from home, tired of the taste and fragility of plastic. It was one that she'd taken from her mum's house, after she died, a solid brown mug with a cream interior and a handle that looked like it had been stuck on as an afterthought. A hairline crack was forming on the mug, running downwards from the edge. She'd have to be careful, she pondered, the whole thing could give way one day and she'd be scalded.

She set the mug down gently on the table to her left and then she looked at the man in the bed and she smiled.

'How are you, Daniel? Can I get you anything?'

The man in the bed grunted. That meant that he was in pain.

'More meds, love? Shall I ask for more meds?'

He grunted again, and winced.

Maggie got to her feet, smoothing down the front of her trousers, and stuck her head around the door. Outside, the plush, carpeted corridor was empty. She turned her head from left to right. It could be a hotel when it was empty like this, she thought, a kind of two-star airport hotel possibly, with its eighties colour scheme of peach and spearmint, its upholstered seating of tubular metal, framed watercolours of French fishing villages and plaster-moulded up-lighters.

She padded down the carpet towards a small glazed work-station where two women in white overalls sat leafing through paperwork.

'I'm sorry to disturb you,' she began, in her gentlest, most considerate voice – who knew what onerous task she might be distracting these women from? – 'Mr Blanchard, he seems to be in some discomfort . . . when you're free, not now, when you get a minute . . .' she tapered off.

One of the women – Maggie thought her name was Sarah but couldn't be sure, there were so many people here, they came and went and it was hard to keep track – smiled patiently and put down her paperwork. 'Of course,' she said. 'I'll come right now.'

Maggie had never been to a hospice up until two weeks ago and she felt the same sense of awe about it as she'd felt about midwives on birthing units after she'd given birth to her first child, twenty-five years ago. *Wow*, she'd thought, *people do this*. She'd toyed with the idea of being a midwife herself for a while after she'd had her children, wanting to be part of the miraculous work they did, but the desire faded. Now she felt the same way about the men and women here. To be present at the far side of the spectrum, to give dignity and grace to these fading moments, to witness the exit of a whole human existence. It was truly inspiring. She felt at home here now. She felt like she belonged.

She followed the nurse back to Daniel's room and watched as she fiddled with the dials on the equipment to which he was attached.

'Thank you,' she heard him whisper, as the morphine drained into him. 'Thank you.'

'You are very welcome!' trilled the nurse. She paused and pushed her hands into her pockets, stood for a while and gazed down upon him, smiling. 'Can I get you anything else, Mr Blanchard? Some juice? A paper?'

Daniel smiled, a small pucker of his lips, and shook his head, just once.

'OK!' sang Sarah. 'I'll just leave you here with your friend then, let you get some rest. You should start to feel a lot better very soon.' She gave his hand a squeeze where it lay against his white bed sheets, and then she left.

Maggie picked up his other hand and held it inside both of hers. She watched him for a moment, watched the lines of tension start to ease from his face, his beautiful face. She still remembered the first time she'd seen that face. Just over a year ago. He'd appeared to her like an apparition, a grimacing angel, above the desk that she manned twice a week at the physiotherapy practice.

'Good morning,' he'd said, and she'd immediately been enthralled by his accent, a soft, milky French affair. Then she'd caught the strong angles of his face, the cushiony lips, the black hair streaked with silver, the olivey skin, the turquoise eyes, and felt her stomach collapse in on itself. It was rare, as a woman of a certain age, to find a man of a comparable age who made your stomach sag and your heart begin to pump more purposefully.

'Good morning.' She'd smiled, feeling glad that she'd treated herself to that teeth-whitening session a month earlier, feeling prettier for it. 'Can I help you?'

'It's my back.' He winced. 'My friend recommended this place. He said I should see a Candy Stapleton?'

'Ah, yes.' She smiled again, showing off her lovely white teeth. 'Of course. Would you like me to make you an appointment?'

He straightened himself and stared at her, disconsolately. Maggie's heart ached for him. 'I was hoping to see her now. Today. I was hoping for immediate attention. My back is so . . .' He winced again and clutched his lower back.

Backs. Always backs. Knees in skiing season, backs the rest of the time. She looked at him sympathetically. 'I'll see what I can do. Take a seat.'

He was there for nearly three hours in the end. Long enough for some unforced conversation to surface, long enough for her to find out that he was indeed French, that he had lived in England for nearly thirty years, that he had never married and that his back had been troubling him to a greater and greater extent for the past two months. Maggie made him a cup of tea from her kettle and told him that she was divorced with two grown-up children and that she'd been working at the practice for nearly five years. Just for pocket money. Her ex-husband looked after her very nicely, she didn't really need to work. She tried her hardest to make herself sound interesting. She had made the assumption that because he was French he was intrinsically more interesting than her. It occurred to her that there were probably boring people in France too but it seemed somehow unlikely. England was just the sort of boring place where boring people came from, Maggie felt. And she included herself in that.

He wasn't much of a smiler. He didn't smile once for the full three hours he was in the waiting room, not even when she gave him his tea. But then, she'd concluded, who smiled with a bad back?

He came in every day after that, to see Candy. The therapy didn't seem to be helping much; if anything his back grew worse and worse as the days went by. Eventually Candy referred him to a specialist at the local hospital and Maggie knew that she might never see him again so she did one of the bravest things she'd ever done in her life and said: 'Maybe we could . . .'

And he had smiled and said: 'Yes, we could. Tomorrow night? We could have dinner? Yes?'

She'd smiled gratefully at him. She'd been about to say that they could meet up for a cup of tea, but dinner was really what she'd been after. She was glad that she hadn't misread the signals. She was glad that he wanted to take her out for dinner.

That first dinner had been a muted affair. Daniel's (for that was his name) back had been an issue. He'd numbed the pain with red wine and little white pills that he kept in his jacket pocket in a clear plastic pot. By the time their desserts had arrived he'd been straining to get out of his chair so they'd retired to a corner of the bar where they had a small low sofa and some flattering lighting, and things had improved for a while. Daniel had complimented Maggie on her hair: 'It is very lovely hair, Maggie, you look after yourself.' And she did look after herself. She'd not been a good-looking teenager and then in her twenties she'd let herself get fat with the babies, sat around like a pudding really for the best part of a decade. Then she'd got divorced and lost the weight and suddenly there she'd been, thirty-six years old and a very attractive woman, like a stranger who'd been hiding inside her all along. She'd got more and more attractive as she headed towards her forties, her bones finally fitting well inside the flesh of her face, keeping her make-up modern and fresh like they told you to in the magazines, professional highlights and a good diet. She'd never looked better than she did on her forty-second birthday. She'd peaked and then it had started to go and she'd thought: *No, not yet, I've only just got used to being attractive, I'm not ready to let go of it yet.* So the odd little procedure, the teeth whitening, a tiny bit of Botox and some fillers, expensive supplements and creams, and now she was fifty-three and, in a soft light like this, away from the cruel scrutiny of English daylight, she could still pass for forty-two, she really could.

But although Daniel had praised her hair and her general levels of personal upkeep, he had not tried to kiss her that night, nor any of the other nights that followed. And then one night they'd met, for Chinese she recalled, she'd deliberately packed some Polo mints into her handbag to mask the garlic, just in case, and he'd said: 'Maggie, I want to thank you for being my friend. I am a lonely man and I have lived a lonely life and I do not have many friends. But I count you, Maggie, as a good friend. A very good friend.'

Maggie's smile had frozen in place. He was going to dump her, she'd thought, dump her before he'd even kissed her. She'd felt her heart ache with sadness.

'So I hope that you won't mind if I burden you with the fact of my condition? Which I learned of only today, so excuse me if I am not quite myself. But it appears that I have a large tumour, in my lung. This is what has been causing the pain in my back. And beyond that it also seems that I have secondary cancer in my legs and in my stomach. So . . . it *seems*,' he laid his large hands flat upon the table, 'that there is not a lot that can be done for me. It seems that I am to die.'

Maggie had clasped her hands to her mouth and stifled a squeal. Then she'd let them fall to her lap and stared at Daniel in mute horror. 'No,' she'd said, 'no!'

He'd smiled then. It struck her as a strange time for him to expend a smile, when they were seemingly in such short supply. It was almost, she'd felt, as though he were happy about it. No, not happy, just relieved.

'It is fine, Maggie, it is fine. It is *destiny*, you know? I never saw myself as an old man, and now . . . well, sixty would have been nice, but fifty-three? Fifty-three will just have to do . . .'

But inside Maggie's head, a little voice was still saying: No, no, no. Inside Maggie's head was the sound of shattered dreams and a broken heart. Fifty-three would not do, would not do *at all*.

They'd managed two more dinners after that, before Daniel had had to go in for chemotherapy. He'd told her not to visit him in the hospital but she had, catching him in his cotton pyjamas – pale-blue edged with cream piping. His slippers were tucked underneath the bed and a copy of the *Telegraph* lay on the tray in front of him and he was wearing half-moon reading glasses. She'd never seen them before. They made him look, of course, more intelligent, but also more vulnerable. Her heart turned over with love. But he'd removed them with a haste that suggested vanity when he saw her approaching over the top of them.

'Oh,' she'd said, 'you wear glasses.'

'I usually wear lenses,' he'd muttered distractedly, 'but I thought, on top of everything else, here, in this place, all this,' he indicated the medical paraphernalia surrounding him, 'did I need to be fiddling around with those little things? Also, I thought I would not see anyone who knows me.' She searched his face for a sign that he was teasing her, that really he was secretly delighted that she had disobeyed his instructions and come to see him. But there was none.

'Sorry,' she'd said, nervously, trying not to cry. 'Couldn't bear to think of you here, all alone. And I brought you some fruit, look.' She pulled a carrier from her shoulder bag and took three green apples and two bananas out of it. She laid them on his tray and immediately wished she had not brought the fruit. It looked insensitively healthy. And also clichéd.

Daniel didn't look at the fruit. Instead he looked at her wanly and sighed. She thought he was about to complain about the fruit, tell her she was a fool to bring him fruit, that he was too ill to eat fruit, that he did not even *like* fruit, but he didn't. Instead he took her hand in his and as Maggie glanced at him she saw a single tear roll down his cheek. 'Thank you,' he whispered, 'you are a very good person.'

'You are very welcome.' She smiled compassionately and handed him a tissue. 'Very, very welcome.'

In some ways, she pondered over the intervening months, it was a bit unfair that she had finally, after nearly twenty years on her own, started to fall in love with someone, and then he got terminally ill. If she wasn't such a positive, glass half full kind of person, she'd almost say it was typical. But it wasn't typical. It was atypical. Generally her life ran quite smoothly and in a vaguely upward direction. Generally Maggie got what she wanted, but then, Maggie didn't really ask for much. So instead of seeing the impending death of her new boyfriend as a bad thing, Maggie decided to view it as a gift. An opportunity to make a difference to someone's life. A chance to care. And so, for the last few months, that was what Maggie had done. Instead of being Daniel's girlfriend, she became his carer. Instead of waiting by the phone for him to call and fantasising about engagement rings and white weddings, Maggie did his shopping for him and managed his medication. Instead of sitting opposite him in low-lit restaurants and meeting him for picnics on sunny afternoons, she accompanied him on hospital appointments and cooked him stews.

He was close to the end now. It could be days, it could be weeks, but certainly no more than a handful. He was thin and his face had lost its previous perfect symmetry, hanging slack in places, knotted with tension in others. In the hours when he was in pain, the morphine rendered him silent and still. She missed him then and felt a sense of his life force draining away through his grey skin and into sticky puddles on the floor below his bed. But on good days, when his body held more essential spirit than opiates, she and Daniel would talk until his mouth began to chafe with dryness or sleep pulled him back into silence. Maggie sensed that the conversations they had during these moments were more candid and open than any of the conversations they'd had during the preceding months, when they'd shared wine in restaurants and enjoyed the fanciful notion that both of them would remain alive for at least another twenty years.

In a Thai restaurant on their fourth date she'd asked him about his mother. He'd shrugged, as though someone's mother could not possibly be of any real interest to another person. 'She is very old,' he'd said after a moment. 'She is not the person she used to be.'

'And what sort of person did she use to be?' Maggie had gently urged.

He'd shrugged again. 'A different person,' he'd said. 'You know?'

'Where does she live?'

'In France,' he'd replied, with a note of exasperation.

She'd wanted to push it: where in France? With whom: brothers, sisters, grandchildren, a cat – alone? But she had felt his impatience and she'd let him change the subject. But today he'd volunteered something new: his mother lived in a home. In Dieppe. And then this: he had a brother. The brother lived near the home in Dieppe and visited her every day. 'I feel no guilt,' he said, 'for my mother. She is old. She doesn't know that she is in a home. She doesn't know who she is. But my brother, every day he has to get into his sad little car and drive across the sad little town where he lives and on to the grey highway, to that big house by the sea where it always smells of fish and spume, and sit with a woman with glassy eyes and cold hands who used to be his mother. And she will not know him and then he will leave and feel guilty that she is on her own until he makes the same journey the next day.'

'What about his wife, his family?'

'He has no wife, no family. He is like me. He is alone. So, we die and our line dies with us.' He coughed then and Maggie passed him a cup of squash.

'Oh, well, you never know,' she said, light-heartedly, 'that's the thing with being a man. There might be a little you out there somewhere and you just don't know it.' She let out a small tinkle of laughter and glanced at him, checking she hadn't crossed yet another invisible line.

He pulled his eyelids tight over his eyes and smiled wryly. 'Maybe,' he chuckled. Then he sighed. 'Maybe. After all, anything is possible.'

Maggie smiled too, relieved that she had amused rather than aggravated the man that she loved. And then she watched him, attentively and adoringly, as he drifted slowly back into a thick fug of drug-induced sleep.

ROBYN

Robyn's life had turned into a novel. One of those novels with shoes on the cover. And it was about a girl called Robyn who meets a man in a clothes shop whilst selling him a brown jumper and how he waits outside the clothes shop for her to finish work and then takes her to a beautiful bar in the basement of a smart restaurant in the beating heart of Soho where they drink pretty cocktails with cherry blossoms and pink vodka and talk for so long that the trains stop running and the evening turns to deepest night and they have to walk for half an hour to find taxis to take them home. It then follows the heroine and this man (his name is Jack) on every wonderful, joyous, honeyed, romantic cliché as they meet up again and again in locations such as London parks on sunny afternoons, floating restaurants on canals, pub beer gardens hung with fairy lights, art galleries, sweaty gigs and art-house cinemas to see films with subtitles.

The man called Jack turned out to be twenty-seven years old and, of course, since Robyn's life was now a novel, not a bank teller or a student or a direct marketing account executive but a novelist. An actual published novelist. He did not write fat books with shoes on the cover, but slim books with out-of-focus photographs on the cover and one-word titles. He'd had his first book published when he was twenty-five, his second last year and was now halfway through his third. And because this was a novelised vision of real life, he had, of course, just sold the film rights to his first book for tens of thousands of pounds, so even though his books didn't sell that many copies, his bank account was healthy enough for him to keep on suggesting more and more idyllic locations for their rendezvous and to slip £20 notes into her pockets to pay for cabs, on the nights when she went home.

More and more frequently, though, Robyn didn't go home. She stayed at Jack's, a suitably photogenic shabby little one-bed place in a fat stucco house on a leafy Holloway square with rattly sash windows and gnarled wooden floors and an oversized wrought-iron bed with an abstract painting hung crookedly above it. She did indeed pad barefoot around his shabby but lovely flat in his oversized sweaters, and drink tea out of his giant Starbucks mugs whilst curled up on his scruffy but elegant sofa, with his head in her lap, running her fingers through his glossy hair. She had never felt more beautiful in her life and she had never felt more as if the life she was living was the life that she had always been destined to live, mapped out millennia before in stars a billion light years away.

When she was away from Jack she would pick through the photos on her iPhone of the two of them, arms out-stretched, heads touching, beaming into the lens. She took a lot of photos these days: the view from Jack's window, Jack's hands around a glass, an arrangement of their possessions on a pub table, the back of Jack's head, the dents in their empty pillows caught in the early sunlight of a Saturday morning. No detail was too small or insignificant; no aspect of their union was unworthy of a visual record. Jack teased her about it: 'I've just dropped a lump of hummus on the kitchen floor – quick, take a picture!'

But Robyn couldn't help herself; if her life was a novel then she was making the film of the book. Just in case, she supposed. In case it all went wrong. Because in books with shoes on the cover something always goes wrong. Girl meets boy. Girl falls in love with boy. Boy and girl have a stupid misunderstanding and split up.

But Robyn could not possibly conceive of how this perfect union of two such compatible and uncomplicated people could ever find a way to unspool itself.

And when it did she knew that she was no longer living in a novel with shoes on the cover but in a novel with an out-of-focus photo on the cover and a one-word title.

She'd thought it already, even before Nush had said anything. She'd thought it, if she was honest, from the very first time she'd seen him. She'd made him wait two weeks before sleeping with him, not in some pathetic attempt to keep him on the boil or to assert her feminine wiles, and not, even, to prolong the giddy innocence of those first few dates. Robyn didn't play games and she didn't politicise sex. The reason she'd made him wait was because of a tiny nagging sense of unease deep in the centre of her psyche. She couldn't place it or name it, but it was there, lurking like a strange man in the shadows.

She'd overridden it, of course.

She was in love.

She was gorgeous.

He was gorgeous.

She needed a better reason than nagging unease to reject his advances. And actually, from the moment their relationship was consummated, the feeling passed.

Other things happened over the couple of weeks, but she ignored them as the possibility that her initial misgivings might have been founded on something real was too unpalatable to contemplate.

There was a conversation, on the decked balcony of his friends' shared house in Tufnell Park. He'd already told her that his father was dead. That had been ascertained on their first date. Her father was an anonymous sperm donor. His father was dead, in a car crash when Jack was eight months old. It had bonded them together. 'Poor us,' Robyn had said, 'never seen our fathers' faces,' and they'd made sad faces at each other and then laughed. Not that it was funny, but they were laughing because they were allowed to laugh, because it was their sad thing and they retained the rights over it.

Robyn met Jack's mum, Sam, a month into their relationship. She was a nice-looking woman with extravagantly highlighted hair which she wore piled on top of her head with a big mother-of-pearl clasp. She was luxuriantly middle class, in Sweaty Betty leisurewear and bare feet, and her little two-bed cottage just outside St Albans was a perfect late-nineties stage set of Designers Guild furnishings and antique pine.

She called Robyn 'darling' and greeted her with a kiss on each cheek and a look of fascinated affection. They sat in a battered pine kitchen with a butler's sink and a pale yellow Aga and Sam smoked Marlboro Lights by the back door, blowing the smoke out of the side of her mouth where it was immediately picked up by the breeze and brought back into the kitchen.

'You two look *adorable* together,' she said in her raspy jazz singer's voice.

Robyn and Jack glanced at each other and smiled. They knew that.

'Jack has been talking about you a *lot*,' she continued, throwing her spent cigarette into a flower bed and pulling the back door shut behind her.

'All good, I hope.'

'I'd say. And I must also say as the mother of just one precious boy, that when he comes home and tells me he's fallen in love with a medical student who wants to be a paediatrician and looks like a young Megan Fox, well . . . music to my ears! I give you my blessing.'

She joined them at the farmhouse dining table, fixed Robyn with her direct gaze and smiled again.

Robyn smiled back at her, wondering what she was thinking.

'So, Jack tells me your father was a sperm donor,' Sam began, bluntly.

'Mum!' said Jack in alarm.

'What? You said it was all out in the open. It *is* all out in the open, isn't it, darling?'

Robyn nodded and smiled. 'No secrets in my house.'

Sam squinted her eyes together as though she were trying to throw her image of Robyn into some other sort of focus. 'Absolutely fascinating. Isn't it?' she added, as if seeking confirmation from a third party that, yes, it was indeed fascinating. 'And do you look like your donor father?'

'Well, I don't look like anyone else in my family so, yes, I assume I must.'

'And this was because, well, your father, your dad, the one who brought you up, he had fertility issues, is it?'

'Mum!'

'It's OK,' said Robyn, 'honestly, I'm happy talking about it. No. It wasn't to do with my dad's fertility. They had two daughters before me. It was . . .' She breathed in before continuing. 'My sisters both had Rett Syndrome. It wasn't supposed to happen twice but then they found it was down to a mutation in my dad's sperm. So that meant they couldn't risk having any more babies. Rachel died when she was fifteen. Gemma died when she was seventeen. And they thought about asking a relative to donate some sperm but decided that was too complicated, that it would be easier to use an anonymous donor. And that's what they did – and here I am!' Robyn threw

123

a 'da-da' pose and smiled. She'd told the story a dozen times before: The Tragic Reasons Behind My Miraculous Existence. She could tell it without an aching heart and a tear in her eye because she hadn't really known her sisters. She was four when Rachel died, five when Gemma died, more concerned with school and playgrounds than the two sick girls who lived in a hospital three miles away.

Sam had her hand clutched to her throat. 'Your poor, poor parents,' she said, 'to lose two children. Everything they must have gone through and to find the balls from somewhere to keep going, to make themselves a family. You know, the human race gets an awful lot of flak, but really, most of the time, people are just going around, being quietly, silently, utterly *amazing*.'

Robyn nodded and smiled. She knew exactly how amazing her parents were, not only for the way they had soldiered on so bravely in the face of so much adversity but also for the way they had raised her, the joyful, loving, secure upbringing they had given her.

'And what about you?' Sam continued. 'How do you feel about your donor father? Do you ever want to meet him?'

Robyn shook her head. 'No. Never. Ever.'

'But don't you want to know? Don't you want to know what he looks like? Who *you* look like?'

'No. Honestly. This is me.' Robyn touched her chest. 'This is who I am. I am not my mother. I am not my father. It's like I've made myself a single entity. Like I stand alone. It's like I'm *Eve*.' She laughed.

Sam blinked at her in surprise. 'Original woman?' she asked.

Robyn smiled and shrugged. 'I suppose so.'

'Wow.' Sam let the single word hang in the air unadorned for a moment. Robyn watched her and saw unsaid words working their way around the muscles of her face. At first she thought that maybe Sam had been silenced by wonder and awe. But it then occurred to her that she was trying to work something out. 'You know,' she said a moment later, 'I'd never, ever thought about it like that before.'

'What do you mean?'

'Oh,' she straightened herself up, as though emerging from a hypnotist's trance, 'nothing,' she said, 'nothing really. It's just interesting, isn't it? How we form our identities. How we package ourselves. How we process the truth.'

The mood in the kitchen had become tense. It felt as if a bucket had been knocked over and something sticky and unpleasant were trickling out of it. The subject was changed, a supper of roast chicken and mashed potato was served and eaten, and Robyn had not really given the conversation much more thought until two weeks later when she introduced Jack to her friends for the first time.

It was in a pub in Mayfair, round the corner from the wealth management company that Nush worked for. The get-together was being billed as a celebration of her promotion from receptionist to assistant PA to a director, but was really a 'come and meet Robyn's mysterious new boyfriend' event, which meant a higher than average turn-out, especially for a night outside the Buckhurst Hill comfort zone.

Robyn had felt so proud walking into the pub that night with her beautiful, clever, gentle man. She gripped his hand inside hers and virtually pulled him towards the table at the back of the room where everyone was gathered, desperate to show them the star of the next chapter of her Incredible Perfect Life.

She was happy for her friends with their nice boyfriends with City jobs and sports cars and teacher-training courses and bedrooms in their parents' comfortable Essex homes. And she was happy for her single friends with their Saturday night plans and their Facebook existences. They were happy and she was happy that they were happy. But nobody else had what she had. Nobody had the precious pearl of their split-apart, their soul-mate, a man with wooden floors and published novels and the bone structure of a Titian archangel. Her friends were still finding their way while Robyn sat cosy and warm and aglow with satisfaction at reaching her destination. Robyn was home.

Nush spotted them first and leaped to her feet, a tiny bird girl with dark eyes that were almost too large for her face, and newly cropped hair like a neat black cap on her head. She threw herself at Robyn's neck and squeezed her hard. Robyn said: 'Congratulations!' in a neatly cadenced sing-song, an attempt to maintain the façade that that was why they were here, in a pub, miles from where any of them lived.

'Thank you.' Nush echoed Robyn's tuneful intonation, her eyes darting across her friend's shoulder to Jack.

'This is Jack,' said Robyn, pulling away, 'and Jack, this is Nush, my best friend.'

Nush clasped his hand and then hugged him to her. 'Oh, wow, it is *so* nice to finally meet you. You're lovely!' Nush, it appeared, had started drinking before the arranged meet-up time of eight o'clock. She pulled away from him and regarded him, her eyes still on his. 'You are so pretty,' she said, and Robyn and Jack glanced at each other and laughed.

'No, really, honestly, you are. Oh, wow, you two . . . you're the cutest couple I've ever seen. Look, everyone,' she turned to address the rest of their group, 'this is Jack. *The* Jack. Aren't they the cutest couple you've ever seen? Aren't they? I mean . . .' She paused, turned back to look at Jack and Robyn, then back again to the table and said, 'They could be brother and sister.'

There was a brief silence until she added: 'Oh, God, I mean, you actually could! You could. You could really be brother and sister. Holy shit . . .'

Nush's words got swallowed up by whoops of hilarity from the rest of the group and Robyn smiled apologetically at Jack, who smiled back reassuringly, and the conversation twisted and turned easily away from the subject of Jack and Robyn and whether they might be related, and Robyn did not, in fact, give the concept another thought until later the next day when she'd caught Jack at the sink in his bathroom, his chin angled up to shave his jawline, and thought for the briefest, most fleeting of seconds, that she was looking at herself.

'What did your dad look like?' she asked, almost immediately, a quickening sense of dread leaping from her stomach to her throat.

Jack stopped what he was doing and glanced at her reflection in the mirror. He paused for a moment and then shrugged and rinsed his razor under the tap. 'I don't really know.'

'But you must have seen photographs of him?' she continued.

'No,' he said, plucking a towel from the rail. 'My mum burned them all.'

'She burned all the photos of your dad? God, why?'

'Because she hated him.'

'What, seriously?'

'Yeah. They'd been together for three years, madly in love, then he buggered off the minute he found out she was pregnant. He went to live in a commune in France, shacked up with some eighteen year old, we never heard from him again. Mum took me to the commune when I was about eighteen months old, so that he could meet me, gets there and finds out that he's been killed in a car crash ten months earlier.'

'She just burned all the photos?'

'Yeah. I guess. Or chucked them out or something.'

'She didn't even keep one so that you would know what he looked like?'

'No. Well, I guess she thought that I'd meet him one

day. I guess she thought he wouldn't be dead.'

'But what about his family? His parents? Didn't you ever see them?'

'He didn't have any parents. He was brought up in a children's home. He was a Barnardo's Boy.'

It seemed a detail too far. French communes and car crashes was one thing – an orphaned Barnardo's Boy was another. It was too much of an artistic flourish. Too romantic. It could be true. It probably was true. But then again, it might not be . . .

Robyn's mind darkened then and discomfiting thoughts jostled for space in the shadows. The sheer force of her first glimpse of Jack in Zara all those weeks ago, the way his mother had been so strange with her in the kitchen that day when they'd been talking about her donor father; Nush's pronouncement in the pub the other night that they looked like brother and sister; that moment, just now, when she'd caught his reflection in the mirror and thought it was her own; and now this . . . burned photographs and Dr Barnardo's.

She'd read those stories in flimsy magazines about long-lost siblings meeting up in adult life and falling instantaneously in love. She'd read them with horror and disgust. But surely, she reasoned with herself, even if she did have brothers and sisters out there – and there could be no more than nine, those were the rules – what possible, infinitesimal chance was there that one of them would walk into her branch of Zara on a Thursday night looking for a jumper? It was surely so improbable as to be entirely impossible. But was it any less possible than any other meeting between two people? Between a woman and her soul-mate? Could not the mere suggestion of an invisible connection between two people provide the impetus to propel a person off the pavement and into the basement of a clothes shop? Could not a genetic link in fact predispose two people towards a liking for a particular high-street fashion chain (and Robyn had 'specially applied for a job at Zara because she liked their clothes)? So it might not in fact be pure random coincidence. It could all be down to brown jumpers.

All these thoughts passed through Robyn's head in less than one minute. They left her feeling wounded and bruised. She looked at Jack again – she studied his face as he turned from the mirror and walked towards her, smiling. He was not her twin. He had his mother's startling turquoise eyes, and her slightly oval-shaped skull. But that nose and those lips . . . They were hers, and he – he belonged to her, like no one else had ever belonged to her. She possessed him and he possessed her, in that calm, unquestioning way of family.

Family.

A chill ran through her and she turned away from him. She did not look at him again for eighteen minutes.

DEAN

Dean sat on the sofa, staring at the same lump on the carpet. Cupped inside his hand was the last centimetre of a spliff, soft with spit and brown with unfiltered tobacco. He pulled the last lungful of smoke from the stub and rubbed it out into an ashtray in front of him. Then he got to his feet and studied himself in the mirror bolted to the back of the living-room door. He was wearing a suit. He'd bought it yesterday, £29.99 from Primark. His shoes were his uncle's, and his tie was from the Cancer Research shop round the corner. He'd sprayed it with Febreze to mask the smell of old people and damp clothes and now it smelled even worse.

His eyes seemed to have retreated inside his skull, his cheekbones were showing and his lips were dry and chapped. He noticed a tube of Sky's hand cream on the shelf above the radiator and squeezed a small blob on to his fingertips. He smoothed it into his lips and as he did so perfume filled the air around him. It was her smell. The smell of her hands. He'd never noticed it when she was alive. He smacked his lips together, tugged at the hem of his Primark jacket, and then he left the flat and went to his girlfriend's funeral.

It was a nice day. Blue and fresh with a sharp breeze. Clouds rolled across the sky busily, as though they were late for an urgent appointment. The church was full. Sky would have been pleased with the turn-out. All of her friends were there, dressed to the nines, sobbing extravagantly. As he walked up the aisle with his mum, people caught his eye, throwing him looks of fevered compassion that pushed him off-balance. It was like this was a film and he was the tragic hero, like when the credits rolled his name would come up first in big letters. But it felt wrong, as though he'd stolen the credit from someone who really deserved it. He was a fraud. He hadn't really loved Sky. He hadn't even cried yet. And as for their baby girl . . . he still hadn't been back to the hospital. He couldn't face it. He'd sat in the flat for three weeks, his phone switched off, ignoring the buzz of the intercom. The only person he'd spoken to had been his mum. She'd brought him buckets of chicken and nine bottles of Pepsi Max and told him that everyone was thinking about him, that everyone loved him, that Isadora was doing really well, that she'd been in every day, her and Sky's mum, that they'd fed her with a bottle, that the jaundice was going, that some wires had been unattached, some tubes taken out, she'd opened her eyes. She didn't tell him to get off his arse and go and see her. She didn't tell him to do anything. She just fed him food and love and information. Dean had never loved his mum as much as he had in the past three weeks.

He shuffled along a pew and found himself sitting next

to Sky's cousin. He was ten years older and a full foot taller than Sky. He threw Dean an inscrutable look.

Dean hooked a finger inside the collar of his £3.99 shirt and pulled at it. Sky's mum sat in front of him. She turned when she sensed him behind her and her face was a mask of repressed dislike, out of which she fashioned a smile. She mouthed 'hello' and Dean mouthed it back then she whispered, 'Are you OK?' and he nodded. And then stopped when he realised that he should not be OK, and in fact on many levels was not OK. He finished with a shrug and an apologetic smile. She patted his hand and turned away. She looked awful. Horrendous. She'd taken her grief-ruined face and painted it with too many colours and emulsions, rendering herself into a terrible child-scaring drag queen.

Sky's coffin was white with gold handles. On top of it were the letters SKY spelled out in pink rosebuds. There was a photograph of her, too, a big black-and-white blow up of her smiling. Dean couldn't remember the last time he'd seen Sky smile.

'Beautiful picture of Sky,' his mum whispered in his ear.

He nodded. It was. She was a beautiful girl.

The service rattled on. People stood up to speak. They'd wanted him to speak but he'd said no. Dean had never before spoken in front of people in his life and he wasn't about to start now. This wasn't his day. This wasn't about him. It was about Sky's mum and Sky's sisters and Sky's wailing friends.

There were eleven speeches in all; Dean stopped listening in the end. The words 'angel' and 'princess' and 'beautiful' were bandied around to the extent that he fully expected a rousing rendition of 'Candle in the Wind' to spring from the church organ at any moment. But as it was, he and five other men heaved the lightweight coffin on to their shoulders and left the church to the strains of 'Ave Maria'.

After Sky's coffin had been lowered into the ground and everyone had dutifully scattered the hole with earth and roses and teddy bears, the crowd dissipated but Dean stayed. For a while he stood at the edge of the cavity with Sky's mum and his own and both women draped their arms around him and Dean wanted to hate the sensation of their middle-aged, powdered, perfumed bodies pressed against his, but after a moment he yielded to it and they stood like that for a few minutes until his mum said, 'Come on, let's go, they'll be waiting for us.'

'One more minute,' he said, 'I'll catch you up.' And so he stood alone in the box-fresh afternoon and felt in his pockets for the spliff he'd made earlier. He lit it, inhaled, then sank to his haunches, a foot from Sky's final resting place. He stared down at the dirt-messed stuffed animals, the single stem roses that looked like tragic suicides and there, half-covered with earth, a photo of Isadora. She was staring directly into the camera with her wide-apart eyes and it felt for one fleeting moment as though she were staring directly into his soul, the way it had felt when he'd seen her just after she was born. He gulped and averted his gaze from hers. She was too much for him. Too clever, too strong, too good.

But there was something else in that gaze, something that knocked the wind out of him. It was *him*, his essence. Everyone said she looked like him, but who did he look like? He had his mother's fine-boned build, her pale English complexion, the bump in the bridge of the nose, her elegant wrists and freckled back. But his eyes were not hers, nor his lips, nor his jawline, nor his deep-seated melancholia and distrust of the concept of human connections and community. His mum ran the local community centre, threw parties for no reason, invited people into her house to keep her company, found points of interest in everyone she met, stayed in touch with people with whom she'd made only the briefest, most fleeting connections. Dean loved her for it, but that wasn't his style. That wasn't him.

There'd never been a man in their house. His mum had dated over the years but kept the men away from him, scared in case the man had made Dean love him and then broken his heart by leaving again. He had an uncle but he lived twenty miles away with his wife. Dean had never really felt the absence of a man in his home. And he'd never really given much thought to the man who laid biological claim to being his father, a stranger even to his mother, a man who had sat in a small room and collected his own essence in a jar in return for a few pounds and the knowledge that he was somehow doing somebody some good. Dean had only found that out three years ago, his mum had told him on his eighteenth birthday. Before he had been under the impression that his dad was a random

French guy that his mum had met on holiday at the age of forty-one, a late-blooming romance, in the dying embers of a glorious summer, two lonely people, one night of passion, et cetera, et cetera. The bit about him being French turned out to be true. The rest of it was sweet fiction.

Dean had not felt shocked or betrayed by the revelation. It made more sense somehow. He'd never really seen his mum as the type to have a Shirley Valentine-style encounter with a swarthy foreigner. He'd always had trouble aligning the concept with himself and his existence. The anonymous man in the small cubicle who had had no cause to find any common ground with his mum seemed far more compatible with Dean's notions of himself.

He was conceived just before the law had been changed, before donors were compelled to make themselves accessible to their children when they became adults. Dean had no legal recourse to his father. Dean had no right to see him. And for three years Dean had had no wish to see him and no desire to track him down.

Until now.

He shuffled forward towards the edge of the grave and held the spliff between his lips. He flattened himself to the ground and reached out for the photograph with his extended right hand, but his fingertips did not even come close to the depths where Sky's coffin lay, the photograph on top of it. He would have to leave her there, his baby, just like he had left her at the hospital. He lay there for a while, his head and arms overhanging the unfilled grave, staring at the photograph of Isadora. Above him clouds gathered in the sky and the afternoon began to settle. The breeze seemed to make a discreet exit; he felt it lift and move away, whispering conspiratorially through the trees behind him. Then it was still and quiet, and for the last time ever Dean was alone with his two girls – Sky in her gleaming white box, Isadora in her dirt-strewn photograph – at peace with one another. Tears came at last, fat, heavy drops that fell from his eyes straight into the hole in the ground.

He left her there, with her bears and her flowers and her daughter, and the last gasp gift of his tears, and he went to find his mother, to lose himself in beer and company.

MAGGIE

When Maggie arrived at the hospice on Wednesday morning Daniel was propped up in his bed, holding a cup of tea by the handle and halfway through the *Daily Telegraph*. He glanced up at Maggie as she walked into the room, peering at her genially over the top of his reading glasses.

'*Bonjour*,' he said, a smile in his voice if not on his face.

Maggie was taken aback. When she'd left him the evening before, he had been asleep after a long afternoon of discomfort and rather unsettling mumbling and murmuring about things that had made little sense. At one point he had turned to Maggie, spittle collected at the corners of his mouth, and muttered, 'It's you. It's *you*. You're. Not! Letting me. *Die!*' She'd spoken to the nurses on duty and they'd said, 'It may be that it's spreading to the brain. It may be that his behaviour will become more erratic.' Maggie had been scared leaving the house this morning, scared of what she might find. For all she knew, today might be the day – the day that Daniel died. She'd brought him some dried fruit and yogurt nuts anyway from the new nut place that had just opened up in the station, and he eyed the paper bag with some relish as she pulled it from her bag and placed it in front of him.

'Well,' she said, 'don't you look better today?'

He nodded and laid down his newspaper. 'I am feeling very good today. I am not sure why. Maybe I am going to get better.' He let out a wry rasp of laughter and Maggie smiled uncertainly. Jokes of that nature often threw her off course. Black humour. Gallows humour. Maggie didn't really have the requisite widget for laughter in the face of adversity. The only approach to take to death, she felt, was sombre respect.

'Well,' she muttered, 'you're better today, and that's marvellous.' She watched him reach into the brown paper bag and take out a whole dried apricot. He proffered the bag to her. 'No, thank you,' she said, 'I've had my own.'

She watched him bite into the amber-coloured lump and begin to chew. He had not chewed anything for days. He had not held a tea cup or picked up a paper for days. Death was playing a childish game, tip-toeing around mischievously: 'Here I am! Oh, no, only joking, I'm over here . . . no, over here!' Every time she asked a nurse, 'How long? How long do you think?' she would be met with the same response. *It could be any time.* Death did not just hit you with a stick and then walk away and leave you to die. Death fiddled about with you first. Death forced you head first into the toilet bowl of your demise and then yanked you back by the collar. Death was not as simple as Maggie had imagined.

'Come on,' said Daniel, peeling back his sheets, 'let us go for a walk.'

Maggie looked at him, alarmed. 'Ooh, are you sure?'

'Absolutely sure.' And then he smiled, wide and bright.

He moved slowly, a foot at a time, but he talked quickly. Maggie began to wish she had brought a recording device. His words tumbled out noisily like a jackpot of coins from a fruit machine. She linked her arm through his, and she listened as best she could, some of what he was saying lost in the rapids of his urgency and his accent.

'You know,' he said, 'it is not true that I have not had a child. It is not true at all.'

They were in the garden now. It was colder than was comfortable for Maggie who had left her jacket by Daniel's bed and was left in only a cotton blouse with three-quarter-length sleeves. But the sun shone and they stood by a pond filled with glimmering golden Koi carp, scurrying urgently beneath the jade-green surface of the water.

Maggie looked at Daniel questioningly. 'What do you mean?'

'I mean,' he continued, turning his handsome face towards the sun and squinting, 'that I have children in this world.'

'Well . . .' Maggie stumbled over her words, unsure what stance to take to a pronouncement that intimated sexual relations with other, faceless women, when with her he had never got as far as first base.

'I have four,' he continued. 'Two boys. Two girls. One is twenty-nine, one is twenty-seven, one is twenty-one and one is eighteen. Imagine that! Four children. And imagine, also, Maggie, that I have never met these children. In fact, that I have spent thirty years pretending to myself that they do not exist. That they are just, *comment s'appellent* . . . like fairies? You know: like ghosts? Some people believe in them, some people don't. Unless you have seen one. And because I have never seen these so-called *children* then they do not exist, *n'est-ce pas?*'

'I don't understand,' said Maggie, unlinking her arm from his. 'How could . . .'

'I gave away my sperm, Maggie May. My precious seeds, I gave them away, to strange ladies, and I asked that the strange ladies take the seeds, sow them but never come to find me with their babies.'

'You were a sperm donor?'

'Yes. I was. Can you imagine that, Maggie? Imagine me, doing that? It seems so distant. It seems so . . . *extraordinary* now. Now it seems extraordinary, then it seemed normal, mundane even. Then it seemed like giving blood, you know, a nice thing to do. And now, now I finally understand what I did. Now I am nearly old and nearly dead, it is finally real to me. I made life, Maggie!' He gripped her wrists with his hands. 'Can you believe it? I made life! Me! Daniel Blanchard! I made four lives! And now, you know, maybe those lives have made other lives. Maybe there are more babies, I suppose, yes, *grandchildren*! There are four adults out there and they are living their lives while I am closing mine and we are totally, completely, inextricably linked. It is . . . it is like a *miracle*! Yes, a miracle! And it has taken me thirty years to

141

understand this, thirty years to know what it is that I have done.'

Maggie stood and stared at Daniel. His eyes were shining. He looked crazed. But he looked happy. And she knew his words were true.

'Do you think it is too late, Maggie May? Do you think it is too late for me to know them?'

She caught her breath. She had never seen him like this before, so open, so raw. It made her ache somewhere deep inside, with love, with pity, with fear. She smiled at him, weakly. 'Oh, my darling,' she said. 'Oh, my darling.' She had never called him 'darling' before. His demeanour had never invited it. But she felt it now, that he was her darling, her sweet, darling, beautiful man, and that she loved him with every shred of herself, and that she could just about bear to see him die but she could not bear to see him die with this hole in his heart. 'I don't know,' she said, 'I don't know if it's too late. I don't know how these things work. I mean, what do you know about these children . . . these people? Do you have any way of contacting them?'

He shrugged. 'No,' he said, 'I don't think so. Though the youngest one, the girl, she has my details. She is the only one who could contact me. They changed the rules. I remember the day. I thought: *Well, I will probably be dead by the time this one is eighteen, what harm can it do?*' He laughed, uproariously, louder than Maggie had ever heard him laugh before. Once again, she struggled to see the humour in it.

'So,' he continued. 'That is that. Unless my youngest

offspring decides that today is the day to find her long-lost daddy then all is lost. Because I can feel it, Maggie,' he pointed at his skull, 'I feel it. Not every day. Not every moment. But the blackness, it is inside me now and it is comfortable. It has on its slippers,' he giggled, 'its gown. Its cocoa. Yes. It is at home now. And I am gone soon. It is sad.' He looked at her with wide, shining eyes. 'Yes, it is very, very sad. But now,' he let the sadness drain from his eyes, 'while I have the energy, while I can still stand, let us dance, Maggie May, let us dance.'

He didn't give Maggie a chance to protest. He took her in his arms and he pressed his body against hers, their hands clasped together, and he rested his chin upon the crown of her head and rocked from foot to foot, humming a tuneless lullaby into the silent air. Maggie buried her cheek against the soft velour of his dressing gown and closed her eyes. She followed his steps with hers and breathed in the smell of him, slightly medicinal but still unmistakably him, and she thought, *I love you, Daniel, I love you so much*. And she knew then exactly what she could do to prove it to him.

LYDIA

'Hello, stranger. Fancy coming over for supper tomorrow night?'

It was Dixie. Lydia hadn't heard from her for weeks, not since Viola's *Welcome to the World* party three weeks earlier. It was her fault, she knew that. Lydia certainly had the time and the headspace to find ways to see her friend and her new baby. Lydia could have been going over to visit every week, every day, if she'd so wished. Dixie was the one with the good excuse not to see her. But for some reason Lydia felt oddly repelled by their family unit. She'd felt it that night at her house, the first time they'd brought Viola over, a sort of co-dependency that had never been there before between Dixie and Clem, with Viola right at the centre of it. That was what happened, of course, when people procreated. Whatever the circumstances, a new dynamic was shaped and other things around that dynamic had to bend and twist to accommodate it. It was inevitable that things would change; Lydia just had not been expecting to feel these rather overwhelming stirrings of repulsion. Rejection yes; distance, yes; disgust . . .? Well, that had taken her somewhat by surprise.

It had struck her at the party, watching the baby being bundled around the room, from person to person, each person touching that baby, holding that baby, as though it were an amulet, possessed of some divine power. Their faces were greedy and soft, as though they were drawing something out of the baby. And the baby itself was like a saggy lump of meat, submissive and strangely noiseless. It was not a pretty baby. Not that that should matter. But it wasn't. It had a blue-tinged complexion with red patches and eyes that never seemed fully open, and its hair was thin and full of powdery flakes of dry skin. It had been dressed in a white cotton dress with a pink rose printed on the front, white tights and a pair of small white leather shoes, and was supposed, Lydia assumed, to look appealing. The trick seemed to be working on everyone else, but not on her. She had avoided the infant all day long and stifled the urge to grab her coat and leave.

She stayed for hours beyond her comfort zone, hoping that the other guests would peel away and that she would be left alone with Dixie and Clem, or more specifically with Dixie. She pictured the two of them, tired and a little drunk, collapsed together in the debris of the party, finally having the open and honest conversation that they had not had for so long. But their other guests did not leave and at six o'clock bottles of vodka were being opened and music was being selected on the iPod and Lydia remembered that this was what Dixie and Clem were like; they were social and spontaneous and there was no reason why having a baby should have short-circuited that. So she collected her coat and she kissed the few people she knew by sight and Dixie saw her to the door, the baby clasped to her chest and fast asleep so that there was not even the opportunity for them to hug, and they had said words about meeting up – *Yes, we must, we really must* – and then suddenly Lydia was on the pavement in Camden Town and she was alone.

She had glanced up at the window of the flat and seen the flicker of movement, of people, of *life*. The world went on without her. She was her own worst enemy. And then she had spent a Saturday night alone, in her empty house, and had not spoken to Dixie again since. It did occur to her that maybe her friend was cross with her, for not holding her baby at the party, for leaving early, for being a drag and for not being in touch for so long, but the longer their disconnection continued, the less able Lydia felt to do anything to bridge it. And now this, an invitation to supper. Lydia felt her spirits lighten at the prospect. She had been living inside herself for too long. Her life had grown very dense and difficult to negotiate and for weeks now the only spots of sunshine in it had been provided by Bendiks and the slightly peculiar friendship stroke flirtation that had developed between them since their moment of bonding a few weeks back.

Lydia texted back almost immediately. *Love to. What time and what shall I bring?*

8 p.m. After the bairn's gone down. And bring something fizzy. ☺

So she arrived the following evening, wrapped against

a chill wind in a down-filled coat and clutching a bag with two bottles of Bollinger to her chest. She knew that Dixie had meant Prosecco or Cava or a bottle of Tesco's own brand plonk, but Lydia also knew how much stupid money she had sitting in her bank account, bringing joy to nobody's lives, least of all her own, and had experienced a flutter of pleasure as the two bottles were rung through the till and the counter assistant had said: 'That'll be ninety-eight pounds, please.'

She was quietly pleased to learn that the affable Clem was out; as fond as she was of him, this was an important night for Dixie and Lydia. And the baby was nowhere to be seen. 'Ooh, Bolly,' said Dixie taking the bag from Lydia's outstretched hands, 'you nutter!'

'Well, I feel like we haven't really celebrated the baby coming yet . . .'

'You mean apart from the actual baby party that we had here three weeks ago? With champagne and balloons and stuff?'

'Well, yeah . . .'

'Yes. I know. Not your thing. It's OK. Come in, come in, and *excuse the mess*. Seriously, I can't believe I ever had the time to put things away and stuff. It was fine when she was tiny because she just slept all day, but now she's awake all the time and the moment she sees me going anywhere near a broom or a pair of rubber gloves she starts on at me. It's like she *wants* to live in squalor.'

'I could send Juliette over?' The words were out before Lydia had a chance to censor them. Dixie looked at her curiously, trying to gauge whether or not she was joking. Lydia smiled, unconvincingly, and shrugged. 'Well, it's not as if she's got much to do half the time, it's . . .'

'No, it's fine,' Dixie cut in. 'Honestly. I'm happier just mucking along, you know?'

Lydia did know. She knew Dixie better than she knew anyone else. It was stupid of her to have suggested it. She watched her friend push one bottle of champagne into the over-packed fridge and then set about opening the other. 'No champagne glasses,' she said, 'the last one got broken at Viola's party. And, in fact . . .' she gazed into the depths of the glass cupboard '. . . no wine glasses either. Tumbler or shot glass?' She held up the options.

'Oh, God, tumbler, definitely.'

Dixie brought the tumblers and the bottle into the living room and laid them on the coffee table. Also on the table was a packet of Huggies wipes, something called Infacol in a teat pipette bottle, a plate of old toast, a two-day-old newspaper and a packet of Fruit Pastilles.

'Yes, welcome to my life,' said Dixie, watching Lydia examine the rubble. 'This is the central operations area, right here. This is where the breast-feeding occurs, where I take my meals, where I sleep during the day and where Clem quite often sleeps at night. This is where I attempt to read newspapers and watch more than twenty minutes of a TV show at a time. This is where I live.'

Lydia looked at her aghast.

'*But*,' she continued, 'let me tell you this, before you get the wrong idea and think that I have ruined my life . . . it is worth every single minute. Honest. It really, really is. Cheers!' She brought her glass towards Lydia's and smiled.

'Cheers,' agreed Lydia, 'and sorry.'

'Sorry for what?'

'For being such a crappy friend.'

Dixie's face screwed up in confusion. 'What do you mean?'

'Oh, you know what I mean. I've been useless. I haven't phoned or texted or come over with food for you or anything. I've only seen Viola twice since she was born. I've been shit.'

'Oh, honestly, Lids. For God's sake, I promise you, it's not a big deal. I know you. I know babies aren't your scene and you were so sweet having us all over when we were all yucky and newborn and you bought Viola that lovely outfit. It's me who's been useless. Seriously. I just cannot get my act together. You know, I knew Clem was going to be out tonight a week ago and it took me until last night finally to get round to inviting you over. It's just, everything's . . .'

'Different?' suggested Lydia.

'Yes,' said Dixie, 'everything's different. But I can feel myself climbing out of it now. I mean, look, I can put her down at night now. That's new. Up until two weeks ago she was up with me until I went to bed, asleep on me, I'd be pinned to this sofa for hours. And now, well, it'll only be a few hours, she'll be awake again at midnight, but at least I know I get this bit of the day to myself.' She smiled and rubbed her elbows. 'So, look, I did not invite you over here to yabber on about baby shit. What's new with you? You look different . . .'

'Do I?'

'Yeah, have you lost weight?'

Lydia put her hand to her face and considered the question. 'Yes,' she said eventually, 'yes. I probably have.'

Dixie laughed. 'Only you, Lydia Pike, could lose weight and not even think about it. I'm still carrying half of Viola's afterbirth around with me, I'm sure I am.' She grabbed her spare tyre and sighed. 'So how's it going with the personal fitness trainer?'

Lydia flushed a little at the thought of him. The very notion of Bendiks left her feeling like she'd just had sex. She could not possibly tell Dixie how she was really feeling about her personal fitness trainer. Dixie would think she'd lost her mind. She cleared her throat. 'Good,' she said, 'fine. Starting to get used to it now, doesn't feel quite so alien any more. And much better now I don't have to go to that pretentious gym any more.'

'So he comes to you, does he?'

'Yeah. Or we train in the park.'

'Wow,' said Dixie, her face wistful for a life she'd never actually lived. 'And how's work?'

'Oh, it's, well . . . ticking along.'

Dixie and Lydia never talked about her work. Dixie was the one with the interesting job, she always had been. It was a silent given that any conversations about work would be about Dixie's job. Not Lydia's. 'How about

you?' she countered, 'any chance of getting back to work?'

'Oh, God, no. No no no. I think I'm going to take a full year. I'm so far away from even imagining being back on a job, let alone actually doing it, it seems like another world. Hard to believe that all those people still exist, that they're all getting up every morning and doing that stuff while I'm here, with Vee and all these screwed-up tissues.'

'Have you taken her home yet? Have you taken her to the village?'

Dixie nodded. 'Yes, a few weeks back.'

Lydia blinked the thought of 'home' from her consciousness and forced a smile. 'And how was it?'

'Yes. It was grand. Never has a baby been more tickled, sniffed or adored in the whole history of creation. And it was just lovely to get out of town, you know, to breathe in that scrumptious air and hear those jangly night-time sounds and just, well, just be at home. With my family.'

'Did Clem go with you?'

'Yes, he certainly did. No way was I doing that drive with a baby all by myself! Yeah,' said Dixie, smiling wryly, 'we'll probably end up back there, you know. In fact . . .' she paused, and Lydia waited '. . . we're planning another trip next month. Maybe look at a few places.'

'Ah.' Lydia returned her wry smile.

It didn't need discussing. Dixie knew how Lydia felt about their homeland, and Lydia knew how attached Dixie still was to the place. They had always agreed to disagree on the merits of Welsh life.

'Don't you ever . . .?' began Dixie '. . . get the urge? You know. Don't you ever miss the place? The feel of it? The people?'

Lydia laughed and shook her head.

'Now that we're getting older,' Dixie told her, 'I don't know . . . I thought I was a proper Londoner. Thought I'd found my place, my pace, that this was where I belonged, but now I'm nearly thirty, it all seems a bit . . . unnecessarily *big*. Do you know what I mean? Unnecessary amount of shops and restaurants and roads and people and noises and smells and . . . I don't know, I just don't need so much of it any more. It's all wasted on me. And I just kind of think, if I'm going to cloister myself away in my little London village, just see the same few people, buy the same food from the same few shops, walk the same walk across the same expanse of green, wave at the same people as I cross the road, why not go and live that village life somewhere where I can afford a really nice house, and a garden, and where my mum can help me look after my baby?'

'But what about work? Your career? Not much call for film directors in Walterston.'

'We've thought of that. We'll take it in turns, me and Clem. I can work out of Cardiff. Do some telly. He's got mates here who'll have him on their sofas if necessary. It would work out. Well, it could work out. But it's all still a notion rather than a plan. We haven't made up our minds, not yet.'

Lydia nodded, knowingly. It was just a matter of time, a matter of when, not if. Her friends would go. They would empty this flat of themselves, buy a charmingly ramshackle cottage, take their scrawny baby with them and be Welsh again. And then she would never be able to see them. Because Lydia would never go to Wales again. She'd known that from the very moment she'd boarded the train to London Euston seven years ago with all her stuff in a trunk at her feet. Wales was where she drank too much. Wales was where her mother had died and her father had died and where her childhood had died when something strange and unpalatable had happened on a balcony in a tiny flat in a tiny village in the middle of nowhere. London was where she'd left all that behind and moved forward, onward, up and beyond. Lydia was grateful to London in a way that she'd never been grateful to a human being. It had given her more than any human being and been more loyal and inspiring and kind to her. She may be lonely and apart from the world here, but she'd rather be lonely and apart in a city that understood her than in a village that didn't.

'Will you come and stay, if we do move?'

Lydia flinched. 'Yeah,' she said, 'sure.'

Dixie threw her a look that said that she knew, and Lydia knew, that she would not come to stay but at this point in both their lives they would have to pretend that she would.

'And I'd be back all the time.'

'You could stay at mine.'

'Well, yes, I was going to say that. Might be a bit cramped, though?'

'Well, yes, I'd have to open up the west wing for you, obviously . . .'

'But of course.'

'And then this flat, wow, it'd be gone.'

'Forever. Some other youngsters would live here.'

'Free and footloose and without a care in the world.'

'Partying, carousing, bed-hopping, pill-popping.'

They laughed out loud in unison and then fell silent, still smiling.

'It was good being young, wasn't it?' said Dixie.

'It certainly was.'

'But I'm looking forward to the next bit now. The big, grown-up bit. I think it'll be fun. I think I'm going to like being middle-aged. I think it'll suit me.'

Lydia agreed. Dixie had always had something of the cottage-dweller about her: she followed *The Archers*, baked cakes, dusted. Now Lydia thought about it, it was inevitable that her friend would have a baby before she was thirty and relocate herself to the sticks. In the same way that some people had a brief lesbian fling in their youth and then settled with a man, Dixie's time in London being a Camden hipster had been just a phase, something to get out of her system.

And where did that leave Lydia? Alone. With her Philippine housekeeper and her Latvian trainer and nobody in her life whom she didn't actually pay to be there. And it struck her as she looked at her fresh-faced friend in her trendy teenage outfit of skinny jeans and oversized t-shirt with a spray-painted sketch of Debbie

Harry on the front of it, that even though Lydia herself was the one in the elegant Whistles t-shirt and Autograph jeans, with the big tasteful house and household staff and bank account in seven figures, inside she was still an awkward teenager who would never be able to take on the responsibilities that Dixie had.

Lydia left the flat two hours later. She had not mentioned the letter from her uncle Rod or the Donor Sibling Registry or her growing crush on her (probably gay) personal trainer. She had barely talked about herself at all, in fact. She had not felt that it would help her situation. Dixie had already removed herself from Lydia's life by becoming a mother. Now she was removing herself physically as well by moving back to Wales. To ask her to get involved with the dark, swirling machinations of Lydia's inner existence would be pointless and disappointing.

So instead she went home and she poured herself a gin and tonic and she sat at her computer and prayed to it: 'Please, please, please, today, let there be someone there today. Please.' And she opened up her e-mail account and there was an e-mail from the Registry. She stopped. There had been e-mails from the Registry before, letting her know about changes to the way the website worked and monthly newsletters. But this looked different. She gulped another neckful of gin and tonic and then, with lightly shaking fingers, she clicked the e-mail open. '**Wigmore Fertility Centre**: Donor 32 has a new listing on the Donor Sibling Registry.'

Lydia gasped. She pushed herself backwards on her

wheeled chair, physically away from the computer, from this miraculous development. She clasped her hands to her cheeks and then she laughed. Not because it was funny, but because she was so overwhelmed with shock and nerves that she could find no other response, like the time she'd crashed into the back of a woman's station wagon crammed with small children on an A road in Finchley and laughed so hard she'd been unable to give the woman her details.

She pulled her hands from her face and then she breathed in deeply, quelling the rising hysteria that threatened to engulf her. And then she clicked on the link and waited to see who she was going to find on the other side.

ROBYN

A week after Robyn had seen herself staring back from Jack's reflection in the bathroom mirror, they celebrated the six-week anniversary of their first meeting. It was Jack's idea. He, of course, had absolutely no idea what was crashing around inside Robyn's head. Jack thought it was business as usual. Robyn was trying very hard to pretend that it was indeed business as usual. She'd almost managed to convince herself that the whole thing was ludicrous, that she was mad even to have thought such a thing. After all, look at Paul and Linda McCartney, Brad Pitt and Angelina Jolie; they'd all instinctively and naturally found themselves attracted to people who resembled them. It was normal. It was inevitable. It was probably a very good thing. It did not mean that Jack was her brother. It did not mean anything. But still, it was there. The doubt. And behind that doubt lay an unpalatable possibility. And as a result of that tiny, infinitesimal possibility, Robyn could not touch Jack.

She'd pretended she was having a period. 'A very heavy period,' she'd said, gravely. 'The heaviest I've ever had, I might even have to go to the doctor about it. And pains,' she'd added, as an afterthought. 'Really bad pains.' She'd massaged her abdomen with her fist and winced.

Jack had squeezed her shoulders gently and said, 'Yes, you must, you must see a doctor.'

'And I just feel generally, you know, *rough*,' she'd said a moment later when he tried to kiss her. 'I'm really, really sorry. I really am. I'm sure I'll feel better soon.'

He'd kissed the top of her head and she'd thought: *That's fine*. A brother would kiss their sister's head. She accepted her hands being held and squeezed shoulders and stroked hair and even a gentle nose-rub. Because in spite of all her fears and doubts and misgivings, she still loved Jack more than life itself.

'What is this?' she asked, as he handed her a tissue-wrapped parcel.

'Open it,' he said. He was perched behind her on the back of the sofa with his arm around her shoulder. The sun was bright through the window behind him and the whole room was bathed in a kind of optimistic light. She saw her fingers on her lap, clutching the delicate gift, which was held together with spirals of frangipani-hued ribbon. She'd bought him nothing. She felt sadness engulf her and breathed deeply to banish it. It was Saturday night. She was with her one true love. He'd bought her a gift. She pulled her shoulders back and began to unfurl the ribbons, peel back the paper. Inside was a cube of fabric, burnt orange, shot taffeta. She unfolded the cube and revealed a dress. *The* dress. The flame-coloured one she'd admired in the window of that shop all those weeks ago, just before she met Jack, when her life had felt normal and set on a predictable though dazzling course. She'd talked herself out of buying it with her birthday money. And now here it was, in her lap. The same dress.

Jack felt her silence as disapproval and leaned down towards her. 'Is it OK?' he said. 'Do you like it? I can take it back if you don't. They said that would be fine. Only I saw it and I could just immediately see you in it . . .'

'No, no, it's fine. I love it. It's just . . .' She turned and looked up at him. 'I saw this dress in a window. Just before I met you. And I nearly went in to buy it.'

'What! The same dress?'

'Yeah.' She fingered the fabric thoughtfully.

'Wow,' said Jack, quietly. 'Well, there you go then. Clearly we were meant to be together.'

She smiled and attempted to laugh, but it wouldn't come. Boys had bought her stuff in the past; underwear, perfume, even a pair of cubic zirconium earrings from Elizabeth Duke. The underwear had always been wrong; the wrong size, wrong colour, wrong type. The perfume had always been wrong, too, and as for the earrings . . . no one had ever bought her clothes before. Her mother had learned a long time ago that buying her daughter clothes would only lead to sadness and a return trip to the clothes shop. Robyn was a woman who knew what she liked and what she didn't like.

She stared at the dress in awe. What did this mean? She imagined for a second that Jack really was her brother. Not merely another child sired by the same man who had sired her, but her actual elder brother who had lived with her since the day she was born. Would her real brother have been able to pick out the single most perfect dress available on the high street and present it to her? No, her real brother would probably have totally forgotten it was her birthday and then dashed around the corner to pick her up a box of Ferrero Rocher from the corner shop. So was the fact of this dress actually a *good* thing? Did it in fact mean that their connection was based purely on romance and animal attraction and not on shared DNA?

'Are you going to try it on?' asked Jack, getting to his feet.

'Er, yeah, sure.' Robyn stood up slowly and headed towards the bedroom with the dress in her hands.

'You don't have to be shy,' he laughed.

'No, I know. I just, er, I need to use the bathroom, too.' She forced a smile. 'Back in a minute.'

The dress fitted her perfectly. She'd known it would. She gazed at herself in the full-length mirror and admired the way the fabric clung to her waist and pushed up her breasts; the strangeness of the colour against her skin tone, the way it clashed with her hair. She was the only other person she knew who could have seen how well such a dress would have suited her. She decided she would wear it tonight, even though she was in sneakers and not heels. Jack's face broke into a smile when she walked back in a moment later. 'Wow,' he said, admiring her, 'I am *good*. Check out my hitherto undiscovered dress-buying skills! You look amazing. Come here.'

She came to him and allowed him to hug her. She pressed her face against the softness of his sweater and smelled him through the layers of his clothes, that soothing, elegant, sweet smell of her lover. *This is fine*, she thought, *this is right. There is nothing wrong with this scenario. My brother would not have chosen me this dress. My brother would not smell this good.* And for the hundredth time that week she pushed her concerns to the very furthest reaches of her mind and slapped on a smile and tried to get on with the business of being in love.

'Got you something else,' said Jack, pulling gently away from her and smiling.

'Oh, God, what?' she replied, more harshly than she'd intended.

'Well, it's not a gift as such, it's a suggestion. I was going to wait until dinner, but now that the dress has proved such a blinding success I'm all buoyed up, so . . .' He reached into the back pocket of his jeans and pulled out a tiny parcel wrapped in the same creamy tissue as the dress and tied with the same blossom-pink ribbon. 'And no, don't freak out, it's not a ring.'

She smiled nervously and pulled the ribbon from the parcel. Inside the tissue she found two brass keys on a small brass ring.

'For here,' said Jack.

'Keys?' said Robyn, somewhat redundantly.

'Yes. They're for you.'

'Oh,' she said, 'right.'

'I was thinking . . .' He paused then and she could see

nerves plucking at the muscles beneath his skin. 'I hate it when you're not here. I mean, not that I can't live without you or anything. But all the planning and stuff, just to be together. And all the travelling you're doing, back and forth. And your college is literally half an hour away. I just thought it would make more sense for you to, you know, maybe *move in*?'

Robyn blinked.

'Live together.'

She blinked again.

'I mean, I know we've only been together for a few weeks, and I know you're only eighteen. But I would not tie you down, I promise you. You could come and go and do your own thing and go out every night if you wanted. But just for me to know that at the end of all that you would be here. With me. That's all.'

Living together. She let the concept settle in her mind. Living here, in this picturesque flat, waking every morning in Jack's arms, strolling down his tree-lined avenue to the tube station, coming home from college to find Jack at his computer, tapping away at another well-regarded novel, opening a bottle of wine, drinking it in each other's arms on the sofa while watching films and interesting documentaries. And doing that every day. She wanted that. She really, really wanted that. She'd wanted that since the first night they'd met; felt the pointlessness of the hours they spent apart, felt the futility of her solitary journeys home on the train, watching everything she cared about dashing away from her through the window in the wrong direction.

And now he was offering it to her. And she couldn't take it. Because everything was wrong. She sighed. And then she smiled. She took the keys from their wrapping and held them in the palm of her hand. 'Can I think about it?' she said.

He looked shocked, but it passed in less than a moment. 'Yeah,' he said, 'of course you can. Take as long as you like. It's a big deal. I know that. But keep those.' He pointed at the keys. 'Keep them. They're yours.'

He folded her hand over the keys and then kissed her on the lips.

She let him.

Hi, it's me. Don't turn me into a stalker. Tell me what's going on. I can take it, whatever it is. I just need to know, J.

Robyn sighed and switched off her phone. She felt sick. She had not eaten a proper meal in five days, subsisting on apples, cornflakes and Diet Coke. She had not seen Jack since Saturday. They'd had sex that night and now she couldn't shake the memories of it from her consciousness. It had felt fine. She'd put everything to the back of her mind, thought about the dress, reassured herself that she wasn't doing anything wrong and let herself enjoy it. Then the following morning she'd dropped the keys into her handbag, folded her taffeta dress into a carrier bag and left Jack's flat wondering when or indeed if she would ever come back. If she did in fact discover that Jack was her half-brother then she would have to live with the fact that not only had she knowingly had sex with him, but she'd deceived him, too, by allowing it to happen. Every time she closed her eyes it was there, the two of them devouring each other. At the time it had felt like passion; now it felt like they'd behaved like *animals*. They'd had two female dogs when she was small, mother and daughter: most of the time they were indifferent to each other, but occasionally one of them would mount the other and hump it as hard as it possibly could. She thought of those two dogs now, doing something so random and so unnatural that had no actual evolutionary or anthropological point to it, and it made her think of herself.

She switched the phone back on and looked at the message again: *Dear Jack*, she imagined herself replying, *I cannot talk to you at the moment because it is possible that we have been incestuous. I am waiting to hear back from the clinic from whence I was sired to discover the identity of my real father so that I may happily eliminate this possibility from my mind. In the meantime, every time I think about what we have been doing together, I feel like I am going to throw up. Lots of love, Rx*

Instead she typed: *I'm really sorry. I'm not feeling well. It's nothing you've done, I promise. I'll be in touch soon, Rx*

A moment later her phone trilled at her. *As long as I haven't done anything to upset you. I will try to be patient. Missing you, Jxxx*

Finally, the following day, the postman brought Robyn what she'd been waiting for. It was contained within an expensive cream envelope, with a discreet postmark on it: **WFC** in curly capitals. She took the letter to her room and sat cross-legged upon her bed, regarding the unopened missive cautiously. Here it was. The first step on the road. Inside the innocuous cream envelope was a whole new world, a world she'd never wanted to set foot in, a world that terrified her. She breathed in deeply and then sliced it open with her finger.

Dear Miss Inglis,

Thank you for your enquiry regarding Donor 32. According to our records, there are three other live births relating to this donor. A girl in 1980, a boy in 1983, and a boy in 1989. There have been no further live births relating to this donor since yourself. We hope this information is of some assistance to you.

Yours sincerely,
Wigmore Fertility Clinic

Robyn let the letter drop on to her bedcover.
A girl.
Two boys.
A girl.
Two boys.
A boy born in 1983.
The same year that Jack was born.
Everything inside her curdled as this fact weighed upon her.
Suddenly every doubt she'd had about her fears and her concerns evaporated, leaving her with nothing

but stark, bitter certainty. Somewhere out there was a twenty-seven-year-old man who was her brother. And it was probably her boyfriend.

She stuffed the letter back into the envelope, screwed it into a tight ball and hurled it against her bedroom wall.

Robyn's mum folded up the evening paper she'd been reading at the kitchen table and got to her feet. 'How about signing up to the Donor Sibling Register?'

Robyn pulled the paper towards herself and stared at her mother in confusion. 'Why?' she asked. 'He's not going to be on there. He thinks his dad was a Barnardo's orphan killed in a car crash in France. If he is a donor baby, he doesn't actually know.'

'No, not to look for Jack. But if you find two boys and a girl on there, then you'll know. You'll know that it's not him.'

Robyn shuddered. She hated the thought of this other woman somewhere who shared her genes. She never wanted to meet her. Robyn would hate her, she knew she would. But it made sense, what her mum was saying. If she signed up to this Registry thing and found another man on there who was born in 1983 then she could dash to the train station, sprint down Jack's Holloway avenue, leap into his arms, throw her arms around his neck and never, ever let him go.

'You're right,' she said, pushing the paper away from her again, 'you're totally right.'

She pushed the thought of the woman who shared her

genes from the front of her mind and headed upstairs to her laptop.

UK Donorlink was initially rather forbidding. Robyn downloaded a leaflet and felt winded by the amount of information she needed to process before she could even begin the registration process. And then she felt herself deflate as she realised how many hoops she was going to have to jump through before she was able to find out anything at all about her genetic siblings, male, female, or otherwise. First she would have to fill in a form, then she needed to undertake a DNA test, and then she would have to wait for the agency to get permission for any genetic matches to share their information with her . . . and everything was carried out in writing. It could take days or even weeks for her to find out what she needed to know. And in the meantime, she still had her boyfriend's front door keys in her handbag and a huge gaping hole in her heart where he was supposed to be. She sighed, pulled her chair closer to the desk, and began to do what was necessary.

Three days later a letter arrived. Robyn didn't dare hope that it could be the Donor Sibling Register already. She had crawled her way through the weekend, painfully, as if over shards of glass, imagining Jack in his light-filled flat, bumbling around lost without her. She ripped it open, sparing not an ounce of patience. And there it was. One match. A female. She didn't read on. She let the letter drop to the floor and then she let herself fall heavily upon the bottom stair. She felt she was going slowly insane.

Two weeks ago, before she'd seen her own face in her boyfriend's reflection, she had been walking a path through Nirvana. Two weeks ago she'd known exactly who she was and where she was headed and she'd had a man by her side who was going to help her get there. Now she'd come careening off the path and landed face down in a ditch. She felt wrong and misshapen, like all the angles and nuances of her most interior self had gone askew. Being with Jack had somehow loosened her bond to her parents. Meeting him had opened her up to the possibility of a life beyond being just a daughter. And now she was home again, a daughter again. And it wasn't where she wanted to be. She'd had a taste of adult life and had it snatched away again. She wanted to go back to Jack. But she couldn't go back to Jack. And she couldn't even tell Jack why she couldn't go back to him because he would freak out. And meanwhile the only chance she'd had of putting her mind to rest had turned out to be a big fat nothing. A woman. A bloody boring, horrible woman.

She stared at the abandoned letter on the floor. She was furious with the Donor Sibling Registry and she was furious with the woman claiming to be her genetic sibling. Useless. Pointless. Conniving and conspiring to decimate her life totally. And then she felt angry with the man too, her donor father. He was a wanker. Literally, pejoratively, in every conceivable way, a wanker. What sort of man goes around giving his sperm away to strangers? What sort of man allows his DNA to be replicated and abused and ricocheted around the world without a backwards glance? What sort of man could abandon his offspring to the universe, toss them into the air like a pack of cards and then walk away before he'd even seen where they'd fallen?

All her life she'd been grateful to this man. All her life she'd put him on a pedestal, admired him, been grateful for his altruism. Altruism – the first four-syllable word she'd mastered as a child. She'd been born out of altruism. Altruism. Yeah, right. He was no better than some small-town Romeo, spreading his seed around the village without a care for the consequences. He was just another jack-the-lad. An idiot. Selfish, short-sighted, cretinous and cruel.

As these angry thoughts circled her mind Robyn found herself sobbing violently. Everything rose to the surface then: her poor lovely sisters; her parents who had never really lost the faded bruises of sadness behind their eyes, no matter how hard Robyn had tried to make them glad and proud; her beautiful Jack, sitting alone in the flat he'd offered up to her, wondering why she didn't want to be in love with him any more.

Robyn sobbed for about thirty minutes. It was the first time she'd cried since she was seventeen. Robyn didn't like to cry. It wasn't her style. But these tears were over-due and these tears were necessary and the house was empty so she let them come for as long as they needed to. Until she was stopped in her tracks by the sound of the doorbell chiming. She blinked at the front door. Who could this be? Nobody ever came to the house during the day except the postman and he'd already been. She mopped her face with a tissue, examined the carnage of her red-raw facial features in the mirror next to the door and then sniffed a tentative: 'Hello?'

'Robyn?' It was a woman's voice, loud and direct.

'Yes? Who is this?'

'It's Sam. It's Jack's mum. Can you let me in?'

'Oh,' said Robyn, almost in a whimper.

She took another look at her face. She looked like a girl who had been crying for half an hour. She would need to find a reason.

'Hold on,' she said to the closed door, while she hurriedly de-smudged her eyes and flattened her hair, 'hold on.' And then she pulled the door open and tried her hardest to smile a totally normal smile at her boyfriend's mum. 'Hi!' she said, 'Sam! What are you doing here?'

Sam gave her a strange look, almost patronising.

'You know why I'm here,' she said.

Robyn laughed, nervously. *Here it is*, she thought, *here it is*. 'Do I?' she asked, as lightly as she could.

'Of course you do. Now, are you going to let me in or what?'

DEAN

Dean took the shot from Tommy's outstretched hand and necked it in one. It tasted like petrol, like paraffin. It burned at the back of his throat. It issued vapours from his nostrils. It rang in his ears. It numbed all the excruciating corners of his mind. He sucked on the spliff that Tommy had just passed him and then he let his body collapse against the back of the sofa and the world recede away from him, just for a few moments.

Tommy was his cousin. He'd been in the army for the past four years and now he'd signed himself off and was back in London. It was good timing. Dean and Tommy had grown up together and the people you grew up with were the easiest people to be with, Dean always thought. And right now he needed someone easy to be with. Tommy was the looker of the family. Dean had always liked going out on the town with him because the combination of Dean's dark, other-worldly features and Tommy's Action Man facial geometry (in some ways he could never have been anything other than a soldier) made quite a formidable impression. And Tommy, unlike Dean, liked talking to girls, approaching them, flattering them, pursuing them. Dean liked girls, he just didn't like all the palaver you had to go through to get to them. He and Tommy made a good pair in that way.

They'd been talking all afternoon about Tommy's time in Afghanistan: the bullets, the dirt, the nights under the stars wondering if he would live to see the sunrise. He used a lot of jargon when he talked: medevac, SCUD, sortie. It didn't mean much to Dean but he appreciated the distraction from his own concerns. For the past two hours he'd been in a world where babies were blown up by snipers, not waiting to be taken home from special care, where men were men and women were not really in the picture at all. It was a good place to be. But now, as Tommy took the half-smoked spliff back from Dean and drew on it, Dean knew that The Tommy Show was almost over. A brief silence fell and Tommy sighed.

'My mum told me all the shit that's been happening. Fucking crazy, man.' He shook his head, sadly.

Dean nodded.

'I mean, how old was she?'

'Sky?'

Tommy nodded.

'Nineteen,' said Dean.

'Shit.' Tommy squeezed air through pursed lips and grimaced. 'Christ. You know, that kind of thing happens all the time out there,' he gestured with his arm, to a place that Dean assumed was Afghanistan and not south-east London, 'you expect it. But here . . . You know, modern day and age. You'd just think, you'd think they'd be able to stop it. Young girl, all her life ahead of her. Fuck, man . . .' He winced again and rubbed the spliff out into an ashtray. 'And what about the baby?' he asked. 'Boy, girl?'

'Girl,' said Dean.

'Right. What's the deal with her? My mum said she's still at the hospital.'

'Yeah, that's right. She's been in special care, you know, in an incubator. Wires and shit.'

'Fuck,' said Tommy.

'Yeah, she's doing well, though. She's coming out next month, they reckon.'

'Oh. Right, that's good. And she's all right, is she? I mean, you know, brain-wise?'

Dean flinched. He hadn't even thought about that. With Sky being a premature baby herself it had never occurred to him that a premature baby could be anything other than one hundred per cent normal. The suggestion rankled with him slightly. 'Far as I know,' he replied. 'Yeah. She's fine.'

'Good stuff,' said Tommy. 'That's good. And then she'll be coming here, will she?' He looked around the unsavoury flat questioningly. It had not been a pretty flat when Sky had lived here, but it had at least been tidy and relatively hygienic and home to things like clean bath towels and washing up liquid. Now, after living here alone, during the toughest four weeks of his life, Dean knew the flat was squalid. He had attempted to tidy up when Tommy had said he was coming to visit, but really all he'd done was to kick things from the middle of the floor out towards the edges of the floor; the flat still smelled of mildew, stale smoke and loneliness.

'No,' said Dean, 'not here.'

'Then where?'

Dean shrugged. He had not seen his daughter since the day she was born and had no idea what would happen next month when she was finally discharged from the hospital. His mother had offered to take Isadora. But then so, of course, had Sky's mother, Rose, who felt she had a bigger claim to the child, being her maternal grandmother, and Dean could see her point. In a way he wanted the baby to go to Rose. She was younger than his mother, had other grandchildren, lived in a nicer house and would take the responsibility in her stride. Dean's mum was different. She liked her life the way it was. She was independent and hadn't really had to think about anyone apart from Dean for her whole adult life. She was not geared up for life with a baby. But still, the thought of his baby being brought up by that overly controlling woman in her chichi house with all those shit magazines everywhere and her vain daughters and their spoiled children and TV blaring out MTV all day long, and the plastic fucking fairies in the garden . . . Rose would treat the baby like a doll, put it in a big frilly pram with a rosette on its head and wheel it about Peckham as if it was the holy reincarnation of her princess bloody daughter.

He shuddered at the thought of his daughter becoming another Sky. That woman had already brought four self-obsessed princesses into the world, he didn't want her to do that to another one. But he didn't want to land a baby on his own sixty-two-year-old mother either. Whatever she might say about being glad to do it for him, he knew it wasn't what she wanted. And he knew that Rose would fight her tooth and nail to keep the baby for herself anyway and probably did have more right to it. So there was only one other solution. But all Dean needed to do was take one look around this flat, and one look in the mirror at his gaunt, grey, almost scary face, and he would roll himself another spliff and know that it could never happen. He couldn't even face seeing his child in the safety and security of a modern hospital ward. How could he hope to nurture her here, in this fetid place, to find within himself the nugget of whatever it took to love and care for a new baby? He would never be a father to his own child, he knew that much. He was too small, inside and out. There was not enough within him for this baby. He was not equipped, in any way.

'I don't know,' he said eventually, defeatedly, 'Sky's mum, I suppose. She's got all the kit, you know, she's all set up for it. Makes sense really.'

'And what about you?' asked Tommy. 'You'll visit, will you?'

'Yeah,' he said, reaching for the bottle of Aftershock and pouring them both another measure. 'Yeah, I'll visit.'

He grimaced at the lie. He wouldn't visit. He would stay here and he would fester and putrefy and then one day, hopefully sooner rather than later, he would die.

'Cheers,' he said, raising his shot glass to his cousin's, 'good to have you back.'

They knocked their glasses together grimly, both of them aware of but not acknowledging the sheer weight of deep, heavy, unknowable shit that had been left untouched behind the light façade of their conversation.

Dean awoke the following morning in bed with a girl called Kate. She had red hair. He had never slept with a ginger girl before. He blinked at her through tacky eyelids, his vision blurred with sleep. Her hair was proper, bright orange. Carrot. It was simultaneously alarming and amazing. He almost put out a hand to touch it but realised that his arm was trapped beneath her sleeping body, that his arm was in fact totally dead. He pulled it from under her, inch by inch, wincing with discomfort. Finally the arm was free and he shook it violently from side to side, trying to regain some feeling in it. It crawled with pins and needles and distracted him for a moment from the throbbing inside his head. His thoughts contained no real clues to the journey that had brought him to the bed of this woman with orange hair.

He knew he'd been dragged to the pub last night by Tommy at some time after ten o'clock. He knew that it was club night at the pub, that a female DJ with pigtails and a school uniform on had been installed in the corner, and that he had danced to 'Ride on Time' by Black Box with a bottle of Budweiser in his hand. He knew that Tommy had been scanning the place for girls from the moment they'd walked in and declared it 'full of rough as fuck minge' but still managed to ferret something half-decent out of the scattering of women lining the bar. But he did not know where this one had come from. Just knew that her name was Kate. He only remembered that because it was his grandmother's name. He remembered saying that to her, last night: 'You've got the same name as my grandmother.' But not adding: And the same as my baby daughter's middle name.

He peered around Kate's room. It looked like a student's room. She had a dressing table covered in junk jewellery and photos of friends, a guitar against the wall, a laptop, a sari pinned across the window. And there, on her bedside table, a mug half full of thick cold tea with the words 'Deptford University' printed on it.

The girl began to stir and Dean held his breath. He had no idea what to expect. But as the girl rolled towards him he was pleasantly surprised to see that she was pretty. Not as pretty as Sky, but then not like that ginger one from Girls Aloud either. She had delicate features and the right kind of freckles and her lips were a kind of strawberry colour. 'Urgh, God,' she said as her eyes alighted upon him. Then she rolled away from him again and grunted.

'Yeah, nice to meet you, too,' said Dean with as much humour as he could muster.

'Urgh, God. Not you,' she groaned. 'Not you. *This*.' She pointed at her head. 'Hurts. Hurts bad.'

Dean sat up and flopped his legs over the side of Kate's bed. 'I'll get some painkillers. Where do you keep them?'

She pointed him silently towards a plastic Tupperware box on her dressing table. He unpeeled the lid and brought her over a packet of Ibuprofens and a glass of water from her desk.

'Thanks,' she said, heaving herself into an upright position and pulling her hair away from her face. It occurred to Dean as he watched her and also considered his own appearance that they were both wearing underwear. He had on his boxers and Kate was wearing a grey vest over a bra.

'So,' he said, 'you and I? We didn't . . .'

'No. We didn't.'

'Oh, right.' He tried to dredge something up from the bottom of his brain that might remind him what exactly they had done, but found nothing.

She tipped the pills on to the back of her tongue and swallowed them frantically with the water. 'Remember?' she said. 'We talked?'

'We talked?'

'Yeah. We sat up until stupid o'clock in my kitchen talking.'

'Right.'

'Yeah, and smoking. We smoked a *lot*. My throat feels like I've been swallowing glass.' She put her hand to her throat and stroked it tenderly.

'So, what were we talking about? You and me?'

'Oh, anything and everything. Your dead girlfriend, mainly. And your sick baby. Oh, and your sperm-donor dad.'

'No!' Dean spun round and looked at her in shock.

'Yeah. For real. I mean, all I wanted was to meet a nice boy and maybe have a bit of a cuddle. Bloody typical for me, I end up with Mr Dead Girlfriend doing a Jeremy Kyle in my kitchen.' Her words sounded cruel but Dean could tell she was only being flippant. He could remember now. He could remember seeing her pretty face by the light of a candle, watching her filling the kettle and stirring a teabag around a mug. He could remember ham sandwiches on plastic plates, and filling and rolling and filling and rolling a dozen fat spliffs, sending hazy veils of smoke into the air around them. And he could remember talking. Not just chatting but really talking. And he remembered saying this: 'It's so easy talking to you, I feel like I've known you, like, *forever*.'

He didn't feel like he'd known her forever this morning. He felt like he'd never met her before in his life. He felt awkward now, knowing that he'd opened up to this strange girl with orange hair and freckly shoulders.

'Sorry,' he said, after a moment. 'Didn't mean to dump on you.'

She smiled then and he liked the way her face looked when she smiled. He could see for a moment why he might have felt able to open his soul to this girl. 'Not a problem,' she said, pulling her thick hair back into a wild bun. 'Glad to have been of service. I dread to think how many typos there were in that form we sent off, though. Holy shit. It must have looked like it had been filled in by psychotic six year olds.'

He smiled at her curiously. 'What form?' he said, a creeping sense of unease growing within him as a memory began to unfurl in his head.

She turned and glanced at him. 'You don't remember?'

'What?'

'Going on the internet last night?'

He glanced at the laptop on her desk and then at the plastic swivel chair pulled up in front of it and the small wooden stool to the left and, yes, he remembered sitting on that small wooden stool watching Kate tapping away at her keyboard, he even remembered thinking: *She's good at typing.* And as that memory revealed itself so too did another.

Kate and he in the kitchen, Kate putting mugs into the sink, pouring tap water into glasses, saying: 'Come upstairs. It's in my room.'

He could remember the pale minty green of the walls on the staircase and a photo of a cat wearing a raincoat and rain-hat taped to the outside of the bathroom door. And, before that, the conversation that had preceded their ascent to Kate's room.

'Don't you ever wonder? Don't you want to know?'

'What? Like brothers and sisters and stuff?'

'Yeah. You know, people who are related to you. God, if I thought there were people out there who were my actual family, I just wouldn't be able to resist it. I'd have to find out. I'd have to know.'

'Yeah, it's never really bothered me. I mean, there's even a place now, apparently, they set it up last year, where you can trace your genetic siblings. My mum told me about it. But I still never really thought about it. I suppose, you know, with the baby coming and then

everything that's happened since, I just wasn't too fussed about it.'

'What's it called?'

He shrugged. 'I don't know. Sibling Register or something.'

'Is it online?'

'Yeah. Yeah, it is. My mum said that's what you have to do, if you want to join. You have to do it online.'

He could remember a sense of excitement and adventure coming upon him then. A sense that he was in the right place at the right time with the right person. That this was meant to be happening. Suddenly he'd felt the possibility of another life galloping towards him across the open meadow of his imagination. He'd felt light and fresh, like a house that had been locked and shuttered for too many years being opened up to the elements again. He'd thought it was the most brilliant idea that anybody had ever had. He'd almost run up Kate's stairs in his haste to move his life along to this new place. Yes, he'd thought, yes. Let's do this. *Let's rock and roll.*

And then he'd sat on that stool and watched her do it, tap-tap-tap, page after page of personal details. He'd been expecting something at the end of it. A fanfare, maybe, or a bugle call, flashing lights and a ream of photographs of men and women with the words YOUR BROTHERS AND SISTERS! typed underneath.

He'd been deflated when he realised that he would have to wait, that actual human beings would have to read through his application, verify his details, check that everyone involved was happy to have him informed of their existence, and that there certainly wouldn't be any photos.

'What a con!' he'd said. 'What a fucking con!'

'Yes, but it's there now. It's in the system. You've done it. At some point over the next few days you're going to find out whether or not you've got any brothers and sisters out there.'

'Fuck.'

'I know,' she'd said.

And then they'd had another smoke and gone to bed.

This morning, in the harsh light of a bright spring morning, conscious of the smell of old smoke and unbrushed teeth, Dean felt appalled by this development. Kate was pulling on a hooded sweatshirt.

'I can't believe we did that,' he said.

'Yeah,' she said, smiling, 'it's cool, isn't it? Beats Ouija boards any day!'

'But can I, you know, can I change my mind? Did it say?'

'Yeah, I reckon so. I think they'll let whoever's already registered know that someone new has registered and then they'll ask you both if you want your details shared. I suppose you could always say no at that point.' She turned and looked at him, her fists still furled inside the sleeves of her oversized hoodie. 'You won't, will you?' she asked, thoughtfully. 'You won't say no?'

He shrugged. He couldn't get his mind around it just now. 'I don't know. Depends, I suppose. Depends on what they say.'

Kate sat herself down on the edge of the bed next to Dean and held her chin in her hands. She looked at him from the corners of her eyes. 'You have to tell me what happens, you know that? I'm not asking for your phone number or to be your girlfriend or anything like that. I mean, fuck, you're the last person I'd want to go out with. You're just, like, a complete car crash. But you have to at least just text me. When something happens.'

Dean nodded, absent-mindedly. 'How did I meet you?' he asked suddenly. 'Last night?'

She laughed. She had good teeth. 'You don't remember?'

'No. I remember dancing in that pub. I remember sitting in your kitchen. I don't remember where you came in, though.'

'I was sent,' she said, mock-seriously, 'by the dark, unknowable forces of destiny, to change the course of your life forever.'

Dean laughed, uncomfortably. He didn't get her humour, but he could tell that she was funny and clever. Cleverer than him. 'No,' he said, 'really.'

'Really?' she said. 'Your friend was sick on my shoes. You helped me clean them up.'

Dean laughed. 'You mean Tommy?'

'Yeah. The squaddie guy. He was trying to tell me how redheads make him extra hard and go for longer then he just upchucked all over me, big time. It was blue.'

'Blue?'

'His sick was blue.'

Dean had another vivid memory. Opening the lid of Kate's flip-top bin and disposing of a pair of blue-stained canvas shoes.

'So, will you take my number, Mr Dead Girlfriend? Just a three-word text will do: *Have nice sister*. Or, *Met my brother*. Or, *Changed my mind*. Just so I know.'

'Yeah, sure,' he said. ''Course I will.'

'Good,' she said, and smiled a satisfied smile and patted his hand. 'Come on,' she said, 'let's go down. Let's have a nice cup of tea.'

He followed her down the stairs, past the photo of the raincoat-clad kitten, past the minty green walls, and back into the kitchen where the night before he'd made a decision that would change his life forever.

MAGGIE

Maggie sucked in her breath, squeezed shut her eyes and grimaced. Her friend Jeannie ripped the fabric away from her skin and threw the tufted strip into a small bin on the floor. Maggie bit down on a yell. Jeannie smoothed another strip of fabric down against the inside of Maggie's buttock and once again Maggie drew in her breath.

'Just pull there, will you, Mags?' said Jeannie, indicating a haunch of thigh. Maggie gripped it and held it taut while Jeannie ripped some more hairs from a place that Maggie tried not to spend too much time thinking about. She let a small howl issue from between her clenched lips and said: 'Are we nearly done?'

Jeannie scrutinised Maggie's undercarriage through heavily mascaraed eyes and ran her fingertips over her bikini line. 'Yes,' she replied, vaguely, 'nearly done. Another few minutes, I reckon.'

Jeannie had been waxing Maggie for about twenty-five years. Neither could really remember if they'd been friends before Jeannie had first pulled pubic hairs out of her thighs or if they'd become friends as a result of it, but they'd certainly been acquainted. Maggie was not the sort of person who would let just anyone see her from that angle.

Maggie came to Jeannie's house once every month. It was daft really as nobody ever got to see her naked these days and she didn't even use the swimming baths in town any more, since she'd been spending all her free time at the hospice. For a while she'd hoped that maybe Daniel might one day countenance her naked form, but that was not now going to happen. But still, it was important, Maggie felt, to be properly groomed, everywhere, at all times. She felt clean when she was waxed, she felt hygienic.

Jeannie finally pronounced herself finished and smoothed oil over Maggie's thighs. 'How's your friend?' she asked, snapping off her rubber gloves and letting them fall into the bin.

Maggie smiled sadly. *Her friend.* That's all he'd ever be now. She felt engulfed by grief every time she thought of the lovely journey that she and Daniel would never get to share. 'Daniel?'

'Yeah.'

'Oh, well,' Maggie rolled herself from Jeannie's treatment table and retrieved her tights, 'not so good. You know. It's a very strange process, I must say. Very strange to be so close to someone who's basically . . .'

'Dying?'

'Well, yes.' Maggie didn't appreciate that rather brutal use of the word. She was sure there was a better way of putting it. 'But it's odd. Some days he just seems like there's nothing wrong with him at all. Other days I expect to walk into his room and see an empty bed, you know, all neatly made up with tight corners and fresh pillows. All ready for the next poor soul.' She shuddered, delicately. 'I feel so sad for him. It's all so protracted and unpredictable. In a way it would be better . . .'

'To get knocked down by a bus?'

'Well, no!' Maggie laughed nervously. 'No! I mean, that would be terribly painful, after all. And you might not . . . pass away immediately. You might end up in a wheelchair. Or brain-damaged. No! But, maybe, you know, the Swiss approach. A little injection. All over.'

'Well,' Jeannie wiped her hands on a paper towel and pulled off her white overall, 'that's kind of what they're doing in there, isn't it? Palliative care? Lots and lots of little injections, killing you off a tiny bit at a time?'

'No!' protested Maggie. 'No! They're just helping him with the pain!'

'Yes, but they're not trying to keep him alive, are they? They're not trying to help him get better?'

'No, but that doesn't mean they're killing him. You know, he danced with me the other day. He did. He took me for a walk in the gardens and he asked me to dance. I mean, if he really was being "put out of his misery" by the hospice, surely he wouldn't have been able to do that? Surely it would just be a slow decline rather than all this jumping about? And . . .' She paused. She'd been living with the strange knowledge of Daniel's revelation for almost a week now. She hadn't spoken to anyone about it. Mainly because she didn't really talk to anyone much these days, her life being as consumed by Daniel as it currently was. She looked at her old friend; possibly, apart from her children, her mother and Daniel, the closest person to her in her life, and she felt the words bubble up from within her.

'He told me something amazing, Jeannie,' she said, pulling up her black sheer tights. 'But if I tell you, you have to promise that you won't tell another soul?'

Jeannie raised her eyebrows at her. 'Who the hell do I know who would have any interest in your friend Daniel when none of us have even met him?'

Maggie bridled. 'Well, you just never know. So promise me.'

'I promise you.' Jeannie sighed and smiled at her old friend.

'He was a sperm donor, back in the eighties and nineties.'

Jeannie's over-plucked eyebrows leaped towards her hairline. 'Wow,' she said.

'And he has four children. Two boys and two girls. All in their late-teens or twenties.'

'Oh, my goodness.' Jeannie rearranged a cushion behind her back and stared at Maggie agog.

'I know. And he's never met any of them. Knows nothing about them apart from their birthdays and genders. And now that he's so, well, you know, close to the end, he says he wants to see them. Or at least find out about them. And obviously, in his current situation, there's not much he can really do about it.'

'So you want to get involved?'

'Well, yes, I suppose I do. Though I haven't got a clue where I'd start. I mean, where would one start? It'll be like finding a needle in a haystack. Or actually four needles.'

'Did he tell you which clinic he donated to?'

'No,' said Maggie. 'No. I didn't really ask him anything about it, after he told me. I didn't want to push it too far. Not in his condition.'

'Well, if you're serious about doing this for him, you'll need something to go on.'

'Yes, yes. I know. Of course, you're right.'

'When are you next seeing him?'

'Later. Six-ish.'

'And you're serious about doing this for him?'

'Totally.'

'Well, then, you can't afford to hang around. Take in a notepad and a pen and ask him everything. If the cancer is spreading to his brain, tonight could be your last chance.'

Maggie shuddered, lightly. But then she nodded. 'I know,' she said, feeling a deep well of sorrow building inside her at the thought of Daniel's poor calcifying brain. 'I will. Tonight. I'll talk to him. Tonight.'

They were wheeling around the drinks trolley when Maggie arrived at the hospice just after six. 'Wine? Beer? Sherry?' asked a cheery woman wearing a pink rose in her hair. There was a matching rose in a vase on the trolley and some chocolate fairy cakes sprinkled with silver balls, a gift from a well-wisher. Cakes often appeared in the corridors around here. Cakes and books and cases of wine. It was remarkable to Maggie that there were so many generous-spirited people in the world, quietly sprinkling silver balls on to freshly baked fairy cakes and parcelling them up in Tupperware boxes, finding a space in their days to drop them off, not hanging around to hear whether or not they were considered delicious but coming back the next week to collect the Tupperware boxes, all for the sake of simple human kindness.

Maggie had always thought of herself as a good person. She smiled at everyone she met and gave to charity collectors and always told people that they looked nice. She recycled and held babies for people and gave generously when friends asked her to sponsor them to do a charity run or hike. She'd even done a fun run herself a few years earlier. Just a mile. In a pink tracksuit. For breast cancer. But still. She liked to think of herself as human sunshine, a person to brighten up your day, a distributor of good karma. But she wondered about this assessment of herself more and more these days, confronted by the rich soup of endless giving and contributing and doing and caring sloshing around at this hospice every day.

'Can I get you a glass of wine, Mr Blanchard?' the lady with the rose in her hair asked gently as she edged her way into the room.

Daniel smiled. 'Yes,' he declared, happily. 'Yes. I think today I would love to drink a glass of wine. What do you have?'

'Red or white,' said the lady, whose badge, Maggie observed, named her as April.

Daniel smiled again, a special smile, Maggie had noticed, that he used when an English person amused him in some indefinable way. He used it on her a lot. She'd given up asking him what he was smiling about. He could never explain.

'In which case,' he continued, 'I will have a lovely glass of your finest *white*. Thank you.'

April poured the wine into a small rounded glass, the type they used to serve wine in in pubs in the old days. The glass was scratched and too old to keep its shine, and the wine had a look of not being far off room temperature. But still, thought Maggie, a glass of wine is a glass of wine when you're trapped in bed in a hospice. If it were her in that bed with cancer running round all over her insides, she'd do nothing but drink wine all day, she mused, warm or cheap or otherwise. There'd be no reason not to.

April poured Maggie a small glass of red wine and then left them each with a fairy cake on a paper napkin, which both she and Daniel already knew they would not eat, and then they were alone again.

Despite his enthusiasm for the concept of wine, Daniel did not look like a man who wanted a drink and, indeed, barely touched it. His face had grown slack new contours overnight and his hair was looking thinner, wirier; less like hair and more like stuffing. His entire form looked flat, like a cartoon character gone under a cement roller. It was as though his body was taking on the textures and the shapes and the lines of his bed, as though he and his bed were somehow growing together, like layers of compost. He put the wine glass down on to his tray and Maggie had to leap to her feet to steady it as it wobbled perilously in his unsteady grasp.

'Thank you, Maggie. My arms feel like twigs. They do. I cannot believe that once I used to carry heavy books in these arms. I built a garden wall with these arms. I carried my mother in these arms, down two flights of stairs. And now . . .' He let his words fade away.

Maggie wanted to leap upon these facts about the heavy books and the garden wall and the carried mother. When? she wanted to ask. Why? What books? What wall? But she could sense Daniel's weakness and knew that she should only really make him think about things that were vital, and right now the precise history surrounding the building of a garden wall was far from vital.

'Listen,' she began, first tucking her hair behind her ear and then pulling from her handbag a small notepad and pen, 'what you were saying the other day, remember, in the garden? About being a sperm donor? About the children?' She stared at him anxiously, willing him to remember. A light flickered inside his eyes and she breathed a sigh of relief.

'Yes,' he replied. 'Of course I remember. You do not easily forget the first time you tell another human being your deepest, oldest secret.'

She smiled, grateful for his remembering and for the fact of his confidence in her. 'Good,' she said, taking his hand in hers, 'I'm glad. But listen . . . and you are absolutely allowed to say no to this . . . I was wondering . . .'

'Yes,' he interrupted. 'Yes. I want you to do it.'

'Do what?' Maggie held her hand to her throat in surprise.

'Find them. If you can. I want you to find them. I want to know that they are happy and bright and beautiful and glad that I allowed them to be. You know, that they are not angry. Or even that they are.'

'Really?' said Maggie, smoothing down the open pages of her notepad. 'Oh, gosh, that's so brilliant. I've been meaning to ask you for days and been too worried in case you didn't want to talk about it again. I mean, the last thing I'd want to do is upset you.'

'Oh, Maggie.' Daniel smiled and squeezed her hand. 'How could you ever upset me? I shouldn't imagine you've ever upset anyone in your life!'

Maggie smiled, knowing somewhere deep down inside that this was probably true and something of a point of honour.

'Yes,' he continued, 'I give you permission. I think I have time. But knowing that this could be possible . . . well, I will make myself the time. I read an article, last year. There is now a website for children of donor fathers. I remembered this suddenly in the middle of a dream a few days ago. It is possible, I suppose, that my children may be on this website, that they may even have met each other. They may all be somewhere now, having a cup of tea or, perhaps, a very tiny glass of warm wine,' he laughed out loud, 'wondering who exactly this so-called father of theirs is. It is worth having a look, I suppose. But all these years I thought it didn't matter and now I am almost gone and, well, my timing is terrible. I can see that. Truly, truly terrible. But even if you only find one. Even if you find out just that one of my children is alive. Maybe the colour of their hair. Or their name. Or the title of their job. Just one fact, however small. It would be the greatest gift to take with me to my ending. It would be the greatest thing anyone has ever done for me.'

He smiled down at his bed sheets, at their entwined hands. His eyes were wet again. They rubbed their fingers together like good luck charms and Maggie blinked away her own tears. She didn't ask him how he would feel if she found no one. Neither did she ask him how he would feel if she found someone when he'd already drifted too far out into the ocean of his own demise even to be aware of it. Nor how he would feel if she found someone who was sad or damaged or full of hate and anger. She just smiled and stroked his hand and said, 'Leave it with me, Daniel, I'll do everything I can.'

Daniel's flat was formed from the top two floors of a large detached house just on the outskirts of the town centre. The house sat behind a gravelled carriage driveway and was at the uglier end of Edwardian architecture. But still it retained several pleasing features such as some ornate stained glass in the front door, leaded windows and a highly polished brass plate in which were embedded six glass buttons, each coupled to a doorbell. The button for Daniel's flat read: M. D. Blanchard. Maggie's natural instinct was to press the button but inside her handbag was a set of keys. Daniel had handed them to her in the hospice the night before with precise instructions about a further key to be found hanging from a nail knocked into the wall behind a desk, and a small drawer into which this key would fit, and a green folder entitled 'WFC', inside which Maggie would find everything she needed to contact the fertility clinic and identify him sufficiently to access the Donor Sibling Registry. Maggie had been to Daniel's flat before. Once to have some champagne on his terrace on a particularly beautiful early September evening ('This could be our last chance to sit out for a very long time, we mustn't miss it') and once to help him pack for his stay at the hospice. She'd cleared out his fridge and opened his drawers and unplugged his television, but all under his supervision. She felt like an intruder now, here on her own.

The air inside his flat was still and dense. His cleaner had been in a couple of times during the past month so the place was not exactly as it had been left, but still it felt like an intrusion to be here, to disturb the dust motes and the Hoover tracks in the carpet, to mark the place in any way. It was unlikely now that Daniel would ever return to this place but if he ever did, if there was a God and he did cast down a miracle (stranger things happened, every day), then it would be nice for him to find the place untouched, waiting, like an old dog.

Daniel's flat was not the flat of a middle-aged French-
man, more the flat of an elderly Englishman. His walls
were hung with reproduction oil paintings and his furniture was heavy and brown. His curtains were cream
jacquard and his sofa was a Chesterfield. His bookshelves
were lined with British classics and his kitchen smelled like
stale Mazola and Ritz crackers. A dried out blue J-cloth
hung stiffly from the swan's neck tap. It was a nice flat.
Maggie had pictured herself maybe living here one day, a
long time earlier, when Daniel had simply been a serious
man with a bad back. All the lamps had been on then, the
air had been thick with late summer and birdsong, and
she'd been pleasantly elevated by champagne and the
proximity of the most handsome man in Bury St
Edmunds. Anything had seemed possible back then.

She rested her handbag on a small table and unfurled
her long silky scarf. She looked around her, trying to
locate a 'small walnut desk'. She found it lurking behind a
large overstuffed armchair. It was home to a collection of
glass paperweights containing swirls of chartreuse and
cranberry, and some small framed black-and-white
photographs of people (his parents, she assumed) getting
married a very long time ago. She crouched down and felt
the wall behind the desk from inside the knee-hole, until
her fingers located the key, hanging from a piece of green
twine. She then found the small drawer hidden away
inside another drawer behind a secret panel, and there it
was, as promised, a light green folder, musty and faded,
marked with the letters WFC.

She took the folder to the armchair and settled herself against the heavy upholstery. She held the folder for a while on her lap, feeling the full enormity of her task, the totality of Daniel's trust in her. There were lives contained inside this folder. People. Stories. And, more importantly, there were secrets. Maggie didn't care for secrets. Or lies. She didn't have the right sort of mind for juggling all the requisite bits and pieces, the things you shouldn't say, the people you shouldn't mention certain things to, the words that had 'never been spoken', the events that had 'never taken place'. It was all too confusing and nerve-racking. A life without secrets and lies was a simple path to walk. Inside this folder were lives with so many layers of complexity that it made Maggie dizzy just to contemplate them.

Daniel did not have a computer. 'Who am I going to send an *email* to?' he'd protested. 'What is there on the internet that I cannot find on my bookshelves? *What?*'

'But what about booking holidays?' Maggie had countered.

'Holidays! Ah, yes, holidays,' he'd replied. 'I do not go on holidays. I have the sea an hour from my door and I live in one of the most beautiful towns in this country. I take my holidays on my terrace.' He'd smiled, and Maggie had smiled and thought that she'd never met anyone as simultaneously fascinating and utterly prosaic as Daniel in all her life.

She would need to take the papers home, back to her house, use her own computer. Her work here was done.

But still, it struck her that maybe there was more she could do. She may never come back to this flat. She had no legal right to enter it. She was not included on any of Daniel's official paperwork. It was likely that she would be the one to deal with his affairs when he was gone, but it was not definite, and supposing, she pondered, supposing she traced a child or two and supposing that child or two wanted to make contact with Daniel and supposing this all happened too late, that Daniel was comatose or, worse, that he was gone. What would she be able to tell that person about the man they'd wanted to meet?

She could recount her own memories of him, retell her own few meagre anecdotes. But that would not be enough. She had only known this man for a year, and for most of that time he had been dying. She knew so little about him. He was so opaque and impenetrable. She knew that he had an elderly mother, a bachelor brother, that he'd once been a doctor, that he'd retired due to ill health. (He hadn't elaborated but she'd suspected that the illness had been more mental than physical. People generally liked to talk about their physical ailments. Mental illness on the other hand . . .) She knew that he had a boat by the sea at Aldeburgh, a dinghy, called *Clarissa*. (She did not know why it was called *Clarissa* and she had never had the opportunity to see the boat as Daniel had stopped taking it out when his back started to trouble him, at exactly the same time that he had come into Maggie's life. She felt it again, that stab of hurt that she really had missed the best of Daniel by such a small margin.)

She knew that he liked to read and he liked to drink and he liked to eat, that most of the restaurateurs of Bury and the surrounding hamlets knew him by name and shook his hand warmly when he walked into their establishments. She did not know how he could afford to eat out so regularly or how he had afforded to furnish his generously proportioned home so finely or how he paid for the champagne and the wine and the smart clothes and the private physiotherapy. She knew nothing about this man that would really be of any help to a child asking questions and she would hate to pull someone out of their blanket of ignorance and then be unable to give them anything more than a vague sense of a person that they would never get to meet.

So she went into Daniel's kitchen and she found a stash of crumpled carrier bags and she then went about filling the bags with what she could only describe as mementoes. It seemed a terrible thing to be doing, stripping the essence of the man away from his home, without his permission, without his knowledge, and it was ordinarily not at all the sort of thing that Maggie would ever do. But this situation was far from ordinary. Daniel had not asked her to do an ordinary thing. The normal rules did not apply.

She put into a bag the two small framed photos of the long-ago married couple. ('And this', she imagined herself telling a dumbstruck twenty year old, 'is a photo of your father's parents. Your grandparents, I suppose.') She put in a bottle of his aftershave (something in a ribbed glass bottle from a shop called Trumper's, that smelled like cucumbers and cut grass). She found some old Boots photo packets stuffed with pictures of Daniel in various guises: on his boat, sitting on a bench with a lady friend, at the Henley Regatta in a straw boater, holding someone's King Charles spaniel. She only flicked through them cursorily, having no desire to study them in depth without their owner's permission. She took a photo album filled with tiny black-and-white photos of long-dead relatives in flapper dresses and long-nosed cars. She took notebooks filed along a shelf, although she did not open them to see what they might contain, feeling that that too went some good way beyond the pale. She took a framed map from the wall, a watercolour representation of the area around Dieppe from where he came, and she took a small blue address book from the telephone table. And then she straightened up the cushion on the armchair to remove the imprint that her behind had left in it, took one last look around the place, and quietly, respectfully, pulled the door closed behind her and headed for home.

LYDIA

Lydia had bought a cat. It was blue with a squashed face and fat cheeks. She'd bought it from a dealer on the internet who bred them in a semi-detached house just outside Kettering. The house had been cold, ugly and not warm enough, but the lady had been kind and loving and had seemed almost tearful to say goodbye to the bear-faced cat she'd called Samsara. The cat was a British Blue. Lydia had seen one on an advert for room deodorant and fallen instantly in love. A blue cat that looked like a bear. She'd always been a dog person. But now she was a cat person. It made sense really. Everything about her screamed CAT. Her big empty house, her crush on a gay personal trainer, her faltering friendship with her only real friend, her high-powered job. CAT CAT CAT.

She called the cat Queenie. The cat was three years old. The breeder had kept her from an earlier litter but it turned out that she was infertile and would not be able to earn her keep. It also meant that she was toilet-trained and not entirely obsessed with balls of string and endless play. From the moment Lydia had unlocked the door on Queenie's box, it had been clear that she had found herself the right animal. Queenie had delicately shaken out each leg in turn, surveyed the room, spied the white leather modular sofa in the glass extension and immediately jumped upon it, the most expensive piece of furniture in the house. The sun had picked her out, turning her fur duck-egg, and Lydia was sure she saw the cat smile with pleasure, as if to say: 'Finally, I am in surroundings in keeping with my status as a small blue goddess.'

The presence of the cat in her home had given her existence some much-needed soft edges. Queenie slept in Lydia's bed at night and woke her gently in the mornings by pressing her nose against hers and padding her chest gently with her soft feet. The cat then followed her from bed to shower, from shower to dressing room, from dressing room to kitchen and from kitchen to office.

Juliette hated the cat. She'd recoiled in horror the first time she'd seen Queenie sitting imperiously upon the bright white sofa, studiously licking her own anus. The cat and Juliette had exchanged a knowing look and Juliette had clutched her chest and said something in Tagalog that sounded like a curse, before turning on her heel and leaving the room.

Lydia had taken full responsibility for the litter tray and the small plastic bowls that Queenie ate her biscuits from. (Lydia loved to watch her eat biscuits. She especially loved the particular tone of the crunch the cat made as she smashed them between her tiny teeth.)

Queenie was currently sitting on the armchair in Lydia's dressing room, watching her with interest as she tried to examine the contours of her bottom in the mirror behind her. Lydia had not devoted much of her life to thinking about her bottom. But today she was wearing new gym trousers. They were very fitted with lots of seams and contours and constructed from a hi-tech fabric with a slight sheen to it. They were not for the faint-hearted and Lydia, when it came to her appearance, was very faint-hearted indeed. She spoke to the cat (what use was a cat to a single woman if you could not speak to it?): 'I think I can get away with this. Don't you? I mean, it's not as if I'm exactly fat. It's just, you know, lumpy bits. But honestly, anyway, what does it matter? He's gay. Isn't he? Do you think he's gay? You've met him. What did you think?'

Queenie threw her a slightly embarrassed look and then turned away.

Of course she's embarrassed, thought Lydia, *I am a woman. And she is a cat.* Lydia sighed and smoothed her hands down her buttocks one last time. She would wear the shiny leggings. If Bendiks was gay (of course he was), then he would not be perturbed by the sight of a few fleshy hillocks in the contours of her behind, but he *would* be pleased that she had thrown out the baggy fleece-lined joggers with the frayed drawstring waist. Lydia pulled her dark hair back into a tight ponytail and gave her overall appearance one last look before she and Queenie headed downstairs to greet him at the door.

Bendiks looked different today somehow. He looked less groomed. His face did not look like it had been recently exfoliated and slathered with rich cream. His eyebrows did not appear to have been plucked and combed and his eyes were untroubled by any form of concealer, leaving his sockets looking grey and exposed. His hair was overgrown and he smelled, for once, of perspiration. 'Hello, Lydia,' he said. 'How are you today?' He dropped immediately to his haunches to pet the cat who had already wound herself around his legs. 'And how are you, Miss Queenie? How are you today?' He scratched behind her ears and Queenie's already smiling face stretched out even further. Lydia's cat had the same taste as Lydia in everything, it seemed, from sofas to music to men. Bendiks' smile, on the other hand, was small and unconvincing. If Lydia had not known that Bendiks was an East European she might even have suspected that he'd been crying.

'How are you?' she asked as he stood up.

'Oh, I'm fine. You know?'

Lydia sensed a window inside the slightly pathetic 'You know?' for her to address his sadness. 'You look . . .' she began.

'I know,' he said, sadly. 'I look terrible. It's OK. You can tell me. I tell you when you look terrible. It is OK for you to return the compliment. I have not slept. In fact, I have not even laid down in order to sleep. I have been up all night.'

'Well, yes,' said Lydia, 'you do look very tired. Is everything OK?'

'No,' he sighed. 'Everything is not OK. Everything is appalling.'

'Oh, God,' she said, trying not to sound too captivated by the notion of his plight. 'God, come in, come in. Do you want anything. A tea? A coffee?'

'Ha! A vodka would be better, I think.'

'What, really?'

'No,' he laughed gruffly, 'no. That is the last thing I should be doing. A coffee would be nice, though.'

Lydia peered into the kitchen and asked Juliette very apologetically if she would mind making two double espressos and then led Bendiks on to the back terrace where the spring sunshine was playing on the decking and warming the cream cushions on the rattan furniture. Bendiks sat down and Queenie leaped balletically on to his lap, where she turned three times before settling herself into a ball and staring contentedly at Lydia. Bendiks dropped his chin into his chest and then buried his face in the cat's body. 'Shit,' he said eventually, raising his face again and letting his head roll back on his shoulders. 'Heavy, heavy, heavy.' His voice cracked, just a touch, and Lydia froze. She wasn't sure she was prepared for someone else's tears right now. She watched him and waited for him to speak again.

'Today,' he began, eventually, 'I am a bankrupt.'

Lydia's eyes widened.

'Today, I have been to the court and been told that I am a bankrupt. That everything I own is no longer mine. That I am no longer allowed to work in this capacity and that all my credit cards are to be shredded. Today I have ceased to exist.'

'Oh, my God, Bendiks, that's terrible.'

'I know, I know.' He sighed and dragged his hands over his strained face. 'It is totally terrible. I am destroyed.'

'Oh, you poor, poor thing. How did this happen?'

Bendiks shrugged and plucked at the cat's fur disconsolately. 'Credit cards. Overspending. The usual stuff. I've been really, really stupid. A real idiot.'

'But,' Lydia began gingerly, 'isn't being bankrupted a good thing when you're in debt? I mean, like a fresh start?'

He shrugged again. 'Not where I come from,' he said. 'I have been reduced to the status of a child. No more credit. No more self-employment. I will have to go back to working in a gym, be an employee again. And I have had to give in my notice on my flat.'

'Oh, no, why?'

'Because it was too expensive. It was another stupid decision. I chose a flat I liked rather than a flat I could afford. I have been juggling everything in the air, you know, paying for my whole life on credit so that I could use my wages to pay for this stupid, beautiful flat. And now I will have to live on just my wages. So bye-bye beautiful one-bedroom flat in Willesden. Hello shitty flatshare in Wembley.'

'You've already found someone to share with?'

'Well, no. But I'll have to do that. Probably someone from the gym. And I've seen their places. They're shitholes.' He shuddered delicately and looked sadly at the floor.

Lydia stared at him desperately. Her heart was breaking for him in a way that she hadn't thought was possible.

Lydia's heart was a sedate organ generally. It sat silently within her and kept her blood flowing smoothly around her body. It occasionally leaped at the sight of an attractive animal or a beautiful man. It sometimes ached dully with loneliness or longing. And once it had even raced with nervous anticipation, in the run up to a live radio interview when she was a student. But most of the time her heart did nothing, felt nothing, sat in its box under her ribs, tick-tick-ticking away the seconds and the moments and the days. So this sensation, she would call it compassion, was a new one for Lydia to contemplate. Bendiks looked broken, there on her rattan sofa. He looked like the child he'd been reduced to in the bankruptcy hearing. She could not bear to think of him packing away his things into boxes and moving them all to a dank house full of people in some far-flung corner of London. She wanted him to feel good about himself. She wanted him to retain some pride. Because his pride was one of his most attractive features.

'Stay here,' she said, the words out of her mouth and hanging in the air before she'd had a chance to wonder what she was doing.

'What?'

'I can rent you a room, for the same as you'd pay for the shitty flatshare. You'd have your own bathroom. Run of the house. Come and go as you please. Just while you're sorting yourself out.'

Bendiks' face fell into an expression of soft amazement. 'No,' he said, one hand clasped to his chest. 'Are you serious?'

Lydia nodded. 'Yes,' she said. 'Why not? I mean, this house, it's always been too big just for me.'

'Yes, but Lydia, your privacy, your space . . . I would hate to infringe on that.'

'It's fine,' she insisted. 'I spend most of my time in my office anyway. We'd probably never even see each other.' She ended her words with a small, sharp laugh. Even as she was speaking she was lining up the potential pitfalls of her rash suggestion. Awkward meetings in the kitchen in the mornings with last night's fungus still coating her tongue and her hair flat and pillow-stale. Passing each other in corridors in states of incomplete dress. The possibility of strange men, women or both passing through the house and mangled sounds of coupling floating through walls at ungodly hours. And, worse still, the terrible prospect of unsolicited conversation, chatter, words, at unexpected junctures. Lydia was accustomed to a very small amount of speech in her day-to-day existence, and she liked it like that. Conversation was overrated, in her opinion.

Her smile began to wither and wane as these misgivings flooded her thoughts. Would the distinct advantage of being able to see the fragrant Bendiks every day in an informal and intimate environment be quickly outweighed by the disadvantages of sharing her house with a man she barely knew?

He seemed to have noticed Lydia's frozen smile and was looking at her thoughtfully. 'You have not thought this through, have you?'

'No!' she chimed. 'I have! It's fine!'

'Look,' he said, 'I love this house, Lydia. You know I do. And I would love to stay here with you. It would solve all my problems. It would be perfect. But I do not, under any circumstances, want you to feel uncomfortable or unhappy. Please, do not be afraid to say so if you'd rather I didn't come to stay.'

Lydia's smile softened again. This would be fine. It would have to be fine. Because she could not say no to this beautiful man.

'Honestly,' she said. 'It would be a pleasure. I want you to stay. I really do.'

Bendiks beamed. 'In that case,' he said, 'I would love to accept. Thank you, Lydia. You have made me very, very happy.'

She could not remember the last time she'd made anyone happy. She went through life touching no one, making no impact. And here it was, like a small, strange miracle. This man had walked into her home ten minutes ago looking grey and lost. Now his face had regained its colour, his whole demeanour was bright and energised. And she had done that. With one, rash, unplanned gesture. And when she looked at him, she felt more than compassion. This, she reminded herself, was a man who understood her. This was a man who had experienced loss. This was a man from a foreign land who had come to London and made a life for himself. This was a man that she felt comfortable with and actually, now she thought about it, this was a person she might quite like to have around as she stumbled towards the most nerve-racking and peculiar experience of her life.

Because there were now two matches showing on the Donor Sibling Registry.

Two.

A man and a woman.

The male match had come up last night.

The female match had still not responded to her request for contact. It had been three weeks since she'd tried, but still there was nothing. Lydia was trying very hard not to take it personally. Why would you sign up to an agency like that if you had no interest in making contact with your siblings? It made no sense. No, she reasoned with herself, this person was on holiday. Yes, that's what it was. She was away. She was eighteen years old so maybe she was having a gap year. Or studying abroad. She pictured this girl sitting in an internet café in Delhi, accessing her e-mails, finding one from the Registry. She imagined her with a female friend, saying, 'Wow, look at this, I've got a sister!' and then going off to see the Taj Mahal or something.

Or maybe she was ill? Maybe she'd been taken suddenly unwell and was now in a hospital ward some-where, fearing for her life, unaware of the contact request from the Registry. Maybe her gravely concerned mother couldn't bear to bring it to her attention in her current state. Or maybe she'd just lost her internet connection. Or maybe she'd gone to the countryside to stay with an elderly aunt. Or maybe she was doing it, right now, filling in the form, giving the agency her permission to share her personal details. Lydia still checked her e-mails obsessively. The preoccupation with waiting to hear from her sister had taken the place of the preoccupation of waiting for a match. Was this what this experience was destined to be? she wondered. Waiting and waiting and waiting?

And just as she'd fully assimilated into her existence this desperate game of waiting and making excuses and inventing more and more unlikely scenarios for the lack of contact, there was another one. A man this time. Twenty-one years old. Now the whole thing would begin all over again. Her nerves were ragged. She could no longer concentrate on anything for longer than about half an hour before it came hurtling back to the surface of her mind. Brother. Sister. Contact. Waiting. She almost wished she'd never signed up in the first place. She hadn't expected it to be like this. She hadn't expected it to be such agony.

Juliette walked out on the terrace then, two small cups and saucers balanced on a tray with a selection of biscuits and two glasses of water. Lydia jumped to her feet to take the tray from her. Juliette tutted good-naturedly and said, 'No, you sit. Sit.'

Lydia felt a small wave of embarrassment for the overly formal and solicitous nature of the delivery of the coffee. It was all so unnecessary. She didn't need all this five-star frippery. She just wanted someone to keep her house nice for her.

'Juliette,' she said, to break the awkwardness, to

humanise her, 'I'm not sure I've ever introduced you properly. This is Bendiks. Bendiks is my fitness trainer. Bendiks, this is Juliette. Juliette looks after me.' She ended this on a nervous laugh. *Looking after her* made her sound like a crazed old maiden aunt with a tendency to walk out of the house in her nightdress.

Juliette smiled suspiciously at Bendiks and barely brushed the solid hand he offered her to shake. 'Nice to meet you,' he said.

'Yes,' said Juliette, circumspectly, before turning on her heel and heading back into the house.

Bendiks laughed. 'She is very protective,' he said.

Lydia considered that and thought it was probably about right. Lydia paid Juliette to look after her and her house, and anything not written into that original agreement – cats, visitors – was dismissed off the cuff.

'Yes,' she agreed, 'but she is very, very good at her job. As far as I'm concerned she's an investment. I pay her to keep my house looking exactly the same as it did when I bought it. If I lived here on my own it would look like a student house share. You know, I've lived here for a year and there is not a speck of limescale *anywhere*. And it's things like that that make a house keep its resale value.'

Bendiks smiled at her. 'It is OK,' he said. 'I'm not English. You don't need to justify these things to me. Where I come from, anyone who could afford a housekeeper would have a housekeeper. Where I come from, people would think you were mad if you didn't. You English. You're very strange about these things. So ashamed of money and success. So ashamed of your trappings. You should celebrate! A beautiful young woman, self-made, set for life. Wow. You should be shouting it from the rooftops! You should be proud of yourself!'

Lydia blinked at him. Had he just said that? she wondered. Had he just said she was beautiful? Lydia had no idea if she was beautiful or not. The mirror told her different things every time she looked in it. Nobody had ever told her she was beautiful. But then nobody had ever told her she wasn't. It had been left to her to draw her own conclusions, and she had failed to do so. But this compliment from Bendiks, it acted as a small weight in the balance towards believing that maybe she was nice-looking. He had no reason to say that to her. Nothing to gain from it.

And as she sat there on her terrace, the sun warming her face, her cat smiling at her dreamily from Bendiks' lap, Bendiks himself looking at her with a mixture of pride and affection, and a growing sense within herself that maybe she wasn't a freak after all, it occurred to Lydia that for the first time in her life, the pieces of her own personal jigsaw were coming together. It was almost as if she were finally starting to make sense of herself. The cat, the trainer, the potential new housemate, the letting go of Dixie, the fact that she did not share her DNA with a man she hated, the siblings she was hoping to meet, even this house, this stupid big house: it all felt like it meant something. The stage was set. The timing was right. Now all Lydia needed was for someone to get in touch with her and say they wanted to meet her.

ROBYN

Sam gazed at Robyn over the top of her bunched up knuckles. Her eyes were serious and sad. By her elbow was a mug of peppermint tea that Robyn already knew she would not drink. There was too much talking to be done.

'Why are you hurting my son?' Sam asked, quietly.

Robyn flinched. She had not been expecting those words. She had expected Sam to know exactly why she was hurting her son. *Because he's my brother, of course!* a small voice inside her head shouted out.

'Do you not know?' she asked, picking at a loose thread in the tablecloth, unable to meet Sam's intense gaze.

'Know what?' asked Sam.

'I thought you knew,' she muttered.

'I'll tell you what I know, young lady, and that is that my son has never felt the way he feels for you about any-one else. He's a sensitive young man, a beautiful, gentle, wonderful man, and he's given you his heart in a bag. And he thought – and I thought – that you felt the same way. It's been clear to me that you're both crazy about each other . . . and now you've just left him in limbo and I know he's a grown man and I know it shouldn't be any of my business and I shouldn't be here and that I should just butt out but I can't, because he's my only boy and I love him so much and I can't *stand* what you're doing to him. I can't *stand* it!'

Her voice caught on the last words and Robyn looked up at her. She was crying.

Robyn looked away again. 'Look, it's not as simple as that,' she began. 'It's – I thought you knew. Do you really not know?'

'Know what?'

'Jack's father – was he really a Barnardo's orphan? Did he really die in a car crash?'

Sam blinked away her tears and glanced at her in horror. 'What?' she asked, blankly.

'Is it all true? The story about Jack's dad?'

'Of course it's true.'

And as she said the words, Robyn knew they were true and she felt everything inside her fall and flood, like a sluice sliding open in a dam. Her legs weakened and her heart slowed and then it picked up again as she felt a huge burst of maniacal laughter forming in her chest. She swallowed it and smiled calmly at Sam. 'Really?' she said.

'Yes. Of course it is. Why on earth would I lie about a thing like that? And what on earth does it have to do with you and Jack?'

Laughter bubbled under the surface. Robyn's smile widened. 'I thought – you're going to think I'm mad – but I thought he might be my brother.'

'What!'

'Yeah, I know, it's nuts, isn't it? But there were so many things . . . we look so alike, and then I signed up to the Donor Sibling Registry and they told me I had a brother born in 1983. And I just thought . . . And you!' she remembered suddenly. 'You were so weird, that night at your house, when we were talking about me being a donor's child. You were looking at me so strangely . . .'

Sam blinked at her and shook her head. 'Was I?' she said.

'Yes! Like there was something you were thinking. Like you'd used a donor yourself.'

Sam laughed. 'Really?' she said. 'I honestly don't remember. But if I was looking at you strangely it was probably because I just find anything to do with parentage interesting. Because Jack doesn't have a father. I suppose I'm always subconsciously looking for reassurance, for other views, for different ways of looking at things. Because I've felt guilty all my life that I couldn't give him a dad.'

Her strong face softened then and she put one large hard-skinned hand against Robyn's. 'Oh, sweetie,' she clucked. 'Sweet girl. I can't believe you've been going around all this time, thinking that you were doing something wrong. You should have come straight to me, sweetie. I could have put your mind at rest a long time ago and saved you all this pain. Because you and Jack, well, you're perfect together. And, trust me, I will do anything it takes to support the pair of you. I believe in you two, and that is a hard thing for me to say. This is my boy, my only child, no one was ever going to be good enough for him. But you are. I honestly believe that. I mean – why else would I be here?' She paused for a moment, her mouth still open from her last syllable, her hands spread wide in front of her. And then she leaned back in her chair and laughed.

Robyn smiled. Finally. It was over. She felt all the wrongness inside her melt away. She had not slept with her brother. She was not a pervert or a freak. She was normal. She was totally, splendidly, beautifully, utterly normal.

'So,' Sam continued, leaning back towards the table, 'is that it now? Are you reassured?'

'Yes,' smiled Robyn. 'I am. But promise me one thing? Please?'

Sam looked at her, expectantly.

'Don't tell Jack. Please don't tell him. I'd hate to think of him knowing about all the weird shit I've been worrying about. I just want everything to go back to normal . . .'

Sam smiled and nodded. 'Don't you worry,' she said, 'your secret is safe with me.'

The first thing Robyn did when Sam left half an hour later was to call Jack. 'I'm sorry,' she said. 'I'm so sorry. I've been freaking out. And I've been crazy. But I'm not crazy any more. I'm totally sane. I've missed you. I love you. I've got your keys in my hand. I'm ready to go. Can I still move in?'

There was a moment's silence and then Jack laughed. 'What, now?'

'Yes,' Robyn said, breathlessly, 'why not? I can be packed and there by early evening.'

Jack laughed again. 'Wow,' he said, pensively.

'You OK?'

'Yeah,' he said, 'I'm great. I'm good. I'm just, shit, I don't know. I've been so . . . God, I can't even put it into words. I've just been totally desperate. I've missed you so much. I thought . . .' He paused and sighed. 'I thought it was all over.'

Robyn smiled and breathed lovingly into the phone. 'I hate myself,' she said. 'I hate myself. And this – this isn't me. Honestly. I don't do this kind of thing. But then, no one ever asked me to live with them before.'

'It's my fault. I knew it the minute I said it. I knew it was too much. You're so young. We've only just met. I was an idiot.'

'No!' she cried. 'No! You weren't an idiot. I was an idiot. An idiot ever to think it wasn't a great idea. I've been ill. I've lost half a stone. I look awful. I love you. I really love you. I'm going to pack. I'll see you in a few hours. I love you.'

'I love you too,' laughed Jack.

'Shh, now. Let me go. I love you.'

'I love you.'

'Stop telling me you love me! I love you!'

'I love you more.'

She sighed. 'You win. I'll see you soon.'

She switched off the phone and she rested it on the kitchen table and she grinned at it. She tried to stop smiling but she could not. Her smile was stuck. She glanced then around her parents' kitchen. She looked at the biscuit-coloured tiles impressed with purplish bunches of grapes, the chunky ceramic pots in a line: TEA, COFFEE, SUGAR, with their fat cork lids. She looked at the magnetic noticeboard studded with plumber's bills and dental appointments and receipts for wheelbarrows and car batteries, at the stable door hung with stained aprons and rusty barbecue forks. This had been her kitchen since the day she was born. The kitchen had changed not one iota, just tarnished and faded and cluttered itself. But Robyn had changed. Not slowly, not in barely perceptible increments, but overnight, from the moment she met Jack. And now that change was taking her away from here, away from Essex, from her parents' home. And she was ready now. Ready to be an adult. Ready for Jack. Well and truly.

Except, it wasn't that simple. Because somewhere inside the grubby chaos of the past few weeks she had brought something else into her world. Two brothers. And a sister. She'd never wanted to know about them. She'd had no interest in these people. They were not relevant to her journey. But now they were here. The 'sister' person had requested her information. And now there was another one. He'd signed up just last week. It was the younger of the two brothers. And there they were, in black and white. Real people, fleshed out from translucent shadows to two dimensions, one click of a button away from standing in front of her complete with smells and voices and blemishes and preconceptions and needs and wants. She kept trying to force them back into the box of her past but they refused to stay, bursting out of the sides like excess clothing in an over-packed suitcase. She'd breathed life into these people and now that she was done with them they refused to die. Sister. Brother. Brother. Sketchy, indistinct, sinister as ghosts.

'What are you going to do about them?' her mother had asked her the night before.

'Nothing,' she'd replied, knowing even as she said it that it wasn't true. However much she wanted it to be.

Her mother had stopped stirring the gravy granules in a Pyrex jug on the kitchen counter and Robyn had seen her inhale, breathing away her natural reaction. A moment passed and then slowly she'd begun to stir rhythmically at the gravy again. She was trying to find the right words.

'Well,' she'd said, eventually, resting the jug in the middle of the table, 'maybe not now. No. Maybe later on. When you're more settled.'

Robyn took her mother's well-intended words and let them sit with her for a short while before saying, circumspectly, but not without feeling, 'Yes. Maybe later. Maybe soon.'

The conversation was over. Dinner was served.

DEAN

He could hear her in the background. A small, keening noise, like a bird on a windowsill. It shocked him. He'd never heard her cry. The last time he'd seen her – the first time he'd seen her – she'd been muted by tubes and machinery. There'd been no lusty cry of indignation as she was pulled from her mother's belly, just pathetic silence. The sound both alarmed and reassured him.

'Is she OK?' he asked Rose.

'Yes, she's fine. She's just wanting a cuddle, aren't you, sweetheart?'

He heard Rose move closer to the keening sound, and then he heard snuffling and waffling sounds of flesh against speaker, and then the keening sound stopped and he heard Rose saying. 'There, there, my beauty. There, there, my angel. That's better, isn't it? There.'

There were half a dozen different sentiments buried inside Rose's tone of voice and Dean could read them all. Listen, she was saying, that is the sound of your motherless daughter crying. Listen, this is the sound of me instinctively knowing what your crying daughter wants because I have done this so many times before and am doing a much better job than you or your feeble mother could ever hope to do. But listen also to the sound of parenting, *this* is what you should be doing right now. I should not be soothing this crying baby. You should be soothing her. Although, the subtext continued, *I don't want you anywhere near this baby, you hear me.* This is my baby. My baby's baby. You have lost any stake in this baby with your gutless and self-centred behaviour of the past ten weeks.

As much as Dean disliked his late girlfriend's mother, he had to concede that she had a point. He was only on the phone to her now because the council had been in touch about getting the flat back from him and he needed the baby's birth certificate to try and take it over in his own name. It was a cowardly and feckless thing to be doing because he knew deep down inside himself that he had no intention of ever living here with the baby. The best he could conceivably envisage was that the baby might come here for the odd overnight stay if Rose needed to be elsewhere. But really, this flat would never be a home to his daughter. And he would never be her father. The truth was that he was using the fact of the baby's existence to try and wheedle himself a home out of the government. He was a loser. He could see Sky now, with her big swollen belly, sitting on that chair opposite him, saying: 'You're pathetic, you know that? You're fucking pathetic.' And she was right.

'What d'you want her birth certificate for?' asked Rose, suspiciously.

'I need to, er, it's for, like, child tax credits or something. I had a letter through.'

'Send it to me. I'll deal with it,' Rose barked.

'No. It says it has to be the registered parent. It says I have to apply.'

'Hmm,' she murmured, dubiously. 'I don't remember ever having to do anything like that with the rest of them . . . Saffron, I've got Dean on the phone: did you ever have to send off the kids' birth certificates to apply for your tax credits?'

Dean held his breath, heard Sky's sister in the background saying: 'No idea. Don't think so, though. Think the government gets all the information through computers and stuff.'

'No,' said Rose to Dean. 'I'm not letting you have her birth certificate. End of.'

'But she's my kid. It's my name on that certificate.'

'Yeah, well, you're lucky it's on there. To be honest, I was that close to saying "Father unknown", because, quite truthfully, Dean, you may as well be.'

And then she hung up.

Dean stared at his phone for a moment. He was not surprised. She'd been quite civil considering. And he didn't have the energy or the wherewithal to fight back. So that was it. The flat would be taken away from him. He'd be back with his mum. And a small deep-seated part of him was glad. This whole moving out, getting a job, having a baby thing, looking after himself . . . it had never felt right. It had always felt too soon. He rested his phone on the table and looked around the bare flat. Yes, he thought, yes. His conversation with Rose had sealed it. He would move out. Back with his mum. He would pretend none of the past twelve months had ever happened. He would start all over again. And maybe, in starting all over again, he might discover what exactly the point of himself was.

Dean and Tommy sat side by side in the Alliance, just across the road from the benefits office. Tommy had just been in to sign on – 'For the first time in my life,' he'd muttered disconsolately. Dean had signed on, too. Not for the first time in his life. Dean had been unemployed for nearly a year now. Once he'd moved in with Sky he'd let things slide a bit with the driving job. It hadn't seemed worth getting up for, really. His mum always gave him a few quid every week and in the past he'd saved it up, for his future. Ironic that the moment he started building a future he'd thrown it all away. It was almost as if he'd known there wasn't going to be one.

It was 3.35 and on the table in front of them were two pints of Dutch lager and two packets of crisps, torn from top to bottom and displaying their silvery, oily innards. Both men stared into the middle distance in silence. Tommy was all or nothing. You either couldn't get a word out of him or a word in edgeways. It didn't bother Dean either way.

He let the silence draw out for a while and pulled together his thoughts. There was something he wanted to talk about but he didn't really know where to start. So he started at the place he knew Tommy would find the most interesting.

'So, I went home with that redhead on Friday night,' he said.

'Oh yeah, I thought you might.' Tommy winked at him. 'How was it?'

'Yeah,' he said, 'it was all right. She's a bright girl.'

'A bright girl, eh?'

'Yeah. She's a student.'

'Wow. What the fuck did you talk about?'

Dean laughed.

'Oh, right, I see. No talking required, eh?'

'No, it wasn't that. We didn't even . . . you know?'

'What? Seriously?'

Dean shrugged.

Tommy picked up his pint. 'Yeah, well,' he said, 'I reckon it's fair enough. A bit soon probably. A bit soon for all that. You're probably wise not to get involved.'

'Well, yeah, it was a bit more than that, though. I mean, I liked her. She was cool. And something happened.' He inhaled and threw Tommy a quick glance from the corner of his eye.

Tommy looked at him quizzically. 'Oh, yeah?'

'It's a bit weird really, and I haven't told you any of this before but while you were away my mum told me something. She told me that my dad wasn't who she'd said it was. That my dad was . . .'

'A donor. I know. My mum told me. Years ago.'

225

'What, you knew?'

'Yeah. Sworn to secrecy. I wished she hadn't told me.'

'Fucking hell! I can't believe you knew that all along and you never said anything.'

'Christ, I nearly did, a hundred times. My mum should never have told me. But that's great. Your mum finally told you.'

'Well, yeah, I guess. And it's cool and everything. I wasn't really bothered or anything. Sort of made sense really. But that night, with that girl, Kate, we were really wasted. I mean, like, completely fucked, and we went on to the internet and she signed me up with this Donor Sibling Registry thing.'

'Fuck, right. And?'

'And there were two matches. Girls. Women. Sisters. One's eighteen. One's twenty-nine.'

'Holy shit,' said Tommy, putting his pint glass back down on the table and staring at Dean with wide eyes.

'Yeah, I know. I didn't mean to do it. It just kind of happened. And now one of them wants to get in touch.'

'No way! Which one?'

'The one who's twenty-nine. She lives in London. Somewhere up north. And she's single, not got any kids, lives alone. Her name's Lydia.'

'Lydia?' Tommy tested the name against his tongue, almost like he was checking its credentials. He nodded, approvingly. 'Lydia,' he said again. 'Sounds posh.'

'Apparently she's Welsh.'

'Oh,' said Tommy, dismissing his theory.

'Yeah, she wants to meet up.'

Tommy blinked at him. 'Fuck, man,' he said.

'I know. It's just, I don't know. Part of me really wants to? But part of me is really really really shit-scared.'

'Have you told your mum?'

'Yeah. She thinks I should just sleep on it for a bit. See how I feel. You know what she's like, she never lays it down.'

'Yeah, I know. But shit. That is massive. That is totally massive.'

'I know. I know.' Dean drank some lager and chased a few crumbs of crisps around the empty packet with his fingertips. 'What would you do?' he asked eventually, turning to his older cousin with hopeful eyes.

'Fuck, I'd go. God, yeah. But then, I'm up for stuff like that. I'm not as, you know, sensitive as you. And I don't want to make light of it. It's a big deal. But if I were you, I'd do it. I mean, it's your blood. You've got more blood in common with this woman than with me. The worst thing that could happen is that you don't get on. The best thing that could happen is that you have a sister, for the rest of your life. All for the sake of a tube journey north and a few hours out of your day. Yeah, if I were you, I'd go for it. What have you got to lose?'

Dean nodded. He'd known that's what Tommy would say. And somewhere deep inside he knew that Tommy was right. He should do this. He should meet this woman, Lydia. And he should try to contact the other one, the teenager. His life had come completely untethered from its moorings. His girlfriend was dead, he had no job and his daughter had been taken to live with a woman he couldn't stand. Maybe it would take something like this to help him see what the point of anything was. Because certainly, from where he sat now, it was very hard to see one.

He nodded, his gaze casting out across the room into the fug of the early-afternoon gloom. He thought of another pub, across the river, maybe one like this or maybe a posh gastro one. He thought of a woman: he imagined her tall and regal, wearing a mackintosh. He imagined approaching her, examining her profile which would be aquiline and elegant. He saw her turn to him and smile and say, in a voice like that girl off *Gavin and Stacey*, 'Hello, Dean, I'm Lydia. It's lovely to meet you.'

And then the image was gone and he was here again, in Deptford, nursing a pint with his cousin Tommy and still no surer about what to do next.

Dear Lydia,

My name is Dean. I am twenty-one year's old and I live in Deptford, that's south-east London. I dont work right now. I've had a tough year. And I'm between houses, just moved back in with my mum. My mum told me three years ago about my dad. When I turned eighteen. It come as a bit of a suprise. I used to think my dad was a man she met on holiday when she was forty-one. It didn't bother me much. I thought it was quite cool actully. How did you find out? And what did you think about it?

Anyway, I think I'm feeling ready to meet up with you, if you are? As I say, I don't work so I can be free and easy, realy. Maybe you've got a local? I can come up your way? Or somewhere central? You tell me. Hears all my details. I'm not good on the phone so best to text or something. Let me know.

Yours faithfuly,

Dean Higgins

Dean re-read the email. He thought it sounded quite good. Friendly, but not scary-friendly. And kind of intelligent but not like he was making too much of an effort to sound intelligent. And a bit of information, but not so much that they wouldn't have anything to talk about when they met up.

'Mum,' he said, over his shoulder. 'What do you think?'

She appeared in the room, halfway towards being dressed for a date with a man she'd met on the internet. Her straight hair was sleek and shiny after a session with her ghd straighteners, and she was wearing a printed black-and-white sleeveless dress that showed her cleavage. Dean thought that her arms were probably a bit meaty and slack for a sleeveless dress and her cleavage had seen better days. But she looked pretty enough in a smattering of make-up and some dangling pearl earrings.

'It's all right,' she said, 'I'm going to wear a cardigan.'

'No,' said Dean, 'you look nice. Honest. You look really nice.'

His mum smiled at him and squeezed his shoulder.

'Thanks,' she said. 'If you keep saying things like that then you can stay for a bit longer.' She hadn't taken too enthusiastically to the news that he was moving back in. 'I suppose,' she'd said, softly, 'while you sort your life out. Yes. Why not?' Dean had been surprised. He'd always imagined that his mum was lonely here on her own, that she'd quite like to have him back. But it seemed that a lot had changed in the year he'd been away. Not least his mother's attitude towards dating.

'Let's have a look at this then.' She pulled another chair towards her desk and squinted at the screen while she read. 'It's great,' she said a moment later. 'You might want to run a spellchecker over it. But it's fine.'

'Fine?' said Dean.

'Yes, love. It's fine.'

'You mean it could be better?'

'No, honestly, it's fine. I mean, it doesn't need to be any more than that, really, does it? I mean, you'll do all your talking when you actually meet up with her, I suppose.'

'You think it's crap, don't you?'

'No. I don't think it's crap. It's just a bit uninformative, that's all. But, as I say, you'll have plenty of time to really get to know each other in the flesh.'

Dean sighed. He was still only half-convinced that this was a good idea. Still only going through with it because the people whose opinions he valued the most highly – his mother, his cousin and Kate with the red hair – all thought he should do it. But really, what would he and this posh bird called Lydia have in common? She was a scientist. He was an unemployed van driver. She was Welsh. He was English. It was going to be a disaster.

He ran a spellchecker over the e-mail and then, with an odd sense of trepidation, nausea and excitement in his belly, he pressed send. In his mind's eye he saw the tall lady with the aquiline nose, sitting in a quiet study in her large stately townhouse. She was wearing a stiff white blouse with the collar turned up, and fingering a string of pearls that sat high on her throat. He saw her click on his e-mail to open it and he saw her reading it, with a small smile playing at her lips. He tried to imagine what would be going through her mind as she read his words. He wondered if she would be feeling as nervous as he was or if she would be feeling nothing but cool contempt for this half-educated yob from Deptford.

'All right, love,' his mother said, her feet now planted inside navy strappy sandals and her arms covered by a white fitted cardigan with silver buttons, 'I'm off.'

She smelled of something he'd never smelled before. At first he thought it was perfume but then he realised it was something else; heat, vibrancy, nerves. 'You OK?' he said, turning in his seat to address her.

''Course I am,' she said, brightly.

'And this guy . . . he's OK, is he?'

'He's fine, Dean. Honestly.'

'And you'll be out in public, yeah?'

'Yes. It's only our second date. Come on.' She laughed and squeezed his shoulder. 'What do you take me for? And you, are you going to be all right?'

He turned and glanced at the monitor. 'Yeah,' he said. 'Yeah. I should be OK.'

She smiled at him tenderly. 'Oh, Dean . . .'

He looked at his mother and was alarmed to see that she looked a bit tearful.

'I never thought about all this. I never thought how this was going to impact on you . . . I feel so bad.'

'What?'

'This,' she gestured at the document on his computer screen, 'putting you through all this. You must be so scared. And it's all my fault.'

Dean stared at his mother affectionately. 'What are you talking about?' he said with a laugh.

'I mean,' she sighed, 'that twenty-two years ago I made a totally selfish decision and now you're having to pay the price for it.'

Dean laughed again. 'Honestly, Mum. It's fine.'

She stared at him intently. 'Really?' she said. 'Is it really fine? Because to tell you the truth, Dean, half the time I feel so guilty.'

Dean blinked at his mother and exhaled.

'Honestly. I brought you into this world and it's done you no good as far as I can see and I just think, I don't know, doing what I did, to make you, I could have tried a bit harder with you, given you some more opportunities, then maybe, oh, I don't know . . . I just feel like I've done everything wrong.'

Dean sighed again and then took his mother's hands in his. They were clammy and soft. 'Mum,' he said, 'I love you, OK? I love you and I'm glad you did what you did. I like being alive. And this,' he gestured at the screen, 'this is good. Yeah? It's going to be great. It's all a part of life, isn't it? The life that you gave me.'

His mum smiled gratefully and squeezed his hands. 'Having you was the best thing that ever happened to me,' she said. 'Truly. Honestly. And I'm so so proud of you.' She leaned towards him and kissed him on the cheek. Then she leaned away from him again and appraised him lovingly.

'I'm glad you're back,' she said after a moment. 'I didn't like you being on your own in that place. All alone. With all those memories. You stay here as long as you need to, OK?'

She bent then to hug him and he hugged her back. His lovely mum. The best woman in the world. He watched her leave, her wide hips straining against the printed fabric of her dress, her chunky ankles incongruous atop the delicate shoes, off on a second date with a man called Alan. His heart suddenly ached for her and he smiled weakly. He waited until he heard the front door closing behind her and then he went into the back garden and made himself a spliff. He smoked it slowly and deeply and sent the smoke from inside himself out into the world, imagining it crossing the London sky, south to north, like an offering from a peace pipe, passing through the tall thin windows of a tall thin house and into the private rooms of a lady called Lydia Pike.

MAGGIE

Maggie asked her friend Jeannie over for dinner the following night. She invited her for three reasons: firstly because she wanted a pedicure, secondly because her eighteen-month-old granddaughter Matilda was staying the night and, as much as Maggie might have given birth to and raised two children all by herself, she still felt a little untethered when left alone with a child she had not directly brought into being. But thirdly, and mainly, because she wanted her help with signing Daniel up to the donor website. She'd had a quick look at it last night when she'd got back from his flat, and quickly switched it off again. It had looked horribly convoluted and she hadn't known where to start in terms of correlating the information in Daniel's folder with the information needed on the form.

It was 7.30 and Jeannie was upstairs with Matilda, having offered to read her her bedtime story while Maggie got on with dinner. Maggie could hear Matilda overhead, scampering up and down the landing, screaming with high-pitched excitement, and realised that Jeannie had fallen into the oldest trap in the book: attempting to endear herself to a small child by making it laugh, prompting an endless cycle that resulted, on the whole, in hysteria and ended shortly thereafter in tears. Maggie raised her eyebrows and smiled. It was nice to hear life in her house. She did enjoy living alone, but it was at moments like these that she remembered what it had felt like when her house was full of other people's lives.

On the hob was a pot of *coq au vin*, though Maggie realised it was a little old-fashioned to call it that these days; chicken stew would probably be more de rigueur. On the kitchen counter she tipped some green leaves into a smart white bowl (she'd got rid of all the patterned stuff when her husband moved out, and replaced it with this over-sized white stuff, like they served on in trendy pubs). She opened a bottle of French dressing and then she sliced a fat French loaf (known as a *'Rustique'* according to the accompanying signage in Waitrose) into ovals. She unfurled a John Lewis brightly spotted tablecloth on to the kitchen table and laid it with more white plates and matching spotted paper napkins.

She had already opened a bottle of wine. It was one that Daniel had recommended to her many months ago, French, of course, and she'd developed a fondness for it that was less to do with the wine itself and more to do with the memory of a charmed moonlit night in a bistro in Aldeburgh, involving fresh razor clams and samphire, flickering red candles, and a slow and balmy walk back to the car park through cobbled streets accompanied by the sounds of seagulls circling overhead in the almost darkness.

She'd spent three hours at the hospice today. Daniel had been sweetly spacey, his face relaxed into a kind of compacted smile for most of her visit. Maggie liked to think it might partially have been inspired by her presence, by the soothing charm of her measured conversation, but knew in reality it was just the drugs. He hadn't wanted to talk about anything serious and she'd been unsure about bringing up the subject of the Donor Sibling Registry in his current state. The nurses were happy with his condition. He had stabilised, they said. Which brought to mind an image of a speeding car applying its brakes just a few feet from a cliff face and then sitting there with an idling engine, the driver tap-tap-tapping the steering wheel before putting his foot to the accelerator again and hurtling off the edge. This was the best she could hope for, an idling engine. She just hoped that Daniel's engine would remain idling long enough for her to make contact with at least one of his lost children.

Jeannie finally came downstairs half an hour later. She looked flushed and her wavy hair was dishevelled. She grabbed her wine glass from the kitchen counter and filled it to the top. 'And there was me, thinking I was ready to be a grandmother,' she laughed.

Maggie laughed too. 'Exhausting, isn't it? Especially at our age. I don't know how those old mothers do it, you know, those ones popping out babies in their forties. It's a young woman's game, in my opinion.'

'A very young woman's game,' agreed Jeannie.

'Cheers.' She held her glass out towards Maggie's. 'To being old and child-free.'

'Oh, yes, indeed.' Maggie smiled and clinked her glass against Jeannie's. 'And cheers to you, too. Thanks for coming over. And thank you for my lovely toenails.'

'Always a pleasure doing your trotters, Mrs Smith. They're the nicest ones I know.'

The women sat down then and enjoyed a pleasant meal of stew and bread, the sounds of Matilda's deep-asleep breathing on the baby monitor accompanying their gentle conversation. They talked about Daniel and they talked about their children and they talked about the Italian holiday that Jeannie was taking that summer with her new boyfriend. After dinner they took their half-full wine glasses through to Maggie's living room and they settled themselves in front of her laptop. (Her son had picked it out for her and set it up last Christmas. It was an Apple Mac, in deep rose pink. Maggie was very fond of it.)

On the table in front of them was Daniel's paperwork, arranged into piles according to relevance. Maggie had pulled out all the really personal stuff, the photos and such, and put it away. Not for Jeannie's eyes. Only for the eyes of Daniel's children. And then together the two friends filled out a form that was intended to be filled out by the man slowly fading away in a big white bed, in a small modern building, half a mile away from where they sat.

Jeannie left at eleven o'clock and Maggie walked around her small, neat house, turning off the lights, tidying her desk, drawing the curtains across the living-room windows.

She always found this time of night unsettling. The trees outside grew manes and limbs in the dark night breezes, and people passing by her window on their way home looked panicky and rushed. Maggie's heart always beat a little faster as she pulled her curtains together, some primal echo of the drawing up of footbridges, the battening down of hatches, the padlocking of gates. Caves had no windows. Wombs had no windows. Windows were inherently just holes in a house.

She took the stairs quietly and tiptoed into the spare room where her granddaughter slumbered. She was the wrong way round in her travel cot. Either Jeannie had put her in the wrong way or she had managed to turn herself the full one hundred and eighty degrees. She was dressed in a red babygro: Maggie's daughter, Libby, was not fond of pink; had, in fact, quite strong political objections to the colour pink and the brainwashing of little girls into worshipping at the altar of pink. Maggie didn't really understand why it riled her so much. It was only a colour.

Matilda had a thick mop of auburn waves, exactly the same colour as Libby's, and her face was a square brick of plumped, creamy flesh implanted with two enormous green eyes, just like her father's, and a tiny little whorl of a pink mouth which apparently had something to do with her great-grandmother on her father's side. There she lay, her fists curled inwards towards her ears, a living, breathing amalgamation of a hundred thousand different people, all of whom had at some point in their lives had a night of passion with somebody else and made another one, outwards and onwards in ever-increasing circles, an unstoppable force of humanity extrapolating itself across millennia. Until here, in a small cottage in a Bury St Edmunds backwater, it was all distilled down into one perfect, creamy pearl – Matilda.

In a way, what Daniel had done, into a small jar in Wigmore Street all those years ago, and what those mysterious women who'd used his sperm had done, had subverted the natural order of things. Maybe there was meant to be a pre-ordained pattern to these things, a vast human dance, if you like; take your partner by the hand and then make a baby, take that baby by the hand and make another one, and so on and so forth ad infinitum. Where did anonymous sperm donation fit into that dance? Maybe what Maggie had set into motion tonight was a way of re-choreographing the dance, of joining up the dots, of normalising something distinctly unnatural.

Maggie pulled Matilda's cover up around her chest and resisted the temptation to stroke her big apple-cheeked face. She blew her a silent kiss instead and then backed from her room towards the bathroom. She thought of the four children Daniel had helped to create, lying in their beds tonight, in places unknown. She hoped that they were as safe and as happy as her little Matilda. She hoped their mothers loved them as much as Libby loved Matilda. She hoped that they had fathers, maybe, or grandparents who showed them photos of their own ancestors, of long-faced men and women in cumbersome clothing, of small children in sailor suits or sooty-faced youngsters outside working men's terraces. She hoped that they knew who they were and where they'd come from. She hoped that finding Daniel would be just the crowning conclusion to a perfect existence and not the final step in a long and painful journey to self-knowledge. She had started a process tonight on her rose pink Apple Mac, a process that could end up anywhere. She had opened Pandora's box.

In her bathroom mirror Maggie washed away her happy face of foundation, Touche Éclat and sapphire eyeliner. She had not had a facial in over six months. The Botox and the fillers had long since faded away and her skin was pale and dry. She removed the make-up quickly and efficiently, trying not to look for too long at the old, lonely woman in the mirror staring back at her.

A few days later Maggie headed off to the hospice with a small Jiffy bag in her handbag. It had arrived this morning, recorded delivery. What a thing to sign for, she'd thought to herself as she'd scribbled on the driver's little computer screen. What a very odd thing indeed.

She held her breath as she pushed open the door to Daniel's room. She needed him to be good today. She needed him to be normal.

'Good morning, handsome,' she said, leaning in to kiss his cheek. Strangely the less handsome he became, the more comfortable she felt about suggesting that he was.

'Good morning, Maggie May.' He smiled at her and she knew immediately that today was a Good Day.

'I brought you some Starburst and some satsumas.

There.' She unloaded a carrier bag on to his tray and unpeeled a satsuma for him. 'How are you today?' she asked benignly.

'I am feeling very young and silly,' he said. 'If it wasn't for the fact that my body is glued to this bed, I would be doing something reckless.'

'Oh, yes,' she smoothed the seat of her skirt before sitting down, 'like what?'

'I don't know, Maggie May, maybe like taking you in my arms and kissing you on the mouth.'

Maggie flushed and looked at him in surprise. 'Oh,' she said.

'I never did kiss you, did I, Maggie? All those lovely evenings we spent together, and I never did kiss you. And now it is too late. I am a fool.' He smiled wryly, and then he patted the side of his bed.

Maggie moved herself from the chair to his bed and smiled at Daniel uncertainly. 'I don't know what to say.'

He clasped her hand and squeezed it. 'I don't expect you to say anything. Except I want you to know this: if I had my time all over again, I would have kissed you that night, remember, in Aldeburgh?'

Maggie smiled. 'How could I forget?'

'The air was so warm and you were wearing a lovely white . . .'

'Yellow. Pale yellow . . .'

'Yes, that's right, a yellow dress with your hair tied back. And your skin was tanned and smooth and I wanted to eat you.'

Maggie put her other hand to her chest and stared at him in amusement and awe. 'Well,' she began, 'I mean, gosh. I had no idea.'

'No, well, why should you? I was . . . too slow. Too cold. I thought my life had run out of possibilities. I thought if I kissed you, you would vomit.'

She laughed. So many things she wanted to say in reply, but not one of them made it to her lips. Instead she said, 'Oh, how silly!'

'No, not silly. You are an exquisite woman. I am a damaged man. I did not want to inflict that damage upon you. So I kept myself distant from you. But now, well, the irony, I cannot damage you any more because I will not be here for long enough to do so, but I am too disgusting and decayed to take you in my arms and do the things I want to do.' He sighed, he shrugged and then he smiled.

Maggie squeezed his hand once and then moved back to her seat. She felt moved by his words, but also unsettled. He had changed the entire shape and flavour of the last year of her life. She had thought herself the hanger-on, the one waiting in the wings to be found attractive by a man she desired. But all the while he had been desiring her too. How different things could have been. But also, maybe, how much more tragic.

'Well,' she said, eventually, 'I must say, Daniel, that if at any point in the last year you had taken me in your arms, I would not have tried to get away.'

'I know, Maggie. I know. And that makes it even worse.'

'But thank you,' she continued, 'thank you for telling me how you felt. It will help . . .' She paused. She finished the sentence silently in her head. *It will help when you're gone.*

'Well, it may help you but it will be of no use to me whatsoever!' Daniel laughed and the laugh became a cough. He leaned away from his pillows and coughed into his fist. Maggie passed him a cup of water. 'Oh, Maggie,' he said, once he had recovered himself. 'What a stupid man. What a stupid life. What a fool I have been, again and again.'

'No,' she said gently, 'you have done your best. It's what all of us do. Day after day. Just our very best. And besides,' she paused, having finally, she felt, found the right moment to address the issue of the Jiffy bag in her handbag, 'you've done more than most.'

'I have?'

'Yes. You were a donor. You helped four women become mothers. You gave the gift of life.'

Daniel smiled. 'Well, this is true, I suppose. Though of course I have no idea what form that life has taken. My children may be rapists and terrorists for all that I know.'

'Well, that's highly unlikely, I'd've thought.' She found the joke a little dark for her tastes. 'But listen, I've been asked to do something. By the Donor Sibling Registry. They need to test your DNA. They sent me a little kit.' She reached into her handbag and brought out the brown envelope. 'Look,' she said, 'it's ever so simple. I just need to swab the inside of your cheeks, with this little stick, and then pop it in here and send it back.'

He looked at the kit with semi-amused interest. 'Oh, goodness, so now I am like a yobbo on *The Jeremy Kyle Show*! I am to have my paternity tested.' He chuckled.

'Are you happy to do this?' she asked.

'Yes, I suppose I am.'

'And then,' she continued, 'they need your birth certificate. I found it at your flat. Oh, and a household utility bill. I'll send it all special delivery. Extra secure.'

He laughed again. 'So this is what it comes down to. Utility bills and bureaucracy. Everything in this life comes down to paperwork eventually.' He sighed.

'We don't have to do this,' she said, 'you can change your mind?'

'No no no!' he said in a louder voice than she'd imagined he still possessed. 'No. This I have to do. I need to do. And the sooner the better. I cannot take you in my arms and ravish you, but I can do this thing.' He smiled. 'Come,' he said, 'remove my DNA. Scrape it from me. I am ready.'

He opened up his dry, cracked lips and offered her the pink, moist insides of his cheeks.

LYDIA

Finally Lydia could feel the long, cavernous days of winter ebbing away. Through her office window she could see a smooth blue sky and she could feel the warmth of the afternoon sun warming the carpet by her feet. Queenie sat right in the middle of it, as if it belonged exclusively to her, this long-awaited pool of golden light. Lydia stretched her legs out in front of her and stared in dismay at her winter feet. They had the semi-opaque, greyish-whiteness of lard and her toenails were tinged yellow. She needed to sort out her feet. Now that she was sharing her house with another human being, it was vital. How could she display these bony, misshapen lumps of meat and bone to another human being? She had already invested in new pyjamas. Not sexy pyjamas. The last thing she would attempt to be at seven in the morning was sexy. But just smart pyjamas. From Toast. Smart, but kind of cool. Pyjamas that spoke of scraped-back hair and reading glasses and serious bedtime literature.

Lydia sighed. Bendiks had moved in four days ago. He had arrived with three very smart suitcases, one of which appeared to be a real Louis Vuitton. He'd unpacked silently in his room, emerged at six o'clock all spruced up and smelling of expensive aftershave, and then not returned until some unimaginable hour the following morning. She'd heard him about the house since, his door opening and closing every few hours. And she had stood, for a short while, outside his bedroom door that first day, her knuckles poised beside it, steadying herself to ask him how he was doing and if there was anything he needed, but she'd lost her nerve and backed away, silently, towards her own room. And then she'd bumped into him yesterday morning, thinking, wrongly, that he'd already left for work, when she was wearing her Toast pyjamas and looking like a total fright. She'd slept so deeply the night before that her face felt like a full sponge. She'd jumped at the sight of him, pristine, fresh, and on his way out of the door. He'd smiled at her broadly and said, 'Good morning, Lydia! At last I see you! I was beginning to think that you had moved out!'

'Oh, no!' she'd replied, over-brightly. 'Just here. Just, you know, *hanging* around. Working. That kind of thing. Everything OK?'

'Yes,' he replied, simply, 'yes. Everything is OK. I will see you later. OK?'

'OK!' she'd babbled.

She was constantly on edge.

The edginess was compounded that moment by a gentle knock at her door. She jumped.

'Lydia,' came a low, male whisper, 'it's me. Can I come in?'

She quickly tucked her ugly feet away beneath her office chair and picked up a sheaf of paperwork. 'Yes!' she said, in that strangely high-pitched voice. 'Come in!'

And there he stood, in a simple t-shirt and distinctly heterosexual jeans, his hair messed and whorled like the coat of a guinea pig and his bare feet smooth and tanned.

'Hi,' he said.

'Oh. Hi.'

'Is this a good time?'

She looked at her desk, somewhat pointlessly, and then back at Bendiks, shrugged and said, 'Yes. It's fine.'

'Good,' he said. 'Is it OK for me to come in?'

'Er . . .' She glanced around her office again, searching for errant items of discarded underwear or rotten food or bunched up gym socks or anything that could in any way be construed as an indication of sluttishness or freakishness. Finding none, she returned her gaze to Bendiks' and said, 'Yeah, sure, come in.'

He sat immediately on the leather chair in the corner and pulled his feet up on to the seat. She looked at them momentarily and tried not to allow any strange noises of longing or desire to escape from between her lips. 'So,' he began, running his hands up and down the arms of the chair in a way that seemed designed deliberately to stoke the coals of her imagination, 'I just wanted to say hello. I've hardly seen you. And it feels a bit strange, to be living here in your house and never to see your face.'

'Yes,' she agreed, 'I know. It's just, well, I suppose I

don't really get out much. What with work and the fact that Juliette does all my shopping and . . .' She drifted off as she ran out of normal-sounding reasons for rarely leaving her house and started to run up against the weird ones, like the fact that she had no friends and no family and no hobbies and no interests.

'Oh,' he smiled and folded his arms across his chest, 'good. Because I was starting to think you were trying to avoid me.'

'Oh, no. No no no no. Not at all. I'm always like this. Honestly. Just a little hermit. Locked away in my office. You know. It's nothing personal, I promise you.'

'Good.' He smiled again and then leaned forward and appraised her so frankly with his dark brown eyes that she felt herself blush. 'Because I am so grateful to you for everything, and I would hate it if I was making you feel uncomfortable by being here.'

'You're not! Really! It's good having you here.'

He looked at her quizzically, clearly still not entirely convinced. 'Well,' he said, rubbing his chin and smiling at her, 'that is OK then. But you, you are a very hard woman to read. It is impossible to know what you are thinking.'

Lydia smiled, partly with relief. It was a blessing, she felt, that Bendiks could not see what she was thinking as for most of the time when she was in his company she was thinking about him lying on top of her.

'So,' he said, rearranging his feet, 'how are you? How is everything going?'

'Oh, fine. Not bad. I'm, er . . .' she smiled at him apologetically almost, as if she was about to break some bad news '. . . I'm seeing my brother this afternoon!'

'No way!'

'Yes! He got in touch! Last week! And we're meeting for a drink this afternoon.'

'Oh my God, but that . . . that is amazing. You must feel so happy.'

Lydia considered his choice of words for a while. It had not occurred to her to feel happy. She had felt only fear mixed with mild excitement. Her brother's name was Dean. He'd written her a very sweet e-mail the week before. Sweet, but not exactly inspiring. She hadn't really known what to expect. It was probably unrealistic of her to imagine that these people should be particularly interesting just because they were her genetic siblings. But then again, she reasoned, a lot of people weren't that expressive with words. Maybe when she met him she would be pleasantly surprised. She did hope so.

'So,' said Bendiks, 'what time are you leaving?'

She looked at the clock on her computer screen. 'In about forty-five minutes,' she replied.

'Oh, my goodness,' he said, leaping to his feet. 'Then I must leave you alone, to get ready. To prepare yourself.'

'Oh, no, honestly. You don't have to . . .'

'Well, actually, I am going out now too,' he said, 'to meet a client. I might just jump in and out of the shower before I go. But, listen, wow, good luck for this afternoon. I'll be thinking of you. And I'm going to send you a text message. What time are you meeting him?'

'Five-thirty.'

'Good. Then I am going to text you at exactly five-forty-five. If you do not like this boy, if you want to come home, just tell him that it's an emergency and you have to go, OK? But if you're happy, please reply, so that I know.'

Lydia smiled. She was touched by his instinctive desire to protect her. 'Thank you, Bendiks,' she said, 'that's really sweet. And I will, I promise.'

'How are you feeling?'

'Sick,' she replied.

He smiled. 'I'm not surprised. I am feeling sick too and it is not even me who's going to meet his brand new brother.' He smiled and then he put his hands in his pockets and turned to leave. 'Good luck, Lydia,' he said, 'this is an amazing thing that is about to happen to you.'

Then he was gone and Lydia slowly unfurled her feet from beneath her office chair and exhaled. She waited in suspended motion until she heard him leave his bedroom ten minutes later and then the front door bang closed behind him and then she ran down a flight of stairs and into her bedroom to watch him from the window. He had on a denim jacket (gay?) and white trainers (more gay?) and carried his gym bag over his shoulder. He was talking to someone on his mobile phone and he was laughing. He turned the corner and Lydia let herself flop down backwards on to her bed.

She ate a peanut butter sandwich just in case it turned out to be the sort of night that required a lined stomach, and then she showered and changed and brushed her teeth and tried to ignore the distorted feel of her stomach and the knot in her bowels. She'd already decided what to wear. Jeans. Just ordinary blue jeans. And a billowy long-sleeved black jersey top and wedge-heeled sandals. She combed out her dark hair and she applied a little mascara and a little lip gloss and she stared at her face in the mirror for a little too long, until it looked warped and wrong and not at all the sort of face to be showing to a twenty-one-year-old man who just happened to be your brother. The edges of her world became more and more vague as she went through these ordinary machinations. She felt normality drifting away from her, like a dissembling dream. But it did not occur to her for a moment that she would not go. She was going. That was about the only thing that felt real.

At 4.50 she left her house and walked to the tube station. She was meeting Dean at a bar in the London Bridge Hotel, a pleasingly bland-looking place she'd uncovered on the internet on being informed that this was where his suburban train brought him. Dean lived in Deptford. As a relative newcomer to London, Lydia wasn't entirely sure where exactly Deptford was but felt it had a slightly loutish ring to it. Just the sound of the word as compared, for example, to a word like Chelsea, put her in mind of tower blocks and juddering overhead rail lines.

She arrived at the Borough Bar at exactly 5.30 and scoured the room. Dean had been unable to e-mail her a photograph of himself as apparently he didn't own a digital camera and his phone didn't have a camera on it, but had described himself as tallish and slim with short brown hair. Lydia deduced that there was no one in the room who could conceivably be him so she headed for the bar and ordered herself a large gin and tonic. She took the drink to a small round table positioned close to a window so that she could scan the street for his arrival and, as she rested the tumbler on the table and was about to sit down, she saw him.

He looked like an overgrown lemur, thin and lean with a face full of eyes. He scanned the room with those big, scared eyes, hands at the ends of long arms stuffed into the pockets of a thin cotton jacket, long legs draped in over-large denim, a small silver stud in his left earlobe, big feet in blue trainers, and a carrier bag hooped into the crook of his arm. He had the face of a 1960s rock star, all lips and eyes and cheeks and skull, and his body was so spare it might easily have been made of nothing more than bone and muscle. He looked malnourished and shrunken but, beyond the cheap clothes and downtrodden demeanour, he was undeniably and ethereally beautiful.

He spotted her and smiled. He took a hand from his pocket and raised it to her in a kind of awkward salute. She raised hers to him and echoed his smile.

'Dean,' she said as he approached. She got to her feet and offered him her hand to shake, as though he were a student hoping for work experience rather than her own flesh and blood.

'Nice to meet you,' he said.

His hand was clammy and his face was set with fear.

He's more nervous than I am, she thought.

But she saw his features soften as he looked at her. 'You've got my nose,' he said, and she could hear a hint of childish delight in his voice. 'Look.' He turned to the side to show her his profile. 'Don't you think? It's the same?'

It was.

She turned sideways too and he examined her nose and smiled.

'Yeah,' he smiled, 'yeah. I was kind of hoping there'd be something, you know, something the same. Just to make me feel like this wasn't just . . .'

'Meeting a total stranger?' she offered.

'Yeah.' He smiled and sat down.

'Let me get you a drink,' Lydia said. 'What would you like?'

'Oh, right, yeah. What's that you're drinking?' He pointed at her glass.

'Gin and tonic,' she replied.

'Yeah. I'll try one of those. Thank you.'

Lydia brought the drink back to the table and Dean took it from her with two outstretched hands like a toddler reaching for a cup of juice.

She watched him peel off his thin jacket to reveal a shirt. Worn 'specially, she couldn't help thinking, to impress her.

He lifted the glass to his lips and took a sip. He grimaced. She lifted her glass then and held it aloft. 'A toast?' she suggested.

'Yeah, why not?'

'To us.'

'To us,' he concurred, and they knocked their glasses together. Matching drinks, matching noses.

'Couldn't believe it when I found you on there,' he said. 'I have to be honest with you and say that I was pretty wasted when I signed up.'

'Me too.' Lydia smiled.

'What, really?'

'Well, actually, no. I was wasted the first time I went to sign up, but I didn't go through with it then.'

He nodded his understanding. 'I don't even remember doing it.'

'Wow.'

'Yeah, I know. Luckily the person I was with when I did it remembered.'

'Pretty impressive that you could remember all that detail, though.'

He tapped his head with his index finger. 'It's all up there. Donor number. Clinic. Address of the clinic. It's been sitting in there for three years.'

'That's when you found out?'

'Yeah. When I was eighteen. My mum told me. What about you?'

'Three months ago.'

'No way?' His thick eyebrows pressed together. 'That late, huh?'

'Yes. Been in a state of ignorant bliss up until then.'

'So what . . .?'

She shrugged, and then appraised him with widened eyes. 'I got an anonymous letter. Well, not even a letter. Just some paperwork. From the clinic. And an article about the Donor Sibling Registry.'

His eyes widened in sympathy. 'Jesus,' he said, 'and you've got no idea who from?'

'Not really. All I know is it was someone in Wales. Someone from home. Which could be absolutely anyone, I suppose. My mum and dad are both dead and I've totally lost touch with all my relatives so,' she shrugged, 'I don't suppose I'll ever find out who it was. But I have my suspicions.'

'Oh, yeah?'

'Yes, my uncle Rod. My dad's brother. He was very close to my mum and dad. If anyone had known about this it would have been him.'

'And your dad? Did he know?'

'I don't know,' she said. 'He never told me he knew, but now I think back on it, he obviously did.'

Dean shook his head slowly from side to side, in disbelief. 'And I thought my life was fucked up.'

Lydia smiled at him. Of course his life was fucked up. You could tell just by looking at him that his life was a stinking mess. But for now his face was sweet and soft and Lydia could tell that he was enjoying her company and that this experience was turning out better than he'd imagined or hoped. She felt the same way too. From the moment he'd turned sideways to show her his nose, she'd felt fine about everything. And the longer she looked at him, the more she shared with him, the more relaxed and comfortable she felt, not just about this meeting, but about herself. Dean was her, ten years ago; too thin, badly dressed, hunched and apologetic for her existence. And then she felt it, *plunk*, another piece of the jigsaw falling into place. An overwhelming sensation enveloped her, took the breath from her. It was new and it was remarkable and it was something she'd waited all her life to feel.

She felt *maternal*.

Here it was finally, for the first time since her dog had died, a sense of love and affection. She wanted to touch this boy. She wanted to hug him. She wanted to hold him to her bosom and keep him safe.

She finished her gin and tonic and Dean finished his and then he went to get them some more. She watched him at the bar. He was a pathetic specimen. Pathetic and beautiful. She smiled fondly at his back. *Her brother*. Her baby brother.

He put down another gin and tonic in front of Lydia and a pint for himself. She wouldn't let him buy another round. He was clearly penniless. She remembered only too well the sense of painful extraction she'd felt paying for drinks in pubs when she had no money. She remembered the days of pulling out a solitary £10 note from a hole in the wall and squeezing every last drop out of overdrafts and borrowing crumpled fivers from friends. She remembered it all as though it were yesterday. She had, after all, been poor for a lot longer than she had been wealthy.

'So, what made you decide to go through with it?' she

asked him. 'I mean, I know you signed up when you were drunk, but afterwards, when you had to get tested and stuff. What was your motivation?'

She saw something flash through his eyes. It looked like pain.

'Oh, God,' he said, smiling apologetically. 'I don't know where to start. It's been . . . Fuck.' She watched him struggle to find some words to use. 'Three months ago I was living with my girlfriend and we were about to have a baby together. Then she went into labour early and started losing blood and next thing I know, she's, well, she's dead.' He shrugged and smiled at her pitifully.

Lydia felt her gut twist itself into a knot. 'What about the baby?' she whispered.

'Baby's fine,' he said. 'Baby's good. She was in hospital for ten weeks, you know, until her due date.'

'And where is she now?'

'With my girlfriend's mum. Yeah.' He tapped the side of his pint glass with blunt fingertips.

Lydia was speechless. 'God,' she said, eventually. 'That is . . . I don't even know how you must be feeling. I mean, you're *so young*.'

'Yeah, well,' he said, 'shit happens. Happens to everyone. Maybe I just got my shit out the way early. And that's part of what this is about.' He gestured to Lydia and then to himself. 'Everything's *gone*, you know? My flat. My girlfriend. My job. My future. Even my mum, a bit. She's getting used to me not being around, doing her own thing, dating and stuff. It's all going or gone and I think I just wanted to start something, you know? And the minute I saw those people . . . you, and the other girl, the young one . . . it, I don't know, it felt like *the next thing*? Not to say I wasn't totally crapping myself about this. I haven't eaten since yesterday, you know? I just kept thinking . . .' He paused. 'I was really scared you'd be . . .'

'What? A cow?'

He laughed. 'No, not a cow. Just thought you might be a bit . . . *aloof* ? Had this image of you. In pearls and stuff.'

Lydia laughed out loud. 'Never worn pearls in my life!' she said.

'Yeah, well.' He smiled, 'I can see that now.'

Lydia's phone made a twittering sound and she pulled it out of her handbag, smiling apologetically at Dean. It was a text, from Bendiks, the escape text he'd promised her. *All OK?* it read. She smiled again and typed the simple response: *Very OK*. She switched off her phone and slipped it back inside her bag. 'So,' she said, turning her attention back to Dean, 'your baby, who does she look like?'

He smiled, understanding her need to ask the question. 'She looks like me.'

'And who do you look like?'

He paused, seemed about to say something, then stopped. He stared down at his feet and then he looked up again. He appraised her, uncertainly, and then he said: 'I look like you.'

Lydia fed her brother that night. She bought him a pie at the bar and watched him eat it with some satisfaction as she herself fiddled with a wooden board piled with unhappy slices of salami, cracked olives, coiled anchovies and a cluster of punch-bag-shaped caper-berries. She put her card behind the bar and, when it was time to settle the bill, she did it surreptitiously, gently dismissing Dean's objections.

It was nine o'clock when they left the hotel and it felt like they had covered only a small fraction of a percent of the things they wanted to talk to each other about; that if their relationship was a slice of cake, their time together so far had been a mere crumb.

Lydia had considered the idea of inviting Dean back to her house but lost her nerve on the cusp of saying it. He was her brother, that had been proved scientifically, anecdotally and officially. They had the same nose. But still, she reasoned with herself, he was a stranger.

So they parted with a promise on both sides that they would meet up again, very, very soon.

'Maybe that other one will be in touch by then,' Dean said, hopefully.

'The girl, you mean?' asked Lydia.

'Yeah. The young one. Then all three of us could meet up.'

Lydia smiled. She couldn't quite imagine it. She felt that she and Dean had formed a kind of exclusive club of two tonight. It seemed less likely than ever that there was another member, let alone another two.

'I wonder who the fourth is?' she asked.

'Yeah.' Dean touched his chin and pondered the

concept. 'The mysterious fourth. The other boy. Maybe he doesn't know?'

'I guess so,' she agreed. 'Or maybe he doesn't want to know?'

Dean shrugged.

They were outside London Bridge station. It was getting dark. People passed either side of them, seething like rapids, homeward bound. It was time to say goodbye. They smiled awkwardly at each other. They'd drunk enough to lose their initial reserve, so they pulled together in an embrace. Lydia tried her hardest to give her body a more yielding form. She was not designed to be hugged and she didn't want to give her brother the sense that she was resisting him. But as they came together she felt it coming from him too, the strange stiffness of a person uncomfortable with physical affection. They came together like two coat stands, digging into each other with sharp elbows and stiff arms. But inside the gauche embrace there was real affection, and as they separated they smiled at each other warmly and with emotion.

'I've really, really loved meeting you,' said Lydia.

'Likewise,' said Dean.

'Next week?' said Lydia.

Dean shrugged again. 'Yeah,' he said, 'any time. I'm not exactly busy, you know . . .'

'Me neither,' said Lydia.

They laughed and then touched each other's arms and Dean turned away first. It seemed that should be his role as the youngest. And her role as the eldest was to watch him leave, cover his back, to see him safely into the mael-strom of the commuter station.

Lydia stood for a moment after he'd gone. She had one hand in the pocket of her jeans, the other holding the strap of her handbag. As the sun fell behind the hori-zon, leaving its lingering residue of inky blues across the city, the temperature fell and Lydia felt the late-evening breeze chill her skin. She unfurled her heavy scarf and covered her shoulders and her arms with it, then hitched her bag closer to her body and stepped out on to the street, her eyes peeled for the reassuring glow of a vacant taxi.

Lydia's house greeted her like an old friend as she approached it thirty minutes later. After the strangeness of the evening, it looked safe and familiar. She felt her body relaxing as she walked up the front path towards the front door. She pictured herself in less than a minute, collecting a glass of water, kicking off her shoes, padding up to bed, peeling off her clothes, laying down her head, closing her eyes, pondering the evening, letting it all sink in while making new sense of her life. But as she turned the corner into the kitchen she saw that Bendiks was sitting at the table there, wearing a white t-shirt and combat shorts. He had lit a candle and was reading a paperback which was held in the crook of one knee, and when he heard her walking in he looked up slowly and smiled. 'You're back,' he said, somewhat unnecessarily.

Lydia smiled at him uncertainly. 'I am,' she replied.

'I stayed up,' he said, again somewhat unnecessarily.

'Yes,' said Lydia, unhooking her handbag from her shoulder. 'I can see.'

Bendiks closed his paperback and uncrossed his legs. He looked at her warmly. 'I know it is silly,' he began, 'but, I don't know, I was *worried* about you. I know you sent me that message but that was a long time ago. And I just wanted to . . . well, make sure you got home all right. And that you were feeling OK. Are you,' he continued, 'are you feeling OK?'

Lydia put down her handbag and smiled a smile of relief. 'Yes,' she said. 'I'm feeling absolutely OK.'

Bendiks' smile also softened and he leaned across the table towards her. 'So,' he said, 'how was it? How did it go? Unless you'd rather not talk about it?'

'No.' Lydia sat down and ran her hands across the smooth table top. 'No. I do want to talk about it. I'm just not sure what to say.'

'What was he like? Was he nice?'

Lydia looked at Bendiks' expression of concern and felt a rush of pleasure soar through her. *How sweet*, she thought, *how very sweet*. 'He was,' she said. 'He was really nice. Quite shy. Quite quiet.'

'Ah,' Bendiks laughed and leaned back again against his chair, 'just like you then!'

'Well, yes, I suppose,' she said. 'He was very like me. Very like me when I was his age. But lovely. Really lovely.'

Bendiks eyed her thoughtfully, almost dreamily. 'Wow,'

he sighed. 'This is amazing! You know that, don't you? What is happening to you, it's amazing.'

Lydia smiled. 'Yeah,' she said. 'I know. It feels like a dream.'

'It *is* like a dream. It is like an amazing dream. And now, you still have two more to meet. The other brother and the sister.'

Lydia rubbed her elbows and shrugged. 'Doesn't seem quite real,' she said. And it didn't. The sister seemed less real than ever in the light of her meeting with Dean.

Bendiks smiled at her and then got to his feet. 'Can I get you anything?' he said. 'A cup of coffee? Maybe a herbal tea?'

'No, thanks, I'm fine. I think I'd better get to bed actually. I'm feeling a bit tired.'

'Something stronger?' he suggested playfully. 'A schnapps, maybe? Come on, we could take them out on to the terrace, it's not too cold out.'

Lydia considered the offer and then Bendiks' motivation. He was staring at her not quite beseechingly, but certainly with some depth of intent. She wondered why he wanted to drink schnapps with her on the terrace and almost asked him, almost said: But why? Why would you? She cast her gaze around pathetically, looking for a suitable response. Part of her wanted nothing more than to sit on the terrace with the object of her desire and for them to get slightly drunk together. Another part wanted to grab her handbag and scamper upstairs to her room, closing the door firmly behind her.

'Er, OK then,' she said, somewhat involuntarily. 'Yes, why not?'

He beamed at her and clapped his hands together. 'Good,' he said, 'great. I will be back in a minute.' She watched him through the kitchen door, taking the stairs to his room two at a time. She watched the muscles in his thighs straighten and harden with each flex and felt a lurch in her stomach at the possibility that lay ahead of her; that she might one day get to feel those thigh muscles straining against hers. She gulped and turned away from the door, staring through the blackness of the kitchen window and trying to talk herself down from a state of heightened nerves. When she heard him returning she breathed in deeply and greeted him with a fulsome smile. He was clutching a tall, thin bottle of clear liquid. She fetched two shot glasses and followed him out on to the terrace.

Lydia sat down first, and Bendiks chose not the seat opposite but the one right next to her so that his body was only a few inches apart from hers. He poured the schnapps into the shot glasses and told her something about its provenance but Lydia was not listening. She was instead running a scenario through her mind, in which she would open her mouth and say, 'Bendiks, are you gay?' And he would look at her askance and say, 'No! Of course I'm not!' And then he would prove it by bending her backwards over the arm of the sofa and kissing her neck urgently whilst simultaneously running his hand up and down her bare thigh. She shook it from her head as she sensed that he was waiting for her to answer a question, and said, 'Sorry? What?'

He raised his eyebrows at her and laughed. 'Nothing,' he said, 'nothing. I can see you are miles away. And it is perfectly understandable, given the evening you've just had.'

She smiled at him wanly. 'Well, yes,' she said, grateful for his misinterpretation of her silence. 'It has been quite a night.'

'Well,' he said, handing her her glass and picking up his own. 'I propose a toast. To your brothers. To your sister. And of course to you: the amazing Lydia.'

'Ha!' she snorted. 'Right!' She hadn't meant it to sound so disingenuous. She genuinely did not know why anyone would refer to her as amazing. But he swooped on her self-deprecation anyway and quickly shooed it away. 'You *are* amazing. You may not think so, but I can assure you, from my perspective, as an objective onlooker, you are quite remarkable. Seriously, it is rare to meet a woman like you, so independent and clever and sexy and young.'

Sexy. Lydia stared at him. 'Oh, stop it,' she said.

'Why?' replied Bendiks. 'It is just the truth.'

Lydia felt almost nauseous with the density of his compliment. It was as though she had eaten six donuts in a row after years of living on cabbage. Delicious and remarkable, but too much. She smiled at him awkwardly and his expression changed. 'I am really sorry,' he said. 'Have I offended you?' And as he said this his hand moved towards her and caressed the skin of her arm. It was an innocuous gesture, no more than you might make to a stranger you'd brushed past in the street, by way of apology. But as his skin touched hers it was as if every light in the dark house of her body had suddenly been switched on. It was as though electrodes had been wired up to every nerve ending and activated. It was as though she'd been asleep and now she was awake. Wonderfully, terrifyingly awake. She brought in her breath so deeply and so quickly that it was audible. Bendiks looked at her in alarm. 'Are you OK?' he asked, once again bringing his hand down against her skin, this time leaving his hand there, this time caressing her lightly.

'Yes,' she said, quietly, 'I'm fine.'

His hand remained. And so did his gaze.

'You can see it,' he said, 'in your eyes. You can see something . . . *foreign.*'

She blinked at him and laughed.

'Seriously,' he continued, 'in most ways you are so very British. But when I look at you, like this, in there,' he pointed out both of her eyes, 'I can see something different. Something exciting.'

She flinched slightly at the word. She did not want anyone to think she was exciting, because she was not exciting. And anyone thinking that she was would be horribly disappointed.

'I am sorry,' he said, pulling away from her, releasing his grasp from her arm. 'I am embarrassing you. I apologise. I am just . . .' He turned away and searched for words. 'I am just slightly in awe of you. And slightly, well,

I don't know how to put it. I think a lot of you. That is all. Please forgive me.'

She smiled at him. 'Of course I forgive you,' she said. 'There's nothing to forgive. I'm just tired, that's all.'

'Of course you are,' said Bendiks. 'Of course. You said you were tired and I still dragged you out here to drink with me. I just really wanted to spend a few moments with you, because I feel we are constantly like ships passing. And it would be a shame for me to move on from living with you not knowing any more about you than I did before I moved in. But if you'd rather just stick with the passing ships, just tell me. I won't take offence.' He threw her a sweet smile.

She smiled too and said, 'No. I don't want to stick with passing ships. It's lovely having you here. And we should do this sort of thing more often.'

'Good,' said Bendiks, pouring another shot into each glass. 'Good. Then another toast. To you and me. More than just ships. But hopefully also friends . . .'

'Yes,' she said, 'friends.'

And as she said it the luscious, illicit thoughts of legs entwined and lips parted and bodies conjoined slipped from her consciousness and away from her. *Friends*.

She tipped the schnapps down her throat and tried to look like she wanted nothing more.

ROBYN

Robyn stared at the paper pinned to the wall outside her homeroom with a sense of dread and disappointment. She had failed again. This was the third monthly exam in a row she had failed. The work was never-ending, three hours of study a day, plus lectures, tutorials, and more study to take you through the weekend. This weekend just past, she had been expected to read and memorise five chapters of text on physiology from a book so big it had made her hands ache just to hold it. She had got as far as the beginning of chapter two and given up. Her brain, which had always been better than everyone else's, which had always absorbed facts and information without too much effort, was simply not up to the job of retaining all this terminology. And she herself had too many other things preying on her mind to find and practise new ways to learn. She was failing, Robyn Inglis was failing, and she had no idea what to do about it.

She unpinned the paper from the cork board and bunched it up inside her shoulder bag.

*

Robyn lifted the lid of the shiny silver bin in Jack's kitchen – no, not Jack's kitchen, *her* kitchen, she had to keep reminding herself – and recoiled. It was piled to the very rim, mountains of rancid rubbish, squashed down like a garbage Dauphinoise, slivers of paper and card forced down the sides, congealed teabags jammed into crevices, scrapings of flabby old cereal coating everything. It was a bin that should have been emptied at least twelve if not twenty-four hours earlier. Jack had left early this morning, 9.30, for a breakfast meeting with his agent at some trendy members' club that Robyn felt she was supposed to have heard of but hadn't. He was not due back until after lunchtime. Which meant that Robyn either had to sit in the flat with this rancid overflowing bin, or empty it herself.

Robyn had never emptied a bin in her life.

Which was not to say that she was unaware of bins or of the fact that they required emptying from time to time. She had watched her mother a hundred times, a thousand times, tear off the slinky black rectangle, divide it with her fingertips, whip it across the room, engorge it with air and then feed it effortlessly into the box that lived beneath the sink. She'd watched her pull a bulging bag from the container under the sink, sometimes it seemed with some effort, deftly manipulate the rim into a tight knot and then take it away. Somewhere. Robyn wasn't entirely sure where.

Her parents had never asked her to empty a bin.

She studied this bin. It was twice the size of the one in her parents' house.

She pulled out a few drawers, her eyes searching for a black cylinder. She went to the window to survey the front of the house for signs of places to put large bags of rubbish. She began to feel vaguely panicky. She should be able to do this. She was nearly nineteen years old. She was studying medicine. She should be able to empty a bin. She failed to find a bin bag but found a large carrier bag that seemed as though it would suffice. She took the top off the bin and then she started to tug at the edges of the bin bag.

'Urgh, yuck,' she hissed as her fingers brushed against soggy cereal.

She pulled again and the bag lifted a few inches. She pulled it halfway to the top of the cylinder and then let it fall. It appeared to be full of concrete and lead. She bunched up the corners and tried again, and finally, with some effort, she yanked it free of its container. As she did so the bag bulged ominously and then exploded at her feet. Jack's waxed floorboards were awash with shavings and trimmings and scrapings and skins. A murky liquid trickled darkly from the mulch and dribbled away between the floorboards. The smell was acrid and Robyn put her hand across her mouth.

She was tempted then to pick up her handbag, leave through the front door and not come back until Jack was home. But instead she cried for five minutes and then found a pair of rather large yellow plastic gloves in a cupboard beneath the kitchen sink. She pulled them on, still sobbing, and proceeded to scrape the obnoxious compost from the floor and into the large carrier bag. She knew she was being pathetic. She knew there were barefoot children in India picking through other people's rubbish for twelve hours a day in intense heat. She knew that she was spoiled and silly. But everything just seemed so hard these days.

On the tube on the way home from college last night the train had stopped for slightly too long in a tunnel and the carriage had quickly heated up to the point of discomfort and Robyn had felt her heart quicken unpleasantly beneath her ribs. The driver had made an announcement across the Tannoy to the effect that they were stuck and he had no idea when they would be moving again. She'd looked around the carriage at the strangers who surrounded her. She'd spied an empty seat a few feet away and wondered about the logistics of getting from where she was standing to there without drawing too much attention to herself. Her heart had quickened further until she was certain the man standing next to her would be able to hear it in her chest. Her peripheral vision began to cloud over and she saw herself collapsing against the side of the carriage; she envisaged being taken to a waiting ambulance, wrapped in a grey blanket, everyone staring at her. She saw all this and her heart beat faster and faster until she felt she was about to scream out for help when finally the train hissed itself back to life and she felt the carriage jerk forward and then they were moving again and her heart slowed down and she was safe. But for those few moments she had felt what it must be to lose your mind, to have no control over yourself. For those few moments she had lost sight of herself completely.

She had no idea why she should be feeling so disjointed. Here she was, back in the heart of her very own romantic novel. Here she was in her Holloway flat with her novelist boyfriend and her perfect face and perfect body and perfect life. She was Robyn Inglis, the luckiest girl in the world. But her world felt like that tube train yesterday: stuck in a tunnel. She could not seem to move on from the dark place she'd been in when she'd thought that Jack was her brother. She felt nervy and unhappy and strange. The only time she was happy was when Jack was here and it was just the two of them. The rest of the time she was lost.

She took the heavy bin bag and she bounced it down the staircase outside their flat, bang bang bang against each step. She pulled it down the garden path and found to her surprise two large green bins, just slightly shorter than she was, parked side by side near the garden gate. They were painted with the number of the house. She lifted the lid cautiously and was assailed by yet another rich and unhappy stench. She attempted to launch the bag from the pavement to the mouth of the tall bin, but failed. A middle-aged man passed the house on a bike. He slowed down and eyed her curiously and for a moment she thought he was going to stop and offer to help her. But he didn't. He cycled on. Robyn watched him disappearing down the street and wanted to hurl the rubbish bag after him. She tried three further times to heft the bag into the bin, but eventually gave up and left it there on the pavement.

When she returned to the flat she considered the possibility of doing some coursework, catching up with herself, but decided instead to return to bed. The sheets were still tepid from her and Jack's bodies and the bed was flamboyantly unmade. She remembered waking up this morning, she remembered the feeling of contentment on seeing the nape of Jack's neck and then the feeling of disquiet and vague panic when he'd reminded her that he was out for the morning. She remembered how her day had broken in half at that very moment.

She lay with her head against Jack's pillow and she inhaled his smell. And then she cried again.

What had she become? She hated this new version of herself. She'd turned into exactly the sort of person she despised; needy, clingy, hopeless. She could not empty bins. She could not travel alone. She could not function without her boyfriend. Every time he walked out of the room she collapsed. Only the smell of his pillow could rouse her momentarily from her misery. She was pathetic.

She cried herself into a rather fractious slumber. A dream unfurled itself inside her sleep, a dream of her sisters, their gaunt faces in their final days, their ravaged bodies inside the pretty, trendy dresses her mother insisted on buying for them. And then she dreamed of a boy. He was pushing one of her sisters in her wheelchair. He was smiling. And whistling. He stopped when he saw her and said, 'Hop on,' and she did, on to her sister's lap. Except it wasn't her real sister any more. It was another woman, taller than her, with long legs and long hair. She was aware of the contact between them and she felt the woman's arms embrace her. She could hear the boy whistling, and saw that they were approaching a pair of doors in front of her. There was a sign on one of them but she couldn't read it. She knew that if she wanted to get away from this whistling boy and this long-legged woman she would need to jump off the wheelchair before they reached the doors, but then she found herself relaxing, leaning back into the woman's embrace, being wheeled slowly towards the doors. She clasped the woman's hand in hers and thought that she smelled nice, she smelled like Jack. The doors opened and then Robyn was awake.

Her phone was ringing.

She sat forward and swung her legs from the side of the bed so fast that she felt her head spin.

'Yes,' she whispered into the phone.

'Hello, love.' It was her mum. 'Are you OK?'

Robyn relaxed. 'Yes,' she said, 'I'm fine. I just had a strange dream.'

'You were asleep? But it's nearly eleven.'

'I know. I know. I've been up and everything. I just, I don't know, I was tired. I didn't sleep well. I haven't been sleeping well.'

'Are you sure you're OK?'

'Yes. Honestly. I'm just . . .' she moved her phone to her other ear. 'I don't know. Everything's a bit . . .'

'Are you alone?'

'Yes. Jack's at a meeting.'

'Do you want me to come over?'

Robyn paused. She wanted to say yes. But then Jack was due back in an hour anyway. She sighed. 'No, I'm fine. Honestly.'

'Something just arrived for you, Recorded. I signed for it. Do you want me to find out what it is?'

'OK,' she yawned.

'Oh,' her mother said. 'I think I know what it is. It's one of those kits, you know, a DNA kit. It's for your DNA test.' She sounded excited. 'What do you want me to do with it?'

Robyn considered the question. She'd filled in the form two weeks ago and ticked the box about being willing to undergo a DNA test. She'd only done it for her mum. 'What harm can it do?' she'd said. 'You still don't need to make contact with anyone. But at least you'll know who they are.'

Robyn imagined the box in her mother's hand. And then she thought about her dream: the happy boy pushing the wheelchair, the cuddly woman with the long arms, the doors leading to a mysterious place. She thought about how the dream had made her feel; uncomfortable at first, and then happy as she allowed herself to get close to the woman and to let the boy push her to a different place. It was one of those dreams that felt like more than a dream; that felt like a signpost. She was lost and the boy in the dream seemed to be showing her where to go. She felt something like an invisible rope bridge being thrown then from her consciousness to the box in her mother's hand. That was where the answer lay.

'Come over,' she found herself saying, somewhat breathlessly. 'Come over now. Bring it with you.'

'Are you sure?'

'Yes. I want to do it. I want to meet them.'

'I'm on my way,' said her mother. 'I'll be there in an hour.'

DEAN

Dean emerged into the brightness of a crisp May afternoon from St John's Wood tube station. When he'd left Deptford it had been overcast and looking like rain. Maybe this was what the weather was always like in St John's Wood, he considered. He followed a rough map he'd drawn on the back of his hand to a short wide road opposite Lord's cricket ground. Each house was set back discreetly from the road, some behind large electric gates, some behind neat box hedges. The houses were old, Victorian in scale and design, but with the scrubbed, gleaming look of new-builds. And they were gigantic. Dean had never seen so many large houses in a row. In his part of town, houses like this stood alone, usually abutted by squat shops or cheap apartment blocks. He walked slowly, taking in the ambience, the feel of another world. But then he saw a man in a window, watching him suspiciously, and he picked up his pace.

He found Lydia's house at the furthest end of the road. It was as wide as four buses and the colour of ground bones. The windows were pasted over with opaque film so that you could not see inside from the street. The front garden was spare, planted with black tulips and spiky plants, the ground in between covered over in grey stone chips. Hard concrete steps led to a fat grey door fitted with modernist furniture and the number twenty-seven was picked out in the fanlight above in more opaque film.

Dean stood on the pavement for a moment with his hands in the pockets of his jeans and appraised the house. His jaw fell open without him realising. The house was astounding. The house was nothing short of a miracle. He stepped gingerly on to the footpath which was lined on either side with tiny inset halogen lights. Within seconds of his pressing a bell connected to a small TV, Lydia's face appeared on the screen. 'Come in!' she said. He pushed open the door and there in front of him was a small Asian woman wearing an apron. She looked at him in horror.

'What you want?' she bellowed.

'I'm, er . . .'

'He's here to see me,' said Lydia, descending a wide set of stairs carpeted with vertical stripes in beige and brown.

The small Asian woman looked at Lydia as if she had lost her mind and then back at Dean. 'Are you sure?' she asked.

Lydia smiled. 'Positive, thank you, Juliette. This is my brother.'

Juliette's face softened then and she unleashed a wide smile. 'Ah,' she said, nodding enthusiastically. 'Your brother!' She beamed at Lydia and then she approached Dean with her arms outstretched. She took both his hands in hers and shook them up and down. 'I did not know you had a brother! So nice to meet you. So nice to meet you! Yes. Yes. I can see it now.' She pointed at his face and then at her own. 'I can see that he is your brother.' She turned to Lydia and wagged her finger. 'You did not tell me you had a brother,' she chastised.

Lydia smiled apologetically at the Asian woman but did not say that until six weeks ago she did not know she had a brother either. Dean and Lydia smiled at each other conspiratorially and then Lydia showed him to an incredible room which was like a glass brick stuck on to the back wall of the house. There was nothing much in it, just a huge white leather sofa, a low table and a palm tree. The glass box framed a wide, ornate garden full of puffball trees and square furniture and what appeared, from this distance, at least, to be an actual kitchen. Somewhere in the distance Dean could make out the form of a man in a scruffy polo shirt doing something to the leaves of a small drooping tree.

Beyond the other end of the square box, looking back inside the house, Dean could see a black lacquer dining table around which stood twelve clear Perspex dining chairs. In the middle of the table was a turquoise bowl filled with grass. A vast chrome lightshade hung above the table, and the walls were painted a dark charcoal grey, including all the cornicing and skirting.

'Amazing house,' he said, lowering himself on to the startlingly white sofa.

'Yes,' Lydia replied, dreamily. 'It is a bit. Not my work,

though. It was like this when I bought it. All I did was go out and buy some soulless furniture to fill it with.'

'No,' he said, 'I like it. It's minimal, isn't it?'

'Totally. Too minimal. But then I don't actually spend any time down here. I'm always in my office. Or in my bedroom. All this is just . . .' she spread her arms out '. . . for show.'

'And what's the deal with her?' Dean gestured towards the kitchen at the other side of the house.

'Juliette?'

He nodded.

'My, er, housekeeper.'

'No way!'

'Yes. Indeed. I have a housekeeper. I know. It's nuts. I never thought I'd have a housekeeper.'

'Or a gardener?' He pointed into the garden.

'Well, yes, though he's not staff. I mean, he just comes once a week. For a few hours. Whereas Juliette's here all day every day.'

Juliette appeared in the doorway at that moment and smiled fondly at Lydia and Dean. 'Can I get you anything?'

'No, thanks, Juliette, it's fine. We're not here for long. We're going out in a minute.'

'OK, OK. I will bring you crisps. And mineral water. One minute.'

They both watched her leave and then laughed.

'Well, you know, I never had a mother, so I suppose I feel she's like a gift to myself, in a way, to make up for it.' Lydia laughed again and Dean smiled at her.

'So what . . . what happened to your mum?' He'd wanted to ask her that night they'd met up in London Bridge but hadn't liked to. It had felt a bit soon to be asking her about things like that. But this was their third meeting and they'd been e-mailing and texting too and now he thought she might accept the question.

Her smile didn't waver. 'Depends who you ask,' she said, pulling her legs up beneath her and stroking her kneecaps with the palms of her hands. 'According to my dad, she killed herself; according to other members of the family, he pushed her off our balcony. Either way she died on the concrete outside our flats.'

Dean winced. 'How old were you?'

'Three. I don't really remember her at all.'

'And what do you think happened?'

Lydia shrugged. 'No idea. I think they took my dad in for questioning. No one ever got arrested. No one was ever charged with anything. And after that my whole family just imploded. No one would talk to anyone. And Uncle Rod just kind of disappeared.'

'The guy you think sent you the anonymous letter?'

'Yes. That's the one. I didn't see him again until my dad's funeral, when I was eighteen. But he didn't stay. I just saw him leaving. So yes, basically, I have no idea what happened to my mother . . . whether she jumped, whether she was pushed. And if she jumped, I don't know why she jumped. And if she was pushed, why my dad would have done that. And I've found it easier over the years not to ask myself too many questions about it. I decided a long time ago just to put the whole thing in a little box and for-get about it.'

Lydia brought her fingertips together and stared at them. Dean watched her from his end of the sofa. He wondered if she was going to cry. But she didn't. Her face had set into a kind of plaster of Paris mask.

Juliette walked into the room bearing a small tray hold-ing a bowl of Twiglets, a bowl of cashew nuts, a bowl of olives and two glasses of sparkling water. She smiled maternally and laid these things down in front of them. Dean saw Lydia shuffle uncomfortably as she watched her. 'Thank you, Juliette,' she said in a strangely bright voice that Dean hadn't heard her use before.

Juliette left the room and Dean turned to Lydia.

'Do you think that's a good idea?' he said.

'What?'

'Your box thing. You know, putting stuff away in it?'

She shrugged and leaned forward to scoop up a hand-ful of cashew nuts. 'No idea,' she said. 'But I don't really know what else I can do. I'm estranged from my family. My dad's dead. And even if I knew, what difference would it make to anything? You know. I'd still be Lydia Pike. I'd still be me. But I'd be me knowing that my dad wasn't just a cruel, cold-hearted, unloving old git, but that he was also a flipping *murderer*.'

'I wonder if you were there?' pondered Dean. 'You know, when it happened?'

She shrugged. 'If I was there, I've blanked it out. Totally. But I think I must have been there, because of my phobia.'

'What phobia?'

'My paint thing. You know, the smell of it. My mum had been painting my bedroom when she fell or got pushed or whatever. She still had paint on her hands. I must have been there because even now, if I smell fresh paint, I kind of freak out. I have to leave. And that was why . . .'

'You invented your special paint.'

'Exactly. Not to get rich. Not for all *this*,' she gestured at her opulent home, 'I never wanted all this. I just wanted to be able to paint my home without giving myself panic attacks.'

Dean helped himself to a fistful of Twiglets. He loved Twiglets. He hadn't had them since he was young. 'You must have been there, then,' he continued, desperate to uncover facts from this vague recollection. 'It makes sense. If you can remember the smell of the paint? If you associate it with her death? You must have been there. You might even have seen it happen.' He was pushing her. He knew he was pushing her, maybe a little too far. He watched her reaction. But her face was still blank. She picked a cashew out of the palm of her hand and popped it into her mouth.

'Have you ever thought about hypnotherapy, or anything?'

She laughed then, but not a laugh of amusement, more a laugh of desperate hopelessness. 'Er, no,' she replied. 'No. I have not. As I say. Past, in box, done.' She wiped salt from her hands and then patted her thighs. 'Come on then, let's go.'

'Where are you taking me?' asked Dean.

'I'm taking you to eat. Lots. I want to fatten you up. I want you to put on at least half a stone tonight. Maybe more.'

Dean looked sadly at the untouched olives in their little glass bowl. He felt guilty leaving them there after that woman had gone to all the trouble of putting them out for him. He looked at his glass of sparkling water. He didn't even like sparkling water but he drank half of it, just to be polite. And then he grabbed another handful of Twiglets and got to his feet.

As they passed the kitchen on their way to the front door, Dean popped his head around the door. 'Goodbye,' he said to Juliette, 'thanks for the snacks.'

Juliette beamed at him. 'You are welcome,' she said. 'You are very welcome indeed.'

Lydia took him to a restaurant called Rotisserie. 'I had a feeling you might like meat,' she said.

The restaurant was brown and dim and snug. They were given a booth, shut off from neighbouring tables at both ends by wooden panels and sheets of etched glass. Dean felt like he was in some kind of dream. A few weeks ago he'd been living in that damp flat with the grey carpet. A few weeks ago he'd been nothing. Just a man of twenty-one without a job or a home or a girlfriend. Now he was Lydia's brother. And Lydia was totally amazing. He adored her. He adored her inscrutable face, the way she kept herself all contained and calm. He adored her sarky smile and her Welsh accent. He adored her house, her success, her housekeeper. He adored her e-mails, all the words perfectly spelled. All the grammar and punctuation just so. He adored the way she looked at him, as though she adored him too. And he adored her for bringing him to this posh restaurant, as if it was a perfectly normal thing for him to be doing on a Wednesday evening. But mainly he adored her because behind all the gloss and the glamour, behind the gym-honed body, the shiny hair, the designer jeans and the minimalist mansion, there was a person, just like him. She was an outsider too. She was a loner. She got him. She totally got him.

When he'd arrived home from their first meeting, his mum had been waiting anxiously for him.

'So,' she'd said, before he was even fully in the room, 'so? What was she like?'

He'd smiled and said, 'She was absolutely fucking perfect.'

He ordered half a chicken and chips and a bottle of lager. Lydia ordered grilled king prawns and salad.

She was looking at him with that look of hers, kind of arsey and cool.

'What's the matter?' he asked.

'Nothing,' she said. 'Just wondering about you.'

'What about me?'

'About what's going to become of you.'

He laughed nervously. 'What do you mean, become of me?'

'You know what I mean. I mean – your baby, Dean.'

He flinched. He'd been expecting her to say it, but still it took him by surprise. There were only two people in his life who talked to him about Isadora. One was Rose, but Dean didn't really hear Rose's voice. It registered like a distant lament to his ears, like an oil tanker sounding its horn miles from shore. The other person was his mother. But his mother had never pushed him to do anything in his life. She'd let him coast through school, not said a word when he'd given up playing football after school even though his coach had said he showed promise. She'd let him drift away from a college course in catering and hospitality and into a van-driving job, and now she was doing nothing to make him take responsibility for his baby daughter. Every now and then she'd say she'd been to visit the baby. She'd show him photos of Isadora on her phone, and she'd say something innocuous like: 'She's ever so sweet, Dean. She's a little dolly.' Dean would glance cursorily at the photo, and grunt. He didn't really look. He didn't want to look. He would discern some hair, a button nose, a pink t-shirt, and, the last time, a smile. 'She's smiling now, Dean. Like a little angel.' But he did not see the whole. If he saw the whole then he would have to let her into him. If he let her into him then she would be there forever, whatever he did, wherever he went, like a scar.

This was the first time that someone who wasn't Sky's mother or his own had referred to Isadora as 'your baby'. Tommy always called her 'the baby'.

'What about her?' he countered, cautiously.

'You know what I mean. She's your baby. You haven't seen her since she was born. What are you going to do about it?' Lydia's voice was measured and even. She sounded kind, not harsh. But still the question upset him and he found himself clenching his fists beneath the table against an oncoming rage. 'I'm not gonna do anything about it,' he said, hating the sound of his own voice as it filled the space between them, hating that he was showing Lydia this other side of himself, this rough, unmannered, childish aspect.

She didn't say anything for a moment, just looked at him with her head tilted slightly to one side.

A waitress brought them two glasses of beer and a basket of bread. He picked up his glass and drank from it nervously.

'You can't do *nothing* about it,' Lydia said eventually. 'Nothing is not an option.'

'Why not?' he said.

'Because she's your child.'

'Yeah, well, life's not that straightforward, is it? I mean, look at us. With our *mysterious* French dad and our sister we haven't met yet and some other brother who doesn't even know we exist and you with no parents and me with a baby with no mother. It's all fucked up, isn't it? The whole fucking thing. What makes me any different? What makes the baby any different?'

'You,' said Lydia, simply. 'You're what makes the baby different.'

He looked at her through slanted eyes. Her answer had

taken his breath away. 'Not in a good way though,' he continued. 'What have I got to offer a baby? No home. No job. No family. No future.'

'That's not true, is it?'

'Of course it's true. I'm a fucking waste of space.' The people in the booth behind theirs eyed their table surreptitiously. Dean lowered his voice. 'You know something,' he said, quietly. 'When I first saw that baby, when they first pulled her out, she looked at me and I could tell, even then, even with her all tiny and scrunched up and blue and covered in blood and stuff, I could tell that she was clever. And when I saw that, I already knew that I couldn't do it. Even then I knew that I wouldn't be good enough for her . . .' He stopped and caught his breath deeply, dragged it into his lungs so hard it hurt. But it wasn't enough. A tear left his right eye and splashed on to the leg of his jeans. He watched it soak into the dark fabric and then rubbed at it with his thumb. It was soon joined by another wet mark, and another. He pulled a napkin from the table and put it to his cheeks.

'Fuck,' he said. 'Fuck. I'm really sorry, I just . . .'

'It's OK,' said Lydia, covering his hand with hers. 'It's totally OK. Let it out.'

'Ha!' he said. 'You're a fine one to talk.'

She blinked and smiled. 'Yeah, I know. I know. The pair of us. But honestly, Dean, you've got nothing to worry about. You've got me now.'

'What do you mean?'

'I mean, whatever happens, with you, with your baby,

whatever you decide to do, I've got your back. It's not just you any more, is it?'

He was about to protest, to say something negative. His mouth was halfway open, full of words of dispute. You don't even know me, he wanted to say, you don't know anything about me. You don't know what it feels like to be nothing. You with your big house and your maid. How can I trust you to be there for me? How can you trust me not to let you down?

'I'm going outside,' he said, 'just for a minute.'

She nodded, and then she smiled and took her hand from his, letting him go. 'OK,' she said, softly.

He found a small turning three shopfronts down from the restaurant. Once away from the streetlights he quickly assembled himself a spliff. He huddled down against a damp wall on his haunches and lit it. He was freaking out. Suddenly and totally. He'd gone from being Mr I've Got a Cool New Sister to a nervous wreck in the space of ten minutes. He felt the tension lift as he pulled the smoke into his body, and he let his head flop back against the wall. He hadn't factored this into the equation, he thought. He hadn't factored in the possibility of meeting someone who would care about him enough to make him do something about the mess that was his life. He hadn't thought he'd meet someone who would love him. And it was there in Lydia's eyes, the same look of defiant intelligence as in his daughter's. And the same look of expectation. Lydia had high hopes for him. In a world where no one had high hopes for him, where no one had ever expected anything from him, it was a difficult concept to accept.

He stared into the jagged red tip of the spliff and he remembered how he'd promised Sky that he'd stop smoking. That he'd finish what he had and then stop buying it. And that would be it. He hadn't meant it for a moment. Not for a second. He'd said it to shut her up. He was always saying things to shut Sky up. Because the thing with Sky was that she was quite stupid. She would talk and talk and talk and it was all just noise because there was nothing substantial behind the noise. Just gas and air and bullshit. He never had to make his mum shut up because she never said anything he didn't want to hear. But it was different with Lydia. He couldn't make her shut up, because everything she said meant something. Because she was worth listening to. She was saying things that he needed to hear. But he did not want to hear them.

A dark-haired couple walked past him then, in their mid-thirties, smartly dressed, laughing uproariously at something. 'You would not do that!' the woman was saying through her laughter. 'Oh, yes, I would!' said the man and the woman laughed even louder and then they both turned and saw Dean crouching down in the shadows and their laughter stopped and the woman grabbed the man's arm and they looked at him nervously. He heard their shoes echoing against the pavement as they hurried on and then he heard them resume their conversation, their shrill laughter rebounding once more around the quiet street, their momentary brush with the dark side over.

Dean finished his spliff and then crushed it roughly against the brick wall. He felt like a small animal. He felt like a rodent, a grimy stray, something to be scooped into a plastic box and removed in a white van, taken somewhere to be put down and then thrown away. He didn't belong here, he didn't have a place in this world. He walked to the window of the restaurant and he saw Lydia leaning back against her chair, staring through the restaurant window, looking for him. Then he saw a waitress appear at the table and ask her something. Lydia shook her head and smiled, and then she nodded and the waitress walked away. He saw the people at the table nearest the window look up from their meal and glance at him, anxiously. He didn't want to go back in there. He didn't want to eat a chicken and drink a beer and pretend that he was someone he wasn't. He wanted to slink away like the rat that he was, back through the sewers and the underground, beneath the black currents of the river and into the safety of his mum's house where he could just continue to exist in his pointless state forever.

He ducked into the nearest shadow and pulled his phone from his jacket pocket. He wrote a text to Lydia. It read: *I'm really sorry. I had to go. Take care. Dean.* He pressed send and then he turned up the collar of his jacket against the quickly descending evening chill and found his way back to St John's Wood tube station as quickly as he could.

MAGGIE

Maggie sat on the bench and watched her daughter push her granddaughter on a swing. Matilda gripped the bar of the swing with her two fat fists and leaned down low, her face staring at the black rubber matting beneath her, marvelling as it came in and out of focus, smiling every time she looked up and saw her mother's face in front of her.

Maggie smiled. How many hours of her own life had she spent beside children's swings? How many pushes, how many 'just ten mores', how many cold winter afternoons and sunny spring mornings spent in that swaying, rhythmic dance? She'd known even as it was happening that it would end too soon. She'd known her children would first learn to swing themselves and then not ask to be brought here any more. She'd appreciated every last push.

Libby had had Matilda when she was twenty-two. Younger even than Maggie had been when she'd had Tom. Libby had been devastated. A year out of university. Five months into a new relationship and only four years into adulthood. Maggie had been secretly delighted. This way, she'd thought, I might even get to be a great-grandmother. And this will keep her here, she'd thought, keep her in Bury. Not that she wanted her daughter to be tied down young, but still, it would be nice to have her around. And Maggie did love small children. She'd once read that David Attenborough had been asked what was the most incredible animal he'd ever seen, and he'd replied: A two-year-old child. She agreed with him. Babies she liked and older children were fascinating, but a small child, a toddler, a creature that had spent a year learning to walk, that was beginning to talk, that was incapable of lying or of knowing that it was being lied to, utterly without guile or malice, was a rare thing. A precious thing. An all-too-fleeting thing.

Libby pulled Matilda from the swing and set her back on the ground. She saw ahead of her a pigeon and made after it, her fat arms extended before her. Libby turned to Maggie and smiled.

'What are you thinking about?' she asked, joining her mother on the bench.

'Oh, nothing much. Just children. Just life. The cycle of it. You know.'

'You're getting all philosophical in your old age.'

'Less of the old age, if you don't mind,' teased Maggie. 'And, yes, I suppose I am. It's all this business with Daniel. You know. Him being so ill, these children he's had. All the babies. All the dreams.'

Libby looked at her curiously. 'What's going on there? With Daniel and the Registry?'

'Well, nothing yet. I've sent off all the paperwork.

Haven't heard anything back yet. I pop over to his place from time to time, check if anything's been sent. But not yet.'

'And how much longer . . .'

'I don't know. Weeks, they say. But, I mean, that could be a fortnight, it could be three months. It's the brain, you see. It's in his brain. And it depends how quickly it grows in there and how much damage it does. It's not got much bigger so far. But who knows? Cancer. It's a tricky bugger.'

'Is he still, you know, compos mentis?'

'Well, yes, I'd say he is. On the whole. I mean, the drugs can do funny things to him sometimes. And he's a bit more . . . oh, what's the word? He's a bit more forth-coming, I suppose. He's more open, tells me what he's feeling, has a little joke. He's more human. And I don't know if that's the drugs, the tumour, or if it's just what happens to a person when they know they're, well, when they're getting ready to go. But he's ever so sweet. He told me . . .' She paused. She never wanted to be one of those mothers who blurred the line between friendship and parenting. She never wanted her children to see too deeply into the reality of herself. 'He told me that he wishes things had been different. That we'd been – together.'

'Aw,' said Libby. 'That's nice.'

'Yes,' said Maggie, dreamily. 'It is nice. It's very nice indeed.'

'But better in a way, though? Better that you didn't get too close?'

Maggie smiled sadly. 'Ah, well, actually, I don't think that makes any difference. Actually, I think that what's happening now, me sharing these days with him, I think that's making us closer than any amount of kissing and cuddling would have done. And now with me trying to trace these children for him . . . that's not an experience that many couples get to share. I think what we're doing now, well, it's going to make it very hard for me when he's gone. Very hard indeed.'

Maggie let a small tear slide from her eye and Libby looked at her aghast. 'Oh, God, Mummy, I didn't mean to . . . I'm sorry. I just thought . . .'

'It's all right, sweetie. Honestly. It's fine. I'm bound to feel like this from time to time. It's all so draining.'

Libby put her arm around Maggie's shoulders and gave her a small squeeze. Libby was not an affectionate girl. She had not been an affectionate child either, so Maggie appreciated the gesture. 'Funny old world, isn't it?' said Libby. 'Just minding your own business and then suddenly, twelve months later, you're spending every day in a hospice and helping someone track down their long-lost children.'

'You're not kidding,' said Maggie, enjoying the strange proximity of her youngest child, wanting her daughter never to let go of her. 'If someone had told me a year ago . . .' She let the sentence fade away. A year ago, she thought sadly to herself, she was falling in love.

Matilda came bounding over towards them then, her hands brown with gravel dust. In her enthusiasm to grab hold of her mother's knees, she tripped over her own feet and landed face down in the grass. Maggie never got to tell Libby what she'd have said if someone had told her a year ago how different her life would be now, because Libby was consumed with the business of persuading her toddler that she was fine and administering magic kisses. Instead they slowly gathered together their bits and pieces and headed away from the playground and back towards Libby's little flat in a converted terrace near the town centre.

Maggie stayed for long enough to watch Libby delicately spoon some tomato-ey pasta into her daughter's mouth and complain a bit about Matilda's childminder. (Maggie believed that these complaints were in fact a subtle attempt to coax an offer out of her to look after the child during the week. Maggie loved being a part of their lives but she had no desire whatsoever to spend entire days alone with her granddaughter. She was not one of those modern types of granny.) Libby's partner came home at about three o'clock. He seemed to be a bit grumpy. Libby's partner often seemed to be a bit grumpy and Maggie had no idea whether that was because he found her presence displeasing or if that was just his everyday demeanour. Either way, she was ready to go, the flat was too small for the four of them, and she collected her handbag and headed off in her small red car to Daniel's flat.

She didn't linger now in Daniel's home. It was always strictly business for her there. In, check the doormat, check the sinks, out again. Today there was a larger than usual pile of mail on the floor, including, she was inappropriately excited to note, something with a French stamp on it and a hand-written envelope. She sorted through the pile efficiently, pulling out flyers for pizza firms and window cleaners (although his windows did need a clean, she couldn't help but notice). She stuffed the mail into her handbag and then went straight to the hospice where, she was alarmed to note, Daniel's bed was empty.

'He's in the music room,' said a large girl called Pippa who was passing her in the corridor in the opposite direction. Maggie brought her panicking heart to a resting beat and smiled gratefully at her. 'Thank you,' she said. Daniel was sitting in an armchair plucking at the strings of an acoustic guitar. He was wearing a sweater over his pyjamas so at first glance it looked almost as if he was dressed. His hair was neatly combed and apart from his grisly pallor and the fact of the bag of his own urine contained on a pole at his side, it seemed almost impossible that he was ill at all.

'Hello.' She smiled, kissing him on his cheek and stroking his arm.

'*Bonjour.*' He smiled, brushing gently at the guitar strings again and sending a diaphanous chord of music across the space between them. 'How are you?'

'I'm absolutely fine,' said Maggie, taking a seat opposite him. 'But more to the point, how are you? I wasn't expecting to see you up.'

'Yes, I am vertical! But don't be deceived. I am not always going to be vertical from now on. And getting me in here was not an edifying spectacle, I can assure you.'

'So what made you decide to come in here?' she asked, looking around at the room which she'd not been in before.

Daniel shrugged and slapped his hand against the strings, causing the guitar to issue forth another melancholic shimmer of sound. 'I heard a nurse mention it. I hadn't seen it. I didn't even know it existed. So I asked to be brought here. They tried very hard to make me change my mind.'

'I didn't know you could play the guitar,' she said.

'I cannot play the guitar,' he laughed.

'Oh,' said Maggie, slightly nonplussed.

'I can play no musical instruments. Yet another regret, another failing in my miserable life.'

'Oh, now,' began Maggie, 'that's not . . .'

'You must stop taking everything I say so literally, Maggie May! Of course I do not believe that my life has been miserable and a failure! But I do wish I could have left this place knowing that I could at least strum a little "Jailhouse Rock" on a cheap guitar . . .' He stroked the strings fondly and smiled. 'So!' he said. 'Tell me about the other place.' He indicated the outside world with his heavy eyebrows. 'What is happening beyond these walls?'

'Oh, nothing much,' she said. 'I've been at Libby's all morning. With the baby. That was nice. Oh, and I went to your flat. There was some mail. Just the usual junk. And this.' She rifled through her handbag for the handwritten envelope. 'Look,' she said, passing it to him. 'It's from France.' She attempted to keep her voice buoyant, but she knew even as she passed it to him that the letter might not be a welcome development.

She watched his face carefully and saw it tremble and then sink. He sighed. 'Ah,' he said eventually, nodding his head up and down, very slowly and knowingly. 'Here it is.'

She looked at him expectantly.

'It is my brother. Either my mother is dead or she is about to die or my brother is dying or maybe I am wrong and something truly *wonderful* is happening . . .' He sighed again and tore through the paper of the envelope with one gnarled finger. She watched him read, his dull eyes skimming the lines fast and then slow and then fast again. He came to the end of the missive and then he laid it down upon his lap and stared at it unhappily.

Maggie caught her breath, her fingers lightly touching the skin of her neck.

'Well,' Daniel said eventually, 'he is coming. My brother is coming.'

'Oh,' said Maggie, who had expected worse, 'really?'

'Yes. Next week. He is coming next week. And expects to find me in my nice cosy flat, waiting for him with a bottle of Sancerre and a cheery welcome.'

'He doesn't know that you're ill?'

'No. He does not. This is the first I have heard of my brother in almost five years. Last time we were in touch I was fit as a flea.'

'Oh, your poor brother, he's going to get such a nasty shock.'

'Pah! No! It is I who will have the nasty shock, not he.

I was the one who chose to live elsewhere. I was the one who chose not to be there any more. And now he is coming here. To my place. Never once in thirty years has my brother come to this country. It is all too much. He cannot speak a word of the language. He has never left France, except once, to pick up a dog in Belgium. Some small thing, I don't know, with hair like this . . .' He described a quiff with his fingers. 'Anyway. No. It is I who should be worried. It is I who will be *invaded*.'

'Can't you just . . . *not reply*?' Maggie suggested, though it went against her nature. 'He'll never know where you are.'

'No.' Daniel closed his eyes for a count of three and then opened them again. Maggie feared that she was trying his patience, and swallowed. 'No,' he continued. 'He is my brother. I am dying. The fact that he has chosen this time of all times to come and see me . . . it must mean something. I am weak. I will see him. But, Maggie May, please can I trouble you once again? I am so sorry but please could you send him a message, from your computer? I will write it down for you, in French. Please. Just this and then nothing more. I will ask you for nothing more. You have already done too much.'

'No!' said Maggie, with unexpected emphasis. 'No, I haven't done too much. I haven't done anything, Daniel.'

'How can you say that? You have been my God-sent angel, Mrs Smith. Truly. Now, please, can you ask that lovely fat girl called Pippa to come in here and help get me back into my wheelchair? My vertical time is officially over. It is time to be horizontal. Although, sadly, not with you . . .'

Maggie's school French was sufficient for her to translate at least eighty per cent of Daniel's clumsily scrawled message to his brother.

My dear brother,

I thank you for your (typical?) letter. I have received it in (horrible?) circumstances. I live in a hospice(?), and I do not wait to live a long time. It is my *poumons* (lungs, possibly). You have a reason. It is a horrible habit. When you come, if you could communicate with my friend Maggie, she will show you my apartment and bring you to see me here. Five years, it is long to have been in contact. If you could please wait/hope(?) *au pire* (for fire??).

Your brother,
Daniel

It was fiddly trying to insert all the little characters with their accents and cedillas but Maggie wanted it to be totally perfect. She read and re-read it three times before she pressed send. His brother's name was Marc. Marc Blanchard. She wanted to add a short note at the end, something friendly and welcoming, but he could not speak English and she could not speak more than a few rudimentary words of French and didn't trust those computerised translator things not to make her sound like a complete ass, so she typed, simply: *Je suis Maggie! A bientôt!*

She pressed send and then she went into her neat, nail-polish-red kitchen (another post-divorce treat to herself) and made herself a stir-fry of king prawns and broccoli which she ate alone in front of a re-run of *Ten Years Younger*.

LYDIA

Lydia barely noticed the first time she lent Bendiks £50. She liked to carry cash. Every time she passed a machine she would pull out £100. Having a sheaf of paper money in her purse made her feel secure, in the same way as having a fully charged phone about her person. If it dwindled below £30 she felt uncomfortable, like she was driving a car with a low petrol gauge.

So handing over two twenties and a ten to Bendiks the previous week had barely made a dent in her consciousness. He'd said, 'You can take it out of next week's money, if you like?' but she'd said, 'No, no, don't be silly. It's a loan, pay me back when you can.'

Now here she was, for the third time in ten days, hurriedly retrieving her purse from within the depths of her handbag once more, pooh-poohing his words of apology: 'No, no, it's fine. Of course I understand.'

'But, really, Lydia, I feel so bad. I still have not paid you back what you lent me last week.'

'Honestly, it's fine. Please . . .' She held the notes out to him, and he looked at her apologetically from beneath his extravagant eyelashes and said, 'Are you sure?'

'Yes. Totally. Take it.'

He took the notes and then bowed, very slightly. Then he lifted her right hand with his, and placed a very small, very dry kiss against the back of it.

'Oh,' said Lydia.

'Thank you,' said Bendiks.

He sauntered away from her and collected his gym bag before checking his reflection just once in the mirror in the hallway, sliding the notes into his back pocket and leaving the house. Lydia turned to continue her journey towards the kitchen where she had been headed to refuel herself with an artificially sweetened drink. Juliette was standing near the entrance, posing unconvincingly with a tea towel and a bottle of Flash kitchen cleaner in her hands. She gave Lydia a look. Lydia tried to translate it. It seemed to suggest both pity and concern. Lydia bristled slightly and swept past Juliette towards the fridge. She could feel Juliette behind her, unmoving, vibrating with unsaid words. She pulled the bottle of Sprite from the fridge, and while she was there also picked up two slices of pre-sliced Cheddar and a handful of cold green grapes. Then she closed the door, smiled wanly at Juliette and headed back upstairs to her office with her booty.

She didn't know what to feel. Fifty pounds was nothing to her. Indeed, £150 was nothing to her. She could absolutely afford to chalk £150 up to experience. But she wasn't entirely sure just exactly what sort of experience she was having. Bendiks had been living here now for a month. He had been charming, considerate, quiet and friendly. And he had made it clear that he wanted more from her than just a roof over his head. He clearly found her appealing and interesting and worthy of his attentions. And all of this he did in a sincere and genuine manner. The longer he had spent in her home, the more she had grown to like him. The better she got to know him, the more she knew she'd done the right thing in asking him to move in with her. There was so much more to him than just a pretty face and fit body. He had hidden depths and a gentle personality. He was real. But still, he was poor, she was rich. It could all be a big act, to get at her money. The whole wonderful concept of 'Bendiks' could quite easily be an illusion. And she could quite easily be a pathetic fool.

But she would not worry too much about Bendiks and his unpaid debts. Not for now. For now Lydia had more pressing concerns. Three of them; first was Dean. He had disappeared. He replied to her text messages, cursorily, non-committal. He would not commit to a further meeting, using words like 'busy' and 'maybe' and 'I'll be in touch'. Lydia knew what it was. She'd pushed him too far with the grand house and the housekeeper and the chichi little restaurant in the St John's Wood back street. She'd also completely blown it by coming on too strong about the fact that she thought he should face up to his responsibilities to his baby daughter. Too much, too soon. She knew how to fix it but she wasn't sure if she herself was ready to take such a step. The second issue was the other girl. Her name was Robyn, and she had finally responded to Lydia's request and wanted to get in touch. Except that Lydia was now so pole-axed by issues number one and number three that she could not quite put her mind to the concept. Because issue number three was the biggest deal of all.

Her father had registered.

Her father wanted to get in touch.

She had, for some reason, not factored this possibility into her vision of what might happen after she'd put herself on the register. She'd imagined somehow that the 'father' would want no part of a reunion, that the 'father' would be sitting under a palm tree somewhere, giving neither a fig nor a hoot nor indeed a monkey's about the random scatterings of his DNA. But there he was. A man called Daniel. Fifty-three years old and living in Bury St Edmunds.

Suddenly Lydia was crippled by the order of priority. How should she manage this? In what sequence should she live the next few chapters of her life? Realign herself with Dean, meet up with Robyn, then all bundle up together with Daddy Daniel as a big happy gang? Or see each participant in this bizarre scenario individually? Should she allow herself to get to know each player slowly, or schedule meetings one after the other? Would the others have any interest in seeing the 'father'? Or would it be just her? And if that were the case, wouldn't he want to ask her questions about 'the others'? And how would she fend them off? And what of the fourth spawn? Should they wait for him to sign up?

She sighed and wished herself a family. She wished for a brother or a sister or a best friend, someone she could share all of this with. But her only friend was currently packing all her possessions into cardboard boxes and was about to move herself, her five-month-old baby and her bearded partner to a small cottage in the middle of the Snowdonia National Park. Just as Lydia had predicted, once the seeds of moving back home had been sowed, it had been a very speedy process, helped by the fact that their flat was only a rental. No time even for a farewell party, for which Lydia was secretly grateful.

She glanced at the time on her computer screen. It was almost three o'clock. She eyed her bottle of Sprite and looked at the time again. Then she pulled open her filing cabinet and brought out a bottle of Bombay Sapphire. She topped up the green plastic bottle to the brim, probably a generous double measure, she estimated. It would help her to focus. It would help her to think.

By half-past four Lydia had had four more generous doubles (she still assumed they were generous doubles) and was dancing to videos on YouTube whilst Queenie watched her forlornly from the armchair, as though she were thinking: *What happened, Lydia? You used to be like me, you used to be cool and elegant, and now you are dancing really horribly to Biffy Clyro. I am terribly disappointed in you.*

Lydia ignored the cat and felt the untying of her own guy ropes, the collapsing of her internal canvas. Lydia had never been a social drinker. Nor a social dancer, for that matter. She kept this kind of personal abandonment to

307

herself. She didn't feel it necessary for anyone else to see what she looked like naked with alcohol.

She spent an hour on YouTube, picking out favourites, everything from Bowie to Morrissey to Snow Patrol, spinning around the room, stopping occasionally to top up her bottle with Bombay Sapphire, until there was no Sprite left. Then she wandered across the landing towards the spare bedroom and pushed open the doors on to the small terrace there and considered the view for a while. It was 5.30. Darkness would not fall for a while, the late-afternoon light was golden on the leaves of the trees in her back garden and, despite an ominous bank of charcoal cloud looming menacingly on the horizon, it was a glorious evening. Lydia let the lacy haze of drunkenness wash over her for a while. If she let the detail blur she could be back in her flat in Camden with Dixie; she could be sitting on the big scruffy sofa watching Dixie baste a chicken, her bare feet pulled up in front of her, her laptop at her side. She could be listening to the sounds of Camden mayhem rising upwards from the street below and she could be feeling like a normal young person instead of a scary rich woman with a blue cat in a too-big house.

And it was at that moment that she knew what she wanted to do. She could not face the unknown of her newfound sister and father without first knowing herself. And she could not know herself without knowing what had happened that terrible day on a balcony not dissimilar to this one in a block of flats near Tonypandy.

She'd been toying with the idea for a few days, ever

since Dean had walked out of that restaurant the other night and gone cold on her. But now, at last, she felt clear about it. She walked back into her office and she pulled her mobile phone from the desk. She then composed a new text message, to Dean:

Hi, Dean, I need your help. I want to go back to Wales. I want to see Rodney and find out what happened. And I want you to come with me. Maybe tomorrow, if you're not busy. Please say yes. Lx

She waited a beat to reassure herself that this was the right thing to be doing and then she pressed send.

Lydia collapsed in her bed at 8.30 p.m. and slept until 8 the next morning. A full twelve hours, she thought to herself as she awoke, like a baby.

Her head felt a little fuzzy but not as bad as it could have done, probably because she'd had her last drink so early. She was dressed in clean pyjamas, and yesterday's clothes hung neatly in the dressing room next door. She unfurled her bedroom blind and appraised the day. It was bright and the sky was a kind of watered down blue, stained with patches of white. The man on the radio told her that the temperature was to be around eighteen degrees. She slipped into her dressing gown and hurried down the stairs to fetch her breakfast before Juliette arrived at 8.30 and Bendiks emerged and started pulping things in his noisy machine. She piled Weetabix into a bowl, grabbed a carton of milk and a banana, and disappeared into her office. She had a coffee machine there so she made herself a double espresso and then she checked her phone which was sitting charging on her desk (she had no recollection of having set it to charge last night, just as she had no recollection of hanging up her clothes). There was no message from Dean. She was partially relieved. It had felt like a great idea last night but now, sober and in daylight, it probably wasn't such a good thing to under-take. For a start, she had only the vaguest idea of where to find her uncle, and also, what was she actually hoping to find?

She demolished her Weetabix and banana and gulped down her sugary espresso. She was about to switch on her computer and begin her day with a perusal of the markets and the weather and the state of the world when she heard the doorbell issue its computerised chime. She stopped. It must be Juliette, she thought, forgotten her keys. She went to the monitor outside her office and she switched on the screen, and there on the front step, in a baseball cap and carrying a sports bag slung over his shoulder, was some-one who looked very much like Dean.

'Hello?' she said.

'It's me, Dean,' he said. 'I got your text last night.'

'Oh, right.'

'Yeah. Then I got my phone nicked in the pub. Didn't have your number anywhere else so thought I'd better get here early, in case I missed you.'

'Oh,' she said again, 'I see.'

He stared meaningfully into the frog's eye of the cam-era and shuffled from one foot to the other.

'Is that OK?' he said, eventually.

'Yes, of course. Of course. Come in.' She buzzed him in and met him at the bottom of the stairs. He looked at her in surprise, taking in her pyjamas and her uncombed hair. And then he looked behind her and blinked. 'Oh,' he said, 'sorry.'

'Sorry for what?'

'I didn't realise . . .'

'What?' She looked behind her and saw that Bendiks was standing on the landing, topless and in cream draw-string cotton trousers.

'Morning,' he said, flashing white teeth at them.

'Oh, hi, Bendiks. This is my friend,' she began, then corrected herself, 'my brother. This is Dean. Dean, this is Bendiks. My lodger. My trainer.'

'Her *friend*,' said Bendiks, padding down the stairs with his hand outstretched.

Lydia looked from Dean to Bendiks and back again. As much as she wished that Bendiks was significantly more than just her friend, she felt awkward at the notion of her baby brother getting the wrong impression. 'Yes, but not . . .'

'No,' reassured Bendiks, rather too breezily, 'not that sort of friend. Excellent to meet you.'

Dean smiled uncertainly at Bendiks, clearly blinded by the brownness of his skin and the whiteness of his teeth and the sheer size of his overdeveloped pectorals. This was why Lydia always made sure she was not in the kitchen after 8.30. She had once crossed paths with Bendiks wearing, underneath an unbelted cotton gown, a pair of fitted pants in black that appeared to have a kind of seamed pouch built into them to contain in great detail the fullness of his genitalia. Lydia, swollen as she was with urgent carnal longing, had found it slightly too informative an advertisement for things she could not afford.

'Come in,' she said to Dean. 'Have you had any breakfast?'

'Yeah,' he said, 'I got a bacon roll on the way here. I'm fine.'

'Cup of tea?'

'No.' He smiled apologetically. 'I'm good.'

'So,' she said, 'what happened to your phone?'

'Oh, nothing much. Just left it in my jacket pocket, hanging off the back of the chair. Someone lifted it.' He shrugged. 'My own fault.'

'You insured?'

'Nah,' he said. 'Of course not.'

'I'll get you a new one,' said Lydia, the words tumbling from her mouth before she'd had a chance to check herself.

'Don't be daft,' he said. 'It's fine. My mum said she'd get me a new one.'

'Oh,' she said, 'right. Of course.' She'd forgotten that he wasn't an orphan, like her. She left him downstairs with Bendiks on the terrace while she ran upstairs to get dressed. She pulled on some jeans and a t-shirt with a baggy cardigan and trainers. She didn't touch her face or her hair, she was in too much of a hurry to get back downstairs and break apart the unsettling duo of Dean and

Bendiks. As a classic compartmentaliser Lydia couldn't bear the thought of these two disparate characters being together apart from her.

'So,' she said, addressing Dean, 'shall we go?'

'Right,' he said, placing his hands against his knees. 'Sure. Yeah. Let's go.'

'Where are you going?' asked Bendiks.

'Oh, nowhere. Just to see some old family.'

'Yeah, right,' Bendiks slanted his eyes at her, 'and I thought your family were all dead?'

Lydia was taken aback by this. She'd expected him to pass no comment. 'Well, no, not all of them. I have an uncle. I have aunts and cousins . . .'

'You told me you had lost contact with them all?'

Lydia had no idea why Bendiks was acting so confrontationally. 'Well, yes, I did. But now . . .'

Bendiks' face softened, as though he was aware that he'd been pushing too hard. 'Good.' He smiled. 'That's great. And I am so happy for you that you have found your brother. You are very, very lucky.' He smiled sadly and Lydia felt her stomach lurch. Of course, she thought, of course. She had found her brother, Bendiks would never find his. She ignored a compulsion to touch his arm – he was still too naked to be touched – and instead she smiled at him and said, 'Thank you.'

'Did you tell your mum where you were going today?' she asked Dean, eyeing him across the Formica-topped table that separated them in the first-class carriage.

'Yeah,' he said.

'What did she say?'

'Nothing much,' he said. 'My mum doesn't say much about anything usually.'

Lydia nodded. 'Do you think this is crazy? Doing this?' she asked after a moment.

'No,' he replied. 'I think you'd be crazy not to.'

She nodded and turned to look out of the window. She was staring at the back view of London, at squat yards and stacked windows and brick walls and dirt. There were three hours ahead of them. Three hours to talk. And there was plenty to talk about.

'So,' she began, 'did you get the letter?'

Dean's eyes opened wide. 'Yeah,' he said. 'I know. Bit shocking, isn't it?'

She nodded. 'What do you think about it?'

'I think . . .' He blew out his cheeks. 'I don't know what I think. I mean, I was just about dealing with meeting you.' He exhaled. 'Christ. I don't know. I'm freaking out a bit, I think. What about you?'

'The same,' she said. 'I feel the same. That's why . . . well, that's why I want to do this. I need to, you know, clean up the old mess before I get stuck into a new one.'

'You think it'll be a mess?'

She smiled. 'Probably,' she said. 'I mean, look at us. Only three meetings and you went AWOL. Clearly I'm not very good at this reuniting thing.'

Dean looked genuinely upset by her comment. 'No,' he

said, 'God, no. It wasn't you. It totally wasn't you. It was me. It was just . . .'

'I know what it was, Dean. It's OK. I pushed it too far. I shouldn't have come down heavy on you about the baby.'

'It wasn't the baby. Honestly. It wasn't that. It was just . . . I just felt like you were . . .' he looked up at her with his large brown eyes '. . . like you were too good for me.'

Lydia smiled and shook her head. 'Yeah,' she said. 'That's what I thought. And that was another reason why I wanted you to come with me today. I wanted you to see where I came from. I wanted you to understand me and not just be put off by all the bollocks my money has bought me. I'm no different from you, Dean.'

He looked at her sceptically.

'Honest, I'm not. You'll see. You really will.'

He glanced out of the window. 'I really like you, you know,' he said after a moment. 'It's nothing personal, that I've been off radar. I think you're amazing.'

She looked at him and smiled. 'Well, I know you'll probably think I'm just saying this because you're so flipping insecure, but I liked you the minute I saw you and I've liked you more and more ever since. You just need to sort out your self-esteem issues.'

'You can talk!' he teased.

'What?'

'Well, you, you're all rich and super-successful, you're really good-looking, and you walk around acting like you're just some . . . blob.'

'I do not!' she countered.

'You do, man. You're all just, like this . . .' He curled his upper back into a hump and looked at her nervously. 'You're all, *Don't look at me, avert your gaze*. You know?'

She shrugged, feeling suddenly under attack. And then she sighed. 'Well,' she said, 'like I said, we're the same, you and me. We're just the same. Pathetic creatures. Pitiful, really.' She paused and looked at him. And then they both laughed.

After a moment Lydia said, 'What do you think the other one will be like? The girl? Robyn? Do you think she'll be a pitiful creature, too?'

Dean stopped laughing and considered the question. 'Fuck knows,' he said. And then he paused and smiled. 'I hope so.'

Lydia laughed again and they both quietened then and stared through the window at the bland city fringes scenery.

After a while Dean's face became more tense and it was clear he was about to say something.

'You were right, though,' he said. 'You were right about the baby. I'm a loser. I hate myself. Every morning I wake up and I look in the mirror and I see her eyes looking back at me, you know? The same eyes. Every morning she looks at me in the mirror and she goes: You *loser*. And she's right.'

Lydia stared at him as he spoke. She thought of herself at his age. She thought of her life at university, pulling pints and fiddling with test tubes and keeping out the world. Could she have looked after a baby? Could she have looked after an ill baby? On her own? And, more to the point, would she have wanted to?

He was not a loser, but she would not be able to tell him that. She would have to show him that. So she said nothing and let the pair of them return to a state of restful and contemplative silence while the train took them speedily and urgently towards Wales.

It was warm when they dismounted from it. Lydia hadn't expected it to be warm. She pulled off her cardigan and tied it around her waist. Dean replaced his baseball cap and they headed for the taxi rank.

Lydia felt a chill run through her, in spite of the humidity. She wondered how many hours of her life she had spent at the Cardiff taxi rank. She saw flashes of herself at seventeen, at eighteen, at nineteen. She saw herself in a battered leather jacket, Arnie at her side dressed in a blue bandana and a frayed rope collar. She saw herself younger, hand in hand with her father, heading back home after a stressful journey to Bangor to see her grandmother, dying in a bed in her own front room. She felt herself walking side by side with a dozen ancient versions of herself, and she felt every iota of the misery she'd felt every time she'd been here. Apart from the last time. She saw herself then, freshly graduated, liberated from her family and her past, her things in a trunk, her hair in a brand new twenties bob, Dixie at her side, heading away from Wales and towards London Town.

She'd vowed to herself, and to Dixie, that she would

never, ever come back. She remembered sitting on the train, puffing on a cigarette, staring through the window and saying to Dixie, 'This is the best moment of my life.'

For a moment, Lydia cursed herself for breaking her own vow and for tainting the perfection of that moment eight years earlier. But then she looked at her brother, thin and stooped as he followed her towards the taxi rank, and she remembered why she was here.

'Can you take us to Tonypandy, please?' she asked a man who was folding away a copy of the *Penarth Times*.

He eyed her blandly and hit the switch on his meter. 'What takes you that way?' he asked, looking at her in the rear-view mirror a moment later.

'Oh,' she said, 'nothing. Just family.'

'Ah,' he said, nodding knowingly. 'Right.'

'We'll need you for the whole day, if that's OK? Do you have a day rate?'

'Eighty pounds,' he said, succinctly, and then he turned off his meter.

Lydia was glad of Dean's presence in the taxi with her. It kept the focus off making conversation with the driver. Instead she pointed out landmarks to her brother as they drove. That's where I used to work behind the bar when I was a student. That's where we went to collect my puppy from when I was eight. That's the market where my dad used to work. That's the place that does the best fish and chips in Glamorgan. That's the hill where I first got stoned.

'You got stoned?' he asked, whisking his head round to look at her.

'Of course I did.'

He smiled at her, uncertainly. 'You never told me that,' he said.

'Yeah, well, what did you expect me to say? "Hi, I'm Lydia, and when I was a student I used to smoke weed"?'

She watched the scenes of her past flash by from the taxi window and then she stiffened as the outskirts to her village appeared. She stared in queasy awe at the 7Eleven with the wheelchair ramp outside where she used to buy herself treats and fizzy drinks, and then, when her dad was ill, where she used to do all the household shopping. She gazed at the hair salon, once called Hair Today, now painted guacamole green and called The Village Spa. She saw the shops give way to terraces and the terraces give way to sprawling estates and then there it was, her block. Ugly as ever, four floors of pebble-dashed mediocrity, set behind a small patch of grass and a play area.

The play area had been made over, carpeted in springy blue plastic and planted with brightly coloured bouncy ponies and rubberised baby swings. A young woman sat reading a magazine on a bench while her small boy sat at her feet, twirling the wheels on his scooter. A rubbish bin by the bench was filled to overflowing with squashed pizza boxes, empty cans and a balled up nappy. Beyond the grass and the play area there was a paved walkway that encircled the whole building and led to the entrance at the side.

The young mother on the bench looked up as she saw Dean and Lydia walking towards the flats. She smiled wanly, as though she thought she should know them, and then returned her gaze to her magazine.

'Which one was yours?' asked Dean, looking up.

Lydia pointed at a balcony on the third floor. 'That one,' she said.

'And that's the balcony. . .?'

'Yeah.' She glanced down at the paving. Felt her insides shrink together. Her flesh ran with horror. There it was. Still there, after all these years. The smudge of paint. She dropped to her haunches and stared down at the innocuous pink curl. She put out her hand and touched it with her fingers. Her mother's hand. She remembered again the silver swans and the lovesick budgie and the circles in the magazines. She searched around inside her head to see if there was anything else to remember, anything she'd left behind. But she found nothing.

'Come on.' She got to her feet. 'Let's go in.'

The stairwells were empty and seemed somehow less forbidding than they had when she was younger. On the third level she stopped. In front of her was the place she'd called home for the first eighteen years of her life. She pulled in her breath, straightened her clothes and then she knocked, hesitantly, against the door.

It was opened by a slightly breathless elderly man with greasy white hair and a tortoiseshell cat held in his arms. 'Who is it?' he asked, peering at them blindly.

'My name's Lydia Pike,' she said. 'I used to live here.'

The man's face relaxed and he put the struggling cat down. It attempted to squeeze through the front door but the man yanked it back by its collar. 'Quick, quick, come in, before this one does a runner.' They slipped through his door and into a flat that smelled of stale clothes and fried eggs, and the man pushed the door closed behind them.

'So,' he said, appraising them, 'your Trevor's girl?'

She looked at him in surprise.

'I wondered when you'd be back,' he chuckled.

'Sorry?' She began following him into what had once been her living room but was now very clearly the living room of an elderly man. 'Did you know my dad?'

'Yes. I did. I used to live on the other side of the building, over there, overlooking the fields. Then I was made a widower and my son got married and it was just me so I asked for a smaller place. They offered me this and I knew no one else would want it, on account of what happened.' He sighed sadly and looked at Lydia with watery eyes. 'I'm not a believer in all that karma stuff, you know. I don't believe in negative energy, or whatever it's called. And I liked to have the view of the people, you know. I like to sit and look at the kiddies on the swings and watch the world coming and going. I was bored of the view the other side and this suited me just fine. So I snapped it up. Been here on my own ever since.'

Lydia blinked. She had been expecting a young family. She had been expecting nothing to remain here of her past. Yet here it was. Sitting right in front of her.

'So, do you remember me?' she asked, uncertainly.

'That I do.' He nodded, easing himself into his ugly

nylon sofa. 'You had a dog. You were a bit *moody*, if I recall.' He smiled at her.

'Sorry,' she said, 'what's your name?'

'I'm Pat,' he said. 'Pat Lloyd. You might remember my son. Tony. Tony Lloyd?'

She gasped. She did remember. Tony Lloyd had Down's Syndrome and used always to stop and cuddle Arnie when he passed them on the stairs or in the garden.

'I remember Tony,' she said, 'and he got married, you say?'

'Yes, he did. Took us all by surprise that did. But they've been together ten years now, still as happy as the day they met.'

'Wow,' said Lydia, 'that's lovely, that is.'

'So,' he looked from her to Dean and back again, 'what brings you back around here then?'

He was looking for an introduction so Lydia gave him one. 'This is my brother,' she said. 'We've only just been reunited. I wanted to show him where I came from.'

'Oh, right.' He stopped and smiled at Dean. 'I can see the likeness,' he said, 'between the two of you. I can see you're kin.' Dean and Lydia smiled at each other. 'But I thought . . .' his mouth hung open, mid-sentence. He blinked. 'No,' he said, 'no, never mind. Anyway, can I make you both a pot of tea?'

'You thought what?' asked Lydia.

'Nothing. Nothing. Just getting myself confused.' He got to his feet. 'I'd offer you coffee but I'm clean out. Or I think I've got some barley water somewhere.'

'No, don't worry. We've got a taxi waiting, we can't stay.'

He smiled sadly and returned to the sofa.

'So,' he said, 'how's life been to you?'

Lydia nodded. 'I've got a good life,' she said.

'Married? Any babies of your own?'

'No,' she said, 'just a cat.'

'Cat's no substitute for a child. What about you?' he addressed Dean.

Lydia looked at Dean. Watched the pinkness leave his skin. 'Er, yeah, I've got a baby. A little girl.'

The old man smiled, satisfied it seemed that at least one of the strangers in his living room had added to the population. 'Ah!' he said suddenly, rising to his feet again. 'Since you're here, I've been keeping this all these years and not known what to do with it . . .' He headed towards the door of what had once been her father's bedroom. 'Wait here,' he said. He returned a moment later clutching a rather vintage carrier bag. 'Now this,' he began, holding the bag on his lap and opening it slightly, 'I found when I was replacing the fitted wardrobes. It was hidden inside a sort of false cubby hole. Never knew what to make of it and had no one to ask. But now, well,' he turned to Dean and smiled, 'I suppose this should really be for you. Here, take it.'

Dean blinked at him in surprise, wondering what part he could possibly play in this story. 'Are you sure, mate?' he asked.

The man nodded and handed him the bag. Dean

opened it gingerly and Lydia watched him peer inside. 'What?' he said, looking up again at the old man. 'I don't get it.'

'Well, they must be yours,' said Pat, 'being blue and all.'

Dean put his hand inside the bag and pulled out a tiny pair of blue cotton leggings, a blue and white striped jacket and a pair of miniature white socks.

'You mean, for my daughter?' asked Dean, his eyes screwed shut with confusion.

'Well, no, *yours*. These must be yours. From when you were, you know, from when you were a baby.'

'But I've never been here before in my life,' said Dean, with a small laugh.

'Well, I suppose you don't remember it, being so small, but you must have been.'

Lydia interrupted. 'I don't understand,' she said. 'You mean, there was a baby here? A baby boy?'

'Why, yes,' said Pat, his eyes opening in surprise, 'don't you remember? Just before she died, your mother had a baby. A baby boy.'

And as Pat said these words, Lydia looked at the pile of baby clothes on Dean's lap and saw, with a flash of shock and revulsion, on the sleeves of the striped jacket, a smudge of candy pink paint, dried to an immovable crust.

ROBYN

Daniel Blanchard. Fifty-three years old. Bury St Edmunds.
Daniel Blanchard. Fifty-three years old. Bury St Edmunds.

Robyn held the sheet of paper in her hands and stared at it. She had not been expecting this. Donor *Sibling* Registry it was called. For siblings. Brothers and sisters. Not *fathers*. She had not been thinking about her *father*. But he, it appeared, had been thinking about her. And the others. He wanted to make contact. Daniel Blanchard. Her father.

Jack brought her in a cup of tea and placed it on the table in front of her.

'Fuck,' he said, sitting down and resting his hand against her leg.

Robyn grabbed his hand in hers and nodded. 'I knew I shouldn't have done this,' she said. 'I knew it was a mistake.'

'You don't have to see him.'

'No. I know. But then I'll have to go through the rest of my life knowing that he wanted to see me. And that I rejected him. I'll go through the rest of my life feeling guilty.'

'You've got nothing to feel guilty for!' said Jack. 'This was his choice! His choice and your parents . . .'

'They didn't have any choice,' she snapped, defensively.

'No. But you know what I mean; none of this is your fault. You didn't ask to be in this situation and, frankly, if this man wanted children he could talk to, he should have had them the normal way.'

'But he lives in Bury St Edmunds!' she wailed.

Jack looked at her curiously.

'I mean, I've been to Bury St Edmunds! I might have passed him in the street! I thought he lived in France! He wasn't supposed to live here! And now I can never go to Bury St Edmunds again!'

Jack laughed.

'It's not funny!' she cried.

'No, I know, of course it's not funny. It's just, well, you can probably live without going to Bury St Edmunds, can't you?'

'That's not the point! It's just, I preferred it when he was in France. I liked having him there. And now he's here. And I don't like it.'

'I promise you, on my life,' said Jack, 'that I will never knowingly let you go to Bury St Edmunds.' He brushed his nose against her hair and Robyn let him. He was right. She was being silly. But so far none of this had gone according to plan. She'd made contact with both of them. The woman and the boy. And neither of them had responded. This was remarkable to Robyn. She'd been sick with nerves from the moment she agreed to have her information shared with them. Every morning she watched the postman pull up outside the house with his red cart and sort through bundles of post. Every morning she scurried down to the communal hallway and sifted through the pile of mail, and every morning she breathed a sigh of relief when there was nothing there from the Registry. But, at the same time, she was unnerved. She'd just assumed that they would jump at the chance to meet her. She assumed that they'd be slick, professional Registry users, all primed and ready to go. It had not occurred to her that they might be as uncertain as her. It had not occurred to her, she supposed, that they might be human.

And then this morning there had been a letter from the Registry. Her heart had lurched. Which one, she'd thought, which one? Would it be the boy, close in age to her, or would it be the woman, the terrible aged facsimile of herself? Or would it, in fact, be the missing man, the one who was the same age as her Jack?

But it had been none of those. It had been him. The one she hadn't expected ever to encounter. Her father.

Robyn and Jack left the house a few minutes later. They took a bottle of rosé from the fridge and a bag of crisps and some olives and bread and they headed towards the park. Summer had crept up on them and the end of May was tantalisingly warm and sunny. They were meeting Jack's friends, Jonathan and Leo, in Whittington Park for lunch and Frisbee. Wary of being the only girl, Robyn had asked Nush along. She hadn't seen her friend for weeks. She missed Nush. Nush was her handle on her old life, the life she'd had before she met Jack when she was uncommonly self-confident, the queen of the scene, the centre of her own tiny universe. Maybe, she thought, seeing Nush might help her remember how to be that person again.

Nush was already there when they arrived, stretched out in the sunshine on a beach towel, a glass of wine on the grass by her hand and Leo trying frantically, it appeared from this distance, to get on top of her.

'Oh my God,' she said, sitting up abruptly as she saw them approaching. 'Who is this guy? I've told him about a billion times I've got a boyfriend, but he keeps trying to hump me.'

'I'm not trying to *hump* you,' said Leo, mock-hurt, 'I'm just trying to cuddle you.'

Nush looked at him in amused horror. 'But I don't even know you!' she squealed. 'Seriously,' she addressed Jack, 'who *is* he?'

'Get off her,' laughed Jack, pulling his friend away from Nush by the arm.

'I only wanted a cuddle,' he said, pushing out his bottom lip.

'Sorry about him,' said Jack, 'he's a bit like a dog, you know, it doesn't mean anything. Just pat him on the head occasionally and he'll leave you alone.'

Leo smiled sheepishly and opened himself a can of lager. 'It's your fault for being late,' he told Jack.

'We're ten minutes late! And I cannot be held accountable for your rampant sexuality.'

Jonathan arrived a few minutes later and Robyn and Nush sat together, with plastic glasses of wine and sunglasses, like a pair of twenty-somethings, watching the three older men behaving like teenagers.

'So,' said Nush, linking her arm through Robyn's and resting her head against her shoulder, 'how's married life?'

Robyn dropped a kiss on to Nush's shiny black hair and smiled. 'It's lovely,' she said.

'I still can't believe it,' continued Nush. 'Can't believe you're *living with someone*. Seems like only yesterday you were being banged up against the wall by Christian thingy in that club on your birthday.'

'God, yeah, I know, don't remind me!'

'I saw him last week, by the way,' she nudged Robyn in the ribs, 'he asked after you.'

'Euf!' Robyn shuddered. 'I don't know what I was thinking. That seems like another life . . .'

'Yeah, well, I guess it was in some ways. I tell you what, though. We don't half miss you. It's dead up there without you.'

'Oh, now, I'm sure you're keeping up the good work.'

'Nah.' Nush glanced down between her cupped bare feet and pulled at a strand of grass. 'It's just not the same any more. You know, you've gone, I'm all coupled up, it's the end of an era really. We're all growed up.' She smiled sadly.

Robyn smiled back and brought Nush towards her for

a shoulder-to-shoulder embrace. 'Yes,' she said, 'I guess we are.'

'So what do you do?' her friend asked. 'What's your big grown-up life like? Do you do, like, *ironing* and stuff?'

Robyn laughed and rocked back on her folded legs. 'Nooo,' she said, 'but I do do washing up. And I go to the launderette . . .'

'What, do you, like, take Jack's clothes? Do you fold up his *underpants*?'

'No! I take things for a service wash!'

'What's a service wash?'

Robyn smiled. She hadn't known what a service wash was either until two months ago. 'You take your washing and you pay the lady in the launderette to wash it for you.'

Nush wrinkled her nose. 'What, you mean she, like, touches your dirty underwear and stuff?'

'Yeah, and then she washes it and folds it all up for you.'

'Eugh!' said Nush. 'That's nasty.'

Robyn laughed. It had been a long time since she'd had an Essex Princess conversation and she was enjoying it. 'And the other day,' she said, 'I emptied a bin.'

'You emptied a bin?' repeated Nush, blankly.

'Yeah, a really disgusting one, full of, like, old cereal and stuff.'

'Oh, my,' said Nush, her hand against her heart, 'you are now, like, a *goddess* to me.'

The men were showing off frantically, to each other and to the two beautiful teenage girls watching them. Robyn and Nush smiled at each other. 'Cheers,' said

Nush, holding out her plastic cup to Robyn, 'to you, and your big grown-up new life.'

'Yeah,' said Robyn, 'and to you and not having to empty bins.'

'Hallelujah to *that*, my friend,' said Nush. 'And how's college?'

'Don't ask.'

'What? Really?'

'Yes, really. I'm fucking up, big time.'

'What! No way!'

'Yes way. I reckon they're close to kicking me out.'

'Holy shit! But why?'

Robyn shrugged. 'I don't know,' she said. 'My heart's just not in it, not really. And it's so tough. You really really *really* have to have your heart in it if you want to succeed. And part of me thinks, I don't know, maybe I was just fooling myself about all this being a doctor stuff. Maybe I was just . . .' She paused, her thoughts still not fully formed. 'There's just a lot going on in my life right now, and when I started this medical school thing I was one person and now I'm, well, I'm not another person as such, I'm just sort of in a halfway place. You know?'

'What, you mean, like, between girl and woman?'

'Yeah. No. Well, sort of. I just mean, there's stuff. It's complicated. It's . . .' Robyn inhaled loudly and let the daisy she'd been twirling between her fingers fall to the grass. 'It's my dad. My real dad. I mean, my donor dad. He's been in touch. He wants to meet me.'

Nush's professionally threaded eyebrows arched dramatically. 'For real?' she said.

'Yes. For real. Got a letter in the post this morning.'

'Wowser.' She stared at Robyn, wide-eyed. 'But how did he know where you live?'

'Oh, God, well, that's a long story. There's other stuff. There's . . .' She sighed again and then told Nush about the brother and the sister and the Donor Sibling Registry.

'Oh my God! That's so exciting!' said Nush, grasping Robyn's hands in hers.

'You think?'

'God, yeah! Imagine! Your very own brother and sister! And they both live in London. I mean, what were the chances of that?'

'Well, the clinic is in London, so I suppose . . .'

'And your dad! Your actual dad. I bet he's so cool. Because you're so cool. Not that your other dad isn't cool. I love your dad. But, you know, you've always been sort of . . . special . . .'

Robyn blinked at these words. That was how she used to feel. When it was just her. Now she only felt special when Jack smiled at her. 'Yeah,' she said, softly. 'I know what you mean, it's just . . .' She was going to say, What if I meet him and I hate him and it totally destroys my life? But then she remembered that her 'perfect' life was currently sliding downhill like a wooden house in a mudslide. And maybe what she actually needed now was something to come along and stop it. She'd already signed up to meet her brother and sister on the premise that they were going to show her where she was supposed to go next. Now, it occurred to her that maybe the place they'd been taking her in that very vivid dream, the place on the other side of those double doors, was actually to their father. Her life was unravelling and she was letting it. She needed to reel it back in again, and Nush was right; she was special. Her family thought she was special. Her boyfriend thought she was special. She herself had once thought she was special. Maybe her father would be just the person to help her to believe it once more.

'Would *you* do it?' she said, turning to face her friend.

'God, yeah! I mean, he's not even that old, is he? Fifty-three? Younger than your mum and dad. He might be a laugh. He might even be able to help you with whatever problems you're having at college. Don't forget – the man's an actual doctor.'

'Well, yeah, he *might* be a doctor. But he might be a total loser, too. I mean, surely if his life was that great, then he wouldn't be that fussed about us lot, you know, about something he did twenty, thirty years ago?'

''Course he would! Maybe he's only just had children of his own, or grandchildren? Maybe he was waiting until you were all adults? Or maybe he just woke up one morning, in the middle of his perfect life, smiled at his perfect wife, made breakfast for his perfect children, got in his Lamborghini and thought: *Today*? You know, today is the day. Maybe he got in touch *because* his life is totally "that great"?'

Robyn blinked at Nush in surprise. She had not been

expecting such a considered response from her friend. She swallowed, trying to gulp away the sense of impending drama. And then she smiled. 'Yeah,' she said, 'and maybe he's dying and he's only got six months to live.'

Nush threw her a look of exasperation. 'Yeah, well, whatever,' she said. 'But you asked me what I'd do, and if I were you then that's what I'd do.'

Robyn paused for a moment. She rubbed her thumb and forefinger up and down the silken shaft of a blade of grass. 'What if he's a wanker, Nush? What if I hate him?'

Nush shrugged and picked up the half-empty wine bottle. 'Well then,' she said, 'at least you'd know. And that's got to be better than not knowing, right?'

Robyn held out her plastic glass and nodded mutely.

Maybe she was right.

Jack and Robyn got back to their flat at eight o'clock that evening. Jack had managed to shake off Jonathan and Leo who had been hinting quite strongly that they would, in an ideal world, be joining Jack and Robyn back at their place and drinking themselves sick into the rude hours.

The flat felt melancholy when they returned. It was untouched since they'd left almost eight hours earlier. The sun had passed all the way around their terrace, through the front windows, through the back windows, warming the dust, the furnishings, the wooden floors. Now the rooms were cool and dark, silently awaiting their return.

Jack kicked off his flip-flops and pulled two cold beers

from the fridge. He removed their lids on the edge of the wooden counter, like some dude in an American sitcom, and brought them to the sofa where Robyn sat, still and pensive.

She was feeling the arms of her current life wrapping themselves around her, squeezing her in a tight embrace. She was studying the minute details of her home; the worn patches in the terracotta kilim, the dark nodding tulips in a glass bowl on the dining table, the crack in the plaster behind the TV that looked like a bolt of lightning, the ornate ridges in the skirting boards, the tasteful pencil sketch of a woman's head that hung beside the front door, and a framed review of Jack's first novel from the *Guardian*, entitled 'Word Perfect'.

Every detail was so new, yet already so familiar. But still there was that tinge of melancholy about her surroundings. Her life should feel perfect, but it didn't. Her love for Jack should have been enough, but it wasn't. She should have been sailing through her first year at medical school, but instead she'd dragged herself through, painfully, and was now set to fail.

She turned to Jack as he joined her on the sofa. Her voice left her wine-dry mouth sounding bland and flat. 'I want to meet my donor dad,' she said.

Jack's eyebrows twitched. 'Wow,' he said, 'you've come a hundred and eighty degrees since this morning.'

She nodded.

'What made you change your mind?' he asked.

She shrugged and picked at the frayed hem of her cut-off

shorts. 'Nothing, really,' she started, 'just . . .' She sighed. 'Ever since I signed up with the Registry I've been feeling like something's missing. No, more than that – I've been feeling like I'm supposed to be somewhere . . . like there's, you know, unfinished business in my life. And I was so determined to get through my life without meeting this man, so determined for just my mum and dad to be enough, for *me* to be enough, and now . . . I'm not enough, any more. D'you see? I'm just *not enough*.' She started to cry then and Jack took her in his arms. She pushed her face against the cotton of his t-shirt. It smelled of sun and fresh sweat.

'Good,' he said into her hair, 'good.'

She pulled away and looked at him curiously. 'What do you mean, good?' she asked.

He sighed. 'I mean, *good* because I thought it was me.'

'Thought *what* was you?' she asked.

He sighed again. 'You. The way you've been since you moved in here. Well, since *before* you moved in here. I thought you were . . .' He paused. 'I don't know, what happened . . . after I gave you the keys. For a while it was as if you found me repulsive. And then you just went completely cold on me. I thought I'd blown it, you know? I was so angry with myself, for what I'd done, asking an eighteen-year-old girl to move in with me. But then you came back and I was just totally overwhelmed. I thought I'd lost you. But even then, you weren't the same. You haven't been the same. That sparkle you had the first time I saw you, that look you had in your eye, so cocksure and pleased with yourself – it's gone. And I thought it was me. I thought I'd done that to you. That leaving home, leaving your friends, living with me had done that to you . . .'

Robyn wiped away tears from beneath her eyes. 'No!' she cried. 'No. It was never you. It was always me. You've always been the meaning of everything. You've always been perfect, Jack, totally. It's me who's broken down. It's me who needs fixing. And once I've moved on from this, for better or for worse, everything will be about you and me. The world, the universe and everything in it. I love you so much, Jack, so much.'

He smiled at her with joyful relief. He pressed his forehead against hers and clutched her wet cheeks between the palms of his hands.

'Come on then,' he said, 'let's get writing to this father of yours. Let's get fixing you.'

DEAN

'I used to come down here with my dog,' said Lydia, her hands in the pockets of her jeans, negotiating the downward camber of the slope leading to an overgrown railway track.

'You had a dog?' Dean replied.

'Yeah. A German Shepherd. His name was Arnie. I used to come down here with him and get drunk.'

'Cool,' said Dean, trying to envisage the poised woman in front of him skulking around on disused railways with a massive dog, necking Wild Turkey or somesuch straight from the bottle.

'Well, no, it wasn't really that cool. It was pretty tragic actually.'

He followed her down to the bottom of the slope where she perched herself on the grass. He sat himself next to her and viewed the surroundings with his arms wrapped around his knees. 'Quiet down here, isn't it?' he said.

'Yes. Good place to think.' She placed her chin on her cupped hands and stared into the middle distance.

'Got plenty of stuff to think about now, haven't we?' he said, glancing at the carrier bag hooked over the crook of his arm, thinking about its shocking contents.

'I think we should go to the police,' she said.

'What, seriously?'

'Yes, I do. This is fucking serious stuff. This is . . .' Lydia's voice trailed away and Dean gulped. He was still reeling from the events of the past hour. He pulled a pouch from his jacket pocket and assembled a spliff. Lydia eyed him from the corners of her eyes. She said nothing but returned her gaze to the tangle of weeds, litter and brambles on the other side of the tracks. 'I think he killed him. My dad. I think he killed the baby and then I think he killed my mother.'

'No,' began Dean, because his brain could not process such a dark and depraved possibility. 'No, there must be another reason, there must be . . .'

'It fits,' she said, coldly. 'It fits the mould. My dad, he was strange. He was really strange. He wasn't what a dad should be and I always put that down to my mum dying and leaving him alone with me, I always put it down to him hating me for not being my mum. But now, I think about it and I can *see* it, do you understand what I mean? I can close my eyes and I can see him doing it, I really can.

'But what I don't understand is why I don't remember it? I mean, I must have been there. Or I must certainly have known my mum was pregnant, that there was going to be a baby. I must have *met* the baby, you know? And then realised that it was there one day and gone the next. I don't understand how I could have forgotten that? I mean, surely it should be in here,' she pointed at her own head, 'somewhere? Surely I should know this. Surely I should know!' She dropped her head into her hands and groaned. 'My sick, fucked-up, fucking family,' she growled.

Dean looked at her with concern. He wanted to calm her down but didn't want to make things worse. 'Listen,' he said, putting a hand on her upper arm. 'Listen. I don't want to sound like I don't believe you, but maybe it's not as bad as you're thinking. Maybe there's a better explanation.'

'Like what?'

He shrugged. 'Maybe someone took the baby? Maybe it was adopted? Maybe after your mum died your dad couldn't cope with a new baby and he gave it away?' He stopped abruptly. The realisation struck him like a metal weight against his chest: he could be talking about himself. He stopped breathing for a few seconds and then he inhaled. His heart pattered tremulously. He licked the Rizla paper and he sealed the spliff and then he lit it. The first rush of smoke to his bloodstream calmed his nerves for a moment. He imagined Lydia's father. He imagined him big and shiny, like a skinned Rottweiler. He imagined him with rheumy eyes and thick fingers and a snarling mouth. He imagined him ugly and spitting and crazed. The sort of man who could throw a small baby to its death; the sort of man who could kill his wife and then sit back in an armchair and get on with the rest of his life. He imagined, in other words, the man that Lydia remembered. The weird man. The strange man. The ugly man.

And then he wondered what his own daughter would imagine when she thought of him in years to come. The man who couldn't raise her because she was too small and too clever and too fucking perfect. The man who couldn't raise her because he was too small and too stupid and too fucking pathetic. Would she see an ugly man? A spiteful man? Would she hate him so much that she could reasonably picture him throwing babies off balconies?

He blanched at these thoughts, dragged two, three, four times greedily from the spliff before passing it to Lydia.

She took it without comment and he watched with interest as she put it to her lips and inhaled. And as he watched her, all of a sudden he could see her as she said she'd once been, a loner, a drinker, a loser. He looked at her and saw her fade and then reform in front of his eyes into a hunched teenager, with a faithful dog, sitting on the bank of a disused railway, drinking away the pain of her own bitter disappointment. He suddenly felt closer to her than he'd ever felt to any human being. He wanted to pull her to him and hug her, but he could see that she was lost for now in her own terrible thoughts. After a couple of draws on the spliff she handed it back to him with a small smile and then she laid herself backwards against the long grass and crossed her arms across her heart.

He lay down with her and for a while they rested together in silence, studying the astringent blue sky, passing the spliff back and forth until it was nothing more than a tiny brown lump.

The silence was absolute, broken only occasionally by

the twittering of a small bird somewhere out of sight. Dean had not experienced such silence since he was a child, in a place quite like this, somewhere in Devon, lying with Tommy, sweaty and exhausted after two hours of playing soldiers. He could remember the moment clearly: the two of them panting hard and loud, in and out, the grass tickling his neck, his cheeks burnished red, watching the sun pulsating gently overhead. He remembered eating up the feeling, swallowing it deep inside, knowing that it was rare, knowing that it was special. And now here it was again, a perfect cloudless day, a kind sun, long grass and a kindred soul. He closed his eyes and he breathed it in again, wondering how long it would be until the next time he felt so complete.

He let his thoughts wander beneath the blood red of his closed eyelids. He thought of things he hadn't let himself think about for a long time. He thought of the moments outside the room in the hospital when Sky was silently dying behind the doors. He thought of Rose's face as the doctor explained what had happened, the way all the muscles that kept her face looking like a face had collapsed as one, leaving her suddenly a hundred years old. And he thought of the way his daughter had looked in that plastic box, so inhuman, something that a person was not genetically programmed to see, like a two-headed man or a cow with six legs. Wrong and unlikely yet radiantly beautiful, a fleeting glimpse of a celestial angel. He hadn't thought of these things for so long because they had nauseated him, but he could bear to contemplate them here, now.

A sudden breeze stirred the air; it sounded like water rushing over rocks. He opened his eyes and saw that Lydia was gone. He sat up too fast. Blood rushed to his head and rocked his brain from side to side. And then he saw her, standing a few feet away, her hands in her pockets.

'You're right,' she said as he got to his feet. 'I'm being too dramatic. There could be any number of explanations. I need to see Rod. I need to see my uncle.'

He nodded. 'D'you know where he lives?'

'Sort of,' she said, 'I know the name of the village. Once we're there it'll just be a matter of asking around. Thing is, though, it's getting late. By the time we've done this it'll be too late for the train back to London. I'll probably take a room somewhere, in a B&B or something. But it's up to you. I'll get the taxi to drop you back at the station, if you like, or you can stick around with me.'

Dean got to his feet and stretched himself out. He considered the options. He wanted to know what had happened to Lydia's baby brother. But he had the feeling that Lydia wanted to do this on her own. He also felt there were things he needed to do, too, people he needed to talk to. He had learned more about himself in the last ten minutes here in this forgotten hollow full of thick, unsullied air than he had in the last twenty years of his life. He could be more of a man than Lydia's father had been. And he could be more of a person than he'd ever thought possible.

He'd seen now where Lydia had come from, he'd seen her council flat, her dowdy village, the place she came to escape. And he'd seen where she'd got to, the mansion,

343

the housekeeper, the burly fake-tanned trainer. He didn't want a mansion and housemaid and burly fake-tanned trainer. He just wanted more than he had. And for the first time in his life he really believed, not only that he was capable of more, but also that he deserved more.

'It's all right,' he said, 'I reckon I'll get back, if that's OK with you?'

'That's fine with me.' Lydia smiled.

'And he's cool, is he, this uncle of yours?'

She smiled again. 'As far as I recall,' she said. 'I don't remember much about him, but I'm pretty sure he was a sweetheart.'

'Good.' Dean nodded. 'And you'll be all right, staying here?'

'Yes,' she laughed. 'I'm a big girl.'

'Yeah,' he said, 'I know you are. You're brilliant. I just . . .' He stared at his trainers meaningfully for a moment, wondering if he should say what was on his mind. He looked up at her and blushed. 'I've only just found you. I don't want to lose you again. That's all.'

Lydia's face did something strange then. It sort of shifted into a different position, as if she was preparing to impersonate someone famous, and then suddenly she was crying. 'Come here,' she said.

He stepped into her arms and let her hug him. It was still there, that stiffness, that reserve, but less so than before. This felt more familiar. 'I'm not going anywhere,' she said, her lips pressed to his ear. 'I'm right here for you now, forever. OK?'

'OK,' he whispered back into her ear.

And then they headed away from the sweet silence and solitude of this tiny corner of the universe and back towards the waiting taxi.

LYDIA

The first person Lydia asked knew exactly who Rodney was and exactly where he lived.

'Over there,' the slightly vague woman in a blue headscarf had said, 'there, other side of the hall, the cottage looks like it's falling down. Got a weeping willow outside.'

Lydia had smiled gratefully, and also in amusement. She was right to think that nothing would have changed. She was sure that locals would say that it had, that the area wasn't what it used to be, that it was all so different, but to Lydia's refreshed eyes, this place where she'd been bred, this place that had raised her, it was all precisely the same, even down to vague ladies of indeterminate age in blue headscarves.

She stood now in front of the cottage, which was exactly as the woman had described it, crumbly and tumbledown but not without its charms. Not the least of which was the extravagant willow which hung like an upturned head of hair over the small front garden, patterning everything in its shadow with intricate Moorish dappling.

The front door to the cottage was made of wide planks of wood, painted grey. Lydia grabbed a heavy iron ring and knocked it against a matching iron plate. She turned to the cab driver, parked on the road, and threw him a nervous smile.

A moment later the door opened and there he was. Uncle Rod. He was a small wiry man, physically youthful but gaunt and craggy in the face. His hair appeared to be dyed black and he still wore a small silver hoop in his left ear. He was dressed in a band t-shirt, some kind of heavy metal thing involving snakes and crosses, and faded black jeans. He peered at her curiously through round wire-framed spectacles. He looked terrified.

'Hello,' she said, as coolly as she could. 'I'm Lydia.'

'Of course you are!' His face opened up into a smile. 'Wow! Gosh! You haven't changed a bit. Do come in.' He pulled the door open wider and revealed a flagstoned kitchen and a small greasy-haired dog, sitting behind him and panting.

'Is this OK?' she asked. 'Is now a good time?'

'Now is an excellent time.' He smiled again. 'I was just making my supper. You can join me, if you like?'

Lydia looked at this gentle pixie of a man and saw the welcome glow of a comfortable lived-in home behind him. Her stomach felt entirely empty and she could see on the kitchen counter a chopping board spread with fresh herbs and a small uncooked chicken in a roasting tin. She approached the taxi driver and peeled five £20 notes from the large wad in her purse and then watched him leave, heading back towards the city.

'I must say,' said Rod, leading her into his kitchen and

installing her at a battered wooden table covered with paperwork and old newspapers, 'you look very well. The last time I saw you, well, you must have been about . . .'

'Eighteen. It was Dad's funeral.'

'Yes, that's right. I saw you then, but from a distance. I didn't want to intrude.'

Lydia nodded her head sympathetically, as though she understood perfectly why Uncle Rod had kept his distance at the funeral, but she didn't, she had no idea.

'You were just off to university then, weren't you, off with all your A levels, your aunty Jean told me. I bet your dad must have been so proud.'

'He didn't know,' said Lydia, smoothing her hands against her thighs, 'he was in the hospital by the time I got my results. I mean, I *told* him about them but I don't think he could hear. You know?'

Rod nodded and leaned back against the kitchen counter, his legs crossed at the ankle. 'Well, I suppose I can guess why you're here?'

She smiled.

'You got the cutting, then?'

'Yes,' she said, 'I got the cutting.'

'Yes. Sorry about that. Wasn't quite the ideal plan. But it was just, I don't know, I'd been carrying that blessed secret around with me for nearly thirty years, you know? Thirty years knowing too much about you.' His voice trailed away and he turned to the counter where he started rhythmically to untie the chicken, shred herbs, stuff the cavity, rub butter under the skin, slice carrots, peel potatoes and boil water. Lydia watched him hungrily, listening to the words that flowed from him in his sinewy Welsh accent. 'Anyway,' he continued, 'you know how sometimes the time for something just feels right? You leave something and you leave it and you know you should be doing something about it but you keep putting it off, and then something happens and you think, Aha, now I know why I waited, now I know why I put it off, because *now* is the right moment. Well, that's what I felt when I saw that newspaper article. I could live with you not knowing your real father, in a way that was my last gift to my brother, but you not knowing your brothers and sisters, believing that you're all alone in the world . . . well, I may or may not have made a terrible mistake, you may hate me for it forever, but I felt deep down in my heart of hearts that I'd done the right thing.'

He was facing away from her now and Lydia could see the sharp edges of his shoulder blades pushing against the fabric of his black t-shirt. She felt inexplicably sorry for him and found herself getting to her feet and standing alongside him. 'It's OK,' she said, touching his arm. 'It's OK. You did the right thing. Honestly.'

'I did?' he said, turning to face her.

'Yes. Totally. It was a relief to find out that my dad wasn't my dad and, God . . .' She felt the next few words rushing too fast to the tip of her tongue, so laden with joy and happiness were they. 'I found my brother! I joined that Registry, and I found my little brother! He's called Dean. He's twenty-one. He's lovely. And there's a sister, too, but I haven't been in touch with her yet. I think I will when I get back. I think I'm ready now. And then last week the dad signed up. The dad. The donor! And he wants to meet us. And it's been really weird. I won't pretend I was totally happy when I got your letter, I can't pretend I wasn't angry with you because I was. But it's all coming together now. And I promise you, whatever happens, you did do the right thing, you really did.'

'Oh, thank God. Thank God for that. I've been wrestling with myself ever since, you know. Killing myself over whether or not I'd ruined your life. But I just had this feeling. And thank God that feeling was right.'

'But why did you do it anonymously?' asked Lydia, stooping to stroke the greasy and slightly pungent dog who was sitting on her feet, looking at her hopefully.

'I'm not sure really,' he said. 'I think I just wanted it to be something you could ponder in isolation, if you see what I mean? Not think about anyone else. Just your dad and how you came to be. Not worrying about poor old Uncle Rod and how he was doing. And it's not that I haven't thought about you often over the years because I really have, very often. You were such a funny little girl, so stern and serious, and I always had the softest spot for you. I'd take you out to the playground . . . I even took you to the department store once to get you some new shoes – but I don't suppose you remember that.' He smiled and his eyes filled with the mist of nostalgia.

Lydia shook her head. She certainly did not remember that. But there were bigger and more pressing missing memories to confront. She went to the table to retrieve the old carrier bag with the baby clothes in it.

'Listen,' she said. 'I've been here all day, with my brother, wanting to . . . I don't know really, wanting to confront my fear of my past, I suppose. I wanted to show my brother where I came from, show him the flat, show him where my mother died, show him the places I used to go, when I was young. When I was like him. And I'd kind of wanted to work out what happened that day, the day my mum fell off our balcony. I thought maybe if I went there and saw the place again, it might trigger something. That I might suddenly remember. But instead of remembering, I've ended up finding out more stuff that I've forgotten.'

She handed him the carrier bag silently and watched as he peered inside.

'Good God,' he said. He put down a wooden spoon and pulled the clothes out. He held them in his hands and stared at them, blinking behind his glasses. 'Good God,' he said again. He looked at Lydia and said: 'Where did you find these?'

'The man who lives in the flat now, he found them in Dad's wardrobe. He'd had them all this time.' Lydia felt her heart race then as she mentally prepared herself for the truth, whatever it may be.

'Jesus Christ,' said Rod. The colour had left his face. He took the clothes and sat down heavily in one of his paint-splattered, spindle-back chairs. Then he removed his glasses and pinched the bridge of his nose. 'I can't believe your dad put these away. I can't believe he kept them.'

'But whose are they?' she asked, desperate for him to get to the crux of the thing.

He stood up again and opened the oven door with a tattered padded glove. He slid the chicken into the oven and then he came back to the table. He sat down opposite Lydia and smiled at her sadly.

'They belonged to your baby brother,' he said, 'his name was Thomas.'

Lydia felt a terrible jolt of sadness run through her. 'Thomas?'

'Yes. He was a lovely little thing. He really was.'

Lydia's heart quickened. 'What happened to him?' she asked, brusquely.

Rod sighed and slid his glasses back on to his face. 'Oh, God,' he said. 'I don't know where to start here, Lydia, to be honest. This is all so unbearable. It really is. And I swore . . . oh, Jesus, I swore I'd never say. But little Thomas, well, he died.'

Lydia blinked and gulped. There it was. Just as she'd expected. 'Was it him?' she asked. 'Was it my father? Did he . . . did he kill my brother?'

Rod looked at her in amazement. 'What? Trevor? Kill the baby? Good God, no! No! What on earth . . . I mean, why would you ask that?'

Lydia felt a wave of tension lift from her body. 'I don't know,' she said, 'I just thought . . .' She didn't finish her sentence. 'So what did happen?'

'Well, little Thomas was only five days old when your mum died. Tiny little thing he was. And your dad, well, I suppose he had a kind of breakdown. He couldn't cope. Our mum took in the baby, but she wasn't young then, she was in her late-sixties and not well herself. And there was a lady in the village here who said she could take in a baby. . .'

'Oh my God, you mean, my dad gave the baby away?'

'No, not gave it away. That's wrong, that is. That's not how it was. He just let this lady look after the baby. It was supposed to be temporary. You know, just until your dad was feeling more himself. But he never really did start to feel more himself, your dad, because you know he adored your mother so much. Did you know that? He worshipped her. And he couldn't find a way to be happy without her. And so this lady got more and more attached to the baby, started to call him another name even. And then one night, when Thomas must have been about six months old – oh, God, it was a terrible, terrible night – this woman, Isabel was her name . . . she still lives around here, just across the other side of the village . . . she started screaming, screaming in the night like a dying animal, you know? I thought it was foxes at first. Tried to get back to sleep, but the screaming got louder and closer, and then there was a battering at my door and there was this woman, Isabel, with this thing in her arms, looked like a pile of laundry, but no, it wasn't laundry, it was him. It was little Thomas. Died in his sleep, he had. Like an old man. Just closed his eyes and not opened them again, and she'd gone in there because he hadn't woken like he usually did for a bottle or something, and found him like that. Asleep. So little Thomas never came home. And you never got a chance to know him.

'And that was why, Lydia, when I saw that article, saw those sisters all so alike, all so happy, I wanted you to be able to have that. Because it was bad enough when your mother died. I thought that that had ripped the heart out of everything. I thought that that was the worst it would ever, ever be. But when that little scrap of a boy was presented to me there,' he pointed at the front door, 'on my own doorstep, my own nephew, my own family, well, I can't think there's a worse thing to go through, I can't think there's a greater pain to be felt. And your dad . . .' He pressed his hands to his face. 'Telling your dad. Coming to your place in the early hours and telling him that his little man had gone . . . He never recovered. He never ever did.'

'But what about this?' She pointed at the pink stains on the baby clothes. 'How did they get on his clothes? The same paint as in my room, the same paint as on the concrete?'

Rod fingered the blue cotton. 'This is what he was wearing,' he began, 'when your mother died.'

Lydia stared at Rod and waited for him to elaborate.

Rod sighed. 'He'd been crying, in his basket. Your mother had been painting your room. She went to him with paint on her hands. She couldn't leave a baby to cry, not ever, your mum. She was too soft. I was there, and your dad. We were having a bit of a barney, me and your dad. It was pretty strong stuff. We'd sent you down to the playground with the woman next-door.'

'What were you arguing about?'

'We were arguing about . . .' He sighed again. 'We were arguing because . . . well, it was me. I'd just split up with a girlfriend. A proper serious girlfriend. Asked her to marry me and she laughed. Said, "You're not a keeper, Rod." Can you imagine?' He tutted to himself. 'Anyway, I was drunk. I came to see you all, hoping for a bit of comfort. Your mum was there, painting your room. I sat in there with her for a while, watched her with that pink paint. I was always, I think, a little bit in love with your mother, Lydia, if that doesn't shame me to say so. And I think your dad knew that. He teased me about it, but it was never anything serious. But I think, after you were born, he started worrying about things . . .'

'What sort of things?'

'Well, like the fact that you didn't look like him. I don't think he felt he ever connected with you, not properly. I hope that doesn't sadden you, for me to say that?'

'No.' She laughed hoarsely. 'No, that doesn't sadden me in the slightest. I couldn't be any sadder about it than I already was.'

Rod looked at her fondly and continued. 'Anyway,' he said, 'I was there in your room, with your mum. It was hot. She was wearing an old pair of denim shorts and a t-shirt that I'd given her . . . Aerosmith, I think it was. She was sitting next to me on your bed, very close, because, like I say, I was in need of comfort. She didn't touch me, though, because her hands, they were all covered in the pink paint. But still your dad walked in with you and saw us like that and he maybe just got the wrong idea. Maybe there was an atmosphere of intimacy in the room. And in fact there probably was because, well, me and your mum had a secret. Well, we had two secrets, in fact. You and your brother. Because I was the only person who knew where you both really came from.' He paused and fingered the tabletop. 'I was there with her, both times, when she went for treatment up in London.'

Lydia screwed up her eyes and then made a strange groaning noise. 'Thomas was a donor baby too?' she asked quietly.

'Yes. Of course he was. Well, he wouldn't have been your dad's, would he? I mean, your dad couldn't make babies, that was the whole point of the donor clinic. That was the whole point of everything. And no one could ever have told him that. He'd rather have gone without babies than admit that he couldn't sire his own. And your mother wanted babies more than she wanted anything. Babies was all she wanted. And so there were two options; either she could go with another man . . . but your mother would never have done that, she loved your dad too much, she loved the very marrow of him, you know? . . . or she could go for a stranger. And so she did that, and asked me to go with her. I helped her choose your dad. I helped her choose you, and your brother. You both came from the same man.'

Lydia closed her eyes as a whole new realisation dawned upon her.

'So, yes, we had our secrets, big, dreadful secrets, too.

But then this boy was born and you know, strange as it was, he looked like your dad which should have been a good thing, but it wasn't a good thing because, of course, if he looked like your dad, then he looked like me a bit too. And your dad just walked into this room and saw us there and he must have suddenly decided, suddenly *believed*, that his worst fears were true, that me and your mum were having an affair, that both his babies were mine. A fight ensued, and that was when your mother took you to the neighbour's and asked them to take you out of the building.'

'Did I know?' asked Lydia, feeling the oddness of asking someone a question about something she'd experienced herself. 'Did I know what was happening?'

'No,' he said, 'not at all. You were only three. All you knew was you had a new baby brother and your mum was painting your room pink. Anyway, your father, he started accusing me and your mother of all sorts, started saying that she had always preferred me because I was the bright one. Huh! Ironic really as everyone *always* preferred my brother for being the handsome one, but there you go. He was saying, "You two! Always all giggly behind my back, always cosying up to each other, you must think I'm stupid. I know that girl's not mine. I've always known that girl's not mine. And now look at this boy." And he points at the room next-door. "He's the spit of you, Rod. He's the effing spit of you!"

'He had it in his head that because he hadn't made a baby in five years of trying then he must be infertile, and that the only explanation for the babies was that they were mine. And I had to bite my tongue on telling him the truth. But the more Glenys tried to convince him that the babies were his, the angrier he got. And then the baby started to cry. Your mother picked him up. Your father meanwhile . . .' He paused and sighed, tremulously. 'Your father took a knife from the kitchen drawer. Oh, Jesus.' He put his hand to his heart as if to try and still it. He gulped. 'Just thinking about it, still, it makes me feel like I could throw up. He took a knife and he went after your mum. Your mum gave me the baby. I wish she hadn't given me that baby. If she hadn't given me that baby, I could have done something. But you know, Lydia, honestly to this day I don't believe he ever meant to hurt her, I really don't. I think he just wanted to scare her. I think if he'd got near her with the knife he'd have frozen up, because he did love her so much. But he went for her, with this knife, and I stood there with the baby . . . and the whole thing happened so fast. I just stood there, holding the baby.

'First your mother ran to the balcony and then your dad was there, brandishing this knife. And your mother . . .' He sighed. 'I was watching all this, but I promise you it happened so fast, there was nothing I could do to stop it. She climbed on to the wall of the balcony, trying to get away from him. And then it looked to me as if she was trying to make it across to the next balcony, the next one along from theirs, and one minute she was there, and the next she wasn't.' He stopped and drew in a breath. 'And it was silent for just a moment. All I could hear was myself, breathing; breathing so loud. And then it started, the screaming. *Call an ambulance. Call an ambulance . . .*'

'And . . . and . . . I was there?' asked Lydia. 'I saw it? From the playground?'

'No. You didn't see it. The neighbour had taken you around the corner, for a pee.'

'I was peeing when my mum died?'

'Well, yes, probably,' said Rod apologetically. 'And when the neighbour saw what had happened she took you away, quickly, around the back. Took you to her friend's flat.'

'And what was I told? What was I told about my mother?'

'I don't know,' he said. 'The usual stuff, I suppose. "Mummy's gone to live with the angels," that kind of thing. And then you came here to stay with me for a couple of nights.'

'I did?'

'Well, yes, the baby went to Mum and you came here. Only for two nights. Your dad never let me see you again after that. We never said another word to each other after that day. But you were here, with me, while they were holding your dad for questioning. They were going to do him for manslaughter but there wasn't enough evidence, especially with my witness statement. Because whatever happened that day, I know this much: your father did not kill your mother. Your mother, well, I don't know. I don't know what she was thinking. Maybe she thought she was bloody Spiderman, I don't know. All I know is that in less than thirty seconds she went from holding her baby in her arms to being dead on the ground.'

'She died immediately?'

'Oh, yes, instantaneously.'

Lydia lowered her eyes and stared at some old crumbs embedded inside a deep whorl on the tabletop. 'I don't remember anything,' she whispered.

'Well, no, that's probably best, isn't it? A blessing? At least, that's what I thought when you were a child. We just didn't talk about it. We didn't talk about your mother. We didn't talk about your brother. Your mother's family never forgave your father. And they never forgave me for what they saw as letting him "get away with it". Our family went into themselves completely. Nobody was ever the same again. Least of all your father.'

Lydia looked up at him and grimaced. 'Nor me,' she said.

He looked at her sadly and smiled. 'Well, yes,' he said, 'that's what I feared. Everyone thought because you hadn't seen it, because you couldn't remember, that you wouldn't be affected by it. But living all those years with a man who didn't believe you were his, cut off from your family, without a mother . . . It can't have been easy.'

'It was not easy,' she said, grimly. 'It was not easy at all.'

He smiled at her sadly again and then sighed. 'Listen,' he said, 'you and I have got so much to talk about. I'm sure there's a million things you'd like to ask. Why not stay the night? I've got a spare room, it's all freshly made up. I can open a bottle of wine. It'd be nice to have a proper chance to get to know you again. We really were very close once, you and I, as bizarre as that might sound.'

She looked at his gentle, fine-featured face and thought that, yes, she could believe they'd once been close. He was the sort of man a small girl would like to have as an uncle. She could imagine him pushing her on swings and taking her to the shops. She could imagine viewing him as a friend.

'That would be nice,' she said, 'I'd like that. There's so many thing I want to know. About my mum. And the baby. Have you got photographs?'

'I do, yes. My mother passed me down her albums when she died a few years back. All the family photos. Pictures of you as a child, pictures of your mother . . .'

'I've got those,' Lydia interrupted. 'My dad gave me his albums. What I meant was, have you any photos of the baby? Of Thomas?'

'Yes,' he said, 'yes. I believe I do. And, if you like, tomorrow morning, after we've had a nice wholesome breakfast, I could take you to the cemetery over at Penrhys. I can take you to see where he's buried, little Thomas. If you'd like?'

'Yes,' said Lydia, feeling breathless with a mixture of wonder and sadness and awe, 'yes, please. I'd like that. I really would. Because he's not just *my* brother, is he?'

Rod glanced at her quizzically.

'No,' she said, 'he's their brother too. He's Dean's

brother and Robyn's brother and he's Daniel Blanchard's son. I want to see it for them. For all of them.'

'Good,' said Rod, 'good. That's sorted then. Now, I think,' he peered over his shoulder at the clock on his kitchen wall, 'yes, it is! The sun is definitely over the yardarm and I think it's time for a glass of wine. And let me tell you, this will be the single most enjoyable glass of wine of my entire life.'

MAGGIE

Through a rather complicated system of printing off e-mails and taking them to the hospice, getting Daniel first to read them and then to reply to them in hard-to-decipher shakily written French, then typing them at home and sending them to Marc, it transpired that he would be arriving at lunchtime on Thursday, with the intention of staying indefinitely – in other words, and Maggie was glad that it had never been said explicitly, until Daniel died.

She'd bought some Teach Yourself French tapes and had been listening to them in her car as she drove around between home, Libby's, work and the hospice. She was listening to it now: '*J'ai laissé ma porte déverrouillée*', said a woman with a slightly patronising tone of voice. '*J'ai laissé ma porte déverrouillée*,' repeated Maggie with as much verve as she could muster, wondering if she would ever have cause to tell someone in French that she had left her door unlocked.

She flicked her indicator to the left and turned off the main road into the driveway of Daniel's home. Marc was due in an hour and she was going to strip Daniel's bed and put some clean bedding on. She also had some bags of shopping on the back seat, just some basics, some bread, milk, cheese. (Only Cheddar. She'd lingered over the earthily named French cheeses at the counter in Waitrose, but lost her nerve; how could French cheese purchased in Bury St Edmunds possibly compare to the real stuff?) She also had some apples, some bananas and a couple of pots of chilled soup. And a bar of soap. (It was always nice to be the one to start a new bar of soap, even if the existing soap belonged to your own brother.)

She turned off the engine and the patronising lady stopped halfway through saying something about a shoe shop. As she pulled the shopping from the back seat and let herself into the building, Maggie spoke French under her breath. '*Je vais à la maison de Daniel. J'ai quelques achats. Je m'appelle Maggie. Comment s'est passé votre vol?*'

Maggie was wearing her new sundress – it was good at her age that she still had nice arms and that her décolletage had not yet turned to crêpe; it was nice to be able to uncover herself on warm days. The dress was white. The day that lay before her felt so fraught with darkness and uncertainty that she had been drawn subconsciously to a colour that signalled newness and innocence. On her feet she wore putty-coloured gladiator sandals, and her highlighted hair was pinned up away from her face.

As she walked through the front door of the flat she heard a text message arriving on her phone. It was from Marc: *Chère Maggie, je suis dans un taxi. Je serai là en une heure.* Exactly an hour later she came to the window at the sound of tyres over gravel and saw a car slowing as it approached the building. Maggie pulled down her sunglasses. It was a taxi and there was a man sitting on the back seat. She put the sunglasses back on to her head and then decided in a fleeting moment of vanity to put them back on her face. The light was harsh today and she wanted to make a good, and hopefully youthful, first impression.

She'd straightened herself out and then she ran down the stairs and greeted him, with a wide and welcoming smile, on the driveway.

She'd had her first French phrase all planned out and repeatedly rehearsed in her head: '*Bonjour, Marc, ravis de vous rencontrer.*' As the cab pulled into the driveway she went to the passenger door and saw him lean forward to open it. *Bonjour, Marc,* she thought to herself, *bonjour, Marc.* But as he climbed out of the back of the taxi, all the words in Maggie's head just drained away and she was left instead staring at him, with her jaw slightly slack and her hand clutched tight to her chest. Because the man climbing out of the back of a taxi outside Daniel's flat was, in fact, Daniel.

He smiled at her. 'You must be Maggie,' he said. 'It is lovely to meet you. I am Marc.'

Maggie still said nothing, still stared at the man who called himself Marc but was clearly, in fact, Daniel. 'I . . .' she began, but no words followed.

'Are you OK?' he asked, letting the hand he'd put out for her to shake drop back to his side.

'Yes. *Oui.* Sorry, I . . . er . . .' Her brain slowly started to function again and all the thoughts that had been stuck in a logjam began to filter through. This man was not Daniel. This man was too healthy to be Daniel. This man was Marc. This man, then, was not only Daniel's brother, but also Daniel's twin.

'I'm sorry,' she said. 'Daniel didn't tell me, he didn't say . . . I'm sorry, I don't know, what is the French word for "twin"?'

The man called Marc smiled at her and said, '*Jumeau.*'

'*Jumeau?*' repeated Maggie.

'*Oui.* Yes. *Jumeau. Jumelle* if it is a girl.'

'Oh,' she said, and then tried to process another unexpected fact. Marc could speak English. 'Your brother told me that you couldn't . . . that you only spoke French.' The man smiled and laughed, and at the sound of that laugh Maggie already knew that this man may have the same face as Daniel but he was a completely different person. 'My brother,' he said, pulling his wallet from his back pocket to pay for his taxi ride, 'has not seen me for thirty years.' He shrugged as if to suggest that no further explanation was necessary.

He paid the driver and bade farewell to him in confident conversational English, and then he turned and smiled widely at Maggie. 'You are not as I expected either,' he said.

'Oh,' said Maggie. 'What were you expecting? Or shouldn't I ask?'

'No, you should not ask.' He smiled again, that big, dimpled smile that his brother rarely allowed himself to expend. Then he picked up his small suitcase and glanced at the building in front of him. 'So, this is where my brother has been hiding all these years?'

Maggie smiled back. 'Yes,' she said, 'this is where he lives. Come in. Let's get you settled in.'

He followed her through the communal hallway and up the stairs to the front door of the flat. 'I still can't believe that Daniel didn't tell me you were his twin,' she said, as she turned her key in the lock.

'Well,' said Marc, 'it has been a long time. Maybe he forgot?'

Maggie smiled. 'Maybe,' she said. She pushed open the door and let Marc into the flat first.

'Well,' he said, 'this is a very nice apartment that Daniel has. I did not know. I was always maybe a little worried that he might not be living comfortably, that maybe he had found himself a little poor. But it seems not.' He walked slowly around the two rooms on the first level, wandered to the window in the living room and looked down into the leafy communal garden from Daniel's roof terrace. 'This is nice, very nice. And you, do you live near here?' he asked, turning to look at her and throwing her once more into disarray with his facsimile resemblance to his brother.

Maggie averted her face so that he would not see her expression. 'No,' she said, 'I live in town, near the station, that way.' She gestured vaguely to the east. 'Shall I show you the upstairs?'

He beamed at her. 'Of course,' he said.

He followed her up the softly carpeted stairs and she showed him Daniel's small eaved bedroom and the eaved bathroom off the landing. He left his suitcase on top of Daniel's bed and then turned to Maggie and smiled again. 'Thank you,' he said, 'thank you for your help, Maggie. I wonder if it would be possible for me to take a quick shower before we leave for the hospital?'

She started. 'Oh, yes, of course. Sorry. I should have thought. Have you got everything? I mean, I've put in fresh towels and a new bar of soap, is there anything else you'll need?'

'No, thank you, Maggie. That will be enough, I'm sure.'

She backed out of the room and tiptoed down the stairs again. She sat on the terrace while she waited for Marc to get ready and stared across the gardens and into the distant landscape. Yet again, Daniel's reticence to share anything of himself with her had tripped her up. An identical twin. An English-speaking identical twin. A twin who appeared not to have suffered any of the existential damage that his brother must have sustained to have evolved into such a closed box of a person.

She picked at the dry skin around her French-manicured fingernails and she waited. She felt suddenly engorged with questions she wanted to ask. But this was not a day for asking questions. Today was a day for reunions. Questions could wait.

Marc emerged a few moments later, with damp hair and wearing a very smart windowpane-check shirt in shades of blue and a pair of dark indigo jeans. He smelled of soap and cologne, and he looked, as his brother had once done, terrifically handsome. 'There,' he said, patting his freshly shaved cheeks, 'I am now clean. And, I think, nearly ready for the next bit.'

Maggie smiled and got to her feet. 'How old were you both,' she began, 'the last time you saw each other?'

'We were twenty-four,' he said. And with the words came a vague tone of regret. 'Yes,' he said, dropping his gaze to the floor. 'It is crazy. Twins. Divided. My mother, well . . .' he looked up at her with watery eyes '. . . she has a broken heart. But still,' he smiled again and clapped his hands together, 'there is time to talk, no doubt, as we drive. And now, after thirty years, I am more than ready to see him again. So, let us go.'

'Yes,' said Maggie. 'Let's go.'

In the car, Marc stared quietly through the window for a few minutes. Eventually he turned to Maggie and said: 'How bad is he? Really?'

She sighed, and peered into her wing mirror as she pulled into the next lane. 'I don't know, Marc. Honestly, it's very strange. It's so hard to tell. But I would say, well, he's very bad. I would say, let's put it like this, I think you came just in time.' She turned and looked at him, her mouth forced into a tight smile.

He turned away from her and returned his gaze to the view from the window.

She allowed him another moment of silence before speaking again. 'Listen, Marc,' she began, tentatively, 'there's something else I have to tell you. And this will probably come as a surprise to you, but a few weeks ago Daniel told me something, something quite remarkable. He told me that when he first arrived in this country he was so hard up for cash that he, well, he became a donor. Do you know what I mean by that, a donor?'

'No, I am not sure . . .'

'Well, you know, ladies who can't have babies, or rather they have husbands who can't have babies, they can go to a clinic and be artificially, well . . .'

'Ah.' Marc's head nodded in understanding. 'Yes. A *donneur*. I do know what you mean.'

'Good. Well, your brother did that. And he was told by the clinic where he was a donor that his . . . he . . . there are four children. Who are his.'

Marc's full brows rose higher. 'Yes?' he asked in a tone of surprise.

'Yes,' said Maggie. 'And he asked me, and I'm still not sure how much this was to do with the drugs or with the disease spreading to his brain, but he asked me to see if I can find them. And I haven't found them yet. But I'm hoping that I will. And if I do, I'll be asking them to come . . . to come and see Daniel.'

She glanced at Marc to see how he had taken this revelation. He nodded his head slowly up and down and stroked his chin. 'Wow,' he said eventually. And then he laughed, a soft bubble of laughter at first, followed by a few more bursts. His smile grew wider and then he turned to Maggie and beamed. 'Wow!' he said again. 'That is amazing! You mean, I have nieces and nephews?'

'Well, yes, I suppose you do.'

'Oh, this is incredible news! I thought . . . well, indeed, I thought there would never be any such thing. I have no children, and as far as I was aware my brother had no children. And now, suddenly, there are children! This is wonderful! Just wonderful! Thank you, Maggie. I can see that you are a true friend to my brother. I can see that he is lucky to have met you.' He smiled gratefully at her and Maggie felt something peculiar happen to her heart. She ignored the sensation and smiled and said, 'Oh, honestly. It's no big deal. Nothing anyone else wouldn't have done.'

At the hospice, they walked the corridors together, side-by-side. It felt other-worldly, to be walking into this place with the before version of her dying boyfriend, and Maggie caught her breath against the oncoming moments.

Daniel was as he'd been the previous day; slack, semi-conscious, grey. Marc caught his breath as he saw him and for a moment almost seemed to be about to turn and leave the room. Maggie heard his breath catch in his throat and laid her hand against his arm. 'Are you OK?' she asked. Marc had his fist at his mouth and his other hand thrust in his pocket. He inhaled deeply through his nostrils and then smiled tightly. 'Yes,' he said quietly, 'I think I am. I will be.' He approached the bed and Maggie followed him.

'Daniel,' she said in a loud whisper, touching his shoulder gently, 'Daniel. It's me, Maggie. Can you hear me?'

Daniel stirred slightly and his dry mouth opened a crack. A noise exited his lips but Maggie could not make out a word. 'There's someone here with me, someone special.' Daniel groaned again. 'It's your brother, Daniel, it's Marc. He's here. Can you open your eyes? Can you see?'

Daniel's eyelids twitched and then his lips turned up into a smile. He opened his mouth and slowly he uttered the word, 'Marc.'

Marc moved closer to his brother and laid his hand against his shoulder. 'Yes!' he said. '*Oui, Daniel, c'est moi!*'

'Marc,' said Daniel again. He pulled his arm from under the sheets and let his hand drop heavily on top of Marc's. And then, very suddenly and quite unexpectedly, Marc kicked off his shoes and he climbed atop the bed and he rested himself, in what little space there was, against the side of his brother's poor wasted body and he draped his arm across his brother's waist and he held his hand tight within his and then he kissed him on the cheek, just above his ear, hard and passionate.

Maggie was about to say, Oh, be careful, he has an intubation in his stomach, and a catheter, don't hold him too much. But she caught the words in the base of her throat and left them there. And then she turned and walked out of the room.

An hour later they sat together by the Koi pond. The earlier warm weather had dissipated, leaving behind a disappointingly nondescript afternoon of grey skies. With the chill breeze, Maggie had returned to her car to fetch a cardigan. Marc sat and peered at the gravelled ground between his feet.

'I must have known,' he said. 'It is so strange. But I must have known. To have written that letter when I did, after so many years without any contact. I must have felt it. Because, you know, they say, don't they, that identical twins have this, how you say . . . see-kick . . .?'

'Psychic?'

'Yes, this psychic connection.' He tapped his temple with his finger. 'And I remember, I was sitting at work, in my office, and I saw a bird through the window. It was up high and it was flying like this . . .' he drew a circle in the air '. . . round and round he goes. Round and round. And I find myself thinking that I would like this bird to stop flying round and round and to fly straight, straight across the Channel, straight up here, and then come to my brother's window and tell him that I am missing him. And as I think this, I decide to write him a letter. I see it as a sign, yes? And then, well, here I am and my brother is leaving us.' He let his head drop between his knees and then he brought it up again and Maggie saw that there were tears glistening on either side of his beautiful nose. 'And I am here *only just* in time.' He smiled a brave smile and before she could censor her own actions Maggie had taken both his hands in hers and squeezed them.

'Thank you,' he said in a croaky whisper. 'Thank you.'

They sat in silence for a while, their hands still entwined. A shiver ran down her spine and she shuddered.

'Oh,' said Marc, misreading the involuntary move-ment, 'you are cold? We should go inside? Get some coffee?'

Maggie nodded. She'd had no lunch. She'd quite like a sandwich. They walked slowly back into the building and towards the cafe. 'Why did you and Daniel fall out with each other?' she asked, tentatively.

'Fall out?' he said.

'Yes, you know, have an argument, become estranged?'

'Ah, yes, I see. But no, there was no argument. We did not have a fight.'

'Oh. I thought . . .'

'No, no, no. It was because of what happened. When he was at university. He told you about the child?'

Maggie looked at him questioningly.

'He did not tell you?' Marc sighed. 'Oh, dear. Well, it is not a surprise maybe. It is a hard thing to talk about. And that is why he went away. That is why he could not talk to me any more. Why he could not be the man he used to be. Because of this terrible, terrible thing.'

They turned a corner and Marc held open a door for Maggie to pass through. As she did so her body brushed against his and she felt a startling sense of longing, so strong that she had to hold back a low groan. She ignored the feeling, dismissing it as the result of too many conflict-ing emotions jostling for space inside her head.

'What terrible thing?' she asked, probably more force-fully than she'd intended.

'Oh, well. It is hard for me. He has not told you this

thing and now he is so ill, and maybe he has not told you for a reason. Maybe he did not want you to know?'

'No, he didn't want me to know. I was always trying to get him to talk to me about his past, about how he ended up in this country, but he had . . . *has* this clever way of answering a question without actually telling you anything. But I must say, he's shown me more of himself in the past few weeks than he ever showed me before. It's almost as though, well, as though he can't see the point of keeping his secrets any more. As though they've lost their meaning.'

'Well,' said Marc, 'in that case, maybe we should talk. Maybe I should tell you, because it makes me sad to say this but I feel like my brother will not be telling anyone any more secrets now. I think his time for telling them is over.'

They bought mugs of tea and sandwiches at the cafe and took them to the guests' lounge. They sat opposite each other at a black ash table adorned with brightly coloured dried flowers in a black vase. Maggie nibbled at the edges of her sandwich and waited for Marc to talk.

'Well,' he began, 'my brother was in his final year at medical school. He was a student doctor, hoping to become a paediatrician. He was placed in a children's cancer ward in a hospital just outside Dieppe and one night he was asked to administer some, how you say, morphine?'

Maggie nodded.

'And, well, he misread the dosage. It was late. He was tired. He killed the child with an overdose.'

Maggie gasped and brought her hands to her mouth.

Marc shook his head sadly, just once, and sighed. 'So, after this, there was an inquest, he was acquitted of manslaughter, but he could not go back to medicine. He could not go back to anything. He sat in his student room for a month, he saw nobody. And then, our mother . . . well, she is a very unwell woman herself, you know. She has always had the problems with her mind.' He tapped his head. 'Not a stable woman. And she took this accident very badly. She disowned my brother. Said she could not live with a child-killer as a son. And I think he found it very difficult to see me, his other half, so close we were, knowing that I could not feel what he was feeling. And knowing that our mother, she still loved me but she no longer loved him. And then, one day, he just disappeared,' Marc clicked his fingers together, 'like this. Gone. No words, no explanation.

'It felt as if my heart had broken. He did not tell us where he was for another five years. And then he said he was here, in England. He sent me these letters on this paper, with the English address printed at the top, yes? So I know where he is living. But he does not invite me. And I do not ask to come. And I do not know why this is. I do not know why there is this *bridge* that neither of us can walk across. It is almost as if, being a twin, it is all or it is nothing. You are either together or you are not. There is no halfway point between the two. So we chose nothing. And now, well, he is going away and I will never see him again. Not as he was.'

'Poor, poor Daniel!' said Maggie, one hand still at her throat. 'And poor, poor you. That is such a terrible story.'

'I know. It is a tragedy. A clever, caring, good man and one tiny mistake – and *pouf!* Everything turns to dust.'

'No wonder he never told me that. I mean, imagine how he's been feeling all these years, imagine the guilt and the lack of confidence. How would you ever trust yourself to do anything important again?'

'Well, yes, exactly. And see how he has made his children? See how he has let other people take all the responsibility for them?'

'Yes, but also he's given children to people who couldn't have them themselves. It's almost like he was paying the world back for taking the life of one.'

'Yes, that is true also. But I think it is mainly to avoid the risk, you see? His whole life since this accident has been lived to avoid taking the risk.'

'Yes . . .' said Maggie, and then she drifted away, as she realised that this was why their fledgling relationship had never headed down the road they'd both wanted it to. This was why he had never taken her in his arms and kissed her. This was why he had never told her he loved her. This was why they were still just friends. Because he did not want to take responsibility for her or her feelings. Because he did not want to damage her. 'Yes,' she continued, trying to keep her voice steady, 'yes. I can see that. I really can. How sad,' she said, 'how very, very sad.'

LYDIA

Her brother didn't have a middle name, but then neither did she. Her parents had not believed in middle names, for some unknown reason. She stood and faced his small stone tablet, carved from dove-grey stone, and stared at the lettering: *Thomas Pike*. Her brother. He would have been twenty-eight in August.

She'd been here before. She could remember it now, vividly. Her mother was buried here, too, on the other side of the chapel, between Lydia's father and Glenys' own mother. Lydia had been here to visit her mother's grave as a child, and later as an adult to bury her father.

Rodney stood at her side with his hands in the pockets of his blue jeans. 'You OK, love?' he asked.

She turned partially towards him and smiled sadly. 'I think so,' she said.

Her brother's ashes lay beneath her feet. A tiny box of dust. She wasn't really all right. She was bereft.

'Why is he buried over here?' she asked. 'Why is he all by himself?'

Rodney took a step closer to her and shook his head.

'I don't know what your dad was going through back

then. I wasn't there to know. But I suppose, your dad, he just couldn't deal with it. The little tiny grave. And he didn't want you to know about it either. Out of sight, out of mind, you know . . .'

Lydia turned back to the grave and felt cold dread run through her. Her father, again, doing the wrong thing. Always doing the wrong thing. Every single time. How could he have left Thomas here, a small boy, alone and away from his mother? How could anyone ever have thought that was the right thing to do?

'I want to move him,' she said, turning again to face Rodney, her face set with sudden resolve. 'I want to move Thomas, close to our mum.'

Rodney puffed out his cheeks. 'Well,' he began, 'I'm not sure you'd be able to do that. They're all pre-reserved, you know, pre-booked decades in advance by the sort of people who don't want to leave anything to chance. There's no spare plots up there by your mother. All gone.'

'Well, can't he go in with her? Share her plot?'

Rodney shrugged, apologetically. 'I can ask?' he offered.

Lydia nodded. 'Good,' she said, 'thank you. It's horrible.' She shuddered. The morning air here in the cemetery was chilled and dewy and her head was heavy with too much wine and a late night. She and Rodney had sat up until three in the morning pulling apart the threads of their shared history. But still she'd awoken early and resolute, ready to come to this place and feel what she needed to feel in order to move on again.

They'd visited her mother first, her grave still scrubbed

and tended by Rodney and by her own brother. Then Lydia had stood for a moment over the grave of her father and tried to feel something other than muted rage and vague distaste. She tried to summon pity and compassion from her heart but had found none. Life dealt many people a tough hand and not everyone went on to lead the failure of an existence that her father had. Other people, as the saying went, made lemonade.

She turned to Rodney and she smiled. 'I want to go now,' she said. 'I need to go home.'

'Of course you do, love. Go home and absorb it all. Go home and work it all out.'

She nodded, grateful for his insight into her thought processes. That was exactly what she wanted to do.

'I'll take you to the station now, there'll be a train at twenty-past, we should just make it.'

Lydia glanced once more at the grey stone that lay on top of Thomas Pike and she kneeled upon the damp grass and ran her hands over the tablet. She would be back again, she knew that. There was more in this small, proud country for her now than bad memories. For all that she'd lost, she was gaining more and more every day. She put her fingers to her lips and kissed them, afterwards pressing them to the stone. *I'll sort this out*, she promised Thomas silently. And then she and her uncle walked back to his car in the golden light of a just-risen sun.

'Ah!' said Bendiks, standing on the landing at the top of the stairs when she arrived back four hours later. 'You're home! I was just trying to call you.'

Lydia looked up at him in surprise and then at her handbag where her mobile phone was. 'I've just been on the tube,' she said.

'Ah,' he said, and started to walk down the stairs towards her.

'Is everything all right?' she asked.

'Yes! Of course. I was just desperate to know how it went . . . with your brother, in Wales. And, truth be told, I was missing you a bit. It's a big house when you're on your own.'

Lydia smiled. She felt gripped by fondness and affection for him. He greeted her at the door with a kiss on each cheek and gently removed her shoulder bag from her grasp. 'Here,' he said, 'let me.' He smelled of shampoo and soap. But there, underneath it, was that other smell, that smell that always got her, that slightly musky smell of the essence of him.

'You know we have a session this afternoon?' He put her bag down on the stairs and eyed her smilingly. 'Three o'clock?'

'Shit, yes, of course. Sorry, I'd completely forgotten.'

'I expected you to. So I'm not going to hold you to it. But if you'd like, we could still go for it?'

Lydia tried to clear some head space to consider the option. 'What time is it now?' she asked.

'It's nearly one.'

'OK, then,' she said. 'Yes. I think I could do with a workout.'

'Excellent,' said Bendiks. 'Cool. I'll see you here at three then and we can start with a run. And while we run, you can tell me all about it.'

They ran for nearly an hour. They hadn't meant to but Bendiks didn't have another client and the sun was out and there was a soft breeze and the pavement just seemed to unroll in front of them, metre after metre, like an endlessly unfurling carpet. They took an easy pace, gentle enough for talking without breathlessness, and Lydia told Bendiks everything. She told him all about meeting Rod, and the baby brother who'd died in a stranger's house; she told him about the little grave a hundred metres from where it should be, and the sense of letting go of her past whilst simultaneously embracing it. And Bendiks listened and said all the right things at all the right junctures and it was the closest Lydia had come in a long time to really opening her heart to another human being, to revealing the truth about herself without any caveats or exceptions. She didn't worry about how she would be perceived, or what he might be thinking, or if she was boring or sweaty or if her mascara had smudged. And it was utterly, exhilaratingly, liberating.

They tumbled through the front door at 4.30 and went straight downstairs to the gym. And as they walked, Lydia looked at the outline of Bendiks' body through his sweat-drenched clothes, she stared at the tendrils of wet hair that curled against the skin on the back of his neck and she considered the ache in her groin. Before she'd had a second to censor her thoughts she found herself saying: 'Shall we have a sauna?'

She stopped breathing as the realisation that she had said those words out loud hit her. *Shall we have a sauna*? It was worthy of a cheesy seventies porn movie. She couldn't look at Bendiks. A silence of less than a second felt as long as summer. She closed her eyes and waited to see what she had done.

'Cool,' said Bendiks. 'I thought you'd never ask.'

She opened her eyes and stared at him. 'Right,' she said, 'great. I'll, er, get us some robes.'

She pulled robes from the cupboard that Cait and Tom had left fully stocked with robes and towels ('We'll just buy new,' Cait had said, with a nonchalant shrug) and brought them back to the sauna. Her heart was hammering under her rib cage and she felt scared and stupid and strangely excited. 'I'm just going to get changed,' she said, passing Bendiks a robe. He smiled at her in bemusement. Clearly her state of mind was written all over her face. 'Thank you,' he said, taking the robe from her hands. 'I'll see you in there.'

Lydia dashed around the back of the sauna and tried to remember Cait's instructions on how to operate it. There was a remote-control unit screwed to the wall and she pressed buttons randomly until something sounded as if it had been activated and then she quickly climbed out of her sweaty running clothes and into the robe, tying it tight around her waist, adjusting the collar so that her cleavage would not be on show, staring mournfully at her ugly feet and feeling all the sexual energy that had driven her to make this lunatic suggestion in the first place start to wither and die. But then she walked into the sauna and Bendiks was sitting there, legs splayed open, his robe loosely tied, his chest shining in the muted light, and as she closed the door behind her she felt it: sex. It was alive and breathing in this room and she'd just shut the door and trapped it in here with them. Now surely she would find out, once and for all, if Bendiks was gay. Because if he was straight, and not just pretending to be straight to con her out of multiple £50 notes and a cheap room, then there was no way he'd be able to walk out of this room without something having happened between them.

He smiled at her, almost shyly. And then slowly a wall of steam built up between them and Bendiks became a ghostly statue on the opposite bench and for a while they didn't talk to each other. She saw him peel his arms out of the sleeves of the robe and let them fall on to the bench so that now he was uncovered from the waist up. He rolled his head back on his neck and let it rest against the wall of the sauna and his legs relaxed away from each other so that if there had been less steam in the room Lydia would have been entirely up to speed on the appearance of his genitals. She wondered about his slow and measured unpeeling. Was it deliberate? Or was he just hot?

'I *love* a sauna,' he said, 'I forgot how much I love them.'

'I've never been in one before,' said Lydia.

Bendiks laughed. 'You are so funny, Lydia. You buy a house with a sauna in it and you don't use it.'

'I'm Welsh,' she replied. 'Welsh people don't *do* sauna.'

He laughed again. Lydia sometimes suspected that nobody ever said anything funny in Latvia. 'Here,' he said, patting the bench next to where he sat, 'let me give you a neck massage.'

She glanced at him, possibly with an expression of horror on her face, and he laughed again. 'You are so scared of me,' he exclaimed. 'Really, you must not be.'

'I'm not scared of you,' she replied. 'I'm just . . .'

'Come,' he said again, still patting the bench. 'I have been wanting to get those knots out of your neck since the first time I saw you.'

She smiled awkwardly and moved next to him on the bench. She turned her back to him and lowered her gown over her back and shoulders. Bendiks placed his hands against her shoulder blades and gently pushed the gown down lower so that she had to grip the front of it together with both hands. He pressed his hand against the back of her skull and slowly pushed her head down towards her chest. 'There,' he said, 'good.'

And then he took his good, soft hands and he pushed and he kneaded at her damp flesh until all her muscles had turned to sand, and Lydia thought, *Now, now would be perfect*, and just as she thought that, she felt soft lips against the skin of her back and the sweet heat of his breath against her skin and his hands were on her shoulders and he was drawing her against him and instead of wondering what she should do and how she should respond, Lydia just sat there, compliant and intoxicated, soaking up the

sensation of being wanted and being touched by a beautiful man. Not one part of her body remained unaffected by
his touch and she felt, building deep within her, a loud
animal groan of pure pleasure.

As his lips made their way to the crook of her neck, she
opened her mouth and she let it out, and he, taking his cue,
slowly turned her head towards his and brought his lips
down against hers and there it was . . . finally. Their first
kiss. And Lydia thought, *Yes, yes, yes, I knew you weren't gay. I
knew we could do this. I knew I could have you. I knew I wasn't that
stupid.* And as they kissed, she felt it all fall into place; the
big empty house, the blue cat, the lack of friends, the weird
family, her childhood. It all fell into place because she suddenly knew without any trace of doubt that she was not
weird. A man like Bendiks would not kiss a weird woman.
A man like Bendiks would only kiss an appealing woman.
A woman with some kind of charm and beauty. A woman
in whose company he could feel proud. And as she thought
these thoughts he pulled his lips from hers and looked into
her eyes and said, 'All these weeks and months, I have
been dreaming about doing this.'

And she said, 'Me too.'

And he looked at her in wonder and said, 'Really? You
really dreamed of this?'

She nodded and he touched her chin and laughed.
'Wow,' he said. 'That's amazing. I thought . . . I thought you
thought I was just a big meathead. I thought you thought
you were too good for me. And I thought . . .' He paused.

'What?' said Lydia, searching his dark eyes with hers.

'I thought, for a while, and I don't mean this in a bad way, but I thought that maybe . . . you were *gay*?'

'You thought I was . . .?' Lydia stopped. And then she laughed.

'What?' said Bendiks, trailing his fingertips up and down her shoulders and upper arms.

'I thought you were gay, too.'

He looked at her in amazement, then put one hand to his chest. 'Me?' he said.

'Yes, you!'

'But . . . but, *why*?' he asked.

'I don't know,' she said. 'Maybe I was just trying to protect myself from you. Or maybe it was the plucked eyebrows.'

He immediately put his hand to his brow and said, 'But I do not pluck my eyebrows!'

'You don't?'

'No! Well, only a little bit. Just in the middle. And the messy ones around here.' He pointed out the arch of his brows. 'Oh my God,' he continued, 'does that make me look gay?'

'No!' laughed Lydia. 'Just, well, *groomed*, you know.'

'And groomed is gay?'

'No!' she exclaimed again. 'You look beautiful. You look perfect. You don't look gay. Well, at least, not any more. Not after . . .'

'After what?' he smiled.

'After *that*,' she said, indicating their two bodies, still pressed close together.

He brought his nose towards hers and held it there, his eyes gazing into hers, his breath against her cheek, and he smiled. 'We haven't even started yet,' he said.

And then they began.

DEAN

'Here,' said Rose, handing Dean a small plastic bottle full of pink liquid.

He stared at the bottle blankly. 'What is it?' he said.

'It's for your hands. It's germ-killer.'

He blinked and read the label.

'It's the same stuff they had at the hospital, you know, for the preemies,' she explained, brusquely.

He squirted a small amount into the palm of his hand and he rubbed it in. It smelled of pears. He passed the bottle to his mum and she followed suit. They'd already been told to remove their shoes at the front door. 'No shoes in this house,' Rose had said, haughtily, as if this somehow made her a cut above.

Dean had not been to Rose's house since he'd first started going out with Sky. He felt a chill run through him as he followed Rose up the hallway and into the living room. He had thought that he would never come back here again. The walls were hung with huge blown-up studio portraits of Rose and her children and grandchildren. There was one, above the fake Georgian fireplace, of all of them: Rose, the four girls, Sky nursing a huge bump, her sister Savannah holding her pug-faced toddler on her lap with tattooed arms, all of them wearing white. And there was a new one, above the glass-topped dining table, bigger than the rest, of Sky, just a clean portrait of her face, simply shot in black and white. Beneath it was a vase on a dresser with three stems of Stargazer lilies in it, and a votive candle burning inside a red glass jar. Dean gulped at the portrait, remembering once again how pretty she had been and swallowing, as ever, his unacknowledged feelings of loss and grief.

'Come in,' said Rose, gesturing at the leather sofa, 'sit down. I'll make us some tea.'

Her youngest daughter, Sienna, was curled into a matching leather armchair set in the bay window. She looked up and smiled as Dean and his mum sat down. 'Hiya,' she said. Dean nodded and his mother said, 'Hello.'

It was warm in Rose's house. Too warm. It struck Dean that for all her paranoia about germs on hands and on the soles of shoes she should probably keep her house a bit cooler.

Dean smiled at his mum and she smiled back at him. 'OK?' she whispered.

He nodded. 'Yeah, I'm fine.'

'Just heard her stirring,' Rose shouted through from her kitchen. 'You can go up and see her, if you want.'

Dean gulped. A man on the television told a woman on the television to *shut up, you don't know what you're talking about*. Sienna fidgeted and moved her feet to the other side of her. Dean looked at his mum.

'Come on,' she said. 'I know where she is. Shall we go and see her?'

Dean thought of Lydia's dad. He thought of how she'd seen him for all those years, as nothing more than a creature. And then he thought of his baby daughter wired up in a plastic tank, not quite real, not quite ready to exist. He thought of the moment back in March, that cold bleak day, lying with his head hanging over the grave of his girlfriend, trying to reach the photo of his daughter. And he thought of Thomas, his brother, who'd never stood a chance. He smiled grimly. 'Yeah,' he said. 'Yeah. OK.'

They took the stairs together, softly and quietly, so as not to take the baby too much by surprise, he assumed. He followed his mum into a room which appeared to be Rose's. It contained a king-size double bed loaded with furry cushions and velvety throws and was cast in a liverish-red light through claret and gold striped roller-blinds. The room smelled, like the rest of Rose's house, of plug-in fresheners.

At first Dean felt self-conscious, trespassing into the intimate, womb-like environs of Rose's boudoir. But then he saw her, in a wicker basket on a wooden frame at the side of Rose's bed. The basket was lined with pink candy stripes and overhung by a large, faintly oppressive mobile of moon-eyed teddy bears.

The baby was awake and staring up at the mobile, curiously, her hands opening and closing like tiny jellyfish. She was wearing a pink and red striped bodysuit with the words *Cheeky Monkey* emblazoned across the front. Dean blinked at her in surprise. She was so big. Her body filled out the soft cotton of her suit, the buttons straining across her rounded belly.

'Hello!' said his mother, rounding the corner of Rose's bed to reach the basket, 'hello, little one.' The baby turned her gaze from the mobile towards the source of the voice and, when she finally located his mother's face, her mouth curved into a rapturous smile. 'Look at you!' It was said in a saccharine falsetto. 'Look at you! So big! Such a big girl!' The baby kicked her legs, appreciatively, and made a loud chirruping sound. Dean found himself smiling involuntarily. Even though his mum had shown him pictures of the baby on her phone, he had never really managed to override that image of the tiny ice-blue creature in a plastic box. Yet here she was; long, strong, smiling, almost fat.

'Come here, my lovely,' chimed his mum, 'come to Granny.'

Granny. His mum was a *granny*. Dean blanched. It had never properly occurred to him before. He watched her tenderly lift the smiling baby from the basket and rest her in the crook of one arm. The baby had a full head of hair, dark hair, like his. And like Lydia's. His mum ruffled the soft hair with her fingers and then turned to Dean and smiled. 'Look!' she said to the baby. 'Look who's here! This is your daddy! Yes, it is!' The baby's eyes and mouth opened wider and wider the more higher-pitched her grandmother's voice became. 'Do you want a cuddle, love?' his mum asked Dean in her normal voice. He shrugged and smiled shyly. Then he nodded.

They both sat down on the edge of the bed and Dean's mum gently passed the baby into his arms. 'Like this,' she said, arranging his hands, 'so that you're supporting her head. That's it,' she added, smiling, 'that's it.'

Dean looked down into Isadora's eyes and found that she was staring straight back into his. And there it was again, that deep-seated intelligence, that sheer blinding confidence that had thrown him off-kilter back in the delivery room. Yet this time it didn't scare him, this time he could absorb it and hold it inside himself like some kind of wonderful compliment. He looked at her and felt it again, that same jolt of recognition he'd felt when he first met Lydia, that same instantaneous attachment. 'Yes,' said a little voice inside his head, 'yes. It is you. And you are me. And I am you. And we are the same.' He charted the contours of her face, the fleshy mouth, the wide-set eyes, the downy outline of a heavy brow, and he marvelled at the strength of his donor father's genes, that had fought their way past the fearsome genetic outposts of the Donnelly clan.

Isadora wriggled slightly in his arms and Dean instinctively sat her upon his lap where she immediately caught sight of the shiny zip hanging from the bottom of his hoodie and grabbed for it greedily. Dean passed it to her and then lowered his head to her crown. She smelled of bed and strawberries and something else; something that sent his consciousness spiralling backwards through the coils of his own life, back to his own infancy – the musty, exotic smell of new life.

'She's lovely, isn't she?' said his mum, watching him tenderly.

He nodded and smiled and then, without thinking about it, he kissed the top of his baby's head. Her hands were bunched up around the metal zip and his fingers, the whole area a mass of warm drool. He watched her for a moment and then a terrible realisation hit him: she might accidentally bite the zipper off! It might end up untethered in her mouth! She might swallow it! She might die! He gently pulled the zipper from her mouth and squeezed her to him, his precious, precious baby girl.

MAGGIE

Marc greeted Maggie at the door of Daniel's flat on Friday morning and as much as she had been preparing herself for it, his exact resemblance to his brother still took her breath away. She tried to override the sense of shock she felt and forced a bright smile on to her face. 'Good morning!' she said.

'Good morning, Maggie,' said Marc, flattening himself against the wall so that she could squeeze past him.

'Did you sleep well?' she asked.

'I slept very well. In the way of twins, my brother appears to own the very same mattress as myself so it was almost like being at home. And I have just eaten my breakfast on the terrace. Thank you so much for the provisions.'

'Oh,' she smiled, 'you're welcome. I wasn't sure what you'd want to eat so I got a bit of everything.'

'So,' said Marc, 'I am ready to go. But maybe I could get you a cup of coffee before we leave?'

'No, honestly, I'm fine. I had one before I left. Well, two, in fact. I didn't sleep so well last night.'

Marc looked at her sympathetically. 'Now I feel bad,' he said. 'Maybe it is wrong that I slept well.'

'Of course it's not wrong!' she exclaimed. 'It's good. You need to stay strong.'

'Yes,' he said, 'you are right. Oh, and before we go, some letters arrived this morning. The postman rang on the door. I had to sign for one thing. Here.' He turned and pulled a pile of mail from the hall table and handed it to her.

As she flicked through the letters, her eye was caught by the postmark of the Donor Sibling Registry and she stared at the envelope for a moment before carefully opening it. She caught her breath as she unfolded the letter and then she let it out through a half-smiling mouth as the words sunk in.

A girl. Robyn Inglis. She lived in North London and she wanted to meet up with Daniel. A giddy laugh escaped Maggie's mouth. She put her hand to her heart and then she laughed again, more loudly. At last! And just in time! She read on. The girl was studying medicine at a London university and lived with her boyfriend, a novelist, in Holloway. She said she liked clothes and worked part-time in a fashion shop on Oxford Street, that her mum and dad were a secretary in an estate agency and a building services manager respectively, and that she was originally from Essex. 'But I'm not a stereotypical Essex girl, honestly!' She'd given a mobile phone number and an e-mail address and seemed absolutely certain about her desire to meet up with Daniel, but the message was quite restrained nonetheless. Maggie read the letter three times before folding it carefully into three and sliding it back into the envelope.

'It is good news?' said Marc, who had been watching her, thoughtfully.

'Yes.' She smiled. 'It is very good news. I will tell you all about it in the car.'

It was hard for Maggie to stop her expression from giving away the wonderful surprise as she and Marc scurried down the corridor towards Daniel's room at the hospice an hour later. Her mouth twitched, her eyes sparkled. Daniel had asked her to do something for him, something important, something that would make him happy in these closing chapters of his life. She'd done it, never quite believing that at the end of this strange and impersonal process there might be some real people, never truly believing that she might really be responsible for bringing one of these people into three dimensions and into Daniel's sunny hospital room. She had assumed that they would write too late, or that they would not write at all. She had assumed that it could not possibly be that easy. And it was not until they were on the very threshold of Daniel's room that the fear gripped her: what if it was already too late?

The muscles in her face stopped their strange dance and hardened. She had been so busy feeling giddy with relief that it *was not too late*, that she hadn't considered the possibility that it might already be too late. That even as she was ripping through the paper of the envelope with her index finger; Daniel could have been fighting to expel his last breath that as she parked her car outside, jiggling and twitching with anticipation, he might have been closing his eyes for the last time. She stopped at the door and she inhaled deeply. Marc threw her a look of encouragement.

'You are OK?' he asked.

'Yes,' she said, 'I'm fine.'

And then she rearranged her face into its usual innocuous contours and opened the door.

Her heart fell. Daniel looked terrible. He did not turn at the sound of her voice when she whispered, 'Daniel, it's me.' He lay with his head tilted to face the window, eyes half-open, a dry crust at the corner of his slack mouth.

'Daniel,' she whispered again. She gently touched his shoulder and he turned his head just a millimetre or two and moaned.

'How are you?' she asked, still in a soft whisper.

'Very tired,' he replied. He let his head fall back against the pillow and then he closed his eyes.

'Now, I don't expect you to say anything, and please don't try, but I wanted you to know, I've had contact. From the girl. The youngest one. Her name's Robyn. Like the boy's name but with a Y instead of an I. She sounds very nice, I must say . . .'

Maggie watched Daniel for some kind of reaction but there was none. She felt her joy beginning to drain away. This was not how she'd imagined the moment would be.

'I'll just go and get myself a coffee,' she said. 'Marc, will you stay here with him?'

Marc nodded, understandingly. 'Of course,' he said,

settling himself on the side of Daniel's bed and taking his brother's hand in his.

'I'll be back in a few minutes,' she said to Daniel. 'We can talk about it then. About the girl. OK?'

'Yes,' he said, 'yes.'

Maggie left the room quietly and immediately headed for the nurses' station at the end of the corridor.

'Hello!' she said brightly to a small black woman called Cressida.

Cressida looked up from some paperwork and smiled back. 'Hello,' she replied. 'How are you today?'

'I'm fine,' said Maggie, brightly, 'are you busy? Could I talk to you?'

'No. I'm not at all busy,' said Cressida. 'Come in, sit down.'

Maggie sat down and pulled her chair closer to Cressida's desk. 'Now,' she began, 'I know you can't tell me anything for sure, I do understand that, but Daniel . . . he seems very bad today. He seems the worst he's been.'

'Yes,' said Cressida, 'he is very quiet. He's been sleeping a lot.'

'Yes. But he's been sleeping a lot for a while now and still been fairly good when he's awake. Just now, though, he seemed . . .' She searched for the right words. 'He seemed as though the lights had been turned down.'

Cressida smiled sympathetically. 'Yes,' she said, 'it will seem like that. Things are shutting down now, you see. Bit by bit. It's like shutting up a house for the season, if you understand what I mean?'

Maggie blinked. She thought of a story she'd read to Matilda at bedtime a few days earlier: *Teddy's had enough now. Teddy has to rest.* The words were accompanied by a picture of an elderly and over-loved teddy, patched together, its head hanging by a thread. She'd gulped as the words caught in her throat. *Teddy's had enough now.* She thought of her Daniel, his body filled with the poisons of death, his putty-coloured skin and his crusted mouth. *Teddy has to rest.*

'I've just tracked down his daughter,' she said, her voice cracking slightly. 'They haven't met before. She wants to see him. Do you think . . . do you think there's still time?'

Cressida smiled again. 'I don't know,' she said.

'But in your experience . . . when a patient looks like that . . . when they've started to shut down? How long does it usually . . .'

'In my experience,' Cressida interrupted, kindly, 'there is no usually. But I would also say that I have seen people, moments from passing, cling on for hours and even days in order to see a loved one. Does he know his daughter's coming?'

'Yes. I think so.'

Cressida nodded, clearly not wanting to say anything that could be construed as a prognosis.

'There are others, though,' Maggie found herself saying. 'Other people who may want to see him. Should I . . . I mean, do you think they should come soon? Now?'

Cressida sighed. 'It's all so hard to say,' she said. 'Each situation is unique. Daniel might still be here next week.

But equally he could be shutting down faster than we think. For the sake of a few days, it's probably worth making sure he's seen everyone he wants to see. Especially if they've got a long way to come.'

Maggie nodded. She thought of this lovely girl, this Robyn Inglis, in her flat in North London, wondering how quickly she'd be able to get here. Would she throw on a jacket and head straight up? Or would she have commitments, appointments, arrangements to be honoured? Would it take her hours or would it take her days?

Maggie thanked Cressida for her time and then she got herself a coffee and a banana from the counter in reception and took them both out into the garden. She took a bench by the Koi carp pond and remembered how she had stood here just weeks earlier, being twirled and held by Daniel Blanchard. She stared into the inky depths of the pond, letting her gaze follow the erratic golden dance beneath the surface of the water. How had she ended up here? she wondered. How had her life brought her to this theatrical and tragic dénouement? How had she, Maggie Smith, mum, grandmother, receptionist, ended up taking responsibility for the outcome of so many people's lives? When she and Peter had divorced all those years ago, she'd felt that it was probably the most dramatic thing she would ever experience. She'd thought it was more than she could bear: the court case, the brutal conversations, the talks with the children, breaking the news to their friends and family. She'd thought that none of it was really her style at all. But she'd weathered it, come through the other side, smiling and with a whole new trendy interior to show for it. Her subsequent relationships with her ex-husband, his girlfriend and both her own children had survived unscathed. Which was, she'd always secretly thought, almost entirely down to her.

But this . . . this was in another league of human drama entirely.

She unpeeled her banana and found she had no appetite for it. The joy and anticipatory giddiness of half an hour earlier had gone completely. Instead she sipped at her coffee, urgently, as though it might somehow help her cut through the sad fug in her head and decide what to do for the best.

In her handbag was the letter from Robyn. She glanced at her bag, surreptitiously. She glanced at the carp. She glanced back at the bag and then she took out both the letter and her mobile phone and began to compose a message. The message took her half an hour to write. It seemed such a cold and distasteful thing to be saying to a stranger. Eventually she settled for this:

Dear Robyn,

My name is Maggie Smith. I am friends with Daniel Blanchard. He has received your letter and would love to meet up with you but unfortunately his health is not very good at the moment – hence me writing this message. I think, if you would excuse the possibly rather dramatic sense of urgency, that it would be advisable to see him sooner rather than later. If you still want to see him, please reply to this message and I will be able to tell you the name of the hospital in Bury where he is a patient. I look forward to hearing from you.

This, she felt, conveyed the urgency of the matter without any upsetting or possibly off-putting detail. And she'd deliberately used the word 'hospital' instead of 'hospice', in case the idea of rushing to see a father who might then, potentially, pass away within moments of setting eyes upon her, put Robyn off making the journey. Maggie reread the message for a third time and then, with her eyes closed tight against the enormity of what she was about to do, she pressed send.

Hard, hot tears pushed against the lids of her closed eyes. She could feel the end rushing towards her like a tunnel of fire, and she wasn't ready for it, not at all.

LYDIA

The following morning Lydia crept from the silent house before the sun was fully risen. She had not slept the night before, her body was too electrified after her experience with Bendiks and her mind was too overrun with new and remarkable things to think about, so she had lain upon her own empty bed – Bendiks had asked to stay with her, but she had needed some space – and watched the moon trail across the sky, reaching its peak of ice-blue illumination at about 2 a.m. and then slowly fading away as the sun emerged as a thick red band on the horizon. Her house, as she tiptoed through it to reach the front door, seemed riven with the essence of what had happened between her and Bendiks yesterday. It seemed to seep through the bricks and trickle down the stairs. It was in the air, pungent as perfume. She and Bendiks had had sex in this house. Not just once but three times. And not just in one place but in a number of places. In the sauna, in her bed, in the shower afterwards. They had scented every corner. And she loved her house for holding on to it. Because it had changed her, what happened yesterday, changed her from the inside out, and she wanted that change to colour everything else, including her big, characterless house. Having sex with Bendiks had given her house a soul.

She hit a long stride as she walked down her front path and out on to the street. She could feel the thin muscles that ran from her groin to her knees singing out in lovely agony with every step she took and she pulled her stride wider and wider, wanting to feel the sensation even more. The soreness was good. It meant she had been doing things that she had been designed to do, and doing them with whole-hearted enthusiasm.

She was not sure where she was headed, but her long strides brought her, within half an hour, to the outskirts of Camden Town. She recognised the strange smell of early morning Camden: the overflowing bins awaiting collection, the sourness of last night's beer emanating from shuttered pubs. This was the last time she'd been happy, she thought. Right here, in this dirty place, in a scruffy flat with her scruffy friend, running a thriving little business that was just about to make her a millionaire.

She followed the familiar series of lefts and rights until she found herself on the street where she'd once lived, standing beneath the window of the flat she'd shared with Dixie. She glanced up and noticed with a start that there was a For Sale sign nailed to the wall. She felt her heart quicken and a sudden wave of nostalgic longing overcome her. The landlord had not rented the flat out again to some North London slackers, but had put it on the market. She could buy it! She could own it! She could possess her past! But even as she thought it, she knew that she no longer needed to possess her past because her present was becoming more and more the place she wanted to be.

She smiled up at the windows and silently said goodbye.

Bendiks was not there when Lydia returned home from her walk. She noted that his hoodie was not hanging from the coat rack and that his gym bag was gone, and deduced that he had gone to work. Slightly deflated, she went to find Juliette to ask her if she had seen him leave. Juliette was not in the kitchen and Lydia eventually found her in the utility room, pulling hot sheets out of the tumble dryer.

'Erm, hi, Juliette,' she began, filled with her customary awkwardness at being in the same room as someone doing her dirty work for her. 'I was just wondering, have you seen Bendiks at all this morning?'

'No,' said Juliette, rather brusquely. 'I have not.' She turned her back against Lydia and started to fold up fitted sheets, using some scientific approach that had Lydia spellbound for a moment.

'Oh,' she said, somewhat taken aback, 'right.'

She stared at Juliette's spine and noticed a certain tension in her body language. She considered leaving but went against her own instincts. 'I just wondered,' she continued, 'maybe he went to work? Maybe he might have told you?'

'I told you,' snapped Juliette, still facing away from her, 'I have not seen him. I don't know where he is.'

Lydia flinched.

Juliette turned suddenly to face her. 'I want to say something, if it's OK with you?'

Lydia nodded.

'I want to say that I think this man, this Bendiks . . . I don't like him.'

Juliette's usually soft face was contorted with embarrassment.

Lydia nodded again and said nothing.

'You know, I clean his room. I see the things he buys. Two new watches, just since he has been here. I see a bag from . . . what is that place?' She clicked her fingers urgently. '*Marc Jacob!* I see this bag, in his room. I see the creams and the perfumes and the greasy things for his hair, and is all designer, all of it! And then I see him, taking from you the fifty pounds! I am very sorry to be saying these things to you. I am very sorry and I hope I am not making you angry. But, Miss Pike . . . Lydia, I like you very much. You are a very kind lady. You make me happy to work for you. I like your house. I like it all. But that man – I do not think I like him.'

Lydia stared at Juliette, her lips parted, waiting for some words to come and take this conversation to a more comfortable place. But none did and a silence ensued.

'Anyway,' Juliette bunched a sheet together between her hands and smiled, 'anyway, I'm sure is OK. It's just, I wanted to say these things, OK? You are alone. I feel I want to be here, to look after you. I feel that it is my job, too.' Her smile widened with these words and Lydia smiled back. As much as she was stung by Juliette's low opinion of Bendiks and as much as she was slightly thrown by the possibility that he'd been spending her money on designer hair gel, she was also touched and heartened by Juliette's declaration of caring. It served to fill the uncomfortable gap between Lydia's need for someone to look after her house and her awkwardness with the reality of someone looking after her house. It made her feel happy.

'Thank you,' she said, 'I really do appreciate it. And I wanted to say too that I'm glad you're here, and that if there's ever anything I could do for you, to help you or your family, all you have to do is . . .'

Juliette frowned and put a hand up between them. 'No,' she said, 'this is my job. You give me this job. You pay me well for this job. I like my job. My family is happy. I am happy. Thank you.' The smile returned and Lydia bowed her head, in an almost Asian gesture.

'No,' she said, 'thank *you*.'

She tried to resist the temptation of opening the door to Bendiks' room and seeing for herself the evidence of his profligate spending, but she failed. She wanted Juliette to be wrong. She wanted to find an old tub of Pond's Cold Cream and a carrier bag from Next. But as she craned her neck around his bedroom door it was immediately clear that Juliette had not been exaggerating. The room was immaculate, the bed fully made and arranged with overlapping cushions in shades of steel and sage – and there, in almost every corner, was evidence of untethered, high-end shopping. A row of bags with rope handles stood along one wall. A leather jacket with price tags still attached hung from the door handle of the wardrobe. And lying at her feet, as though any further evidence were needed, was a cardboard price tag, bearing the words: Paul Smith.

Lydia turned from Bendiks' door then with flushed cheeks and a sinking sense of disappointment. Disappointment, but not surprise. 'Of course,' said a small voice inside her soul, 'of course. It was all about my money. What else could it ever have been about?' She'd been a fool to think anything else could possibly have been behind his seduction of her. She'd been a fool, full stop.

She stood for a moment outside Bendiks' bedroom, her hand against her heart, holding back her tears. She felt sick with sadness and embarrassment. And then she pushed her hair from her face, took a deep breath and headed back to work.

'Listen, can you talk?' It was Dean. He was speaking with some urgency.

'Yes,' said Lydia, turning on her office chair to face away from her computer screen. 'Yes. Of course.'

'Something mad's just happened. You won't believe it.'

'What? What's happened?'

'I've just had a text message. From her. The other one. From Robyn.'

Lydia opened her mouth but no words came out.

'She thinks we should meet up. Apparently, he's really ill.'

'Who's really ill?'

'The man. The donor. Our dad. He's really ill and some woman texted her to say that she should go and see him now.'

'What?'

'Yeah. I told you, it's mad.'

'But where is he?'

'Don't know,' said Dean, 'she didn't say. Just that she was going and that maybe we could all go together.'

'But why didn't she ask me herself?'

'I don't know, like I said, it was just a text message. I haven't replied yet. So what shall I say?'

'Oh, Jesus, God, I don't know. I can't think . . . do you want to go?'

There was a short silence on the other end of the line. 'I don't know,' he said, 'it's a bit . . .'

'Yeah, I know. It's all a bit sudden.'

'Yeah. I know. I just . . . I mean, what if he's really ill? What if he's dying? You know. And this is it? Our only chance?'

'Well, yes, exactly,' murmured Lydia.

'Yeah,' said Dean, more decisively, 'yeah. I think I'm going to go. I think I will. It just seems . . . all of this seems so obvious in a way. All of it. Sky dying, meeting you, the baby, now this. It's like it's all got to happen and it's got to happen now. It feels . . . I don't know, it feels right.'

Lydia let a silence unfold while she collected her thoughts.

'You still there?' said Dean.

'Yes, yes. I'm still here. I just . . . I'm not sure. There's been so much to absorb already these past few days. My head's all over the place, I don't know if I can . . .'

'Please, Lydia,' he interrupted. 'Please come with me. Please.'

Lydia breathed in sharply. She felt something like electricity jolt through her at his words and the sweet simple delivery of them. *Please, Lydia.* Her little brother. Of course she would go with him.

'Yes,' she said. 'Sorry, yes, of course. Tell her yes. And call me back the minute you've spoken to her. Tell me what she says, OK?'

Dean called her back two minutes later. 'She's going tomorrow,' he said. 'Tomorrow afternoon. We've arranged to meet at Liverpool Street Station, at four-fifteen. Will you come?'

'Yes, I told you, yes! Don't worry,' she laughed. 'And how will we know her?'

'She said that she will be wearing a red dress and dark sunglasses.'

Lydia laughed at the description, picturing her as some kind of 1940s secret agent. 'OK,' she said. 'And what – what did she sound like?'

'She sounded nice,' said Dean, 'she sounded all right. You know. London accent. Pretty friendly. Just like a normal girl, really.'

'Good,' said Lydia, 'good. But will you come here first? Come over earlier. We'll go together?'

'Sure,' said Dean, 'definitely. I'll come over two-ish. Yeah?'

'Yes,' said Lydia, gratefully. 'Yes. Two-ish. I'll see you then.'

There was a short pause and then he asked: 'Are you all right, Lydia?' in a voice tinged with concern.

'Yes,' she said, tightly, 'I'm fine.'

'You sound a bit *sad*.'

'No, honestly, I'm fine. Really. I'll see you later.'

She turned off her phone and leaned against the back of her chair.

And then, quite unexpectedly, she began to cry.

ROBYN

The day that Robyn was set to meet her brother, her sister and her father had begun bright but was now overcast and chilly. The previous day had been cloudless and hot; she'd walked to university in a strapless sundress, the kind of thing she'd normally save for holidays abroad. But today it was another season entirely and she had promised Dean that she would be wearing a red dress. The dress she'd had in mind was too summery so she surveyed her wardrobe, searching for glimpses of red. And then she saw the burnt orange prom dress, the one Jack had bought her for their anniversary. She touched the fabric of it and thought that, in a way, it would be the perfect dress to wear today. Because today was going to be the dictionary definition of auspicious and because the dress itself was auspicious and because in a way she quite liked the idea of wearing something completely inappropriate.

She pulled on the dress and covered her arms with a red zip-up hoodie. On her feet she wore red ballet pumps, and she tied her hair up into a messy sideways-leaning bun, making sure to clear the back of her neck so that her tattoo would be visible. She looked in the mirror and thought, *I look very young.* She applied some black eyeliner and red lipstick. She looked at herself again and thought: *I look like Lily Allen.* And the thought made her laugh, in spite of her nerves.

Jack smiled as she stood in front of him in his study a moment later. 'You look really pretty,' he said.

Robyn smiled.

'And this is the last time I'm going to ask you this, but are you totally sure you don't want me to come with you?'

'Totally. Honestly.' She pulled a piece of fluff from his brown polo-shirt and let it fall to the floor. Then she put her hand out and cupped his cheek. He felt stubbly and warm. He held her hand there with his and then kissed it. 'Now remember,' he said, 'I want you to make notes. I'll need all the detail I can get my hands on when I write the novel of this.'

She laughed. 'Yeah, right,' she said. 'And what would you write about this precise moment, then?'

He leaned back and appraised her with a small smile. 'I would say: *She wore her favourite dress. Her amazing boyfriend had bought her the dress three months earlier. She loved her boyfriend. She was so very lucky to have him.*'

She punched him affectionately in the shoulder and laughed. 'OK,' she said, 'I'm off. Last train back gets me in at midnight. Will you wait up for me?'

'Yes,' he said, 'of course I will. But . . .' He stopped and looked at the floor, as though considering his next words.

'What?' she said.

'Nothing,' he said.

'No, come on, you can't do that – what?'

He sighed. 'Well, what will you do if he's on his way out, and . . . well, I mean, if it looks as though he won't last much longer but you have to go and get your train?'

She shrugged. She hadn't considered that. 'I suppose I'll just have to come home and go back the next day.'

Jack nodded. Robyn could tell he had other thoughts on his mind but she didn't have time to hear them. She kissed him again and left the house. The world reeled towards her like a slightly frightening drunk as she walked the few yards to the tube station. Nothing seemed as it had the day before. Nothing seemed as she'd expected it to seem. In her burnt orange prom dress and dark glasses she felt herself taking on another persona as she walked down the road. For a while she couldn't quite think who it was she was pretending to be, and then, with a start, she remembered: she was pretending to be herself.

Robyn retained this strangely unnatural sense of impersonating herself as she climbed the escalators at Liverpool Street half an hour later. In fact, the closer she got to the appointed meeting spot of 'next to Burger King', the more thickly she plastered it on to herself. She'd been such a reedy, insubstantial thing these past few weeks and she could not possibly come to these new people, her brother and her sister, as anything less than the person she used to be. She checked the time. She was two minutes late. She checked her hair, she pulled at the neckline of her dress, she adjusted the waist. She felt a sheen of perspiration spring to her skin and quelled her sense of rising nerves with a deep breath and a reminder to herself that she was Robyn Inglis, *the* Robyn Inglis, and that this was cool.

She slowed her pace and then she stopped entirely when she saw them. And she knew it was them. There had been no need for anyone to describe dresses or accessories. It was absolutely beyond doubt. A tall thin woman with dark hair in a side parting, and a tall thin boy with dark hair, cut short around his face. The woman was dressed expensively in smart jeans, a blue t-shirt and a fine-knit cardigan, and the boy was dressed cheaply in what looked like Primark casual wear. Standing separately there would have been nothing obvious to connect the two people, but standing as they were, side by side, they could only be brother and sister.

Robyn walked towards them in a daze, all her concerns and pre-conceptions fading away, all her efforts to present a certain façade forgotten. As she drew closer she saw their noses, their hollow cheeks, their full lips, their square jaws. They were not identical, but they were alike. They were like her. She increased her pace now as the enormity of this moment began to well up inside her. She wanted to get closer and closer, she wanted to see more and more of these people. She wanted to be inches from their faces and to stare deeply into their eyes.

The woman looked up then and saw Robyn approaching and immediately her beautiful serious face opened up into a smile. She said something to the boy and he turned, too, and looked and smiled a smaller smile. And then they were all walking towards each other, like particles of metal towards an invisible magnet.

Robyn would remember this moment in minute and full sensory detail for the rest of her life. She would remember the smell of oil and meat coming from the Burger King kiosk, she would remember the disembodied boom of a train announcement from the other end of the concourse, she would remember a slice of sunshine falling from the glass ceiling and on to the marble floor beneath her feet, and then she would remember being held in a brief embrace by a woman called Lydia, who smelled of clean hair, and then by a boy called Dean, who felt like a child in her arms, and she would remember their faces, their eyes, all three of them searching each other for what-ever it was that had been missing for all their lives: that vital sense of recognition. It was almost as though she was watching the meeting from above, as though she was both studying and participating in the moment. It was like something from a dream.

She couldn't really remember what was said; it was all just words. If the moment had been a scene in the film of the book of her life there would have been no dialogue, just a rousing soundtrack playing behind it, maybe something epic like 'Chasing Cars'. But she could remember the overwhelming sense of being part of a gang, and her unparalleled feeling of pride as she walked with her beautiful sister and her handsome brother towards platform nine and on to a train bound for their father.

LYDIA

Lydia gazed at her father in awe.

He stared back at her.

'Hello,' she said. 'I'm Lydia.'

Daniel looked at her intently and then he smiled. 'You are very pretty,' he said, his voice croaking. He turned his gaze from her to Robyn then and said, 'And so are you.'

The two girls laughed, nervously, happily. And then he saw Dean and put out a thin, claw-like hand. 'And you are very handsome.'

He closed his eyes then, as though the effort of keeping them open had been too much for him. But his mouth remained curved in the shape of a smile and his hand still gripped Dean's. The three children stood and stared at him.

The room rang with silence, a silence of shock and awe and coming-to-terms, a silence of absorbing and thinking and not knowing what on earth to say. It was clear that no one was feeling what they'd expected to feel and that everyone was rather unsettled by the terrible appearance of the dying man lying flat against the bed. And it was clear that this was not going to be a moment plucked straight from the dénouement of a saccharine made-for-TV tearjerker. The conversation would not be torrid and affecting but awkward and mundane. Meeting this strange man in the final hours of his existence was not going to change Lydia's life. Nor anyone else's, for that matter.

But of every remarkable thing that had happened to Lydia in the past week, this was probably the most remarkable yet. She was standing with her father. Surrounded by her brother and her sister. And across the room stood a man who was her uncle, and not only that but her father's identical twin. Nearly every person in this room was related to her by blood. The thought left her feeling giddy with fulfilment. She turned to Dean and smiled, and he smiled back at her. She wondered what he was thinking. Unlike Lydia and Robyn, this was the first time that he had ever looked upon a man who could call himself his father.

'How are you feeling, Daniel?' asked the nice woman called Maggie, who had told them in the car on the way from the station that she was Daniel's 'friend'.

He tipped his head slightly to one side to indicate a neutral answer. 'I'm happy,' he said.

The woman called Maggie lit up at these words and tears came to her eyes. 'Good,' she said, 'that's really, really good.'

And Lydia could sense that that was all the blonde woman called Maggie had ever wanted. And maybe, for all her cynicism, there it was, the grand finale, the happy ever after. Those three simple words: 'I'm happy.' And 'good'. A full circle, a story brought to its gentle conclusion.

Daniel's eyes opened suddenly and his strange gaze worked over the three of them again, from face to face, before his eyes once more grew heavy and closed. 'Where is the boy?' he asked, huskily. 'The other one?'

Lydia gulped. She'd known this was going to come up. She smiled sadly and touched her father's shoulder. 'He was my brother. And he died,' she said. 'When he was a baby. It was a cot death.'

She saw her father's eyelids pinch together at her words. 'I knew it,' he said. 'I knew it. Poor little baby boy. How old was he?'

'Six months,' she replied. 'His name was Thomas.'

'Thomas.' He tested the name on his dry lips. 'Poor little boy. How sad. For you. For your mother. For all of us. How very, very sad.'

He turned his face away from them then and let it rest heavily against his pillow. 'Thank you, all of you, thank you so much for coming. I am happy.' He closed his eyes again and Lydia looked to Maggie, for instruction.

Maggie smiled and approached Daniel's side. 'Would you like a rest now?' she asked, taking his hand in hers.

He nodded, slowly and painfully. And then, a moment later, it became clear that he was already asleep. Lydia's heart lurched. Suddenly she was back, back in that stifling hospital room in Cardiff, waiting for her father to die, wondering what on earth death would look like when it finally came.

'Come on,' said Maggie, letting go of Daniel's hand. 'Let's go and get a cup of tea. Let's let him sleep.'

Maggie drove them all back to Daniel's flat at midnight when it was clear that he was still alive and that the last train to London had long since departed. They left Marc at the hospice. He was to spend the night on a guest bed, next to his brother, unable to bear the idea of Daniel dying in the middle of the night, all by himself. It had looked almost cosy in Daniel's room, Marc tucked under a blanket, with just the reading light switched on, everything quiet, everything still; it was hard almost to believe that in the midst of all the peace and comfort was a dying man.

They were quiet in Maggie's car. There had been talking all day long, so much talking. They all needed just a few moments to digest what had happened. Lydia sat in the front seat, hair wrapping itself across her face in the warm wind that came through the open window, her head turned to face the moving scenery. It passed her in streaks and flashes; streetlights and takeaways, bollards and traffic lights. And there, atop it all, a big full moon, staring down at her as though it knew what she was thinking. She gazed into the chalky contours of the moon and contemplated her existence, the arc that had started in a small cubicle near Harley Street and was about to end in a small room in Bury St Edmunds. She thought about the thin, grey man in the bed, the man who had told her she was beautiful, and she tried to find a pinpoint of emotion, something to hook the whole thing on, but there was nothing there. He looked like a nice man. If his girlfriend and his brother were anything to go by, he probably was a very nice man. But he was not much more than that. A man. A nice, French man.

She turned her gaze from the moon to the interior of the car. She looked at her gaunt brother, his face streaked in multi-colours from the lights outside, staring blankly into the distance; and she looked at her pretty little sister, her phone in her hand, texting furiously with her thumbs, and she knew then that this was all that mattered to her. Not her father, but these two. Her brother and sister. She was glad she'd seen her father, glad for the sake of her own personal history that she could strike a line through that particular section of it, but it was not a father she needed, it was a family.

'Right,' said Maggie, stifling a yawn while pulling things from a tall cupboard at the top of the stairs. 'Maybe the girls could share the double bed in Daniel's room? I'll need to change the bedding, Marc's been sleeping there. And you,' she directed her words at Dean, 'could sleep down here, on the sofa, if that's OK? There's a load of blankets in here. Would that be OK?'

Dean nodded blankly and took a blanket from Maggie's outstretched hands.

'There's everything you need in the kitchen; bread, milk, juice, et cetera. And you've got my number, if there's an emergency. If you need anything else, just call. I'm only ten minutes away. I could be here in a jiffy.'

She showed them the kitchen, the terrace, the locks on the front door – and then, somewhat apologetically, she left. 'I'll be here tomorrow morning,' she said, 'early. And if there's any news in the night, I'll let you know.'

Lydia closed the door behind her a moment later, and then she and Robyn and Dean all looked at each other and it was immediately obvious that they were all thinking the same thing. It had been a long, sober and intense few hours and the mother figure of Maggie had just left them all alone. It felt, weirdly, given their ages, that they'd been left home alone. And after the weighty events of the rest of the day, it was almost like they'd been given permission to act their age.

'There was a bottle of wine in that fridge, wasn't there?' said Robyn, a mischievous glint in her eye.

'Two,' said Lydia.

'Yeah, and a whole rack of it over there – look.' Dean pointed behind them at a rectangular rack screwed to the wall above them in the hallway.

'I'm not even tired,' said Robyn.

'Me neither,' said Dean.

Lydia smiled. 'Well,' she said, 'I was tired. But, Jesus Christ, after a day like today, I really need a drink.'

'Shall we do it, then?' said Robyn.

'It's not as if he's ever going to be able to drink it, is it?' said Lydia.

Robyn looked at her in delighted shock. 'Lydia!' she chastised. 'You can't say that!'

Dean laughed and Lydia looked at him. 'What?' she said.

'You,' he said. 'You've got no heart.'

'I have got a heart,' she retorted playfully. 'But it's true, isn't it? It'll just go off if we don't drink it.'

'But what about the brother? He might want it when he comes back, you know, *after* . . .'

'Look!' said Lydia, gesturing behind them at the wine rack. 'There's loads here! We'll just replace it! Come on. He would *want* us to drink this. I know he would. He's French, for God's sake!'

Within a few minutes they had collected glasses, a cork-screw and a bottle of something very expensive-looking from the fridge and were clustered together on the floor in the living room, watching Lydia pull out the cork. Someone had switched on the table lamps and the terrace door was open, letting in wafts of chill night air, and Robyn lit a candle and it all felt very cosy and very natural. The clock on the mantelpiece said it was almost a quarter to one.

Lydia raised her full glass of wine to her siblings and said: 'To us. Whoever the hell we are.' And as she looked at them, she suddenly realised exactly who they were. They were the kids. Just that, pure and simple. 'Not 'kids' like the sort of kids who ran in and out of the same house, belonging to the same people. Not the sort of 'kids' who were referred to by their parents when they weren't around. *Have you seen the kids?* But kids, nonetheless. 'Daniel's kids,' she said, with a smile. 'In all our lovely glory.'

Robyn grinned. 'We are pretty lovely, aren't we?'

Dean scoffed. 'Well, you two are. But I'm a minger.'

The girls laughed, affectionately, and then all three of them brought their glasses together and said, 'Cheers.' Dean found a CD player and put on the only CD in their father's collection that all three of them could countenance listening to: *Reload* by Tom Jones. It made for a jaunty, earthy soundtrack to their laughter-filled conversation, almost party-like, and Lydia felt filled with warmth and affection as she watched their young faces, smiling and animated in the glow of the candlelight. And then she saw, almost like a ghost, another face to the left of theirs, another young man, smiling and laughing, a young man who looked a bit like Lydia, a bit like Dean and a bit like Robyn, a young man with a Welsh accent and a big sister called Lydia. A young man called Thomas.

'Another toast,' she said, breaking into the conversation, 'to Thomas. Our lost brother.'

Their faces grew serious at her words and for a moment she felt guilty for souring the jolly atmosphere, but then they smiled and brought their glasses to hers and said, 'Yes – to Thomas. God rest his little soul.'

Surprisingly, nobody talked about Daniel. It was as though they were in a bubble of their own making, an impenetrable world into which they let only the things that they thought would be amusing or interesting or exciting. Tomorrow morning they would be taken back to the hospice by Maggie Smith and they would probably, presumably, if they weren't too late, watch their father die. But tonight was about them and their secret club of wonderfulness.

'So listen,' said Dean. They were halfway through the second bottle of wine taken from Daniel's fridge and he was making a spliff on the surface of Daniel's coffee table. 'What's with the gay guy?'

Lydia grimaced at him. 'What gay guy?'

'The one who's living with you. The one with all the . . .' He cupped his hands around his chest to indicate over-developed pectorals.

'Bendiks?'

Dean laughed. 'Yeah,' he said.

'What's so funny?'

Dean sniggered again and looked at Robyn, who was also laughing, and Lydia felt the distance of the years yawning between them. 'Bendiks,' he replied, snorting with laughter. 'You know . . . Bend? Dicks? It's really funny.'

'I don't get it.'

'Because he's gay!' hooted Robyn. 'So, you know, he has to sort of *bend* his *dick*. To get it into other men's bottoms!'

Lydia raised her head with understanding and let a smile break over her face. 'Ah,' she said. 'I get it. I can't believe I never thought of that. But he's not gay.'

'Oh,' said Dean, still laughing, 'I think you'll find he is. Totally.'

'No. Honestly. He's not.'

'Who the *fuck* is Bend Dicks anyway?' asked Robyn, impatiently.

'Bendiks is my lodger,' said Lydia. 'He lives with me. And he's also my personal fitness trainer.'

'Oh,' said Robyn making a wide O of her mouth. 'I *see*.'

'What!' laughed Lydia.

'But seriously, Lydia,' said Dean. 'He's as gay as fuck. It's obvious.'

She tutted and smiled and said, 'Seriously. He's not. I thought he was too. But then I asked him.'

'What? For real? And what did he say?'

'He didn't *say* anything. He just . . .' She paused. 'He kissed me.'

Their eyes opened wide and Robyn covered her mouth with her hands and for a moment Lydia felt like their ancient aunt.

'Well,' said Dean, 'I suppose that means that I was wrong. But I could have sworn . . .'

'He plucks his eyebrows,' said Lydia, and Robyn and Dean laughed again. 'Really – men who pluck their eyebrows just look gay. Don't they?'

'Well, *yeah*,' said Dean. 'Tell him to stop. Tell him he's giving out the wrong signals.'

And at that very moment Tom Jones launched into 'Sex Bomb.' All of them laughed at the appropriateness of the soundtrack. Dean had finished assembling the spliff and he suggested that they sit out on the terrace to smoke it. The girls followed him, Robyn with a blanket around her shoulders, Lydia in her cardigan. The air outside was sharp and chilled and the rattan chairs were damp beneath their skin.

'Nice view,' said Robyn, pulling the blanket tighter around her shoulders. 'I didn't notice we'd driven so far from town.'

Dean brought a lighted match to the tip of the spliff and lit it. Lydia watched him, suppressing a maternal desire to tell him that he really shouldn't, that it was bad for him, that he'd said he'd stop. But Dean had a mother. That was not her job.

'What's it like where you live?' Robyn asked her.

Dean laughed.

'What?' said Robyn.

'Nothing,' said Dean, 'just a good question, that's all.'

Lydia sighed and smiled. 'I live in quite a big house,' she said. 'Dean thinks it's funny.'

'Have you been there?' asked Robyn, directing wide eyes at him.

'Yeah. Loads of times. And it's not a "very big house" – it's a stately home! It's got its own fucking postcode!'

'Oh, it does not,' chided Lydia. 'Honestly. It's just a house. A big one. You'll have to come and visit.'

'Cool!' Robyn replied. 'And will I get to meet your gay boyfriend, too?'

'He's not my boyfriend! I told you.'

Robyn threw her a mischievous look and smiled. 'Whatever,' she said, knowingly.

Lydia sucked in her breath as she pondered the possibility of sharing something with Dean and Robyn. She felt again the difference in age between her and her younger siblings and wondered how they would react to hearing her problems. But then she asked herself, wasn't this what it was all about? Wasn't this the whole point of being related to people? 'What do you make of this?' she began. And then she told them about the bankruptcy and the £50 notes and the piles of designer clothes and Juliette's suspicions. 'Did you like him?' she asked, turning to Dean. 'You met him – what did you make of him?'

Dean shrugged, as she'd known he would. 'Just thought he was gay really.'

Robyn stifled a laugh.

'No, seriously. Thought he seemed like a nice guy. A bit intense, you know, but that's East Europeans for you. Didn't strike me as a sponger, though.'

Lydia sighed.

'I'm sure there's a rational explanation,' said Robyn, reassuringly. 'I mean, maybe someone else bought him all the stuff?'

Lydia shrugged. She knew that couldn't be the case. She knew deep inside herself that she was being taken for a fool. 'Oh, well,' she said, 'it was never meant to be anything serious. It was only ever just some fun, you know . . .' She trailed off, hoping that she'd sounded nonchalant and cool, but, judging by the look of pity on her sister's face, failing miserably. 'What about you?' she asked, swiftly changing the subject. 'Have you got a boyfriend?'

Robyn curled her feet up beneath her and shivered slightly. 'I certainly do. And if you think thinking that your boyfriend might be gay is bad, listen to this.'

Lydia and Dean looked at her, questioningly.

'I thought mine was my brother.'

Lydia eyed Robyn with squinted eyes over a cloud of smoke and said, 'Continue.'

She smiled. 'It's not actually very funny at all. But when I first started going out with my boyfriend, there was this one time when I saw him in the mirror and I thought it was me. And then a load of my friends met him and were saying all this stuff about how he might be my brother. Because, well, he might have been, mightn't he? And I didn't even know then that I had two brothers. And I started freaking out. And then I found out that my second brother, you know,' she gestured towards Lydia, 'little Thomas, had been born the same year as my Jack, and I *still had sex with him*. Isn't that totally fucked up? I mean, seriously? I was sleeping with him at the same time as thinking he might be my brother.'

Dean looked at her and grimaced. 'That's fucked up,' he said.

'Er, *yeah*,' said Robyn, raising her eyebrows. 'I know it was. But I just couldn't stop myself. It was like – it was like this uncontrollable force. But after a while I just couldn't deal with it and I dumped him. Well, I didn't dump him, I just sort of cooled off. Didn't see him for a while. Which was *hideous*. But, of course, it turns out that it was fine. You know, that Jack is not, in fact, my brother, and that I am not, in fact, a disgusting pervert. His mum came round to see me and I asked her and she said I was nuts! So it's all cool. But still. You know. Sick or what?'

She cackled with laughter then and it was clear to Lydia that this was the first time she had been able to laugh about such an important thing. It was clear that this was the first time she had found any humour in it whatsoever, and Lydia thought to herself that, yes, this was what it was like to have brothers and sisters; this lightness of spirits, this banter and laughter and the shaking off of unnecessary weight from serious subjects, the peeling back of clouded issues.

'Did you ever tell him?' Lydia asked her. 'Did you tell him what you'd thought?'

Robyn shook her head emphatically. 'No way,' she said.

'Why not?'

She shrugged. 'Because he'd have thought I was a freak. Thinking he was my brother but shagging him anyway. And he'd hate me for lying to him. Wouldn't he?'

There was a doubt at the end of the question and Lydia gave it some thought. 'I don't think so,' she said. 'Why would he hate you? It's not your fault. It's not. We've *all* got these weird, crazy backgrounds, and we have to make these bizarre excuses for ourselves all the time. And if he loves you and cares about you, he'll understand that, surely?'

Robyn nodded. 'I guess so,' she said. 'I know he still feels freaked out about us splitting up. I've never really been able to explain it to him. But maybe I should. Maybe you're right. All this weirdness is part of who I am. He'll have to accept that. And, you know, all this, meeting you two, seeing our donor today, all of it, it's just made me realise what's been wrong with my life this last year. And . . .' She stopped talking for a moment and drew in her breath. Then she smiled. 'And what I need to do to fix it. Because I always thought my donor was a god and I was some kind of deity myself. But really, he's just a man and I'm just a girl and the rest of my life is not carved out in stone and from here on in I am going to *wing it*.' She smiled with satisfaction at her closing words and Lydia felt her own heart fill with pride, seeing someone so young work it out all for themself.

Lydia watched Dean rub the end of the spliff out against the brick wall and then tuck it into his jacket pocket. 'Funny, that,' he said, pushing his hands into his pockets and stretching back against his chair, 'because all this has made me feel completely the opposite. Been winging it too long.' He sniffed. 'Meeting you two, both so clever and so . . . what's the word? You know, *driven* and stuff . . . it's made me wonder what else I could be doing. It's like, no one ever let me think I should be doing anything with my life. Everyone always let me think it was OK just to drift along. The only person who ever thought I should be more than I am was Sky . . .'

'Who's Sky?'

Dean winced and wriggled against the back of his chair. 'She was my girlfriend. Mother of my kid. She died . . .'

Robyn recoiled slightly and said, 'Oh, no, Dean. I'm so sorry.'

'Yeah, well, that's life, isn't it? I wish it hadn't happened. Worst thing that ever happened to me. But it did, and now I'm getting on with it. You know. And I'm thinking maybe I can be the person she wanted me to be. You know, get off my skinny arse and do something. Contribute something. I mean . . .' he smiled '. . . I reckon it's got to be there in me somewhere. In my genes. I come from a pretty bright family, after all . . .'

'And what about your child?' said Robyn. 'Tell me about your child.'

'Little girl,' he replied. 'Isadora. Izzy for short. She's nearly four months old.'

'Wow!' Robyn's eyes were wide with wonder. 'A baby. You've got a baby. And that means . . . that means that I'm an auntie!'

'Yeah,' smiled Dean. 'Yeah. That's right – you both are.'

'Oh my God,' she laughed, and turned towards Lydia. 'Did you hear that? You and me – we've got a niece! We're aunties! That's, just, like the coolest thing *ever*!' She turned back to Dean. 'Have you got a picture of her? A picture of Izzy?'

'As it happens . . .' he smiled and felt around inside his coat '. . . I did bring one along. My mum gave it to me before I left. Here she is —'

He sparked up his lighter and held the flame in front of the photo. Lydia leaned in closely, her head almost touching Robyn's. She had never seen a picture of the baby before either. And there she was, a little half-formed person with wide eyes, a plump mouth and a head of thick dark hair. 'Oh, yes,' said Robyn, touching one corner of the photo with her thumb and forefinger. 'Oh, yes, indeed – she is one of us. Without a *doubt*, she is one of us . . .'

The three of them sat like that for a moment, three dark heads held close together around the soft flame of the lighter, staring in awe and affection at this proof of the power of their connection. This baby, much more than the man fading away in the hospice down the road, was what bound them together. Lydia stared into the child's dark eyes and felt her own eyes dampen with tears. Suddenly she knew what babies were for. She'd never understood before what possible role a baby would ever play in her life. But now she did.

Continuity.

The soothing reassurance that it would all carry on, minute after minute, day after day, year after year, century after century. The knowledge that there was more to life than her own limited experience of existence; that long after she was gone, there would be others like her; that maybe one day, when all that was left of her was a granite block in a Welsh cemetery, a person somewhere might say something like: *My mother's great-aunt made a fortune out of paint, you know.* Or maybe they wouldn't. Maybe she would never be spoken of again, her headstone obliterated by moss and grime. But still, just to know it . . . just to know that there was more than just her. And to remember that without all the reproduction and continuity there was just age and decay. A big full stop. And here, in Dean's hands, was proof that life really would go on.

'She's beautiful,' Robyn said, loosening her hold on the photo, 'really, really beautiful.'

'Yeah,' said Dean quietly, letting the flame of the lighter die out and slowly returning the photo to his inside pocket. 'Which is pretty miraculous really, given that she looks just like me.'

His comment lightened the mood and all three of them laughed.

'So,' said Dean, slapping his thighs. 'Who fancies a bowl of cornflakes then?'

They ate their cornflakes, on their knees, around the coffee table. The clock said 2.30 a.m. yet still it seemed too early to call it a night.

They were family now. Lydia knew that, and she sensed that the others knew it too. It would be surprising if they didn't come together as a threesome again over the years to come – but this, what they were doing here tonight, this would never be repeated. The combination of factors that had brought them all here . . . the fact that they were in their father's home waiting for him to die, the lateness of the night, the fullness of the moon . . . but more than that – the newness of it all. This was their first date and Lydia didn't want it to end.

They ate in silence, just the sounds of their spoons hitting china, the crunch of the cereal between their teeth, breaking the peace. When they'd finished they immediately returned to the kitchen and poured themselves second bowls, and then, when they'd finished those, they opened another bottle of wine, rolled another spliff and headed back out to the terrace. The sky was already losing its blackness and the moon had shifted out of sight. It would be dawn before too long.

Lydia shivered slightly and Robyn pulled the blanket from around her shoulders and draped it across their knees. And then she snuggled up against Lydia and rested her head on her shoulder. Lydia stiffened slightly. The gesture was reminiscent of Dixie's in the early days of their friendship – 'touchy-feely', Lydia had called it, and in return Dixie had laughed and called her the Tin Man. Lydia thought of those moments now with the weight of Robyn's head against her shoulder, the tickle of her hair against her cheek, the hard points of her knees against her thigh, and she reached deep down inside herself to find something she knew was in there somewhere, something basic and human and raw, and as she did so she felt it rushing through her, from her heart to her feet to her hands. Lydia put her arm around Robyn's small, neat shoulders and pulled her closer. And then she rested her head against Robyn's head and breathed in the smell of her, the smell of her sister.

'Budge up,' said Dean, rising from his seat. Lydia and Robyn moved over and he squeezed himself down next to them. He put his arms around both of them and brought their heads to his. 'This has been the best night of my life,' he said softly.

Lydia and Robyn smiled and pulled him to them, and

there they sat, Dean, Lydia and Robyn, a human triangle, three lost children united at last.

'Let's never go to sleep,' said Robyn, yawning widely.

'No,' said Lydia, 'let's never.'

They did fall asleep eventually. They grabbed armfuls of blankets from Daniel's airing cupboard and made a campsite of his living room. At four o'clock they finally turned off all the lights and even then they did not sleep immediately. Even then there was still more to talk about, still more to laugh about ('Here,' Dean whispered dramatically into the silence, 'do you reckon that Maggie woman will shack up with the twin once the other one's dead? I mean, it's a bit like having a spare.'), still more to learn. But finally, as the sun began its ascent above the flat Suffolk skyline, Robyn and Dean fell silent and their breathing grew heavy and Lydia knew that it was just her now, awake in her father's house. She watched them both for a while, their young, smooth faces, soft with sleep, Robyn's beautiful black hair spread around her head, Dean's hands tucked beneath his cheek like a child. They were safe.

She slept.

DANIEL

Through the narrow opening between his eyelids Daniel can see a flicker of green, a swirl of yellow, a shiver of movement. If he turns his head to the left he can see whiteness, lines, angles, a face. The face seen from here is an abstract blob of pink with some darker bits in the middle that move in and out of focus as he gazes at them. He knows this person is Maggie because he can hear her voice. At times he knows what she is saying. At times he is able to hold on to the substance of the noises coming from her mouth and use his strange new mind to turn them into meaningful words. Some time earlier (today? Yesterday? He doesn't know), she had been talking about the children. *The children*. He had responded in some way to that. He isn't sure if the response had been decipherable. He'd wanted to express a feeling of joy and excitement. It is possible that Maggie had taken it as an expression of discomfort. She had asked for a nurse and one had come, a warm, radiating sensation to his right-hand side as she leaned across his body, the solidity and reassurance of heavy human flesh. No one seems to touch him any more. Not even Maggie. Just these little squeezes to his hands. Sometimes it hurts. Sometimes his hands hurt, like they are open wounds. But he isn't hurting now. He feels fine now. He feels like a jar full of honey.

So then, the children came. He remembers that very clearly. Three beautiful humans. They had looked at him with pity and curiosity, but not with love. He had not expected love. Though he felt also at some point, either before or in between, that he had died. He was sure he had died, but then he hadn't been dead at all and had awoken at the arrival of his children and even said some words. So, no, he had not been dead. Although maybe he was dead now. But no, he would not be able to see these outlines and hear these voices if he were dead. And the children are back again.

The man is there now, too, next to Maggie. It's his brother. Marc. Before (today? Yesterday?) his brother had held him on the bed. His brother had kissed him. And as his brother had kissed him, Daniel's strange new mind had taken him away from this room for a while – his strange new mind is always taking him away from this room and put him into the room in which he and his brother had slept together as children. The room had oak shutters at the windows and a tiled floor underfoot. Daniel and his brother slept there together, side by side, in a small double bed, coiled against each other just as they had been in the womb. They would awaken every morning, chest to chest, breathing in each other's stale breath; they would open their eyes and they would smile with pleasure at the sight of each other, at the dawning of another day of being together.

Daniel had fallen asleep like that again, with his brother's arm around him, their hands layered over each other. Every time he falls asleep he finds himself surprised to wake again. Sleeping now feels so close to dying that he cannot imagine how he will tell the difference once the time comes. When he awoke from this sleep – he assumed it was this sleep and not a different one – his brother had not been on the bed any more and the room had been empty. This is the only time that Daniel feels anxious about what is happening to him, when his room is empty. The more ill he becomes, the less he finds himself alone. Possibly because he sleeps for much longer but also because people do not like to leave the dying in case there is no one there to see them go. Like waiting for a bus, the more time you invest in awaiting the outcome the harder it is to walk away.

But the room is not empty now. It is filled with Maggie and Marc and with his children. He opens his eyes another millimetre and for a moment it is like looking at a snapshot from his past; he and Maggie standing side by side in the dark, outside some restaurant, waiting for a taxi, his jacket around her bare shoulders, but not touching. Never touching. There is the same distance between Maggie and his brother now, a few inches. Daniel has grown unused to having a double. Now he looks at his twin and thinks not, That is my brother, but, That is me. His brother has become a mirror image of

Daniel himself, rather than an extension. He lets his eyelids fall shut again and inhales. His breathing now, it sounds so ugly, like the raspings of a devilish beast. He feels his blood rushing around his body. Remarkably urgent. Remarkably vital.

The children. She is talking about the children again. He tries to hold on to her words.

He manages to expel a noise. The noise is loud and alarming, even to his own ears. *Who?*

He sees them turn towards him, as one, like a choreographed movement in a dance.

'Who?' he says again.

Maggie is alongside him now, holding his hand, like she always does. 'The children,' she says. 'They're here. They wanted to see you again.'

'All of them?' he croaks.

'Yes,' she says, brightly. 'All of them! Dean. Lydia. Robyn.'

He strains against the pull of sleep for as long as he can but finally allows himself to be pulled back down into unconsciousness again, away from the memory that has sat like an ominous sentry inside his mind for most of his adult life.

There is movement all around him. Through the arrow slits of his eyes he can see something flame-coloured. It makes a noise as it moves, a kind of rustling sound, like a brown paper parcel being unwrapped. Atop the orange-red mass is a head, some dark hair, a pair of big eyes looking into his, the smell of sickly perfume, a glimmer of silver at the earlobes.

'He's opening his eyes,' says the girl in the rustling red dress.

Daniel senses more movement, a sea of blobs suddenly propelled towards him, like satellites towards a mother ship. He sees a white top with some kind of writing on it. There is a dark head atop this too. And then another dark head, this one attached to a lithe, bendy body dressed in colours from the bottom of the sea. It is a man and a woman. He wishes he could focus more clearly. But even without seeing, he knows that these people are Dean and Lydia. He feels pain shooting through his legs; it feels like bullets being fired from his pelvis down to his toes. He wants to wince, but knows that any facial signs of his discomfort will be met by a visit from the nurse and more morphine and then he will be gone again, and right now he needs the pain to keep him awake.

He concentrates on his eyes. They have to open. They have to focus. But still, all he can see is blurred outlines, a *pointilliste* watercolour of blobs.

'Do you want some water?' It is the girl in the red dress. He remembers the dress from yesterday. Her name is Robyn.

He nods and she carefully brings the straw to his lips. He has not had water for many hours, maybe days; he no longer needs water as he is about to die, but he wants to take water from this girl, because she is his daughter.

'Can you see me?' she says, putting the cup back on his tray.

He shakes his head and smiles.

And then: 'Red dress,' he manages to say.

'Yes!' she says, delighted, looking around her at the others. 'Yes. I'm wearing a red dress!'

She moves away and now the other one approaches, the woman, Lydia. 'Hello, Daniel,' she says. Her voice is strange somehow, as though she is singing to him. And then he remembers that she is Welsh. Then the other one comes, the boy, Dean. He has very short hair, like a cap on his head. He is thin too, all his children are very thin. He approaches in a less confident manner. Daniel wishes he could reassure him. But there is nothing he can possibly do. He smiles instead. 'Morning,' says the boy.

Morning? Is it?

Daniel can feel it rushing back. The sea of sleep closing over his head as if he is a heavy weight plummeting to the ocean bed. Then the boy touches his arm and there is a sudden terrible pain. Daniel contains it. Pain is good. While there is pain, he is still here, still present. He thinks of things he wants to say: he wants to say that he is sorry, sorry for his cowardice, only to ask to meet them when he knows he will not be asked to do anything more. He wants to say that they are beautiful, all three of them. He wants to say that he is proud of them and that now he can see what it was that he did. He wonders if the existence of these three miraculous people can in any way ever compensate for the life of the sick child that he snatched away one drowsy, unfocused day in a hospital in Dieppe. He wants to say, 'There is my brother, he is yours, have him instead. He is just like me, only better. Keep him. My gift to you.' He wants to say that he has not had a good life but that now, in these fading moments, he can see that it was fine. And he wants to say *goodbye*. He wants to say it to each and every one of them in turn, to take each face between his hands and hold it and kiss it and make eye contact and then to say it, loud and clear, *goodbye*. But there are no more words.

His dry mouth is no longer his. It hangs flaccidly, as if someone has glued it on to his face, haphazardly. There will be no more words. There will be no goodbyes or eye contact or kisses. There will just be this. This floating mass of humanity, that seems to lift from the ground as he lets his eyes close. The room tilts for a moment. He clutches the sheets with his hand to steady himself. The room tilts back again. He forces his eyes open again. The people around him stare at him. They are talking. He cannot hear what they are saying. But he can feel them, all around him, like a warm embrace. They are all there. And he can go now.

He can hear his own breath again in his ears. It sounds horrible. He wants to stop it but he has already had his last moments of control over his body. He is trapped now and there is no way back. He smiles and lets himself be taken there.

LATER THAT DAY

DEAN

Tommy was sitting at a white plastic table outside the Alliance. He had a pint in one hand and his phone in the other. When he saw Dean walking towards the pub he quickly wrapped up his conversation and turned it off.

'All right?' he said, almost getting to his feet, and then thinking better of it.

Dean shrugged and smiled. 'Yeah,' he said, 'I guess so. Want a drink?'

'No.' He indicated his fresh pint. 'I'm OK.'

Dean brought a pint from the bar back to the table and sat down opposite his cousin. He'd come straight from the train and was still in the clothes he'd been wearing for two days and a night. He felt grimy and stale.

'How'd it go?' said Tommy, eyeing him over the top of his pint.

'He died,' said Dean.

Tommy's eyes widened. 'You're kidding?' he said.

Dean shrugged. 'No. Straight up. This morning. He died.'

'What – in front of you?'

'Yeah. He was awake when we got there on Saturday,

447

he was talking and stuff. It was cool. Then his girlfriend took us to his flat and we all spent the night there, went back this morning and you could tell he was on his way out. Literally an hour after we arrived, he was gone.'

'Shit,' said Tommy.

'Yeah. Well.' Dean stretched his legs out beneath the table and sighed.

'So, what was he like?'

Dean squinted and rolled up his top lip. 'Kind of ill, really.'

'No, I meant – what did he look like?'

'Well, he looked fucking awful, but his brother was there and they're identical twins, so I could kind of see what he – my dad, the donor, you know – what he must have looked like when he was normal.'

'So what did he look like, the twin?'

'A bit like me. A bit like Lydia. A bit like Robyn . . . that's the other sister. And quite a lot like the baby . . .'

'*Your* baby?'

'Yes. *My* baby.' Dean smiled and then laughed quietly to himself.

Tommy looked at him quizzically. 'What?'

'Nothing,' he said, smiling, 'nothing.'

'And so, what happens now?'

'Fuck knows. There'll be a funeral, probably next week. I'll be going to that. And then, I don't know. I'll be staying in touch with all of them, I reckon. The girls, his brother, even his girlfriend seemed like a really nice person . . . And I've decided something else, too. About the baby. About

Isadora. I want to get involved with her. Maybe have her to stay sometimes, take her out on my own. Because, one day, when I'm ready, I'd really like to be her proper dad, you know. Maybe get some qualifications, get a job, get a flat, and then she can come and live with me. Lydia says she'll help out, and the other one, Robyn, she's really into the idea of having a little niece in her life.'

Tommy nodded approvingly, silently demonstrating his unspoken thoughts about the whole issue.

'And it's like suddenly there's all these people around, good people. It's like it's all . . .'

He wanted to break into a massive grin and say: *It's amazing! I've found this new world and I'm totally a part of it and it's kind of a tribe and I've got these stunning sisters and this cool new French uncle and it's like I've joined some exclusive club and I'm a VIP member!* But he didn't say any of that. Because his father had just died and it was inappropriate for him to feel this happy. But he was happy. Happier than he'd ever felt before.

He'd felt it that morning, just after his father had pulled in that shocking last breath then let it trickle back out again. They'd all stood like sentries around him and Daniel's brother had wailed and shouted out something in French and the girlfriend had twittered like a lost baby bird. But he and his sisters had just stood and stared.

'Is that it?' he'd whispered to Lydia.

She'd nodded, tersely and squeezed his arm. Robyn had looked around nervously. 'Oh my God,' she'd said quietly. And then she too had begun to cry. He couldn't

449

remember now how long they'd stood like that. Maggie fiddled with Daniel's hair. His brother pulled down his eyelids. And then eventually they had all left the room. They'd gone outside and stood together next to a pond full of golden fish and, without saying a word, the three siblings had embraced. And it was then that Dean had felt it, the awesome reality of them all. Within their embrace had been unspoken words of commitment and trust. Within their embrace had been the future.

The sun sat overhead, behind a thin veil of cloud, and Dean laced his fingers together across his stomach, and, for the very first time, he considered the universe. He thought about the endless dense blackness of it and then he thought of this one tiny sunlit speck of earth, on top of which wriggled the overwhelming swarm of humanity, billions of people, billions of lives, and for so long he'd thought himself just another speck of dust. But now it was as though a giant hand bearing a giant magnifying glass had lurched towards him, through the cosmos, and shown him what he really was.

He waited until Tommy's phone rang again and then he pulled out his own phone. He scrolled through his contacts until he got to the name Kate, and then, without stopping to think about it, he wrote her a message.

Hi there. This is Mr Dead Girlfriend. Just to tell u that I met them all, sistas, dad, the lot, and everythings cool. Hope your good. Let me no if u want to meet up. Thinking bout college and stuff, maybe u could help?

He didn't pause when he'd finished typing, just pressed

send with a confident smile. He was ready now. Ready for anything: love, fatherhood, family, learning, even rejection.

Tommy finished his phonecall and looked curiously at Dean. 'What you up to?' he said.

Dean smiled. 'Nothing, mate,' he said, 'just getting on with stuff.'

A moment later his phone buzzed. It was a text message, from Kate.

Best news EVA! Love to meet up again soon. How about Friday?

Friday good for me. I'll text u later. And see u then.

Dean smiled, and switched off his phone.

ROBYN

Robyn turned the key in the lock of the front door and drew in her breath. She felt like she'd been away for at least a week and she felt like she was coming home as a different human being entirely. Her heart was filled with love for everyone, but particularly and overwhelmingly for Jack. She pushed open the door, dropped her bag and raced into the study. Jack turned from his computer at the sound of her arrival and they threw themselves bodily at each other, burying their faces in each other's hair. 'I missed you so much,' said Robyn.

'Not as much as I missed you,' said Jack.

'Much more than you missed me, I can assure you,' she laughed. *'Much more.'*

Jack made them some tea and Robyn sat upon his lap and drank it while she told him all about her beautiful sister and her sweet brother and the weird numbness of watching her father pass away whilst standing in the same room as his identical brother. She told him about the fun she'd had with Lydia and Dean in their father's flat, drinking wine, getting stoned and staying up so late that they'd only had three hours' sleep. And then she told him about the conversation she'd had with Lydia.

'You know,' she began, carefully, 'I was talking to Lydia about something, last night. I was talking to her about us. About that time when we split up. Remember, when I went all weird on you?'

Jack looked at her with interest. 'How could I forget?' he said, drily.

'There was a reason for me being weird with you, for me not seeing you all that time, and I never thought I would tell you about it. But Lydia said I should. Lydia said you'd understand. Because you love me . . .'

Jack's expression turned to one of concern. 'Go on,' he said, cautiously.

'Well, there was a time, just after we met, when I thought . . .' She took a deep breath. 'When I thought you were my brother.'

'What!' Jack began to laugh.

'It's not funny!' she said. 'It's true. I thought you were my brother. In fact, I was totally convinced you were my brother.'

'Good God! Why?' He was still laughing.

'I don't know. Because you look so like me. Because you don't know your dad. Because I didn't know my dad. Because your mother was all weird with me when we went to see her that evening, when we were talking about me being a donor child.   And then mainly because the Registry sent me a letter telling me that I had a donor brother who was born the same year as you.'

'What, really?'

'Yeah. Really. So you can see why I might have had my suspicions. And I just freaked out.'

'But why didn't you tell me?'

'I couldn't,' she said, 'I just couldn't. I couldn't deal with being the person to tell you that your dad was a donor. I couldn't deal with us both knowing that we'd been incestuous. I couldn't deal with anything at all until I knew for sure that I was wrong. And the minute I knew I was wrong, I came straight back to you. I mean, literally, within minutes.'

Jack fell silent for a moment. 'So when did you know? That I wasn't your brother?' He stifled a laugh at the end of the question.

'Your mother.'

'My mother?'

'Yes. I asked her. She told me. And, of course, if she had conceived you through a donor, she wouldn't have lied about it, would she? I mean, she *had* to be telling the truth.'

'Unless she secretly *wanted* two-headed grandchildren?' said Jack, with a mischievous smile.

'Well, yes,' said Robyn, feeling her heart lighten with relief. 'I hadn't considered that possibility.'

'She's a strange woman, my mum. You never know.'

Robyn smiled and leaned back against Jack's chest. She felt the last residue of awkwardness leave her body and she breathed out contentedly. 'My real brother was called Thomas,' she said, after a moment. 'He died when he was a baby. But if he hadn't died, he'd have been exactly the same age as you. And maybe you could have been friends . . .'

Jack nodded, sadly. 'I would have liked that,' he said, breathing into the crown of her head.

'Yes,' said Robyn, 'so would I.'

Two hours later, Robyn and Jack sat side by side on a bumpy train. The carriage was mainly empty. At four in the afternoon, very few people had cause to be travelling from London to Buckhurst Hill. Jack held Robyn's hand in his. They didn't talk. Robyn's head was too full of strangeness and wonder to find anything as solid as words in there.

Her parents were doing a barbecue. 'Just some steaks and a potato salad,' her mum had said apologetically when Robyn had phoned this morning to tell her she wanted to see them. 'Is that OK, love?'

Robyn had made her decision as she sat alone on the train, heading back to London. She thought about the way that man had looked as he'd exhaled his last breath. She couldn't shake it from her mind. It was so essentially shocking. She'd never seen anyone dic before. She'd fiddled with cadavers in anatomy classes but she'd never before seen the life pass from someone. It replayed in her head, over and over again, the way his face had gone slack, the sudden terrible silence after an hour of nightmarish death rattle. The whole experience had been overwhelming. She could barely remember what had happened now, barely remember what they'd all talked about while they waited for him to die, what they'd all done. She'd left the hospice before the other two, desperate to get back to Jack and to some semblance of normality.

She shouldn't have gone to the hospice. She was not mature enough to see a man die. And she was not, she now knew with some clarity, mentally prepared to spend the next five years of her life studying medicine.

Her mother was wearing a strappy top and a floral cotton skirt when she opened the door to them both forty minutes later. Her hair was freshly brushed through and hung about her rather fleshy face like a billowing pair of brown curtains. She'd also sprayed herself with perfume and put on a pretty necklace and was quite clearly making an effort for the sake of her daughter's handsome young boyfriend.

'Come in, come in, so lovely to . . . mwah –' she kissed them both effusively on their left cheeks '– see you both.'

Robyn's father was out in the back garden, tenderly prodding a pile of juicy steaks with a large metal fork. He had a cup of tea in his other hand and was wearing a sunhat and shorts. Robyn's heart lurched at the sight of him. He was so big and so soft and so strong and so solid. She thought of him compared to the shrivelled man in the bed at the hospice. That man had been just a vessel, literally, as his soul had passed away from it, but also nineteen years ago when he'd given away his sperm to a stranger. That was all he was. Nothing more than an empty bottle. She'd felt sorry for him, of course she had, he looked like a nice person. She'd liked his brother, been taken aback by the resemblance they bore to one another, but apart from that she had felt absolutely nothing.

'Hello, Dad,' she said, pushing herself into his big solid arms and waiting for the familiar, wonderful sensation of his embrace. 'I love you,' she said into the cotton of his t-shirt.

'And I love you too, little one,' he said, kissing the top of her head. 'How are you feeling?'

She shrugged. 'I'm OK,' she said, sitting herself down on a wooden chair on the patio.

'Nice to see you again, Jack,' said her dad, putting out a beefy hand for him to shake. Jack sat down next to Robyn and then her mother came out with a chilled bottle of Tesco's own brand rosé and four wine glasses.

'So,' she said, nervously, passing the bottle to her husband to open, 'how did it go?'

'It was horrible,' said Robyn, shuddering. 'Totally horrible. I never want to see anyone die, ever again. It was the most shocking thing I've ever seen.'

Her mother pursed her lips knowingly and said nothing.

Robyn sighed. Of course, she thought, of course, my mother has seen both her elder daughters die. My mother understands. 'Sorry,' she said, 'I didn't mean to be insensitive. It's just . . .'

'I know,' said her mum. 'I know. But tell us about the rest of it? About the brother and the sister? What was it like? What were they like?'

Robyn told them everything; about her first incredible sight of them, about their train journey, the way they all talked over each other in their rush to get to know one another and to share their stories. She told them about the other brother, Thomas, who hadn't made it to his first year. She told her parents about the handsome twin and the lovely girlfriend with the pretty blonde hair and how they'd told her that Daniel had never made it through medical school, that he'd never been a doctor, that he'd lived his life mysteriously and alone, never had any children and never been married. She told them about the way she and her siblings had all reached out for each other in a spontaneous embrace by the fish pond after Daniel had died and how nice it had felt and how they'd already arranged to meet up next weekend, for a barbecue at Lydia's house. She told them how her brother Dean had a little baby girl called Isadora whom he was going to bring with him, and how Lydia had a huge house in North London and had invented a special kind of paint and was a millionaire, but didn't act like one, she was so down-to-earth with her lovely Welsh accent. She told them about her strange train journey home, sitting alone on a near-empty train, mulling over the extraordinary events of the day and using those thoughts to plan her future. And then she told them something else. Something bizarre. Something she could barely believe she was about to say.

'I made a decision today,' she said, her hand clutching Jack's knee, slightly too hard. 'A really big decision. I don't want to be a doctor any more. I'm going to leave uni.' She paused. 'The thing is, I never even gave myself a chance to consider doing anything else, just thought it was preordained, that it was in my blood. And maybe it *is* in my blood, but then the other two, Lydia and Dean, they've done their own thing. They haven't based their decisions on our donor or on who he was. So I'm going to see my tutor tomorrow, tell him I'm leaving, and then . . .' She paused, because this was the hardest thing to say: 'Earlier, as I was walking home to the flat, I saw an advert, taped inside the window of a cafe. For a waitress. And I just had this weird, overwhelming feeling that it was, like, a sign. It's a really cute little cafe, tables on the pavement, run by a really nice woman. So I went in and asked about it and, well, she offered me the job! It's only six pounds an hour but I'll get tips, and better still it closes at seven o'clock so I won't have to work evenings, and it's like the hub of the community, you know, so I'll get to know all the locals. I'll really be part of where I live. And maybe while I'm doing that, when my head's clear and the pressure's gone, I might work out what it is that I really want to do. It might just, you know *come to me.'*

She stopped and stared at her parents. 'What do you think?' she said. 'Are you really disappointed in me?'

There was a moment's silence and then both her parents smiled and her father laughed. 'Oh, yes,' he said, his arms folded across his fat belly, 'oh, yes, we're *terribly* disappointed in you. Always have been. Always will be. I mean,' he turned to his wife, 'we really only wanted a child who was going to be a doctor, didn't we, love? Anything less than that, well, frankly, it's a bit pointless . . .'

Her parents laughed then, and so did Robyn. She stood up and crouched between their chairs and held them both around the neck, kissing them on their cheeks.

'How could we ever be disappointed in you?' asked her mother, running her hand over Robyn's hair. 'You're our life. You're our everything. We don't care what you do, as long as you're happy.'

And Robyn rested her cheek against her mother's shoulder and considered her sweet, loving parents, her gentle, beautiful boyfriend, her crazy best friend, and now her child-like brother and her quiet, elegant sister, and she thought that, yes, she was, most definitely, certainly, completely and totally, happy. And she smiled.

MAGGIE

Maggie sat flat against Daniel's sofa and allowed her body to leave a firm and undeniable imprint in the upholstery. Daniel was gone and would not be coming back. She no longer felt it was necessary to leave no trace of herself inside his home. Marc was upstairs, getting changed, and she was waiting to take him back to the hospice, where Daniel's body had been prepared for burial.

When she'd got home from the hospice the night before, she'd been unable to switch herself into the state of normality necessary to find sleep. So she'd pulled out the carrier bags, the ones she'd filled at Daniel's house a few weeks earlier, and begun to leaf through the notebooks. She had brought them with her today. She wanted to show them to Marc because they were written in French and because she thought they seemed, from what little she was able to translate, somewhat significant. Marc came downstairs a moment later and smiled at her. 'I am ready,' he said, 'shall we go?'

She returned his smile. He was wearing a white shirt and beige trousers and looked fresh and scrubbed. But from his eyes she could see that he had quite possibly been

crying. 'I've got some things,' she said, 'for you to look at.'
She held up the pile of notepads. 'I think they might be
your brother's journals. I was wondering . . . maybe you
could have a look at them, if you thought that was appro-
priate? Maybe you could tell me what they're about?'

She made two cups of coffee and brought them out on
to the terrace a few minutes later where Marc was sitting
in the shade of a red parasol, leafing through the books.
He did not look up when Maggie emerged and his hand
found his mug of coffee without any assistance from his
eyes. Maggie sat gingerly on the chair next to his and
stared into the distance. She waited until Marc was ready
to talk and then she smiled at him. 'So,' she said, 'anything
interesting?'

'Well,' said Marc, closing a book and blinking at her,
'these are his journals. They are very, how you say: spo-
radeek? Yes?'

She nodded.

'But it seems that we can now solve the mystery of how
my brother lived such a life –' he gestured behind him at
the comfortable flat '– without a job. It seems that he had
a benefactor. A lady, called . . .' he leafed through the
book again to a particular page '. . . Bettina. It seems they
had a long affair, and then she died and she left him this
flat and all her money. It also seems, my dear Maggie, that
my brother was very much in love with you.'

Maggie blanched.

'Yes. He says it here: "Finally, I have found a woman
with whom I could truly wish to grow old, a beautiful

woman, a refined woman, a woman with class and style and a good, kind heart, and it is too, too late. Oh, Maggie, I do love you. I hope that one day I will tell you this, but knowing me, I will not.'"

Maggie gulped and turned away from Marc so that he could not read the expression on her face. She felt tears pressing against her eyelids, bruising and sore. She felt her stomach lurch, once with happiness at the fact of his love for her, but again with misery as she thought of what she'd lost. She waited a beat until the tears had been forced down and then she turned to Marc and smiled. 'Well,' she said, 'isn't that nice? Oh, and how funny about the rich lady! Imagine that! Only Daniel,' she said, 'only Daniel could possibly charm a lady into leaving him her entire estate.' She laughed, a nervous laugh. She was uncomfortable with this peeling back of the mysterious layers that had surrounded him. Maybe, she thought to herself, maybe she would rather leave him like this. A strange, sad and perfect memory. Maybe she should leave these journals with his twin, let him explore the interior life of his brother. Maggie didn't want to know. No, she really did not want to know. Not now that it was too late to do anything with the knowledge.

'Come on,' she said, 'we should probably get going. Let's go and say goodbye to your brother.' She held out her hand for Marc and he took it shyly.

'Yes, Maggie,' he said, 'let us say goodbye.'

LYDIA

Lydia's empty house echoed with the sound of her arrival. Juliette didn't work on Sundays and Bendiks was out. Queenie ran down the stairs at the sound of her entrance and immediately began to love her, rubbing herself frantically against Lydia's legs and smiling at her with delight. Lydia lifted the cat and carried her through the house, checking rooms as she went, checking them for change, for disturbance, and more than anything for signs of Bendiks. But everything was as she'd last seen it. Clean. Immaculate. Sterile.

Lydia continued her ascent through the house and then straight to her office. It was early afternoon and there was nothing else for her to do except work. She had a meeting the following week with a client. She had been neglecting her work these last few days. Now that everything had been tied up, her siblings found, her father dead, her history explicated and her life made sense of, it was time for her to get back to real life. She pulled a file from her cabinet and laid it open upon her desk. Then she booted up her laptop and scrolled through some e-mails, and then she sighed, raised her eyes to the ceiling and tried to remember just exactly what it was she was supposed to be doing. It all seemed so unconnected to the person she'd been for the past few days, so far removed from the woman who'd got stoned with her little brother and sister on a terrace in Bury, who'd slept on the floor like a teenager on a sleepover, who'd had sex in a sauna and drunk wine with an uncle in Wales.

For years she had lived and breathed her work. For years her mind had been a clean and ordered thing, spacious and open-plan as a minimalist loft apartment. Now it felt like a crazed attic, piled full of intriguing boxes and odd treasures. The inside of her head was now too distracting for her to turn any part of it to the matter of work. Half an hour after sitting down at her desk, she stood up again and decided to go for a walk. She glanced through the window and saw in front of her a place she'd avoided for months. She heard the sounds that chilled her heart: the high-pitched shrieks and cries of small children in a playground. She'd never really thought about her aversion to playgrounds, assuming it was connected with her ambivalence towards children in general. But now she knew exactly why she avoided them, and she also knew it was time to face that fear and overcome it.

She was halfway down the stairs when she heard a key in the lock of the front door and saw the outline of Bendiks through the opaque glass. She caught her breath against a burst of nervous energy and arranged her face into a smile. Bendiks looked at her with surprise as he came through the door. 'You're back!' he said. 'Where've you been?'

She was thrown, as always, by his beauty, and felt a dull throb deep down inside herself that told her that her attraction to him had not waned even a degree in the light of his transgressions. 'To see my dad,' she said, quietly.

Bendiks looked confused. 'But I thought your father was . . .?'

Lydia sat on a step and sighed. 'No. Not that one. My real father. The donor.'

'Wow.' Bendiks stopped and rubbed his jaw. 'Wow. That is a very big deal. How was it? Are you OK?'

She smiled and told him about the hospice and watching her father die for the second time in her life. Bendiks sat on the step below her and looked up at her with sympathy and compassion. 'You are such a strong person, Lydia,' he said, sincerely. 'Really. You are amazing. Is there anything I can do? Would you like to talk some more? I am free tonight – maybe we could have dinner?'

Lydia tucked her hair behind her ear and nodded. 'That would be good,' she said. 'If you're sure . . .'

'Of course I'm sure! I care for you, Lydia. And I want to be here for you . . .' He paused then, and cast his eyes awkwardly to the floor.

Here it comes, thought Lydia, *here comes something bad*.

'Listen, Lydia,' he began. 'I, er, I have to tell you something. I am moving out . . .'

Lydia's heart stopped for a moment and she blinked in surprise. 'Oh,' she said.

'It is nothing personal, I promise you. It is . . .' He paused and looked at the floor while he formed his words.

'It is me. I am weak. I have been spending again, Lydia. I have been building up new debt.'

'Oh, Bendiks . . .' Lydia felt herself soften with relief.

'Yes, I know. I had one card left, that they didn't cut up. And so long as I am living here, in this beautiful house, I can pretend that everything is fine. I can pretend that my life is good, that I am a successful man. But my life is not good. My life is stupid. I am stupid. So today I cut up this card. And I have put on to eBay all my things; my clothes and my shoes and my *toys*. All these *things* that I thought I needed. That I thought were important.

'See, here . . .' He pulled a carrier bag from between his feet and showed it to her. 'I have bought a pay as you go phone. Ha! Like a teenager! And also, I have found a room, somewhere hideous, I can't even remember the name of the place, something Park. It is in Zone 3, Lydia! But it is cheap and every morning when I wake up there it will be a reminder to me that I have to work hard and play fair and stay within my means if I ever want to be the kind of man who could live in a house like this on my own merits. You see? So, no, it is not personal. I have loved living here, with you. It has been an honour. But I have to do this if I am to lead a good life.

'Oh, and also . . .' He reached into his jacket pocket and pulled out his wallet. 'Here,' he said, pulling notes from it. 'One hundred and fifty pounds. Yours, I believe?' He held the notes out towards Lydia and she stared at them mutely. 'Take it,' he said, 'please.'

'No, Bendiks, honestly. I don't want your money.'

'It is not my money, it is *your* money. Which I took from you in bad faith, knowing that I was not in a position to repay you. But this is the money I got for my phone. And I want you to have it. So that I can sleep at peace tonight . . .'

Lydia continued to stare at the money. She didn't need it. She didn't want it. But she knew, for Bendiks' sake, that she should take it. 'Thank you,' she said, holding the notes in her hand. 'You didn't have to. But thank you.'

'No, Lydia. Thank you. Thank you for being so kind to me. And thank you for, well, you know . . .' He smiled shyly. 'And I hope, you know, that we'll still see each other. If that's what you would like? Because I would like it. I would like it very much.'

Lydia looked at him and thought, *Yes*. Yes, I would like to see you again. I would like to have sex with you again. And even though I know that you and I will never be a serious item, that we will not get married and we will not live happily ever after, I hope that whatever happens we can always be friends.

'Cool,' she said, rubbing her elbows. 'I can call you on your pay-as-you-go phone.'

'Yes!' Bendiks beamed at her and laughed uproariously. 'Yes! I will give you my number!' Lydia smiled. And felt all the tiny little bits of her life that had been floating around in a state of irresolution gently slot into place. *There*, she thought, *there. Now everything is as it should be. Now I can get on with it.* But then she remembered there was still one fragment of her life that she needed to deal with.

*

The playground was packed. It was four o'clock, the schools and nurseries had just emptied and the sun was high in a pale blue sky. She sat on a bench, deliberately facing towards the playground, and stared in awe through the bars. *Look at them all*, she thought to herself, *just look at them all*. Where did they all come from? What would they all become? Were they conceived in love, in duty, in passion, in a drunken blur? Did they know their fathers? Did they know their mothers? Did they have brothers and sisters? Maybe half-brothers, half-sisters, cousins, uncles, aunts. Each child represented a whole fascinating story of meetings and feelings and moments and consequences, and each child would go on to make their own stories too. It was mind-boggling.

Lydia had never noticed before the way the whole thing fitted together into a kind of vast network, how each individual slotted in and affected everything else around them. It had always been just her. Just Lydia. Nothing to do with anything or anyone, destined to have no story of her own. And that was why she hadn't ever asked Juliette about herself, because that one single question would have brought forth a whole potential sea of other people to think about. That was why she'd got herself a cat even though she was a dog person. A cat didn't expect you to be friends with it. And that was why she'd been so repelled by Dixie's baby. Because Dixie was extrapolating herself, bringing forth new people and new stories and new connections. Procreating. The most natural thing in the world. Yet, for Lydia, for so long, a terrifying concept.

But now she could see where she fitted into this whole thing. She had connections and a story. An amazing story. A story unlike anyone else's. She had a brother and a sister and a brand new, black-haired niece. She had another brother, buried tiny and snug in a quiet corner of her motherland. She had a housekeeper who was possibly a little over-protective and distrustful but with whom she shared a mutual fondness and respect. She had a kind-hearted uncle on her Welsh father's side and a kind-hearted uncle on her French father's side. And now she had a man who wanted her, who found her desirable and interesting. She had no mother and no father but she had so much more than most people.

She peeled off her cashmere cardigan and let the sun warm her bare arms for a while. She stared through the bars at the children in the playground, innocent and unaware of their own stories, slowly unfolding, leading them day by day to an unknown conclusion.

And then she thought of a small girl, growing bigger and bigger in a cottage in a village somewhere in the heart of Wales.

She thought of Viola Dixon-Parry, her best friend's child, a baby she'd never even held in her own arms.

She pulled her phone from her handbag and she typed in Dixie's number.

Getting to Know
Lisa Jewell

Read on for an exclusive piece by Lisa on the writing of *The Making of Us*, reading group questions, a Q&A, and Lisa's tips for aspiring writers.

Lisa on
The Making of Us

Like most of my books, *The Making of Us* started life in my head as a very different book to the one you have just finished reading. I was emotionally drained after finishing *After the Party*, my rather bleak study of an imploding long-term relationship. It had been an incredibly difficult book to write and then the editing process had gone on for weeks and I was totally desperate to do something light-hearted and fun. My thoughts kept turning to *About a Boy* by Nick Hornby – such a funny, touching book – and I decided I wanted to do something a bit like that, a comic study of a relationship between mismatched people from different generations.

At first Lydia was a man. He lived in Lydia's house and had Lydia's job, he went to Lydia's gym and was friends with Lydia's friends. I was about to introduce him (I can't for the life of me remember what his name was!) to a young man who may or may not have been his brother, but was certainly going to change his life in some amusing way, when I suddenly realised that I wanted him to be a woman. So Lydia was born. Then I started thinking of ways for Lydia and the younger person to come into each other's lives, but nothing seemed quite right until I read an article about the Donor Sibling Registry and realised that it was the perfect route for them to take. And so Dean was born. But as I wrote I realised that there was so much more scope within the concept of donor siblings than I could explore with just these two characters and so Robyn was born. Then I was told that a lady called Maggie Smith had won a 'character name' auction for the charity *Room to Read* and instantly I knew that Maggie was friends with the donor and that the donor was unwell. Once all the pieces of the jigsaw were in front of me, it was obvious what I needed to do with them all and the rest of the book kind of wrote itself. And was absolutely nothing like *About a Boy*!

I didn't do very much research; I wanted my characters' stories to be entirely personal to them and not influenced by anyone else's. But I did read a few pieces in the press, coincidentally to writing the book, and was reassured that my instinct to make Lydia, Dean and Robyn bond so quickly and so deeply was spot on. The sibling dynamic in a donor situation is much more straightforward and clear cut than the relationship between a donor and his offspring, so I deliberately wanted to avoid that aspect. I felt that that was another book entirely.

I had a personal interest in the concept of donor insemination before, during and after writing *The Making of Us* – five years ago one of my very best friends took the incredible decision to go through the process herself. As a result I find it hard to take an objective view. All I have to do is look at my friend's son playing with my daughter, see how happy and balanced he is, and how much pleasure and contentment he has brought to my friend's life, and I know that there is no right or wrong way to have a family. It's how you raise your family that counts.

I also appreciated the chance to write about hospices. My mother died in a hospice in 2005. It was extraordinary to spend so much time in a place so filled with the milk of human kindness. They are places that seem almost not of this world, halfway houses between life and death, where even in the last days of existence, incredible things can still happen. I rarely say I enjoyed writing a book. Generally I really don't. But this one was quite nice. The mechanics of it, the concept of the Donor Sibling Registry, the idea of complete strangers having so much in common, and the characters themselves with their very different backgrounds and personalities: the book had its own rhythm and momentum that carried me through. I really hope you enjoyed reading it!

Lisa x

Reading Group Questions on
The Making of Us

- Lisa Jewell tells the story from each of her main characters' point of view. Did you find yourself relating more to one character than the other?

- Like Robyn's parents in the story, how would you feel if your child wanted to find their biological parent?

- Robyn chooses to get some space from Jack when she fears that he may be her brother. Do you think this was the right way to handle the situation? How would you react in her shoes?

- Do you think that Dean is in the right state to look after his daughter at the beginning of the novel? What about at the end? How has he changed?

- Lydia feels that she and Dixie have much less in common than they used to. Is it much more difficult to stay friends if your lives have taken different paths?

- Maggie has clearly fallen for Daniel. By helping him, is she making things worse for herself for when he eventually passes away?

- Bendicks is an intriguing character in *The Making of Us*. Did you ever doubt his intentions? Or did you trust him throughout the novel?

- Robyn's parents are very understanding when she decides to drop out of university and become a waitress until she knows what she wants to do. Would you be this understanding if your child acted this way? Is there anything you wish your parents had been more understanding about?

Q&A with Lisa

• **Which writers or books have inspired you?**

As a child I read anything and everything, from the children's classics to Dickens to *The Thorn Birds*, *The Grapes of Wrath* and every single Agatha Christie ever published. I read four or five books a week so, on a deeply fundamental level, I have been inspired by a huge and eclectic raft of writers. More specifically I do love Nick Hornby and Maggie O'Farrell, both of whom make what they do look so easy. It was a conversation with a friend about *High Fidelity* that resulted in me writing my first book and you don't get much more inspiring than that!

• **What made you want to become a writer?**

Reading made me want to become a writer. As a child, I had a vague idea about being a journalist, but life took me far away from that and by the time I was in my twenties I was a secretary. I'd married young and started reading a lot again, and my husband told me he thought I'd be able to write a book that other people would want to read. After that marriage broke up, I signed up for creative writing lessons to see if he was right. He was.

• *The Making of Us* **is your ninth novel. Have you found that your writing has changed since** *Ralph's Party* **(1999)?**

I hope so. It's hard for me to be objective. My readers would probably be better placed to comment on that. I definitely have to try harder and harder with each book to avoid repeating myself, which results in new ways of using language and describing things. I have also discovered the joy of a proper storyline. My first few books were very much jumping in at the deep end and seeing where I ended up. These days I'd rather have a structure in place and a solid concept behind the characters.

• **Do you have a particular routine you follow when you write?**

It does tend to change a lot, but at the moment I am enjoying having both my children in school and having the run of the house again. Before, I used to have to rush to the gym to get my youngest in the crèche, and then rush to the café to meet the childminder, then cloister myself away in my room at the top of the house. Now I'm free as a bird, currently writing this in the kitchen. Such joy! But I do most of my writing in the café next to my gym. I like the white noise and people-watching, and not having any access to the internet. They also make much better coffee than me.

• **Which character in *The Making of Us* did you enjoy writing most?**

All of them. Genuinely. In fact, when I delivered the manuscript to my editor I said to her that it was the first book I'd written where I was equally excited about writing from each character's perspective. Every time I got to a Maggie chapter I'd think, Ooh, goodie, it's Maggie. And the same with all the others. For me, that was the joy of writing the book.

• **Your fans often comment on how much they love your characters and how relatable they are. How do you make them so 'real'? Do you base them on people you know or are they purely fictional?**

All my characters are entirely fictional. But also entirely real. They do just tend to arrive in my head fully formed and I just have to find a good name for them (I'm anal about names) and then decide what to do with them. There's no trick to it. At the risk of sounding a bit airy-fairy, it just sort of happens.

• **Do you imagine the reader when you are writing your novels?**

I try very hard not to think about who's going to read my books while I'm writing them. When I was writing the sequel to *Ralph's Party* it was much harder not to think about them because clearly a lot of people were going to be reading the book because they'd read and loved the first one and there was this weight of expectation on me to give them a book that lived up to their hopes for it. Generally speaking though, I just write the book that I feel like writing at the time, that I think I'm capable of writing at the time, that I think is going to sustain my imagination, that's going to keep me ticking over, that's going to give me what I need. I'm quite selfish in that way. I try not to think about what my publishers want, I try not to think about what my readers want, I try not to think about what the book reviewer in the Guardian is going to want. I try just to write the book that I think at that time in my life I'm going to be capable of starting and finishing.

• **What is your next novel about?**

Well, once again it's nothing like the book I thought I was going to write. It was going to be a 1990s Britpop rock-chick fluffy love story but it had no intrinsic structure, and, like I say above, I do need that structure these days (must be getting old!). It is about a young girl called Betty who comes to London in 1995 to try and trace the mysterious beneficiary in her grandmother's will, a woman called Clara Pickle, whose last known address was in Soho. The story is threaded through with flashbacks to her grandmother's secret life in London in the early 1920s. So it's part coming-of-age, part romance and part mystery. It's called *Before I Met You* and it's coming out in July.

Lisa on Being a Writer

How I got into publishing

I never for a moment thought I would end up being a published author. In my early teenage years I had this romantic idea of working as a journalist for the *NME*. That didn't work out, obviously, and I ended up working in fashion retail. Then at some point in my early twenties I had this vague idea that someone should write a book about women like me in their early twenties, which nobody seemed to be doing at the time. But it wasn't until I was in my late twenties, when I had just been made redundant at my job as a secretary, that I seriously considered the possibility of writing a book. It was the Nick Hornby novel *High Fidelity* that inspired me.

It was the first time I'd read a book that really spoke to me, that made me think, 'Gosh, maybe it is possible write a book in simple language about ordinary people who live in London and maybe I don't have to wait until I'm 55 years old and have had lots of life experience. I mentioned this crazy concept to a friend and instead of laughing at me she made me a bet. She said, 'Write three chapters and I'll take you out to dinner.' So I wrote the three chapters and she did take me out to dinner. But at no point during the process of writing those three chapters was I seriously thinking I was writing a book that would be published, or that would stand any chance of being looked at seriously by anyone in the publishing industry. I don't think I really thought of myself as a writer until I signed my first book contract. Up until that point I thought there's no reason to write another book as long as I live and up until that point I was assuming that I'd go back to being a secretary. So, it wasn't until I'd signed my name on the dotted line that I thought, OK, that was a complete fluke, not quite sure how I pulled that one off but now someone wants me to write another one. And that was the point at which I started to believe I was going to be writer. Hopefully for a very long time.

My top tips for writers

I do get asked an awful lot about advice for aspiring writers, as well as how I came to be published myself. When I started to write, I was working as a PA and didn't have any grand ambitions for myself. Writing a book was something I thought I might quite like to do one day when I was grown up. But sometimes it can take just a five-minute conversation with someone to give them the confidence (or the slap round the face or kick up the backside or whatever it is that they need) to do what they want to do. I would never have pushed myself to write my first book if it hadn't been for my friend making me that bet, my husband insisting I could finish it when an agent liked the first three chapters, and everyone around me egging me on. Now that's something I can do for other people. It takes two minutes to have a conversation like that so I never get bored of giving people advice about writing.

My five tips for writing are pretty straightforward and simplistic.

Number One: Read. Don't read the way you normally read, don't immerse yourself in the book but really look at what the author's done, in terms of moving the story along, in terms of building up characters, in terms of making the dialogue natural. Really learn from it.

Number Two (and this is really important): Disavow yourself of any romantic notions about the process of writing. Don't imagine for a minute that it's going to be fun, that it's going to be satisfying or particularly that it's going to be easy. It's going to be none of those things; it's going to be one of the most challenging things you're ever going to do in your life. It's very, very difficult to write a book, even one that's easy to read.

Number Three: Start.

Number Four: Keep Going.

And Number Five: Finish.

Those last three things may sound simple but most people never manage to do it. You'll be leagues ahead of the game if you can just push through to those magic words: The End.

Once you've actually written a book, it's also a bit of a numbers game. The same friend who challenged me to write a book all those years ago subsequently went on to write her own novel. In the meantime she moved back to Australia, left her manuscript with me and asked me to keep sending it out. And so I did. Every week I'd pick another three agents out of the *Writers' and Artists' Yearbook*, take the three chapters up to the post office and post them off for her. I think I probably sent her manuscript out to about thirty agents and received thirty rejection letters until suddenly this letter arrived from some crazed agent saying it was the most brilliant book she ever read and she wanted to get it published immediately. So I would say, while it's important to have realistic expectations, it's equally important to have patience and tenacity and just keep on going, because it only takes one person, just one person to love your book and you're halfway there.

What it's like to be a writer

There are lots of things I love about being a writer. I will tell anyone who asks that it is the best job in the world! Not because of the act of writing, which I'll be quite honest about, I don't enjoy at all. But I like the lifestyle of being a writer. I particularly like the fact that now that I've got children, I can work at home. I can take them to school in the morning, I can pick them up in the afternoon and I never miss out on anything. I can spend half my day being a mother and half my day being a professional writer which is a very nice balance.

The other best thing about being a writer is telling people that I'm a writer. It's incredibly satisfying to walk into a social situation with someone you've never met before and get to that dreaded question, 'So what do you do?' and be able to tell them that you do something that is a dream for a lot of people. It's always terribly interesting for the person you're talking to as well. Suddenly, you've opened the door of this secret world to them and everyone always wants to know how many books I've written and where I find my ideas. So I do like having this identity as a writer; I find it a very comfortable fit for me.

As far as I'm concerned, there are only two bad things about being a writer. The first is writing. If you try and imagine, you've got this vast world inside your head and you don't really know what's going to happen at the end of the story. You're controlling all these people; you're controlling their destinies, and you've got no one you can talk to about it. Nobody knows what's going on in this world in your head except for you. You are the managing director of all managing directors. You've got nobody to go to. It can be quite wearing at times having sole responsibility for this thing. It often feels like you're just pulling words out of your head, word after word after word.

I've heard other writers talk about this state called 'flow', a state I've never actually experienced. This is apparently where you can cut out the outside world and you are immersed in your fictional world and the words just pour out of you onto your keyboard. That doesn't happen for me; for me I find it a kind of industrial process, pulling the words out and getting them onto the page. When you come across a problem in the process of writing, sometimes a little thing happens, often somewhere really banal like in the shower or on the treadmill, when you miraculously work out what you need to do to solve it. When that happens, it feels like magic.

The other bad thing about being a writer is what we call in the industry 'writer's ass'. This is what happens when you spend five hours a day sitting on your bum without moving. It's an industrial hazard and only countered by regular sessions at the gym.

The Truth About Melody Browne

When she was nine years old, Melody Browne's house burned down. Not only did the fire destroy all her possessions, it took with it all her memories – she can remember nothing before her ninth birthday. Now in her early thirties, Melody lives in a council flat in the middle of London with her seventeen-year-old son. She's made a good life for herself and her son and she likes it that way.

Until one night something extraordinary happens. Whilst attending a hypnotist show with her first date in years she faints – and when she comes round she starts to remember. At first her memories mean nothing to her but then slowly, day by day, she begins to piece together the real story of her childhood. But with every mystery she solves another one materialises, with every question she answers another appears. And Melody begins to wonder if she'll ever know the truth about her past . . .

arrow books

ALSO BY LISA JEWELL

AFTER THE PARTY

Eleven years ago, Jem Catterick and Ralph McLeary fell in love. They thought it would be for ever, that they'd found their happy ending.

Then two became four, a flat became a house. Romantic nights out became sleepless nights in. And they soon found that life wasn't quite so simple any more.

Now the unimaginable has happened. Two people who were so right together are starting to drift apart – Ralph is standing on the sidelines, and Jem is losing herself. Something has to change. As they try to find a way back to each other, back to what they once had, they both become dangerously distracted – but maybe it's not too late to recapture happily ever after . . .

arrow books

AND COMING IN JULY 2012

The sparkling new bestseller

BEFORE I
MET YOU

A heartbreaking and unforgettable tale of two women in
two very different times linked by a shared determination
to make their dreams come true . . .

C̄

Century · London

Get to know
Lisa online

Be the first to hear Lisa's news and find out
all about her new book releases at
www.lisa-jewell.co.uk

Join the official Facebook page at
www.facebook/lisajewellofficial

Follow Lisa on Twitter
@lisajewelluk